Sword's Edge

L.S. King

This is a work of fiction. Names, characters, events, and incidents are the products of the author's imagination. Any resemblance to actual persons, living or dead, or actual events is purely coincidental.

Cover Design: Miblart Copyright © 2020
miblart.com

Loriendil Publishing
loriendil.com

DEDICATION

To my son James—the actual recipient of grub guts

CONTENTS

ACKNOWLEDGMENTS

Thanks to:

My family, especially James and Sarah for wading through so many drafts. And my late husband who was, and still is, my inspiration in more ways than he could have possibly known.

Dr. Jonathan Crofts for enduring my never-ending, foolish questions about physics and countless other topics.

Shannon McNear for sticking with me through so many revisions and giving me your honest critique, and for just being the rock I need in good times and bad.

Johne Cook, because, you know... Bro.

Bill Snodgrass for believing in me so completely.

Sylvia Perales, Dawn King, Dee East, Rorie Murphy, Bill Slease, and Paul Christian Glenn for your feedback and encouragement.

All my friends on the Skateboard, in ACFW, the Lost Genre Guild, Ray Gun Revival, and the various other online SF/F communities in which I've participated.

Johnston McCulley and Guy Williams—for my love of capes, swords, and brave deeds.

My friend, Deby Bird, who never stopped nagging me that I just had to start writing again.

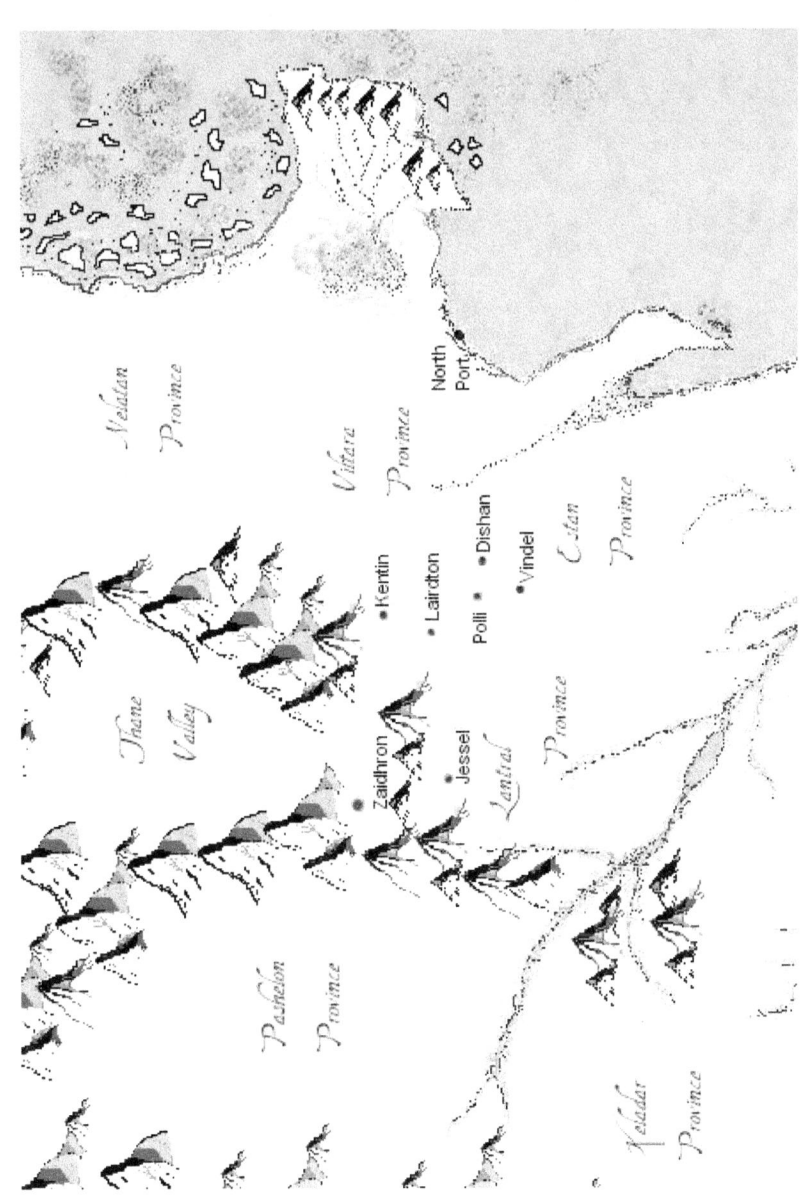

North
Port

Melalan
Province

Vitara
Province

Kentin
Lairdton
Dishan
Vindel

Polli
Utan
Province

Thane
Valley

Zaidhron
Jessel
Lantral
Province

Pathelon
Province

Keladar
Province

iii

PRONUNCIATION OF NAMES

Teldheri:
- ' indicates a glottal stop except when used after ch, in which case it indicates the ch is a hard sound (as in Scottish lo**ch**)
- dh indicates a fricative **d** (as in mo**th**er or **th**en)
- a is **ä** (as in f**a**ther), except in an accented syllable, in which case it is short
- e is short as in **e**gg
- i is short as in p**i**t, except as final vowel, then it is long **e**, as in Teldheri (or when followed by double consonants, such as is common in female names)
- ai is a diphthong, with the separate vowels pronounced as given above: **ä** and long **e**
- ei is a diphthong, with the separate vowels pronounced as given above: short **e** and long **e**
- o is long **o**
- u is long as in r**u**le
- gh indicates a soft g (as in **g**eneral)
- jh indicates a sibilant s (as in mea**s**ure)

Male names:
- accent is on the first syllable except when it is a three syllable name beginning with a vowel with a closed second syllable, in which case the accent is on the second syllable, therefore *El'adhrel* but *Alcan'dhor*

Female names:
- in names such as *Sarinna*, or *Colinn*, the i is pronounced as a long **e** and carries the accent, as indicated by the double consonant after the vowel
- in names such as Amara or Aleta, the accent is on the second syllable
- in names such as Sherel, accent is on the first syllable

"enh?" used at the end of a sentence to indicate a question does not carry a long **a** sound, but rather the nasal enh sound similar to "hein" used by the French.

SWORD'S EDGE

Tam halted amid the bracken and tilted her head, not listening but using her inner sense. She gazed up into the treetops, squinting at the winks of sunlight stabbing through the leaves of the glowing canopy. There—she had felt aright: a tongrah clambered in the branches above. Perhaps meat for evening meal would soothe her father's stormy mood. She nocked an arrow and aimed upward—

A barrage of emotions assaulted her: a jumbling of worry, frustration, doubt. Her throat constricted and she fumbled the arrow, gasping. Her mind whirled and heart thudded. Some stranger—*intruder!*—approached. Tam gulped air and closed her eyes to concentrate on blocking the onslaught. The crushing weight eased.

She exhaled slowly, slung her bow over her shoulder, and squatted among the bushes, waiting until she could see the invader. Ah, there he was—far off, a dim figure in the shadow of the trees.

In her fifteen years, she never knew of anyone finding their home. Her father guarded its location and would not be pleased. She bit her lip. *Oh stars, what will Father say? Or do? Will he blame me?*

Tam ducked into the underbrush and crawled backwards. Once certain she was far enough away to be undetected, she sprang up and dashed through the tangles of wild vines, shrubs, and ferns.

She raced across the clearing where the cottage nestled, realizing too late Father would berate her for such carelessness. He straightened from chopping wood and put down the axe, his face dark with displeasure. She tried not to wince as he seized her arms. Before he could speak, she blurted, "A stranger approaches!"

His grip loosened as he peered toward the forest. He shoved her past him toward the cottage. "Get inside."

Relief swept through her as she ran to the small one-room shack.

Her hand snagged the rough-hewn doorframe to slow her entry. She stood her bow in the corner and hung her quiver on a peg. She fingered her knife, biting her lip. A lass would not wear a weapon, and she must not appear Ranger-Trained. She bit her lip harder and finally unstrapped the knife. Should she pretend to sweep or tend the fire? She glanced about the little room with its meager furnishings. Nay, not yet. She took a deep breath to calm herself, and through a chink in the wall, kept watch.

~:~

Alcandhor strode amid luminescent patches and dark shadows created by the late afternoon sun shining through the forest. His neck and arms still tingled with warning, although his watcher had crept away under the dense foliage and run off. Now, all he need do was follow.

He knew it was not his brother; creeping under the vegetation was not Valdhor's way. Besides, he would have acknowledged Alcandhor as soon as he recognized him—although not gladly. Valdhor did not suffer familial ties. Alcandhor had accepted long ago that no affection would be forthcoming from the man.

Could the furtive watcher be Valdhor's child? The reclusive Ranger had recorded his wife's name, sept, and clan, and her death several years later. Rangers had reported seeing Valdhor with a youngster on the rare occasions they met with him. Valdhor would never take in a waif, so the rumor held that he did have a son or daughter, although failure to record a child's birth was an infraction of the law.

Through foresight—a rare gift inherited by some descendants of the aliens called the Enaisi—their father had ordered Alcandhor to leave be any questions about Valdhor, his marriage, and any rumor of a child. By tradition, a word that rankled him, foresight was given weight as if law. So if a child existed, Alcandhor could face judgment from either side— by following law or by following tradition.

Alcandhor ground his teeth. Orders, law, and tradition all be hanged now! He needed Valdhor; his own foresight in that haunting dream confirmed it. He continued through the ferns and underbrush, sweat trickling down his back. His observer had been Trained well, but few could pass through the woods without Alcandhor's being aware of them, even without using his empathic ability to sense their presence.

Before long, he saw a clearing ahead. With great care he crept forward, pushing aside broad leaves and stepping over thorny vines. He detected Valdhor close to hand, and his heart eased. From a small copse of thick brambles and scrub trees just outside the perimeter of the clearing, he watched Valdhor chop firewood. The Ranger's stance and direction as he split the logs told Alcandhor that his brother knew exactly where he was.

The weathered cottage, with loose chinking and wooden shingles askew or missing in spots on the roof, gave evidence Valdhor only used this as a base. Tall grass grew about the building, and weeds tangled their way into the extensive garden, lending a forlorn appearance. Valdhor had been a loner who enjoyed living in the wild as a youth, and without a wife, he would have little reason to keep a home. But—what of the child?

Alcandhor straightened his shoulders. What welcome would he receive? He stepped into the clearing with a smile, his fist lifting and opening palm forward in greeting. "At last, Valdhor! You hide your home well."

The tall man flexed his shoulders, his leather jerkin tight across his muscular chest. He set down the axe, wiping work-roughened hands on his grey trous. Valdhor tossed his long, dark hair out of his face and back over his broad shoulders, assessing Alcandhor with narrowed eyes, his strong jaw set.

"How fare you?" Alcandhor asked.

"What news?"

A wry smile twisted Alcandhor's lips as he walked toward the sullen loner. Alcandhor held out his hand to grasp Valdhor's shoulder in the traditional manner, but Valdhor crossed his arms and took a step back.

Alcandhor let his hand drop, ignoring the insult. "Not changed, are you? Not a moment to waste on civility? And even less on idle conversation? You look well. I have been fine these many years. You care not?"

"You traveled not this distance for gossip or useless chatter. What news?"

Alcandhor sighed, grimacing in consternation both for Valdhor's cold attitude as well as for the worries that brought him here. "Trouble."

"Let us go inside." Valdhor turned and strode toward the cottage, leaving Alcandhor to follow behind.

A savory smell wafted out the doorway. Alcandhor entered the shabby cottage and stood for a moment, waiting for his eyes to adjust to the darker interior. Little was there, a small table and two chairs near the left wall where Valdhor already sat, and sleeping mats to the right. Alcandhor dropped his pack and added his cloak and weapons to ones hanging on pegs to the right of the door.

Straight ahead at the fireplace stood a thin slip of girl, dressed as though a peasant lad, her straight, black hair cropped just longer than shoulder length. She stirred a pot swung out from the fire. A warm tingling shot down his spine again, and his stomach churned. He brushed aside his apprehension over the repercussions of her existence. So, Valdhor did indeed have a child. And there she stood as if she had been in here tending the food when moments ago she had been spying on his approach with all the skill of a Ranger well-Trained. He eyed the girl, impressed, an idea playing in his mind.

Valdhor glared at him, knuckles tapping the table, his thin lips curled in the familiar sneer. A smile played at the edges of Alcandhor's mouth. So, Valdhor was irritated, was he? Good. Let him chafe. He took deliberate time wiping his feet on the braided mat at the threshold, but his delight at baiting the man faded as he sat.

"Matters balance on the edge of a sword, Valdhor. There are traitors in Laird Hall. I fear perhaps..." he hated to say it, "perhaps even among the Rangers."

A quick intake of breath came from the girl. She sucked on a finger as though she had been burned by the hot soup just ladled into the bowls, her large, oval eyes wide. Alcandhor's gaze lingered on her until the slam of Valdhor's fist on the table brought his attention back.

"I cannot believe that. Not Rangers." Valdhor's growl echoed Alcandhor's own pain and disbelief. Rangers vowed to uphold the highest ideals of their laws. For one to betray that pledge was a disgrace to their clan and a personal heartache.

"Believe it not at your peril. The Laird is in great danger, and we have no way of knowing who in, or near, Laird Hall may be our enemy."

The girl brought over the afternooning, soup and tea, balanced on a cutting board. She placed the food in front of him with dark hands that bore pale scars—scars indicative of sword fighting. More proof of his suspicions. He met her eyes as he thanked her. Dropping her gaze, she finished serving and withdrew to the fireplace. He turned back to his grudging host. "How complete is her Training?"

Valdhor stiffened with a fierce expression, his grey eyes turning dark as coal with anger.

Alcandhor hid a smile, pleased he had provoked a reaction. "Stars, you have the look of a trapped, rabid ballan." His amusement faded. "She watched me come—very stealthily. How complete is her Training?"

Valdhor's nostrils flared, his lips pressed together. "What has *she* to do with this?"

Alcandhor's temper rose; he had not the time or patience for Valdhor's obstinacy. "*She* could be the solution to a very pretty problem. Now, answer me."

Valdhor's jaw set as his narrowed eyes locked with Alcandhor's. He finally blinked, dropping his gaze to the table, his voice low and taut. "She is Trained."

Alcandhor released a long, frustrated breath at Valdhor's antagonism. He motioned to the girl, who watched him with wide, wary eyes. "Come here, please."

The girl approached the table like a wild animal tensed for flight. Her golden eyes—lighter than her skin—met his with apprehension. She had the beginnings of being a beauty. Such dark skin was rare among his people. It was said that those strong with the blood of the Enaisi had the same dark bronze complexion as well, but there had been none thus in generations. Only a few, and only from their own clan, still had such coloring. Where and how had Valdhor met her mother, and why had he kept her apart from his kin?

"Sir?"

Alcandhor shook himself. Speculation later. Now he needed to find out how stalwart she was. "Your name, lass."

The girl glanced at her father as if for permission, but he paid no heed, scowling at the table.

At her continued hesitation, he commanded, "Answer me."

She raised herself up and set her shoulders back, chin defiant, eyes narrow. *Ah, how she looks like her father now!*

"Who are you to demand it of me?" she asked.

Alcandhor sat back and hooked his arm over the back of his chair. His short laugh brought Valdhor's head up with jerk. Alcandhor met his cross gaze with a knowing smile. "Definitely, she is your daughter."

Alcandhor pushed back his chair and stood, moving closer to tower over her. He had backed down many men, but the girl held her ground, eyes fixed on his. Her trepidation fluttered through him; she was not as unmoved as she would have him think. He wanted to smile at her strength of will but remained stern, replying as Thane, not her uncle. "I am Alcandhor. Thane of the Rangers."

Her face paled, and she exhaled silently, her eyes darting over his features with an expression of amazement and awe.

"Well, lass, your name."

"Tamissa, sir. But I go by Tam."

"And you are a Ranger, Tam?"

She dropped her gaze. "My father has Trained me hard, sir. Whether I have been worthy of that Training is yet to be seen."

Alcandhor pressed his lips into a tight line. Hang that man. He should not have been allowed to raise the girl alone. Although Alcandhor knew he could not lay all the blame on Valdhor. As Thane he could have—should have—looked into the matter, despite his father's orders. Well, the girl was not the only one with doubts. He shook loose from self-recrimination and peered hard at Tam. "We will see. I have use for you." He turned to Valdhor. "Can you both be ready to leave by morning?"

Valdhor hesitated, lips thinned and jaw set, before inclining his head. Tam looked from her father to Alcandhor, disbelief on her face.

"Good. We have much to discuss tonight."

Tam backed toward the fireplace, but Alcandhor snagged the stool from the hearth and set it at the table. "Get you your bowl." When she hesitated, he pointed at the seat. Her eyes flicked toward her father, and she brought her bowl and mug to the table, appearing dazed as she sat.

Alcandhor reseated himself and picked up his spoon. The hot soup was welcome to his empty stomach, but he did not expect it to be so toothsome. He licked his lips after swallowing a mouthful. "This is very good."

Tam looked up, her large eyes wide, but she did not answer.

"The correct response"—Valdhor's low, hard voice made the girl jump—"is 'thank you.'"

"Thank you," she immediately whispered to her bowl.

"I see you have raised the girl to be as socially amenable as you are," Alcandhor said.

Tam continued to eat with her head bowed. Alcandhor sipped his tea. Stars, was it good! Very different from the darker brews he was accustomed to, this had a lighter color and flavor. He took a satisfying gulp.

Valdhor tapped the table with his knuckles. "Tell me about the trouble."

Great Bells, did the man ever stop? Alcandhor suppressed his irritation; Valdhor would not goad him as easily as he used to. "Not even a few moments to rest and enjoy a meal, enh? Will it make our departure in the morning come earlier or our journey faster if we take not a little time to relax and put our cares aside?" He turned to Tam with a smile. "Would you mind getting me more tea, Tam?"

With a startled look, she jumped up and took his mug. She tentatively reached for her father's as well, but he shook his head. She snatched her hand away as if burned. Alcandhor fought down his anger at her obvious fear of her father and determined to get her to speak, despite Valdhor.

"'Tis good tea, Tam, but different than any brew I have had," Alcandhor said. "What is in it?"

She filled the mug and brought it back to the table. "I–I experiment with herbs and spices I grow. This blend seems to please...us," she finished with a nervous glance at her father. His attention remained on his soup.

"It is very good."

"Thank you." She sat down and picked up her spoon.

What could possibly draw her into a conversation? Nothing had worked so far. He took another sip of the pleasant tea. "I noticed the large garden. You tend it?"

"Aye."

"You enjoy it?"

"Aye."

"Perhaps before it is dark you could show it to me."

Ah, was that a quick surge of delight from her?

The table and all on it jumped as Valdhor pounded his fist. "Why wish you to waste your time with such nonsense?"

Alcandhor drew himself up, locking eyes with Valdhor. "I will decide what is nonsense." He turned to Tam. "Will you show me your garden when we have finished with our meal?"

She blinked, hesitating. "I...it is full of weeds. We have just returned from roaming the bounds, and I—"

Alcandhor waved a hand. "No matter. I would like to see it. Will you show it to me?"

Her eyes darted toward her father, but she nodded.

"Alcandhor, why wish you to waste time on such things?"

Alcandhor met Valdhor's dark gaze. "Since you seem to be so concerned about the time, you can save us a valuable amount by taking care of the clean up while I look at the garden and discuss herbs with this young Ranger."

"What!"

"You heard me."

"You dare to—"

"Do as your Thane commands." The thunder of authority rang in his voice. He rose, knocking back his chair. "Come, Tam."

She followed him out the side door and toward the garden with a stunned look.

"Something is wrong?"

"N–nay."

He tipped his head to see her face. "You are shocked at my treatment of your father, are you not? He is not only your father but your teacher, and...your hero?"

"I suppose so," she whispered.

He stopped and touched her shoulder lightly. "Be assured, Tam, I have the greatest respect for your father. He is considered one of the best Rangers alive."

Her young face showed amazement. "But not better than you?"

He chuckled. "Oh, aye. Aye, Tam. Much better than me." Humor faded as he groped for words. "You are young, perhaps too young to understand. You have not been raised with family and know not how sometimes..." He let out his breath slowly, wondering how to explain what he did not really understand himself. Weariness permeated his heart and body. "I have reasons for dealing with your father the way I do." He gave a melancholy smile. "But I will try to tread a little more lightly for your sake. Now, tell me about your garden."

They picked their way through the weeds. Tam gestured to plants almost her height with dark green, oval, leaves, pointed at the end. The bright pink, clustered flowers had long, narrow petals that split so that the lower half curved down with a graceful bow, while the other rose in a lofty salute. "This is timora. The flowers are edible, and the leaves have wonderful healing properties for so many different things."

"I know the plant, but was not aware the flowers were edible. Are they tasty?"

"I think they are." Her face lit up as she stepped over a tangle of weeds to a large clump of avalare with its spear-shaped, grey-green leaves and spiked, purple flowers. "This is a wonderful herb. The flowers are edible, can sweeten a room, and be used in an infusion for various maladies. Are they not lovely?"

"Aye." What a joy to see the girl come to life! As she told him about the featherfronds, her face became animated and dimples winked in her cheeks as a smile flitted across her face. In the sun, her hair was not pure black, but had dark brown glints.

She paused, biting her lip, her fingers brushing the thread-like, blue-green leaves of the featherfronds in an absentminded manner. "Sir...you called me a Ranger."

"Aye, I did."

"But I am a girl."

"You are Ranger Trained."

"But...I am a girl."

He laughed. "This conversation is becoming circular." He took her gently by the shoulders and brought his face close to hers. "If your Thane says you are a Ranger, who are you to argue?"

~:~

Tam entered the cottage with the Thane. A candle flickered on the table, and Valdhor sat, waiting for them. His features bespoke his disapproving attitude; it awed Tam that this seemed not to bother the Thane.

"Any ale?" Alcandhor asked Valdhor.

"Nay."

"Well then, Tam, would you mind getting me another cup of your tea, please? Any for you, Valdhor?"

"Nay."

Tam brought a mug of tea for the Thane and sat down. He fingered the mug with a distracted air. His hands were roughened, callused, with scars on them, but unlike her father's broad hands, the Thane's were slender and almost graceful. Like the man.

Worry radiated from him in warm waves. She started, throwing up a block, fearing lest her father suspect she had relaxed enough to sense.

The Thane took a sip of his tea, set the mug down, and leaned back in his chair. "There is much trouble at Laird Hall. There are those who think they can overthrow the Laird and wrest control of the provinces."

"An overthrow of the Laird means also an overthrow of the Rangers. I do not think that would be easily accomplished."

"Nay. But these men were subtle until recently. And the Laird has given his ministers much leeway and not kept close watch on how they administer their provinces, much more so as he ages."

Her father exhaled in a quiet hiss.

"The lords of the near provinces are self-indulgent and greedy. Rumors abound of abuses ranging from nobles snatching land and leaving families homeless to making slaves of the clanless. Rangers have not always been able to gather proof and bring justice and thus are being blamed. The resulting dissension has been growing. We now think we know all the leaders who are stirring trouble in the affected provinces. However, the one that much evidence seems to point to as the mastermind is..." the Thane paused with a grimace, "Lord Krendhal."

"First Minister Krendhal?"

"Aye."

"Impossible." Valdhor waved his hand in dismissal. "He has never had ambitions to power—too hidebound. Loyalty is utmost, and change, blasphemy."

"I know. We feel it is misdirection." Alcandhor sighed, the anxiety keen on his face. "But we cannot act until we know beyond doubt and have all our people in place, lest these conspirators scatter, hiding their tracks. Yet we must move quickly as the dissension is great enough for them to make their move."

Alcandhor stared down at his mug, turning it with a preoccupied

9

expression. "If it is not already too late." He drew in a quick breath, his gaze settling on Tam's father with a desperate urgency. "Valdhor, I need someone I can trust to keep an eye on the comings and goings from Laird Hall and to listen for things no one else would hear. I have no one I could trust as much as you. And if there is anything strange going on that can be seen or heard from without, you are the one who could find it."

Valdhor inclined his head.

Tam's heart swelled with pride. The Thane had come all the way up here because he trusted her father above all others!

"What had worried me is how to infiltrate the hall effectively and find out what is happening on the inside. We must know for certain who is involved and what their plans are. It cannot be a Ranger or anyone known to be associated with us. Who was loyal, yet would not be known or suspected? Then I saw Tam." She flushed as his blue-grey eyes met hers. "Who would suspect a young mountain lass? An orphan left alone. As a Ranger, I cannot leave her upon finding her, yet I must continue my duties, so I drop her at the most convenient place where she can be of service and be cared for. That place happens to be Laird Hall."

Stunned, Tam awaited her father's response.

"You are requiring much from an untested child."

"She is your daughter. She is Trained. Those two qualifications alone recommend her to me."

Valdhor sneered, and Tam dropped her head, shamed that she had failed her father by not meeting his standards in her Training. She always tried her best, but never was it enough.

"Are you willing, Tam?" the Thane asked.

Tam's head snapped up. He would trust to use her when her father thought her inadequate to the task? His eyes pleaded, waiting for her answer. She cut her eyes to her father, but as usual, he did not even glance in her direction. Dare she accept when her father disapproved? She swallowed, her voice soft as she gave the traditional Ranger reply. "I am honored, sir, to be of service."

As the Thane relaxed with a smile, Valdhor ground his teeth. Tam braced for his impending burst of anger, but to her surprise, her father's temper did not flare.

The fear coiled inside Tam slowly dissolved as her father asked, "What think you their next move will be?"

"Provincial and clan wars or assassination. The order depends on how soon the lords betray each other. I fear for the Laird's safety and for the Atheling Randhal, too. The Laird's clan has dwindled rather than grown—"

"Aye," Valdhor said with an impatient tone. "I know."

The Thane lifted his hands with slight incline of his head. "Another fever ran through just two years ago, claiming many lives. Not many are left in Viltara clan who could claim ascendancy to Laird if he and his heir die, and of those, none have the education or training, save Krendhal. Some of the provincial lords who have been sowing dissension not only wish unimpeded control of their own provinces but also have high ambition. I believe one of them, at least, plans on ascending from being a 'mere' lord to the High Lord: our Laird."

"Great Bells!"

"That is why we must move swiftly."

Chapter Two

Tam's thoughts whirled. The Thane slept on a mat nearby, the shadows on his face dancing in the flicker from the fireplace.

The Thane. She never thought she would meet the Thane himself, especially being from a family so diminished in the clan that her father would not even teach her their lineage. She wondered—as she had many times—if her mother had been clanless, or did some shameful event cause their family to be so shunned and her father so tightlipped?

But now—here was the head of their clan, and peacekeeper for their entire world, sleeping on the floor in her cottage. He looked much different asleep. The lines in his face were smoothed out, and he seemed much younger. How old was he?

His kind eyes had seemed sad. Aye, she had felt the sadness in him, when she let her block slip. Though—he had not seemed thus when he arrived. How bold he had looked striding across the clearing toward her father! His long brown hair rippling back over his shoulders, his cloak flowing behind him, one hand raised in greeting. The archetypal Ranger.

He was not the least bit intimidated by her father regardless of his moods, either. That awed her most of all.

And—the Thane called her a Ranger and wanted her to go on a mission! And he thought it not strange that her father had been Training her. What would she be allowed to do? Probably not much, being female. Certainly never Confirmed as Ranger-Trained. But even if not Presented, to be a Ranger at all would be wonderful and more than she ever thought could be possible. She had not known what she ever could be. Her father told her only men were Rangers. She dared ask just once why he Trained her then, and a backhand was his reply.

She forced her mind away from that memory and recalled what she had packed. Not much. Mostly food for the ten-day journey. The Thane said he would get her suitable clothes to wear for Laird Hall. Had she forgotten to pack anything important? She had sneaked her book of herbs into her pack. She could not bear to leave that behind; they might not be home for some time.

At thoughts of her garden, she choked back a sob, but then gazed again at the Thane. He needed her help. Stars, what difference did a garden make compared to that?

12

What would come tomorrow when they began their trek toward Laird Hall? The Thane told her it was dangerous. If she were found out the traitors would not be forgiving. Why did she not feel afraid? He had told her it was all right for her to be afraid. He said that fear was good if kept in control. It kept one alert.

Her stomach roiled. Detection, capture, death—these things held no fear for her in comparison with the thought of failing as a Ranger and failing her Thane.

Afraid he might wake and see her watching him, she turned to face the wall, wrapping her blanket around her like a cocoon.

~:~

After Tam rolled over, Alcandhor opened his eyes to look at her. Much would ride on the girl. Of how stern a stuff was she made? Was her kin's blood in her as strongly as he felt it was?

And Valdhor, what would he do about him? He could not understand that man. He had prided himself on following the law to the letter, yet had broken Clan Law by never sending word of Tam's birth. Without some reason to justify the situation, Alcandhor would be forced to call Question on Valdhor's actions. He would not bring up the point now though; his need of Valdhor was too desperate, and calling Question would probably strip Valdhor of his standing and rank as a Ranger.

Alcandhor put himself in a precarious position by this inaction as well, but he had been driven to Valdhor's home for a purpose, and he would not thwart that. He closed his eyes, fighting the dread that settled on him, but could find no sleep.

~:~

The girl flitted from rock to rock, reminding Alcandhor of a young lithe-limbed hillbeast. Her eyes darted to her father, and she stopped, drawing her knife. She quickly cut several bunches of herbs sprouting from an outcrop.

Alcandhor grinned when she met his gaze as she sheathed her blade. Her contributions of wild tubers, herbs, roots, and greens added wonderful variety to their meals. And she managed it without falling behind.

The bruise on the outside of his thigh twinged at each step, reminding him of the surprising skill Tam had with the staff. He had not expected thus of her and discovered painfully the evening before that the staff was her favorite weapon. Her Training with weapons and barehanded fighting were good—enough to Confirm her as Ranger-Trained.

Tam bent, peering at the ground, and Alcandhor strode over. "What is it?"

"Ka'gua tracks. A young one. But they are about a day old."

Alcandhor smiled. "Very good." The tracks were subtle, barely seen on the narrow stretch of dirt between the rocks. Many a stripling Ranger would have missed it.

A tentative smile touched Tam's face but she did not reply.

She rarely spoke, but was that her, or her father's influence? Valdhor did not seem to approve of her talking and never addressed her except to give her an occasional order. Of course, Valdhor had never approved of talking, or jesting, or anything that would lift the gloom from life. What had it been like for the girl to be raised thus?

Thunder rumbled. Alcandhor glanced up at the swift-moving dark clouds and pulled his hood up, letting his cloak fall forward over his shoulders. Soon, a miserable, cold rain beat down on them as they trudged along.

Tam clambered surefooted down the slope, despite the pelting downpour. He gazed at the girl, his jaw clenched in self-recrimination for ignoring Valdhor as he had, even though he had only followed orders. *You must have known a child existed, Father. Your grandchild. My niece. Foresight or not, why left you her to be raised thus? We could have brought her back, raised her in her clan home.*

A bright flash lit the sky, followed by a booming crack. Alcandhor hunched inside his cloak, grinding his teeth, the storm's turmoil echoing his own. Nay, his father could not answer, but Alcandhor could act. He could be as a father to her and give her the love Valdhor should have. If it was not too late. Had Valdhor already irreparably damaged the child's heart?

~:~

"This will be our last camp." Alcandhor set his pack under a tree. The copse and a small hill protected the spot from the wind. "Tomorrow we should arrive at our city."

Valdhor scowled to himself, and the girl just looked at him with those big, golden eyes, saying nothing.

"I will gather firewood." He turned with a sigh and headed into the trees. It had been a long ten-day's journey. He would be glad to be home. He began collecting kindling.

Valdhor soon approached, his arms full of wood. "I know your mind."

Alcandhor kept his tone light, although he knew the moment testing his Thaneship had arrived. "Do you?"

"Better than any other. You mean to Present her. That is why you insist on me coming with you instead of allowing me to go on ahead to Laird Hall."

Alcandhor shrugged. "She is Trained."

"She is female."

"She is a Ranger."

"She cannot be a Ranger—she is female!"

Alcandhor threw down the wood. Valdhor dropped his armload as well and stepped away from it, his eyes lit, stance ready.

"You know my mind, do you, Valdhor? Forget not that I also know your mind—better than anyone else could. I know what you did, and why. You Trained her as Ranger knowing she never could be one. Why?" He pointed a finger at Valdhor. "Not simply because you wished so badly for a son to Train to take the place you refused for yourself. Nay. But to spite her. You blamed her for being female. You took her womanhood from her—made her a Ranger so that she can be neither.

"You did not want her, but you would not give her to your kin to raise, ah nay, not Valdhor! You refused your traditional responsibility to our clan, but in your pride you kept the girl."

"You know not of what you speak."

"Do I not? Our world is on a sword's edge of change—she will be Presented as a Ranger. Let the clan decide what to do from there. I see the strength in the girl and know her blood—none better."

"They will never allow it."

"Then they can contest you."

"Me?"

"You Trained her."

Valdhor flicked the hair back from his face, eyes dark with anger. "She cannot be a Ranger."

"Why? Is her Training incomplete? Have you done your duty only half-way?"

"Think you I would do less than my best in anything?"

"You have done less than your best in being father to her."

Valdhor lunged at Alcandhor with a raging growl.

~:~

Tam had heard the shouting and crept toward the men, hearing all but understanding little. She stood rooted as they began to brawl. Despite her horror at seeing her father fighting the Thane, she watched their fight with a Ranger's eyes, looking for weakness and judging their tactics. Both were allowing their anger to control them. They could be using much better moves if they were thinking instead of feeling.

Her father would fight in anger when he had instilled in her that a Ranger never fought thus? But he and the Thane both brimmed with fury—it overflowed from them, flooding her with such force that her heart pounded, and she gasped for air.

Valdhor knocked Alcandhor flat. The Thane lay still, a painful grimace on his face. Tam's father stood, breathing like a bellows, pointing a menacing finger at him. "You have no ri—"

Before he could finish, Alcandhor spun on his back and swept Valdhor's leg. Alcandhor dove onto him as he struck the ground, and the two wrestled in unrestrained fierceness. The Thane twisted somehow—with a speed that Tam could not follow—and clamped her father in a painful-looking armlock. Her father lay prone, struggling in vain, face suffused with rage. Tam studied the position—her father's one arm straight up behind him, wrist at a peculiar angle, the Thane's knee in the center of his back. Valdhor's efforts lessened, and he was still.

"I will not be deceived by that. Not this time," the Thane hissed. "What say you?"

Valdhor curled his lip in a sneer, but after a wait and struggling one last time to break the hold, he growled, "Yield."

"And witnessed." Alcandhor looked over at Tam, and the blood drained from her face. Would they be angry she had watched their fight? Valdhor's eyes flicked toward her, and he nodded, scowling.

Alcandhor loosed him and stood. He backed away, still poised to fight. "Any more argument on my decision?"

Valdhor glared at him at he rose to his feet, his face contorted in anger. "Nay."

"Good." Alcandhor nodded at Tam. "Since you are here, Tam, you can help carry this wood."

Tam's mind whirled in confusion as they returned to camp. Why would two Rangers fight each other in a rage? Not a match to test skill, but a real fight, leaving them bruised and bloody.

Tam knelt to build the fire and jumped when Valdhor asked, "Do you truly fear treason among Rangers?" By his voice and manner, the fight never occurred.

Alcandhor sighed, his arms high as he arched his back, stretching. He shook his head, his long hair waving down his back as he did so. "In our city, I do not. However, some of those around or in Laird Hall, I know not. I would not trust anyone too far who dwells within or near

16

those walls, or in Estan. The traitors have sown their dissent most thoroughly."

"So 'tis safe in Zaidhron?"

"Aye. Why?"

"Your plan is to use her as spy, and if she is known in our city and word were to reach Laird Hall—"

Alcandhor frowned. "How can word come to Laird Hall faster than we travel? And I trust those in Zaidhron. She will be safe enough on that account, although—"

Valdhor thrust his face into the Thane's, teeth bared. "My concern is for the mission. It is bad enough you are relying on a girl-child for such an important task. 'Tis folly. You have no regard for the danger to the Laird!"

Alcandhor grabbed Valdhor by two fistfuls of jerkin, teeth gritted and eyes narrowed. "Take care how you speak to your Thane."

Tam tried to make herself small and unnoticed by the fire, afraid they were going to come to blows again. However her father bowed his head. "Your pardon."

Alcandhor let go of him. "Speak not to me again in that tone. Forget not," he pointed at Valdhor, his finger stabbing at each word. "I—am— Thane."

Valdhor grimaced in anger, but slowly it gave way to a thoughtful, approving expression. "Aye. Aye, you are."

Tam's eyes widened in surprise at her father.

~:~

Alcandhor asked Tam questions about Ranger history and Ranger Law after the meal. Valdhor had no texts to teach her from, at least not that Alcandhor had been able to discern, but she could recite much by rote. Valdhor must have taught her their laws all by oral presentation.

But did she understand what she could quote with such ease?

"What does it mean that the Rangers are the law, Tam?" The wind shifted and smoke drifted across Alcandhor's face, the acrid fumes burning his nose and smarting his eyes. He stifled a cough, blinking, as she answered.

"The Rangers are our people's peacekeepers—guardians, law keepers, arbiters, and judges. They represent the law. Without the Rangers to keep the law, there would be anarchy."

Alcandhor offered a gentle smile. "'We,' not 'they.'"

"Sir?"

Sparks flew as Alcandhor poked at the fire, trying to get the smoldering wood to flame. "You said, 'they represent the law' and you should have said, 'we represent the law.'"

Her eyes widened, and she glanced at her father. He sat with arms crossed, staring at the blaze, a scowl on his face.

"I am sorry, sir," she whispered.

The Thane leaned back against a bole with a slow exhale. He could not ask her a simple question or have a conversation without Valdhor's shadow putting a pall on it. Her fear of him was almost palpable. If only he could thrash Valdhor until he knew the same kind of fear he had put in the girl.

Alcandhor would let it go for now. She still only quoted what her father had taught her, but she knew enough to be Confirmed. He would undertake her education after this mission to ensure she had no gaps in knowledge or comprehension.

"Forgive me, Tam. I am too tired to discuss this now."

Was he indeed making the right decision and for the right reasons? His father Saldhor, a great Ranger and scholar, had been the one to emphasize that their society was too hidebound and rigid in its ways.

All the clans nestled in complacency, clinging to the comfort of traditions, suspicious, and even fearful, of change. New ideas were rare. So many of the Enaisi's books were lost, and the aliens themselves had been gone for five hundred years. Without their counsel to know what new inventions or innovations would follow accepted guidelines to safeguard the natural elements of their world, most ideas were squashed. Apathy had set in over the past generations—and stagnation.

Since being Thane himself, Alcandhor continued the barrage his father started. He encouraged his men to marry outside the clan to avoid being considered elitist. He preached against outdated customs and local traditions in both their clan and the world, and urged a return to more of the Laws of the Enaisi, lest the discontent among commoners continued to grow.

Many were embracing these ideas, especially among the younger Rangers, taking wives from outside the clan, reading about the Enaisi, and about their beginnings. The art of scribing was on the rise, and crumbling or faded records were being deciphered and copied before they were lost.

But was their clan ready for a lass as a Ranger? Was he wise to pursue this? And why did he have such resolution? Because it was time for change or to provoke Valdhor? Or perhaps merely selfishness on his part because it would give him what he wanted?

The girl sat against a tree, staring at the fire, her face blank. Did she feel anything? She never laughed or even smiled, and he sensed little emotion from her. He dropped his gaze to the flames to hide the burning anger rising again at Valdhor and at himself. Was there any way to make it up to the girl for not intervening on her behalf when he should have, years ago?

Chapter Three

Despite the drizzle, Tam threw back her hood as they topped the ridge east of the Pashelon Pass, letting the mist dampen her hair. She was now, for the first time, out of Pashelon Province and wanted to clearly see this new place. Unlike the steep, wooded hills and forested high mountains, what she saw was a grassy flatland cradled between two mountain ridges. From her father's teaching, she knew the flatland was called the Settlers' Plain, and beyond, where the two mountain ridges almost met, was the entrance to Thane Valley.

The ridge upon which they stood ran almost due north rising into higher and higher cliffs, culminating into an imposing summit before curving eastward and gently descending in height, ending at the mouth of the valley. From the corner peak, waterfalls cascaded down the precipice into a misty lake, which then emptied into a river meandering southward along the ridge wall, then east, flowing past them far below.

Nestled in front of the lake and so-amazing waterfalls, was the city of Zaidhron. Even under the grey sky, the mysterious, white shimmerstone of the Enaisi made the city glimmer.

The opposing ridge extended southeast in almost a straight line, then broke into lesser spurs and tors, veering eastward. The Settlers' Plain was cut in half by an imposing out-wall which ran in an arc east to west. Towers punctuated the wall at fixed points and abutted the cliffs on each end. A gatehouse and towers guarded a single entrance near its center.

Alcandhor's arm swept across the vista. "The mountain range that surrounds Thane Valley gives it almost complete protection. Its only vulnerability is at the mouth, which, as you can see, is narrow. Zaidhron guards the entrance and both are protected by these high, sheer cliffs that extend on either side and the guarded out-wall as well."

Alcandhor clapped a hand on her shoulder. "Zaidhron is home city of Ranger clan and will be your home when you are not on assignment."

Tam gaped at him. Her home? She would not be returning with her father to his bounds when this was over? She glanced over at her father's impassive face.

The Thane nodded toward Valdhor. "Your father has Trained you well, but you will be under my tutelage now."

Tam could not reply, could not swallow for the lump lodged in her throat. Her garden—she would not see it again. Who would tend it? Harvest it? The featherfrond and sweetfrond seeds were ready for picking. She was going to cut the umaral to make tincture. She breathed deeply, chiding herself. She was a Ranger now—did not the Thane himself say so?—and had no time for such things as gardens.

"We will stop to replenish our food, rest for the night, and get suitable garments for a mountain girl," the Thane said.

Tam dragged her gaze from Alcandhor's face back across the wide, grassy expanse to the white stone walls of the city that was her new home. Her father's bounds contained only a few small villages, which Tam had visited only when she was too young to be left alone. Even in his journeys to herders' dwellings, she waited in their camp for him most of the time. And now she must live in this city surrounded by people, with no trees, no gardens?

She swallowed hard to dispel her heartache and dread before following him and her father. They descended on a gently graded road paved with flat, smooth stone, which wound back and forth down the face of the slope. The sweet freshness of the long, rain-drenched grasses drifted up but failed to soothe her.

At the base of the slope a wide, stone bridge traversed the river and a road cut a swath through the tall grasses, heading north.

They approached the out-wall and Tam, awed at its height and length, did not notice the Rangers on guard until they hailed the Thane, saluting him with fists over their hearts.

"Keeping warm and dry?" Alcandhor called to them. The guards laughed, their eyes on Tam. She ducked her head, her eyes fixed on the paving stones.

Zaidhron loomed larger and larger, cold and formidable. The long azure and silver streamers atop the conical roofs of the towers hung sad and limp, still wet from the rain, no breeze to stir them. Bright, westerly rays broke through the scattering dark clouds, causing the protective outer wall of the city to glitter in the sunlight as if jewel-encrusted. Tam inhaled with wonder, but still, 'twas not at all a place she wanted to call home.

Rangers brought their fists over their hearts as they entered the outer gatehouse and murmurs of welcome echoed as they walked through the dank, vaulted passage.

As they trudged up the incline, Tam craned her neck to see the lofty towers flanking the inner gatehouse, amazed at their thickness and incredible height.

They passed under the raised portcullis, through the massive arch of the inner wall, and into the city. Tam halted in astonishment. She knew from her father's descriptions that the city's six outer walls created a perfect hexagon and it took about a half-hour to cross the diameter. But seeing the vastness of Zaidhron was much different than merely knowing about it.

Vendors under canopies shouted to passers-by. Women hurried along, baskets hanging on their arms and young children grasping their long skirts. Several small boys darted past, chasing each other, whooping and yelling. Two women strolled by, arm in arm, chatting. Their eyes flitted to Tam, and they began to whisper in earnest. The ring of metal on metal from a smithy echoed off the walls. Several Rangers clustered nearby, guffawing over something.

Tam shrank back from the people and noise, but the Thane put a hand on her shoulder, smiling, and nodded toward the open grounds before them. Her heart eased as she took in gardens, grass, and trees throughout. How silly to have thought all would be stone!

She gazed in unabashed wonder as they crossed the city, passing many gardens—some strictly medicinal, others filled with kitchen herbs. Tam breathed deeply of the gossa, sheena, ragal, and other herbs as they went by. In one section a flower garden boasted varieties of flowers Tam had never seen before. She longed to linger, but dutifully kept pace with the Thane. Rows of fruit trees divided many of the gardens. Stone benches sat beneath old, gnarled shade trees.

People passed them on the walkways, bowing their heads to her father and giving her a second look, causing her to avert her gaze, her face growing warm.

Shrieks and laughter came from an area where children played in a large grassy area.

Familiar sounds drew Tam's attention to her left. Beyond a low wall, boys about her age were matching, some barehanded, others with various weapons. They must be stripling Rangers, lads having above twelve years who had entered full Training. A pair fighting with staves caught her eye, and she yearned to stay and match with them.

A small, lean, grey-haired Ranger instructing the striplings called out to Valdhor, fist raising and opening to show an empty palm. Her father simply nodded, returning the traditional greeting, never breaking stride.

They approached a large door in a vast building on the western side, or range, of the city, and the Thane said, "You will be staying here."

Her stomach fluttered. Tall, white, stone walls loomed above her. Not even the flowering vines winding up trellises around the doorway and windows eased her apprehension.

22

The Thane smiled. "Not much like the cottage you are used to, is it? You can wash up here and rest tonight. We will not be leaving until dawn." He put his arm around her shoulders for a moment, his smile broadening. "Come. I think you will like it."

Entering the vast chamber, Tam stopped for a moment, gawking at the size. The aroma of baking bread and roasted meats made her stomach rumble.

Iron candelabras hung from the high, vaulted ceiling. Tapestries with scenes depicted in bright colors decorated the walls along the front and at each end between two enormous fireplaces. Throughout the hall central hearths rose as well. A broad stairway ascended the side of the back wall. The southwest corner beyond the stair contained various musical instruments. Obviously, this was the Great Hall her father had told her about.

Servants spreading cloths on the long trestle tables lining the immense hall looked up. "Where is Sarinna?" the Thane called to them as they started across, then louder: "Sarinna!"

Several women came from various doors in a hallway to the right of the stairs, exclaiming welcome.

One smiled, heading toward them, smoothing back the dark hair that had escaped her netted headcap and straggled about her face. Her mouth dropped open. "Valdhor?" She lifted the skirts of the heavy, maroon bodice-gown and ran to them, throwing her arms around him despite the travel stains and grime on his clothes. Tam stood, stunned.

"Oh, it has been so many years!" Sarinna looked up into his face, frowning. "Valdhor?"

He licked his lips and swallowed. "Aye, Sarinna."

She stepped back, hands on her hips, grey eyes narrowed. "Is that all, you vagabond? Think you that is venial?"

Pain flitted across her father's face. "It is good to see you."

Sarinna tsked and, putting a hand on each side of his face, kissed him lightly on the mouth. She then hugged him, and Tam waited, breathless, for her father's reaction. But he did not stop her or push her away. Instead, he slowly put his arms around her, returning her embrace. Tam stared, mouth gaping.

Sarinna kissed his cheek as they separated and looked over at Tam. "And who is this?"

"Tam," the Thane said. "She is Valdhor's daughter."

Sarinna's face widened into a sunny smile, and she threw her arms around Tam. "Oh, How wonderful! Welcome home, Tam."

Tam froze. The Thane put a hand on Sarinna's shoulder and pulled her gently away. "Do not overwhelm the girl."

"Do not overwhelm—?" Sarinna stopped, looking from the Thane to Tam then over at Valdhor, eyebrow raised, her expression both confused and suspicious.

"Sarinna," Alcandhor said, "we need suites readied for two Rangers for the night."

Valdhor twisted to look at the Thane. "I will barrack with the rest of the Rangers, as is wonted. She"—he nodded toward Tam, voice sneering the pronoun—"can have a spare servant's chamber."

Sarinna raised her chin. "Valdhor! You speak thus of your daughter?"

Tam's father raised up with a haughty scowl, matching Sarinna's glare, but the woman did not back away or cringe. Tam's mind whirled until she became almost dizzy upon seeing a second person unafraid of confronting her father. Who was this woman?

"Rangers," Valdhor said, his lip curled, "do not accustom themselves to luxury."

Alcandhor sighed, grimacing slightly. "A servant's chamber for Tam."

Both Sarinna's eyebrows lifted as her grey eyes darted over Tam, but before Tam could even brace herself for scrutiny, the woman turned away with a swirl of her skirts, saying over her shoulder, "Go on to the barracks then, Ranger Valdhor."

"Wait here, Tam." The Thane put a hand at the woman's elbow and walked with her toward the hallway. "There are things that need to be readied in a hurry..." His voice trailed off.

Tam stood alone, full of questions and confusion as her father stormed out of the Great Hall. She stared at the tapestries, floor, anywhere but the servants who gazed at her with open curiosity.

A lass with a round face and blonde braids looped across her neck soon approached, her eyes raking over Tam as if assessing her. Her dress was plain and cinched at the waist, and she wore no bodice-gown over it as Sarinna did. "My name is Casinn. I'm to show you to your chamber. This way, please." By plain clothes and speech, Tam took her to be a servant, but her gaze had been bold. Was she perhaps Ranger clan, but of such a diminished sept and family—as was Tam—that she worked as servant?

Tam followed her up two flights of stairs and down a hallway. Casinn stopped and opened a door. "This will be your bedchamber tonight. Sarinna said to give you Zaidhron's Chamber."

"Zaidhron's Chamber?" Tam echoed with a frown.

Casinn raised her eyebrows and said with disdain, "You know of our king? The one befriended by the Elders?"

"Elders?"

Casinn planted a fist on one hip. "The *Enaisi*," she sneered. "Do you know about them?"

Tam did not care for Casinn's attitude, but lifted her chin and answered as she felt her father would. "Aye. Our alien mentors. And Zaidhron was the first and last king on this world."

The girl sniffed. "This was the first building the Elders raised when we came here, and this"—Casinn's arm swept through the door—"was the king's chamber. It's considered an honor to be given this room."

Casinn's presumption goaded Tam and she shot back, "Then I am honored." She pushed past the girl and into the hallowed chamber; it consisted of a bed, a wardrobe, a small table and chair, and of course, a fireplace.

"Since you missed afternooning," Casinn said, "I'm to bring up a tray. After you eat, I'm to take you to the bathing chamber, and bring your new clothes."

The door slammed, and Tam was alone. She stood still for a few moments, trying to make her mind adjust to this place. She hung her cloak and weapons on the pegs, then dropped her pack by the wardrobe. A breeze puffed in the windows, wafting the curtains. Tam walked over and pushed them aside to find these windows had glass doors in them and were swung open. How wonderful! Fresh air mingled with cooking smells floated up as well as the sounds of many people bustling in all directions below. A broad walkway followed the edge of buildings that encircled that huge, green area of gardens and trees and fountains. Not the same as the wild, by any means, but beautiful. A refuge from the city within the city. Aye, Tam liked that.

Tam stood, engrossed by all the activity until a knock at the door interrupted her reverie. She let the curtain fall and turned, blinking at the dimness of the room.

Casinn entered carrying a tray and a candle. The girl set the tray on the table. She lit the candle on Tam's table with her own, then left without a word.

Tam's afternooning consisted of a meaty stew with lots of root vegetables and a mug of tea. She ate quickly, then rose and gazed about the chamber, wondering what she was to do now. She returned to the window and watched as men walked along, by the buildings and on the walkways, lighting torches.

Before long, another knock came at the door, and Casinn's voice called, "Are you ready for me to show you to your bath now?"

"Aye," Tam said, striding to the door.

The girl led her past the main stair and down other corridors until they descended narrow steps. Torches had now been lit inside the hall as well.

"Here's the women's bathing chamber." Casinn held open a door looking her up and down with a critical eye. Tam's back stiffened. Why did she resent this girl's appraisal?

"Clothes were to be brought for you. Sarinna said we would have to choose from the store of boys' clothes, as we aren't used to girls dressing as Rangers. Sarinna said if the clothes don't fit I'm to send for more."

Tam nodded, entering the room. The tubs were not like the small thing she had to pour water into from the kettle during cold weather. These were sunken into the floor, with only a shin-high ledge to step over and down into, and were big enough to sit in and stretch out one's legs. The nearest one was already filled with steaming water and screens were angled to allow for privacy. Folded garments awaited on the bench near the tub, along with a small basket of soaps, washing cloths, cleansing balls made from the spongy trunks of the sansil plant, and a comb.

"Just put your things over here." Casinn pointed to the bench. "We'll make sure the other clothes are ready, too."

"Other clothes?"

"The mountain girl clothes."

How did this girl know about that? Ah, the Thane must have told her.

"Did you wish to keep your old clothes? Because if you do, we can have them washed and mended before you leave."

Tam fingered her rough-woven clothes, comparing them to the fine garments that awaited her. She was a Ranger now. Why would she want any other attire? "Nay. I want them not."

She unstrapped her sword and knife, glancing at the girl. Surely she was not going to stay with her while she bathed? Tam paused, meeting her gaze. "I can manage."

Casinn tipped her head with a belittling expression. "If you wish. I'll be outside if you need anything. Just call."

Tam closed her eyes in delight as she lowered herself into the hot water. What a blessed experience! She breathed deeply of the mild, scented soap—nothing like the soft, pale brown stuff she made at home. If only she could prolong the bath, but if she dawdled that girl would likely come in to check on her.

She soon stood, dripping, and grabbed a drying cloth rolled in a basket next to the tub. Stars, such luxury—it was so soft to her skin.

The dark grey trous fit well enough as did the lustrous, dark green silk shirt. She held the leather jerkin out to admire it, feeling its suppleness; she could squeeze the soft, pliable leather as if it were cloth. Silver stitching outlined the armholes, neck, and the beltband at the waist. Embroidered leaves in silver decorated each side of the collar.

Only a Ranger ever wore such a jerkin! Her fingers fumbled in nervous excitement as she laced it. She traced the outline of the Thane's crest embroidered in silver over the heart—a shield with a banner crossing it diagonally, and overlaying both, a sword, tip pointed down, with a circlet hung over the hilt. Her father's and the Thane's jerkins had such a crest, but other Rangers she had seen had not. What did it mean?

Except for her boots, she wore all new attire, and it was the proper grey, brown, and green for a Ranger. She stared down at herself, incredulous. Even if never Presented—surely the Thane had not been serious in stating thus to her father—she was truly a Ranger!

As she strapped on her leg-knife, she heard Casinn through the door. "Are you finished?"

Tam lifted the latch to let her enter. "Almost."

"Good. The Thane has called conclave. I'm to take you there."

Tam met Casinn's incredulous stare as she belted on her sword, her chin set. "I am ready." She followed Casinn down several hallways and outside. They headed north on a road skirting the edges of the range of buildings to their left and the grounds to their right. Shadows and light from the torches played against the walls and tiled path, the soft spitting sounds of flame mingling with night noises of various insects and birds. Tam had given no thought to wildlife in the city, and found comfort in the familiar sounds.

Shouts drew Tam's attention above. Women chatted to each other on balconies. Even in the torchlight, Tam could discern bright displays of flowers and vines overhanging the rails.

Several girls about Tam's age shrieked, racing down stairs that curved down into a small, circular courtyard. They sat, laughing, filling ewers from the water that tinkled almost musically into a fountain while the firelight on the water rippled reflections onto their faces and the walls.

Casinn continued on to another section of buildings which were quiet and mostly dark. A door flanked not only by torches but by banners in Ranger clan colors, azure and silver caught Tam's attention. At the center of each banner was the Thane's crest embroidered in gold and purple.

They entered and climbed the stairs. Casinn stopped in front of a door with the Thane's crest on it, knocked, and departed, leaving Tam standing alone.

Tam swallowed as the door opened. A lean Ranger with long, light red hair caught to the back of his neck in a thong stood in the doorway, his blue eyes wide as he stared, mouth open. He looked over her garb head to foot.

"Well, Andhrel, bring Valdhor's daughter in," came the Thane's low voice.

So this was Andhrel. By her father's instruction she knew the names of their clan's chiefs. Stars, she was to stand before them all! Andhrel held the door wider for Tam to enter. She blinked, biting her lip, then slipped into the room. The Thane sat at the head of a long, polished, wooden table, with her father on his right. Both had hair still damp from their own baths.

Why was her father seated at the conclave table? If the meeting was over her Training and allowing her to be a Ranger, should he not be standing with her? And if not, why was he seated at the table with the chiefs of the clan?

At a table to one side, well lit by candles, sat a Ranger with sun-streaked, light brown hair cascading over broad shoulders. Like most Rangers, he had a moustache and close-cropped chin beard. Inkhorn, pens, a small knife, and paper on the small table revealed he was a scribe. His wide-set, brown eyes scrutinized her. Being unused to such examination, warmth crept into her face, and in a fluster, her eyes darted back to Andhrel. He gestured for her to stand at the end of the long table. His gaze flicked between her and Valdhor, then he walked over and sat, his moustache and chin beard bristling as he pursed his lips.

The four Ranger chiefs studied her. Her stomach knotted, but she forced herself to stand with as calm a demeanor as she could muster at the end of the table opposite the Thane, returning their gazes.

The Ranger next to her father smiled openly at her, a mischievous gleam in his green-grey eyes. Stars, he was tall, even sitting down! A short lock of ebony hair curled impudently down his forehead, and Tam had the urge to rush around the table and smooth it back. A leather thong pulled the rest of his thick, wavy hair to his neck where hung down his back.

Andhrel sat between the two other Rangers facing her father. All three had similar coloring and looks, but the one's hair was lightly streaked with grey: Andhrel's father Lamadhel. So the stocky one on his other side was his younger brother Eladhrel.

The three looked over her Ranger garb as if a mistake had been made. Lamadhel stood, his gaze tearing away from Tam to stare at Valdhor before focusing on the Thane. "Valdhor's daughter is a Ranger?"

"Aye, Lamadhel. This is Tamissa, daughter of Valdhor," Alcandhor said. "Tam is Trained, and I mean to Present her this evening."

She held her breath, bracing herself for an onslaught as Andhrel and his brother lunged to their feet, shouting.

"You cannot mean it!"

"There is no precedent, Thane!"

Alcandhor's eyes bespoke calm as he sat with hands folded. The tall Ranger, who must by default be the remaining chief Haladhon, remained silent although his eyes twinkled. Her father had not moved, but his displeasure was strong—like a knife in her stomach. The protesting Rangers quieted as they received no reaction from the Thane and slowly sat, casting uncertain glances at Tam. She had her own doubts—nay, more than doubts, but dare she speak? Haladhon, who had stayed seated, met Tam's eyes and grinned, winking at her. His amusement bubbled inside her, and she relaxed a little, sensing in him an ally or friend. Stars, she had let her guard down again—she blocked, her eyes flicking to her father.

"There is no precedent for this," Andhrel repeated.

"Then we make one."

"But the law—"

"What law? We have outdated customs and traditions, as we have agreed before. Should we maintain things as they have been when it means taking hard blows, or roll with the blows and strike with changes as we deem them necessary?"

"But this is totally out of our ken!"

"So we must think for once instead of relying on the ways of our ancestors?"

Andhrel looked down with a slow, deliberate exhale.

"No female has ever been Ranger, Thane," the older Ranger said.

"Until now."

"But—"

"Lamadhel," the Thane leaned forward. "Where does it specifically say in our law that females cannot be Trained?"

"I..." Lamadhel sat back, one hand stroking his chin beard, frowning in thought. "I cannot think of any place where it states thus, although Rangers' duties are clearly defined in the law."

"True. But no specific description is given of those who carry out those duties."

"The reference is always 'he' in the detailing of Rangers' duties," Eladhrel said.

"Oh, come, cousin, the masculine is always used for collective pronouns, as you well know."

Lamadhel clenched both fists. "But females are not Trained!"

"Do you then contest Valdhor?" the Thane asked, lifting his eyebrows.

"Contest Valdhor?" Lamadhel repeated slowly.

Tam's gaze was drawn to her father as was Lamadhel's. Valdhor sat with his arms folded, a surly expression on his face.

"He Trained his daughter. Do you contest that Training?"

The room was silent save for the scratching sound of the scribe's pen. Tam's back straightened the slightest bit in pride that her father was so respected.

"But she has not been tested. How do we know—" Andhrel stopped and inclined his head to Valdhor. "Your pardon, Valdhor. I mean not to cast aspersions on your ability to Train, but—"

"Do you not?" Haladhon stretched his legs out under the table and leaned back, folding his arms. "Think you Valdhor would do less than provide us with a Ranger fully Trained to his standards?" His voice mocked, but did he taunt Andhrel or her father?

"It is still traditional to test any Ranger not Trained within the city or at a Ranger hold," Andhrel said.

"I tested Tam on the way here," the Thane said. "Is that not true, Valdhor?"

Tam inhaled sharply—the Thane's attention to her as they traveled from her mountain home now made sense. The sparring, and asking her to identify tracks, and all the questions...

Her father grimaced and shifted in his seat. "It is."

"You have no intention of listening to us, do you, Thane?" Lamadhel asked, his voice stiff and formal.

"Did you not hear him state that he is going to Present her tonight?" Haladhon asked. "He brought us here for the courtesy of letting us know so we would not look foolish when she is Presented. Look at her jerkin collar—it is leaf-clustered. She is Confirmed."

They all looked at Tam's collar. Awed, she had an urge to finger the embroidered leaves on the leather, but dared not move.

"Is that not right, Thane Alcandhor?" the tall Ranger asked, a smug smile on his face.

"It is, you rascal, unless anyone here contests Valdhor."

The chiefs exchanged glances but said nothing.

"Also," the Thane straightened, glancing around the table, "we need to decide if and how the Confirmation of a female affects our laws on heirship and ascendancy to Thane."

They all gawked at him. Tam did not understand, and the strong emotions of these people made it difficult for her to continue to block them all. She could not focus her thoughts.

Eladhrel leaned forward, anxiety in his round eyes. "But Thane," he hesitated, glancing at Valdhor. "What of you?"

Alcandhor settled back with a slight, cocky smile. "What of me?"

Valdhor snorted. "Know you not he would fain be rid of the mantle placed on him?"

"As you were to rid yourself of it?" Alcandhor shot back.

The two locked eyes. In the ensuing silence, tension stretched like a bowstring. Tam's throat closed at their fierce contest. Even the scribe was still.

Valdhor dropped his gaze, and Tam allowed herself to take a deep breath. Who was this man that he could make her father yield?

Alcandhor looked at the Ranger chiefs. "Well? What effect does a female Ranger have on laws of heirship and ascendancy to Thane?"

"You are truly earnest?" Andhrel asked.

"'Tis a valid question we must consider."

"Heirs must go through the male line," Andhrel said.

"Is that a consensus?" Alcandhor asked. "Valdhor?"

"I agree."

Why was her father's opinion asked? Tam frowned, her confusion deepening into frustration. She understood so little and here they were, treating her as if she were no more than a statue. Her jaw clenched.

Haladhon lifted a hand. "We have not asked the girl. If we accept her as Ranger, should she not have a vote? What is her status? Why is she standing there on display instead of sitting here with us?" His eyes narrowed as he looked at each man. "She is accepted as a Ranger, is she not?"

The three Rangers exchanged glances, the older one shaking his head with a frown.

"We have no choice," Andhrel hissed to him.

Eladhrel cut his eyes to Valdhor and leaned over. "He is right."

Lamadhel grimaced, letting his breath out in a slow exhale. He muttered something under his breath then said, "Aye. We accept her."

"So then, she should be sitting here. Only where do we seat her? What rank does she hold? Our rank is usually coupled with our status. Do we now separate the two?"

Valdhor's lips curled. "You are a fool, Haladhon. I sit as Second at Table, and I am not in line for ascendancy to Thane."

Haladhon laughed. "Only because you renounced it."

Tam's head spun. Her father was in line to be Thane, and he gave it up? How could that be?

"And it does not answer my question. Where does she sit at this table?"

31

Andhrel cleared his throat. "I would say seating should be held by status, as has been accorded to Valdhor."

Haladhon stood, grinning, a hand out toward Tam. "Come, Tam. Take your proper place, and welcome."

She took the seat Haladhon vacated. He pulled out the chair to her right and sat, draping his arm over the back. The chair was still warm and his arm against her back more so. She was unused to such unconstrained familiarity, but his easy-going manner kept her from feeling too uncomfortable.

"So now, since Valdhor votes because of his status, then Tam votes too?" Haladhon asked.

The men all exchanged glances.

Andhrel's voice was slow and pensive. "That would seem to follow the same line of reasoning."

Haladhon chuckled and turned to Tam, leaning close. "So, Tam, think you that females Trained as Rangers should be allowed in the line of heirship?"

Tam frowned, staring at the grain and whorls in the wood of the well-worn but polished table. Their whole clan structure was based on male descent. Females traditionally became part of the family they married into. A change would throw their entire clan structure into upheaval. She could not imagine the result would be anything but chaos. She looked up into Haladhon's amused eyes. "Nay, sir."

"So you refuse being Thane then?" he asked dryly.

Valdhor slammed a hand on the table. "That is out of order!"

"It is not," Haladhon replied with a glib air over Tam's head. "You gave up Thaneship to your brother with the stipulation that if you had a male heir, he would be Trained and become Thane. If we amend the law to allow females in the line of heirship, then Tam becomes Thane."

Tam started at the words *to your brother* and stared at the Thane in disbelief. He was her father's brother? Her uncle? Her father had told her his line was ended—that he had no family. But she did have family after all! That kind man was her uncle! Her own uncle!

Chapter Four

Tears smarted in Tam's eyes, and she dropped her head to blink them away before anyone could notice. She surreptitiously wiped the wetness from her hands.

"What say you to that, Tam?" Haladhon asked.

"Pardon, sir?" Her head still spun as she tried to digest the revelation.

"What say you to being Thane?"

"You mock me, sir," she whispered.

Haladhon's tone softened. "Nay, Tam, I do not. I wish you to understand all that is being discussed and to know your honest thoughts."

Sensing kindness, she looked up despite her tears. Gentle eyes smiled at her. She took a breath, hoping her voice would be steady. "We have a Thane, sir. My loyalty is to him."

His eyebrows went up. "Well spoken." He gave her shoulders a squeeze, grinning. "And do not call me 'sir.' After all, you rank me."

"Why do you consider her answer well-spoken? Because she did not wish to usurp me?"

"Aye." Haladhon chuckled. "How many cocksure young Rangers her age would not dive at the chance to be Thane?"

Alcandhor snorted. "None, if they knew the headaches of the position."

The statement drew snickers.

Haladhon grinned, waving an arm. "Besides, if she knows our laws, which she must since Valdhor Trained her"—his voice again mocked—"then she knows she could bring up Question on the law at any time."

"I would not!" She startled herself at her own boldness. The men all stared at her. She gulped, feeling her face flush. "Ascendancy has passed on, and if I were to do so it would disrupt the whole clan."

"Spoken like a true Ranger," Andhrel said.

Lamadhel eyed her then slowly nodded. "Clan first."

Valdhor leaned back, crossing his arms with a sullen grimace. "Is this over now, or are we going to drag this conclave out? It seems all has been decided."

The Thane regarded Valdhor with a cold expression before looking around the table. "Tam is accepted as Confirmed as Ranger-Trained and

33

holds the corresponding status according to her family. Is there dissent?"

No one spoke, and in the silence a musical sound rang out, echoing throughout the city.

"Mealtime horns, Thane," Haladhon said. "Shall we end and go to meal ere we die of starvation?"

The Thane rolled his eyes. "You merely wish to get to the Great Hall before meal so you can watch reactions over our newest Ranger."

Haladhon chuckled.

The Thane sighed and glanced about the table. "So be it. This conclave is over."

Valdhor shot up and out of the chamber. Tam breathed easier. But did she have the courage to ask if what she heard was true?

Haladhon watched the departing Ranger. "As cheerful as ever."

Alcandhor eyed Haladhon with a disgusted look. "One day that mouth of yours might cost you."

"Perhaps, cousin, but I will go down laughing."

"Of that I have no doubt," Alcandhor retorted.

The scribe chortled as the Rangers all rose to leave. Haladhon reached back and swatted at him with a grin.

Tam still sat. She took a breath—she must ask now. "Sir? Is it true that you are my uncle?"

Alcandhor looked puzzled. "Of course, Tam."

"So, I do have family?"

All the Rangers turned to her.

"What do you mean?" asked Haladhon.

"I..." Tam swallowed, hoping to stop the tears. "My father told me he had no family, and I never knew—"

They all gasped, Andhrel exclaiming, "He what!"

Alcandhor raised his hand for silence. "All this time, you never knew? I assumed you knew I was—he never taught you your family lineage?"

"Nay, sir. He said it mattered not because his line was ended, and there was no family."

Lamadhel and Andhrel both spoke at once:

"Alcandhor—"

"Thane, we must—"

The Thane held up his hand again, his blue-grey eyes filled with pain. He came around the chairs and knelt in front of her, taking her hands into the warmth of his roughened, callused ones. "Tam, I am your uncle."

Haladhon's hands rested on her shoulders. Lamadhel stood behind the Thane, smiling at her. "I am your great-uncle." He gestured to

Eladhrel and Andhrel, who flanked him. "These are my sons—your cousins."

"And I am your cousin too." Haladhon squeezed her shoulders lightly. "Your first cousin, once removed."

The scribe stepped up, an intense look in his warm, brown eyes. "I also am your cousin, Tam, although more distantly. I am Maradhor, and we are seventh cousins."

She swallowed hard, trying desperately to stop the tears that threatened to shame her.

"Let me talk with Tam alone, please," the Thane said.

The Rangers filed out. He leaned close. "Go ahead, Tam. Cry. 'Tis not wrong to cry." Tears welled in his eyes, although he smiled at her. He swept her hair back from her face with his fingers and despite all her efforts, she began to weep.

His arms wrapped around her with a firm gentleness. She clutched at him, sobbing. A warmth of affection and peace settled over her. Being touched, held, felt new and strange but comforting. As the crying slowed, she sat up, her breaths coming in jerking sobs. "Why did he never tell me?"

Alcandhor sighed. "Your father has always had strange ideas and ways. I cannot explain him, and I certainly do not excuse him."

She wiped her eyes and her nose on the back of her hand.

"Come. Shall we get you washed up before introducing you to more of your kin?"

Tam nodded and followed him out.

After washing her face in a room downstairs in the back, she took a few moments to calm herself. She could hear voices indistinctly and opened the door.

"...many things, but this went too far," Lamadhel said.

"I cannot comprehend being told one has no family. Imagine thinking you have no family, no sept—not knowing your place in the clan. Stars, how horrible," she heard Andhrel say.

"What a lonely torment for her to have lived with," Eladhrel said.

"What are you going to do about this, Thane?" asked Lamadhel.

"I intend to call Question, but after this mission." His voice lowered and sounded urgent, insistent. "I need Valdhor."

"You dare not put off calling Question," Lamadhel said.

"It rankles me, Uncle. Think you I want to let this go? I want to grab him by the throat and make him answer for what he has done! But I have foreseen that I need him, and 'tis all that keeps him from standing before us now."

Tam chewed her lip. Her father would have to answer for not

teaching her their family lineage! Would the punishment be severe?

"Even though our tradition gives weight to foresight, you put yourself at jeopardy by this postponement," Lamadhel said.

"Aye, I know. I swear to you, I will call Question on all matters after this crisis is over."

A pang of guilt gnawed at Tam that both her father and uncle could be in trouble—because of her. Not wishing to eavesdrop anymore, Tam stepped into the hallway. They ceased their discussion and watched her walk toward them. Their scrutiny drew heat into her face, but she forced herself to look at them. She was a Ranger and had to face circumstances and people. Rangers did not cringe or hide.

As they left the building, Tam was awed that she now walked amid the Thane and his chiefs and to know she was family. She almost stopped—she was now considered a chief of the Rangers by rank! She caught herself and kept her pace, her face composed.

The Great Hall was awash in light from not only candles on the tables, but huge rings of candles overhead and torches along all the walls, and Tam blinked several times, trying to adjust to the brightness. The huge chamber was now in the industrious process of being prepared for the evening meal. Servants scurried in every direction with platters and piles of dishes, the sounds of clattering and chattering filling the air.

"I would wager that many families find excuse to eat here tonight," Haladhon said with a chuckle.

"No doubt," the Thane replied. "Especially since I had the drum tower near Pashelon Pass send word that we would be arriving today."

Sarinna hurried over. "What was that conclave about?"

"You know we cannot discuss that, but you probably have a good idea anyway."

She made a face at him and turned to Tam with a smile. "Welcome again, Tam."

"Sarinna is your aunt—your father's and my sister." Alcandhor grinned. "You have many relatives to meet, so be not afraid to admit if you lose track of which face goes with which name."

"Are you going to whisk her off again, or may I have a little time to chat with her?"

"With evening meal upon us? What time is there?"

"For Tam, I will find time. I want to get to know my niece."

"I need to have a word with you first, Sarinna, about preparations for the morning."

"You have already spoken to me about that."

"I wish to go over it again."

Tam's aunt tsked as she and Alcandhor walked away.

~:~

"What is it?" Sarinna asked as Alcandhor pulled her into the early room and shut the door.

"I needed to tell you something very disturbing. And you must not react overtly about it around Tam."

"What do you take me for?"

"A very strong, outspoken woman, as you well know. But this requires tact. For Tam's sake."

"So tell me."

He studied his sister's face. "Tam is as skittish as a wild animal. Valdhor raised her in the solitude of the wild. She is not used to being around people and she is not sure of herself. You need to go easy."

Sarinna put her fists on her hips. "Think you I have not woven that tapestry already? Tell me before I thrash you."

"I am just making sure." Alcandhor let his breath out. "Valdhor has done something terrible, and it is worse than I first knew." He clasped his sister's shoulders. "Sarinna, he told her he had no family. She never knew until the conclave that she had any close kin."

"What!" Sarinna stiffened, her eyes turning black with fury.

"Calm down!"

"What are you going to do about it?"

"Think you I will not address this? The offense must be dealt with—along with his treatment of her and her birth record. But with this crisis, I have need to postpone calling Question—"

"Why did you not address it at the conclave?"

"We discovered it after the conclave was over."

Sarinna crossed her arms. "Explain that, please."

Alcandhor sighed, combing his fingers through his long hair. Thane of the Rangers and he answered to his sister. "We adjourned, and Valdhor left. We all were getting up to leave when Tam asked me if it were true I was her uncle."

"Bells and stars in heaven!"

He frowned, weariness stealing over him. "I doubt my wisdom on following Father's instructions in dealing, or actually not dealing, with him."

"The past you cannot change. But you can now offer Tam what she has never had—family."

"I can offer?"

Sarinna's face softened, and she smiled. "We can offer."

He grasped her extended hands, his smile an absent afterthought.

"The trouble is, I cannot call conclave. I never even brought up his treatment of her, or of having never registered her birth. I need him too badly right now."

"I know. You had sight. And the others know, I am certain."

"They do. I have told the chiefs I will call Question on Valdhor when this crisis is past, but they are not pleased."

"You will handle it."

"I wish I had the faith in me you have."

She touched her hand to Alcandhor's cheek. "That is because you only ever see your faults. And I see both your faults and your strengths, my dear brother."

Alcandhor shook his head. He could see no strengths—only a man who hung on to his duty because it was all he could do.

~:~

The Great Hall bustled as the servants finished setting the long tables and people sought their seats.

"We are going to be trampled!" Haladhon rolled his eyes with a theatrical wave, as two women passed them carrying stacks of plates. He put a companionable arm around Tam's shoulders. "Let us go to table."

They approached the head table, set centrally at the western end of the hall. Haladhon gestured toward the bench. "This is your place Tam. One place from the end." He sat next to her, on her right.

People passed behind the elegantly carved, highly polished wooden chair at the end of the table, their curious glances cast at Tam.

A tall, slender woman with fine features crossed the hall, one hand on the heavily bejeweled necklace at her throat. As she passed a group of young children, she twitched the gold-edged hem of the brocade bodice-gown away, her lip curling with disdain. She drew near, her oval eyes fixed on Tam with a smile.

Haladhon stiffened.

The woman held out her hands to take Tam's. "My dear Tam." Rings dug into her fingers. "Welcome. I am your aunt, Alcandhor's wife. My name is Aleta."

Tam gave a timid smile, suppressing a shiver. Cold emptiness from her aunt chilled her, although the woman was not blocking her emotions. And why did hostility radiate from Haladhon?

"I know not that we will have a chance to talk before you leave," Aleta said, "but when you get back, we will have plenty of time to get to know each other."

She bent and pressed her cheek to Tam's. A sickeningly sweet smell overcame Tam, almost making her gag. She held her breath until the woman straightened and exhaled when Aleta walked away.

"Pay her no heed," Haladhon murmured in her ear. With a quick glance up at his set face, Tam nodded.

The Thane's wife walked across the hall, chin lifted, but received not so much as a deferential gesture or bow. She approached a side table and shook her finger at a little girl jumping on a bench.

The child turned away with a toss of light brown curls and an impertinent wrinkle of her nose. Her eyes widened, and with a squeal, the girl hopped down and ran across the floor to Alcandhor. He picked her up with a laugh and carried her back to the table. After putting her down, he held out his arms.

Two boys dressed in grey, with unadorned jerkins, embraced him. With a shy smile, the younger boy handed a knife to the Thane, who hefted it with an approving nod. He gave it back, clasping the boy's shoulder. Tam understood. The boys were Trainees. The younger son had proven himself with a blade and was now allowed to carry his first real weapon.

The Thane sat and talked to the boys before gathering them both into another hug. The little girl tugged his sleeve for attention. He picked her up again, swinging her into the air. She shrieked with laughter, and he set her down with a kiss.

With a heavy swallow, Tam blinked hard. What would it be like to be picked up and kissed? She pushed the thought away as the Thane approached the table and stood next to the beautiful chair.

He smiled at her. "During the day meals, we eat together as families. But the evening meal is when any business will be discussed so Rangers eat at the center tables and their families to the side."

A gong sounded, and people scurried to get to their seats. Valdhor appeared at the table to Tam's left. Haladhon stood, gesturing for Tam to rise as well. Every table had filled.

Haladhon snickered and whispered, "Amazing how many decided to eat in the Great Hall tonight."

Tam tried not to feel self-conscious with so many people close around and staring at her.

The Thane waited. When it became silent, he motioned for Tam to come to him. She glanced sideways at her father, but he scowled at the table. She rose, her heart beating so hard she felt choked. Only her uncle's smile gave her strength to face all those people. He turned her around to face the hall, his hands on her shoulders. In a clear voice, Alcandhor spoke. "Hear me all! This is Tamissa, daughter of Valdhor. Today Tam has been Confirmed as Ranger-Trained and sits as Third at

Table."

Audible gasps and murmurs filled the Great Hall. Tam looked about at the myriad faces, determined to hide her qualms. The Thane stepped around to face her, smiling wider. When the hall had quieted, he put his fist over his heart, and all the other Rangers followed his example.

"Bow, Tam," Haladhon whispered.

Tam did, eager for the chance to lower her head and avoid all the curious stares. As all the Rangers sat, she almost stumbled stepping over the bench to reseat herself. She dared not look up as her face again flamed. Stars, would she ever stop blushing?

The gong rang again.

Serving bowls and platters were passed around the table, filled with various kinds of meats, greens, roots, tubers, and other vegetables. Tam's stomach growled at the savory smells, and her mouth watered.

Bread was passed—not the heavy, flat bread she was used to, but a round loaf, crusty on the outside and light on the inside. And butter! She had not had butter since she was a little girl. A faint memory of a woman rocking a churn came into her mind, and she tried to see the face that went with it. An ache grew deep inside, and the image faded. She sighed and concentrated on her food.

Haladhon leaned close. "Wine or ale?"

She had never had either, only being used to water or the teas she made from herbs and fruit. Would it be rude to ask for water? Not wanting to appear uncertain, she made a quick decision. "Wine, please."

He filled a stemmed glass and handed it to her.

"Thank you," she murmured, putting it to her lips. She kept from making a face at the aroma that went up her nose, and had to redouble the effort when she tasted the wine. Her mouth wanted to pucker, and she barely kept from shuddering. How did people drink this stuff?

She put the glass down and continued her meal. The food at least was good and served as an excuse for not participating in the conversations around the table.

The young Rangers across from her talked about who had thrashed whom in recent matches, with glances thrown in her direction.

As one youth bragged, Haladhon bent close with a chuckle, murmuring, "What think you of their method of trying to impress you?"

With a timid glance up at him, she whispered, "Deeds speak for themselves and need not a cockerel to crow on their behalf."

Haladhon threw back his head and roared. "Well said, Tam. Well said!" He continued to laugh, and she enjoyed the sound. His laughter was not raucous, but joyful and almost musical.

Tam pretended to sip the wine, surreptitiously regarding the

Rangers around her and noticed something peculiar. Some wore a necklace of tiny beads of various colors that fit close around the neck. No two were alike. Her uncle wore one, as did Lamadhel and both his sons. Haladhon did not. Nor did her father. An older Ranger across the table wore one, and one of the young Rangers. But for what purpose?

Her study was broken as Haladhon handed her a platter of what he called pastries. "Enjoy, these are a treat."

The pastries were not quite like bread, and as Tam took one she found it sticky on the top. She gingerly bit into it, her eyes widening. Oh, it was sweet! She ate it with deliberate slowness to enjoy each bite and, following what the others did, dipped her fingers in the water bowl nearest her and wiped her hands on the edge of the tablecloth.

Haladhon leaned over. "You do not talk much, do you?"

Tam looked up at her tall cousin and swallowed. "I have nothing to say."

He laughed again, and leaning behind Tam, he pushed her father's shoulder. "Aye. You are Valdhor's daughter all right."

Tam cut her eyes to see her father glare over at Haladhon and turn away. She breathed a sigh of relief. Why did Haladhon wish to goad her father? Surely he knew her father's temper.

"So how do you like your place usurped by a lass, Haladhon?" called a Ranger from further down the table.

Tam's face grew hot.

Haladhon leaned back to see him. "Think you I mind, Loch'alan? It is her place. She is a Ranger and ranks me."

"How can a female be a Ranger?" Loch'alan asked. "Who would trust a lass at their back?"

Haladhon's voice mocked now. "Do you contest Thane Alcandhor? Valdhor? All the chiefs at the conclave?"

A hush descended on the Great Hall.

Tam frowned; nay, this was wrong. By laws of the Rangers and the traditions that Tam's father had taught her, this was wrong. Aye, it was the Thane's decision that the young Ranger was questioning, and her father's Training, but now, she was Confirmed as Ranger. She had been Presented. Her standing as Ranger was her responsibility, and it was on her shoulders to respond to this challenge. Her heart beat so hard it pounded in her ears, and she felt like she was choking again, but she had to do what she knew was Ranger Law, despite all the people who would stare.

She stood, her chin set. "It is not the Thane nor my father that he contests, but me." She looked down the table at Loch'alan. He was young with scattered wisps of brown fuzz where his chin beard should

41

be. "You do contest me?"

His blue eyes were round. "But you are a lass!"

"Do you contest me?"

Chapter Five

Tam did not move while Loch'alan's eyes darted around the table as if seeking support. Finally, he glared at the Thane and spat, "Are you mad, Alcandhor? You cannot mean to let this bloody farce happen?"

Her father stood with such a swift jerk that the bench seat jumped. "Is this the irreverent way you speak to the Thane? And of Enaisi blood?"

Loch'alan swallowed, his face draining of color as he stared at Valdhor. His gaze returned to her uncle, and he inclined his head. "Your pardon, Thane. But can you mean to allow this? She is a mere girl. A lass."

The Thane put down his wine glass, his expression expectant. The young Ranger looked over at Tam in disbelief. She locked eyes with him, determined to appear stolid. Lamadhel mumbled that she looked like her father.

Loch'alan threw his arms out. "I cannot fight a lass!"

"You contested her," Haladhon said, his tone mocking, "and she called you out. You expected that not, enh? Are you bested by a lass?"

Loch'alan glared over at Haladhon, jaw muscles jumping. He tore his eyes from Haladhon to pierce Tam and stood. "Aye, I contest you!"

Murmurs rippled through the hall as everyone rose, heading for the wide doors that led outside. Tam's stomach tightened, not at the contest, but that all these Rangers would witness it. Haladhon clapped his hand on Tam's shoulder with a broad grin.

"Do not let me down. Thrash him thoroughly!"

Torches flickered from the walls around the grounds and on poles in the walkways. Tam inhaled the cool evening air, refreshing after the warmth of the Great Hall. Much better. She needed a cool head for this match.

Loch'alan, surrounded by friends, sauntered to a Training area. He had good height, almost as tall as her father—though not as broad-shouldered or muscular. Would he be as hard a fighter?

Haladhon stayed at her side. The Rangers circled to create a huge ring while others stood outside it, peering in.

Loch'alan, already in the middle of the ring, handed his knife to a young Ranger for safekeeping. With a haughty stare at Tam, he tossed his brown hair back over his shoulders. Was he the formidable opponent his attitude proclaimed? Tam gave Haladhon both her blade and sword, which he took with a grin and a wink. Taking a deep breath, she approached the center of the ring weaponless.

She and the young Ranger faced each other with a salute—their right fists over their hearts—and assumed a fighting position.

Loch'alan shook his head with a frown as they circled each other. "I have no desire to hurt you, lass."

"I am no lass but a Ranger, and I will fain prove it."

"Then let us get this over with." He feinted coming in to her right, but closed on the left, grabbing her arm. She wrapped her hand around his wrist, breaking his hold, and with a quick twist under his arm, she flipped him in the air. He landed on his back, rolled, and rose amid scattered laughter. Loch'alan looked around at the crowd, throwing his hair over his shoulders again, his face red.

Someone called, "Give him thunder, Tam!"

She and Loch'alan circled again.

He caught her arm once more, yanking hard. Instead of pulling away, Tam let his momentum carry her forward. Her forearm drove into his chest, and he stumbled back, releasing her. She threw a punch to his face and Loch'alan, still off balance, landed flat on his back. *Stars, how could a Ranger fight no better than this?*

She ignored the titters and whispers around her and backed up a step, ready for him. He got up, glancing about the ring, his face an angry scowl, blood trickling from his nose.

Loch'alan punched. Tam blocked and countered with a kick to his mid-section, following with a punch to the face. He blocked both but her next kick hit him square in the stomach. As he straightened, he lunged with punches to Tam's face and abdomen. She blocked the onslaught easily, then crouched to duck the following kick, but a second caught her in her gut as she straightened, knocking the wind out of her. Loch'alan swept her leg, and she hit the ground hard, renewing the breathlessness.

Murmurs rippled through the crowd, and several Rangers laughed.

Tam struggled to take a breath, to get to her feet. Loch'alan stood, bouncing on the balls of his feet, his head thrown back, eyes glittering.

As she straightened, she felt an intensity from the crowd around them, wanting a finish, wanting...what? To see her defeated? Her chest tightened afresh at the wash of foreign emotions.

Loch'alan waded in with a flurry of hard blows. Tam became defensive, merely blocking, not countering. She blinked as she blocked again and again, Loch'alan beating her back. She gave way, backstepping, sidestepping. The look on his face owned the truth in her own heart—he was besting her. She backed into a Ranger at the edge of the circle and almost gasped, but her throat closed in horror of the truth: she could not think, or fight. Desperation rose inside.

Loch'alan shot a kick to her midsection. Without thought she spun, deflecting his foot and spinning inside his defenses, and caught him in the temple with the back of her fist.

He fell onto his back with a thud, his eyes closed.

She straightened, taking deep breaths as she stared down at him. He seemed very young lying there motionless, bloody and pale, shadows flickering on his face in the torchlight. Surely he was not severely injured. Stars, she had not meant him harm. The spinning fist was an old move, one she'd been taught very young; she had reacted without reasoning. Was such a move even allowed in contest?

She barely breathed, waiting for some sign he was all right.

He blinked and grimaced, struggling to sit up. She sighed in relief, then new worries flooded her. Did this end the fight? If so, had she forfeited or won? He seemed not inclined to rise and continue.

Not sure of protocol, she stood, waiting. He stared at her, breathing hard, drawing his fist across his face. He frowned at the red smear on his knuckles, lips thinned, but then glanced around uncertainly and slowly smiled.

Hesitantly, she extended her hand and he took it, his eyes still locked on hers. She pulled him up. Humor emanated from him, but underneath, a burn simmered also.

He clasped her shoulder in the Ranger manner, gazing about at the crowd. "You may be a female, but I would fain have you at my back. By the Bells above, you are a Ranger!"

With that traditional acceding response, the ring broke with cheers and their seconds came to give them their weapons. Haladhon grinned and swatted her on the back with a wink.

She sheathed her knife and strapped her sword on again. Her eyes darted here and there, searching for her father in the throng. She could not see him anywhere, but the Thane smiled at her, looking smug. His approval was no salve to her spirit. Had he not seen her panic? 'Twas not her skill which won the match, but a chance blow.

As they came back into the hall, she sought again for her father, but did not find him. The Thane sat in his chair, with several men, not all of them Rangers, gathered around him. As she approached, she heard the Thane saying to one of them, "—prorate it for this lunation. And be certain it is listed as full allotment."

She returned to her own place, Haladhon by her side, while servants cleared the tables. Rangers scattered throughout the hall now, talking and laughing. The Thane's children ran to him, and he lifted the little girl onto his lap while the younger boy jumped onto his other knee.

Alcandhor held his hands up as one of the Rangers leaned forward to talk. "Enough! I must leave early and wish some peace tonight for awhile. Will any of you vagabonds play some music?"

Several Rangers joined the men and women who headed toward the southwest corner of the Great Hall where musical instruments were kept. Soon a melody began, a happy tune, and some people sang along with it. Tables were moved to the side and couples began to dance.

Alcandhor cuddled and talked with his children. Tam looked away as the Thane kissed his daughter's nose, laughing with her.

Loch'alan sat across from Tam. He filled her glass and lifted his own, smiling. She stared at him, perplexed.

"'Tis called a toast," Loch'alan said. "We both lift our glasses as a salute and drink."

She lifted her glass and took a sip as he did. The burning in Loch'alan, the resentment, still existed, but his broad smile belied the feeling. He bowed and walked away. Tam watched his receding back. Was the contest truly finished?

Haladhon grinned, nodding after the young Ranger. "'Twas fortunate Loch'alan contested you. He is easy-going, as is his brother, and will not take it personally. I think he also realizes he is the first one to prove you as Ranger and can state thus with pride."

Tam bit her lip. If she contradicted Haladhon, she would be admitting she had not been blocking emotions, so she remained silent.

A few Rangers wandered over and sat, wishing to share a drink as a salute. The table slowly became crowded, and her heart quickened as if assaulted by the nearness of so many people. She took slow, measured breaths to keep the panicked feeling away, glad that Haladhon stayed next to her. His presence gave her assurance.

After the Thane's children left with a young woman, Alcandhor moved over to sit next to Tam. "You vagabonds cease your toasting, or she will be giddy. We leave early tomorrow, and she must have her wits about her."

Haladhon groaned. "Remind me not of the morning!" He slapped a hand on his chest in mock agony. "I leave early as well."

Several of the Rangers chuckled.

"You are not the only one leaving early with urgent duty," one said.

As they all commiserated about dawn departures, even more Rangers joined them. Feeling smothered again, Tam dropped her head, struggling to control her breathing. The Thane put an arm around her shoulders, and a peaceful calm washed over her, dispelling her unease.

Another tune started. She heard peasants and village folk play tunes a few times in travels with her father, but nothing played so beautifully without error, so sweet and rich. Like a serene dream. She closed her eyes in enjoyment.

As the tune finished, Haladhon whispered, "That is the first smile I have seen from you, slight though it be."

Her eyes flew open and she glanced around, her face growing warm. She tried to cover her embarrassment by sipping her wine.

The Thane leaned close and, in a feigned whisper said, "You will have to forgive Haladhon. He says whatever he is thinking, even when he is not."

The men at the table guffawed, Haladhon along with them.

Some Rangers still had children sitting on their laps or next to them. Others paired off with women, dancing, or talking and holding hands. She saw Loch'alan talking to a lass. Anything she had imagined of the Rangers differed from this reality. Jesting, laughing, music. Her father had indeed given her a narrow view of the life of a Ranger.

Most of the Rangers who had gathered at their table had moved off and only the chiefs now remained, close enough as kin and friends to speak in familiar and companionable terms.

"Not what you expected, is it?" the Thane asked.

She met his kind eyes and shook her head.

"We have hard duty, and it causes us to enjoy life when we can. Here we are family and can let down our guard."

Her mind whirled—this was family. This place was home to all Rangers. And she was part of it.

"The contest took care of quite a few arched backs, Thane Alcandhor," Haladhon said in a mocking voice, talking over her head. "Just as you knew it would."

The Thane raised his eyebrows, a very innocent look on his face as he blinked at Haladhon, but smug pleasure not surprise flowed from him. "Indeed, 'twas a fortunate turn of events. Very fortuitous."

The chiefs all joined in the laughter, but Tam bit her lip in bemusement. "Sir?" she asked with a timid glance at the chiefs who were still sitting near. "How could you be sure that someone would contest? And how could you know that I would stand up to a contest, much less win?"

The Thane grinned. "Because Valdhor Trained you, my dear Tam."

Haladhon nodded. "Anyone who would contest Valdhor's Training is a fool."

"And you knew there were fools to hand?" Tam asked.

Tam jumped as Haladhon roared with laughter. Eladhrel sprayed his drink and choked trying to contain his mirth while his brother, Andhrel, pounded him on the back, laughing as well. Lamadhel covered his mouth, chuckling.

The Thane dropped his head to the table, but his back and shoulders gave away his laughter. Tam stared in confusion.

At last the Thane raised his head, wiping his eyes. He took a deep breath, still struggling to keep a straight face. "Tam, I knew someone would be fool enough to challenge, despite the fact that you were Trained by Valdhor. I did not expect it to be an older Ranger, as much as some of them might wish to contest your age or that you are a female, as all of them would know your father. They would respect his word too much to contest his Training whether they agreed with it or not."

The other Rangers murmured in agreement.

"The younger ones however, do not know Valdhor. It takes a brash youngster to stand up and contest the conclave as Loch'alan did, and I had no doubt that you could take a younger Ranger."

"But you had never seen me in contest. What if you had been wrong?"

Alcandhor shook his head.

"I admit I had doubts." The lines around Lamadhel's eyes deepened with his smile. "But you proved yourself tonight."

Tam's stomach tightened. Had they not seen how she panicked? That she only won by chance?

Haladhon grinned. "I knew it was a safe wager, although winning is not usually necessary in a contest. One must simply fight well. However in your case, you needed to win to prove yourself."

Eladhrel raised a hand. "I admit, 'twill take time to adjust to the notion of a lass as Ranger. But as Father said, you have proven yourself tonight, and"—he leaned forward—"'twas a good sight to see that cockerel on the ground."

They all chuckled.

Alcandhor stood, arching his back in a stretch. "Tomorrow starts early, and it is time for some of us to rest. You, too, Tam. Get you some sleep. Night's rest to you all."

He strode away before they could call a night's rest back to him. With a timid bow, Tam left for her chamber.

A fire blazed in the fireplace. Tam lit a taper from the flame and set it in the holder on the table. A new cloak hung in place of her old tattered one and an extra Ranger outfit was neatly folded on the chair. She picked up the new leather gloves that lay on the clothes and tried them on, flexing her fingers and making fists. Nice. She took them off, set them together, and tucked them through the beltband of her jerkin.

She opened her pack to add the clothes to it and gasped. Her book! What should she do with it? Take it with her? If only she could leave it here, safe. But how? With a regretful exhale, she quickly bundled the extra garments into her pack and heard a knock at the door as she began to strap it shut.

She rose to answer and was surprised to see Sarinna smiling at her.

"May I come in for a moment, Tam?"

"Aye."

"I will not keep you." She sat on the bed and patted it. "Come, sit down."

Tam eyed her aunt as she perched near her. What did the woman want?

"What think you of your first day here?"

"I—it is very different from what I imagined."

"Aye, it probably is. You handled yourself well. I was proud of you."

What should Tam say? She was not used to conversations, and this woman seemed determined to have one with her. Before she could think of anything to say back, Sarinna asked, "Are you nervous about your journey and first duty?"

"A little. I think."

Sarinna's eyes were kind, but her gaze was probing, and Tam fought the urge to fidget. With a quick chuckle, her aunt squeezed her hand, her grey eyes sparkling. "You are probably more nervous trying to talk to a strange woman. I forget you were raised by my taciturn brother. My apologies. When you return perhaps we can spend time together and get acquainted. I will leave and let you get some sleep." She stood.

Tam thought of her book and jumped up. "Sarinna?"

"Aye?"

"May I ask a favor of you?"

"Most certainly," Sarinna said.

"I have something of great value to me, and I did not wish to leave it at the cottage since I knew not when I would return, so I brought it with me, but I do not think I should take it away with me when I journey tomorrow." Tam gasped to catch her breath, but Sarinna's smile deepened, affection wafting from her.

"What is it, child?"

Tam knelt down at her pack and took out the wrapped bundle. She set it on the floor and peeled back the oilskin and several layers of cloth protecting her book. She stood and held it out to her aunt, sharing what she never dared ask her father. "I am not sure, but I...I think it belonged to my mother. It is all I have that I value. Will you keep it safe for me?"

Sarinna accepted the book, clasping it to her breast. "I am honored you trust me. I will most certainly keep it for you."

Relieved, Tam timidly allowed Sarinna to embrace her.

"Night's rest," her aunt said as she closed the door.

Tam sighed, closing her eyes. Her book was safe. Although a weight had lifted off her, her limbs felt leaden. She had endured days much more strenuous, why did she feel so exhausted? Just taking her clothes off taxed her.

She crawled into the bed, the first real one she had ever slept in. Tam thought about everything that she had experienced that evening. She rolled over, the softness of the bed as difficult to adjust to as these sudden changes in her life. It was a restless night.

Chapter Six

Pink clouds smudged the grey pre-dawn sky as Tam and the Thane began their journey. She pulled her cloak forward to guard against the chill in the air. By mid-morning the sun beat down, and she welcomed the breeze rustling through the trees, cooling her face.

Alcandhor slowed his pace, snagging green keeberries almost as big as Tam's fist from vines that grew up into the low hanging branches of surrounding trees. Tam did the same. She bit one of the mellow, sweet fruits in half and glanced at the ring of tiny, black seeds inside, wiping her chin with her hand.

"Mild weather and much food in the wild to extend what we have packed," he said. "This is the best time of year. What think you?"

"'Tis a good time, aye," she murmured. "Lots of wild harvest, as you say."

"There is water." He pointed at a small stream trickling over rocks a few paces to the south.

She drank and washed the juice from her hands and mouth. Afterwards, she looked up to see the Thane splashing his face—still raw and bearing bruises from the fight with her father. She bit her lip. Would it be presumptuous to offer help? "Sir?"

"Aye?"

"I–I have a salve that would speed the healing on your face."

Water dripped as he gazed over at her. "Do you?"

"Aye, sir." She pulled off her pack, rummaged through it to find the tin, and held it out.

He smiled and took it. "Thank you." He paused, and his gaze bespoke—what? Kindness? Affection? "And Tam, you need not call me 'sir' unless you are formally talking to me as Thane."

She hesitated. "What should I call you?"

He shrugged, his eyes sparkling. "Alcandhor."

Tam frowned. That was too familiar, too forward.

His smile broadened. "Or Uncle."

She met his smile with a slight one of her own as a warmth wrapped around her. Uncle. The Thane would let her call him Uncle.

As they continued, the Thane asked, "What think you of your kin?"

Tam hesitated, not certain what to say. "They are nice. Especially

Haladhon. I like his laugh."

Alcandhor chuckled. "No gloominess allowed in his presence, is there? And would it surprise you that he is one of my best Rangers?"

Tam frowned in disbelief, and her uncle laughed. "Oh, aye! And how it vexes your father. He believes one should feel the weighty burden of being a Ranger. He and Haladhon have never gotten along."

"I suspected thus," Tam whispered.

Alcandhor grinned, rolling his eyes. "And 'tis not bad enough that their personalities clash, but Haladhon has always enjoyed needling your father. And he loves playing pranks."

"Playing pranks?"

"My poor girl." Alcandhor shook his head. "I am glad Haladhon had the wit not to try any on you so soon. You know not what a prank is?"

"A trick?"

"Aye. It is playing tricks on people."

"That does not seem very nice."

"Haladhon has been known to go too far, but most of the time they are harmless. He caught me not long ago. I had just had these boots made, and he switched them. I was roasting the boot maker for being so lax in his measurements when I saw Haladhon lurking outside, then I knew."

"He would do that to you?" Tam's eyes grew wide. "But you are the Thane!"

"We are cousins, and he is my closest friend. And I am planning revenge as soon as we finish this business and return home." He chuckled, but his humor faded, his expression growing pensive. "Perhaps Haladhon is the one who will find a way to make you laugh."

"He is very different from the way I have imagined Rangers." She chanced being bold, adding, "His behavior at times seems...disrespectful."

The Thane snickered, ducking under a low branch. "Actually, you got off easy, girl. If you were scandalized by Haladhon, imagine if Marcalan had been there too."

"Who is he?"

"Marcalan is a younger Ranger, just a few years over Age. He is a rascal, and loves jesting and pranks more than even Haladhon does. He is your third cousin. When you get home, we will catch you up on our clan tree. He and Haladhon are of a kind. If they had both been there..." He laughed again.

"He was out on duty?"

"Aye."

She noticed his smile fade a little and decided to take him at his word that she could speak openly. "You do carry the weight heavily, do you not?" she whispered. "Despite your laughter and jesting."

"Aye, Tam. Very heavily," he said, his voice quiet, strained. "Rangers' duties are hazardous enough. And at times I have to send men out on special missions. Sometimes they do not come back. And Rangers are all kin. 'Tis hard. When Haladhon's father did not come back..."

Tam's eyes widened. Of course. Her father had told her the news that Chief Bardhor had died what, a year ago? And he would have been— "Haladhon's father?"

"Aye. He was a good man and advisor, as well as my uncle. Lamadhel misses his brother. And Haladhon..." He sighed. "That is why the light-heartedness is so necessary, Tam. Life has to be more than duty...and worry."

She chewed her lip, considering the gaiety she had seen in the dining hall by men who went into danger, and by the families who waited, not knowing if they would come back. Light and darkness. Just as plants need light and a dark resting time, sunshine and rain to grow. "It is a balance."

"Aye. We must find a balance or the grimness would be overwhelming. Never have we had such problems as now. Brigands roam boldly as they never did before. But also there is the unrest that is spreading. Not many Rangers live to an old age. Not in our days, anyway."

~:~

"You know," Alcandhor said that evening, tossing sticks on the fire, "we must discuss the part you are to play in Laird Hall."

She chewed her lip. Her own father did not think her worthy of this task. What if he was right? "I–I am to be a mountain lass."

"Aye. Can you do that? Can you convince everyone that you are an unlearned mountain girl?"

She tipped her head to one side and, using the slurred accent she heard the mountain people use, she delivered the story she had concocted, not that different from her own.

"It were just me and me Fa, sar. Till he fell and hit his head and died, jus' like that." She snapped her fingers.

Alcandhor laughed aloud. "Great Bells and stars, girl, what an ear you have! Your accent is perfect."

Tam relaxed a little at his praise.

"It will be necessary for you to wear the clothes for at least part of the journey. We have to have them travel-worn and dirty enough to be convincing."

"I could put them on tomorrow."

"Best wait until the day after. There is some hard climbing down before we reach the road."

That brought to her mind something else she had wondered about. She enjoyed asking questions. "Why was Zaidhron built so far away, s—Uncle? I would think it would have been better placed nearer Laird Hall."

"Aye, that is so. And many times when journeying between the two places I wished it were. But it serves a special purpose where it is located."

"What is that?"

"The Enaisi's Portal Complex is built in the mountains both above and below Zaidhron. We are its guardians, as we are of almost all their edifices. Though, I really do not understand why. It is impossible to break into those alien structures as far as I know. They certainly do not need us as guard. But it was allotted to us to play sentry anyway."

"There is no way into them? Then why still bother?"

"I did not say there was no way in," he said with a smile. "I said it was impossible to break in. There is a way in."

A shiver rippled down Tam's spine, and her breath quickened in awe and fear. "Have you ever been inside one of them?"

"Aye."

"Wh–what are they like?"

He smiled. "One day I will take you to some of them. It is much better to see them than try to describe them. But, we ought to think about now. Have you a story to go with your accent?"

She took a slow, deep breath, concentrating of her task, not old buildings left by the feared and revered Enaisi. "Yes I do. As I said, it were just me and me Fa."

He grinned. "Who else is there in your family?"

"No one. No kin. It's rough living up there. When me Fa died, I just struggled along and didn't know how I was going to manage. But then, you come and took me away."

"Good girl!" He gave her a quick hug around the shoulders. "Now, as for what you are to do in Laird Hall. I know traitors are inside. Guards, servants...I know not who. I wish you to keep an ear for anything that might point to who the traitors are and what their plans might be. As a girl from the mountains, you know little of politics and can ask questions more readily, but be not too presumptuous and incur suspicion."

Tam nodded, unsure if she should ask for more direction. Listen and ask questions. It seemed simple enough.

"We also have to make sure you know your way around the hall. You need to be as stealthy in there as you are in the wild. We know not whom we can trust." He pulled folded papers from his pack and smoothed them on his leg. "This is Laird Hall: the grounds and all the floors of the keep."

They went over the layout several times.

"Very good. But to be sure, we will go over it again each night."

"Aye, sir."

He arched an eyebrow at her. "Sir?"

She gave a tiny smile. "I was answering my Thane."

Chuckling, he put away the papers. He tossed fresh wood on the fire, sparks flying up. Smoke billowed up from the logs with hissing and popping, and soon, with a quiet *foohm*, they caught, yellow tongues licking around their sides.

He glanced up at the sky. "It grows late. Do you want first watch or second?"

Tam needed give no thought before answering. She hated watch, but would rather get it over with. "First."

The Thane lay down and soon was breathing deep and even. She gazed at him with fondness. Uncle. Her very own uncle.

The night passed and grew more chill. She wrapped her cloak more tightly about her to keep the cold out. A steady shower began that came straight down, piercing the leaves above and drenching both of them. She pulled the hood of her cloak up, trying to keep dry. Alcandhor grimaced, blinked, and sat up with a frown. "There goes my sleep. Do you want to try, or can you not in the rain?"

Tam managed to doze lightly on and off. The rain stopped, and the wind picked up just before dawn. She shivered helping Alcandhor warm food over the smoldering fire.

They drank hot tea with their breakfast, which helped a little against the chill settled in her bones. The rain came and went, but the wind stayed strong and from the east all day, biting them to the bone as they climbed over the mountainside.

"Uncle, why did we not take the road from Zaidhron?" she asked with a yawn as they settled near the fire that night.

"I want to approach from the north, to assess what movement we can see on the road between Kentin and Lairdton. It will add a day as well as hardship to the journey. But I do not apologize, Rangers do not balk at hardships."

Tam assayed a smile in answer to his, and stifled a second yawn.

Their meal was silent, both too tired to talk. The air turned as they ate and swept away the clouds, revealing the nebula. Tam was glad to see the Bells glowing above.

~:~

"This morning you become a mountain lass," Alcandhor said two mornings later. "Where are the clothes?"

"Here." She pulled the bundle from her pack.

"You can change behind those bushes."

She took the bundle, withdrew to the clump of shrubs he had indicated, and unwrapped the rough-woven, used-looking garments.

"Uncle? What is this?" she asked, holding up one of the garments. It had several lacings and a curious shape.

His mouth dropped open. "You know not what that is?"

She shook her head.

"Oh." He drew a hand across his mouth and scrubbed his face with his hand, turning bright red. "It is, uh..." He pointed to one side of his chest and over to the other. "You wear it...I mean, it is for..." He grimaced, looking perplexed. His mouth opened and closed several times, but he said nothing.

Tam had never seen anyone look, or feel, so embarrassed and lost. She tried not to laugh, but her shoulders shook despite her best effort. "I am sorry, Uncle, but your face! I have never seen such a look!"

Alcandhor grinned, and it grew into a chuckle. Before long, he was laughing aloud, and she joined him.

"By the Bells, girl, I am a fool!" He wiped his eyes. "I thought I had planned for everything, but it never occurred to me that you knew nothing of women's undergarments."

"What am I to do with this?" she asked, smiling.

He hesitated before walking over. He took the garment and held it in front of his chest. "It goes here." His face again reddened. Tam tried not to giggle. He kept his eyes on the garment as he tried to explain. "You tie these," he held up one set of laces, "under, um...well, below—you know. Then these others you lace so that..." He swallowed. "Well, you lace them...across. So it is...comfortable," he finished lamely.

Despite Tam's own embarrassment, she could not help but laugh. "I am sorry, Uncle! But you make such funny faces!"

He snickered. "You have gotten the best of me, my dear niece. And without trying."

"I can imagine Haladhon teasing you over this."

"Only if you dare tell him. Now are there any other garments you are not familiar with?"

She looked over the clothes and held up what looked somewhat like trous except they were made of flimsy white material, only came perhaps to the knee, and used a drawstring.

"You wear that, uh, underneath everything."

"And what is this? There are two dresses? But this one is so thin, like these white trous."

"That one goes next, then the underbodice."

"The what?"

"The thing with the laces."

"Then what?"

"The blouse, and the dress goes over all. You cinch the waist with this belt."

Tam sighed. "This seems very complicated and does not look very comfortable."

"Indeed. Definitely a sore trial for a Ranger."

She held up the underbodice, her nose wrinkled in disgust. "I think I am perhaps the first Ranger to have this sort of assignment."

He laughed again. "I think you are right. I will wait for you over there." He went back around the bushes and sat, looking at the ground.

Tam did well until she came to the underbodice. She tried to get the laces to tie in the proper places but it was impossible—the thing had a will of its own. She became increasingly frustrated until she was almost in tears. She peered over the top of the bushes. "Uncle, I just cannot figure this out!"

Alcandhor blinked with a helpless look.

"Would anyone know if I were not wearing this...thing?"

He shrugged. "The underbodice? Perhaps not. You are young and slender still."

"Good!" Her fingers scrambled to undo the lacings. She all but ripped it off and threw it down. The blouse and sleeveless dress posed no problem. At the last, she put on the wide leather belt and laced it, jerking the material of the dress through to allow some give to lift her arms. Wearing trous was much easier.

She put on the sandals and rolled up her own clothes. "Sarinna does not wear clothes such as these. Are her clothes just as uncomfortable?"

"I could not say, Tam," he said, smiling. "If you wish, you can ask her when we return to Zaidhron."

She came around the bushes carrying her clothes in one hand and her boots in the other. "Where will you keep my things?"

"There is a Ranger hold by the town of Lairdton. We will stop there briefly, and I will tuck them safely away for you before we go on to Laird Hall."

She tied the laces of her boots together so she could carry them slung over a shoulder and stored her clothes in her pack. She straightened. "I feel naked without even my knife."

"You cannot be seen with one and there is no way to hide the sheath under that skirt."

"I know."

"I am sorry, Tam. Hopefully you will be able to get some information for us and get out in a matter of days."

"Think you I can find anything out so quickly?"

"Aye, I do not expect you to be there long. From all reports, and my...instincts, they are ready to move. Hopefully you will see something happening."

"I hope we are not too late."

"As do I."

Tam shuddered with foreboding at the uneasiness she felt from him.

~:~

Just west of the town of Lairdton, the Thane and Tam turned north from the main road onto a path that led to an open gate flanked by Rangers. At their backs hung banners with the silver and blue of Ranger clan, edged in gold. As they passed through the curtain wall, Tam took in the small bailey and the white stone battlements of the fortified building at its center, confused. "'Tis not large for a keep."

"It is not a hall's keep, but merely a hold."

"Hold?" He had used that term before, but Tam was not familiar with it.

"Shortened from stronghold. People are fearful of our clan and words like fortress, garrison, and stronghold seem to make them nervous. Hold appears much less threatening."

"Why are people afraid of us, Uncle?"

"For the position and power of our clan, and for our numbers as well. Our clan has increased more so than any other."

"Why is that?"

"The strength of our blood, perhaps. I cannot say for certain."

Inside the building, they passed through a large foreroom with fireplaces at each end and down the hallway to a door on the left. Alcandhor put her belongings in the small room. Personal items sat on a small table across from a cot.

"They will be untouched in there," he said as they left the chamber. She hoped so. That room held not only her Ranger clothes, but her staff, sword, knife, bow, and quiver. She fingered the rough-woven dress she wore, feeling defenseless.

"Thane!" An older woman paused in the hallway to curtsey before walking up to Alcandhor. She had very dark eyes and dark hair, lightly streaked with grey. Tam sensed a proprietary attitude. "I didn't hear you come in."

"We only stopped for a moment, Sherel. How go things here?"

"Strange. Many Rangers whom I have never met were here and have left again." Sherel crossed her arms. "I cannot manage this hold without knowing what is happening." Her gaze swept over Tam with open curiosity.

Alcandhor nodded. "Soon, but now, just obey. Keep sharp watch for anything unusual. Tell all the Rangers that journey in to report to Haladhon when he comes, and they are none to leave this hold. Marcalan and Capalan should be arriving, I wish them to stay to hand to report directly to me. Tanadhon is to receive all other reports for me and coordinate with Haladhon."

Sherel's voice dropped low. "By the Bells! This truly is serious, isn't it?"

"Just do as you are bid. Watch. And listen. You do both so well."

"That I do," she said with a smirk. Her eyes lingered on Tam, but Alcandhor did not introduce them.

"I will return ere long."

A Ranger with piercing blue eyes and dark hair met them on the way out. He bowed. "Thane."

"Tanadhon, remain here. I will return soon and need to speak to you."

"Aye, Thane."

"Who is he, Uncle?" she asked as they left.

"He is in command of this hold and our distant cousin."

"Are not all Rangers cousins?"

He chuckled. "Nay. Some are uncles."

She smiled, basking in the warmth of affection from him.

They entered Lairdton on a side street, shadowed by the overhanging branches of tall trees. Tam craned her neck to see the well built homes, many more like small manors with walls and gates. "Lairdton is large."

"Aye, and this is not all. 'Twas built north of the main road so traffic to the hall would not disturb their homes. But soon more space was needed, so South Lairdton grew below the road, and is where many of the businesses are that cater to travelers, as well as the mill, and many of the more unpleasant crafts, such as the tanners. Those in Lairdton often look down upon those in South Lairdton, although most are commoners themselves."

They crossed over to a busy street, lined with workshops and stores. Women hurried in and out of shops with children following. A cart hauled by an ugly, squat dray beast lumbered over the paving stones. A man stumbled out of a door with a sign hanging over it—the picture bespoke the words printed on it: the Copper Kettle. Tam watched with concern as the man wove off. Was he sick?

The main street of the town curved south at the east end to join the main road just before the woods ended. As they came out on the main road, Laird Hall came into view, set on a rise at the center of a huge clearing.

The same off-world, white shimmerstone was used here as in Zaidhron, and in the sunshine, the entire hall sparkled like a jewel. Purple and white streamers floated above conical-roofed towers, waving a gentle welcome.

She knew the layout from studying it. The inner and outer curtain walls were hexagon-shaped with towers at each corner. The entrance faced west, toward the town. The drum tower, attached to the inner curtain wall north of the gate, rose high above the sentry towers. Servants and guards lived in the ranges on the inner curtain wall, while the Laird and any nobles in residence dwelt in the keep.

They walked up to the gatehouse, the Thane raising his open hand in greeting to the guards. They put their fists over their hearts in salute.

"Where is Vitran?" he asked the nearest guard.

"I believe he is here, Thane, in the Master of the Guards chamber."

"Thank you." The Thane strode forward with Tam trailing behind, her gaze on the towering walls. They entered a room not far down the southern wall from the gatehouse where two men stood in discussion.

One was balding and dressed in black trous and a long white shirt with ruffles at the collar and paned sleeves under a black, skirted jerkin. A huge ring of keys hung at his side, so this must be Vitran, Laird Hall's steward.

The other had thick, wavy, light brown hair and was dressed in dark grey trous and doublet as were the keep guards, but with ornate gold braiding embroidered upon his collar and sleeves. He must be the Master of the Guards.

"Greetings, Vitran and Galran!"

Both men turned and bowed.

"Thane Alcandhor, how are you?" the guardsman asked with a pleasant smile.

"Pressed for time, unfortunately, Galran. Vitran, I have need of a favor."

"I owe you several, what do you need?" the bald man asked.

"I found this girl alone in the mountains as I journeyed here. She was orphaned. I could not just leave her there so I brought her with me. Can she stay here? She can work as servant."

"Why here? Why not in the town? Or your hold?"

"I have pressing business and cannot stay. I have no time to find someone who might be willing to take the lass, and Sherel would be very put out—you know her." He rolled his eyes and Vitran chuckled. "Besides, I know you can use the help here."

"That is true." Vitran gave a wry grin.

"I have taken her under my protection, and as soon as I can return I will. I promised her I would search to see if she has any living kin."

"You're a good man, Thane Alcandhor."

"I am a man in a hurry." Alcandhor said with a chuckle. He turned to Tam. "I will come back for you, lass. Be good and work hard."

"Yes, sar," she muttered.

The Thane strode away. Tam dared not watch her uncle leave, but the emptiness of his absence pressed in on her. She was alone. Truly alone. And on her first mission as a Ranger.

Vitran looked hard at her—she must not show her disquiet. "You are a good worker, girl?"

"Yes, sar."

"Good. I'll put you in the range kitchens."

Being a mountain girl who had never been to such a place, she could gawk openly without arousing suspicion as they crossed the bailey. Despite her temptations to gaze at the gardens, she studied the keep as much as possible, trying to reconcile her mental map of the place with the actual edifice.

When they passed through the propped-open, large double doors to the range kitchen, the heat from the central hearth and fireplaces in the huge chamber struck Tam. Little outside light or air made its way in except through the double doors they had just entered and from the windows, which were all on the inside wall, facing north.

A wonderful aroma of meats and breads filled the air.

Vitran strode over to a heavyset woman berating a girl for how she kneaded the bread. She turned, her face red from the heat, and a set look on her face as if she had been given vinegar to drink.

Vitran shoved Tam forward. "I have a girl for you, Linna. Put her to work."

"What?" She wiped her hands on her apron. "Just like that?"

"If you don't need help, I can find other work for her."

"I can use the help," Linna replied in a surly voice, glaring at Vitran.

"Good."

He left, and the woman scrutinized her. "So. Do you know your way around a kitchen, girl?"

"Yes, mim."

Linna snorted. She tossed an apron at Tam and beckoned her to a table where several other girls were preparing foods. "Chop these vegetables and put them in that pot. You hear? That pot yonder. No other."

Tam walked around the table as she tied the apron, sweat already trickling down her back. She picked up a knife and began her task. Linna soon came back. "Chop 'em finer," she ordered and walked away.

The light-haired girl next to Tam caught her eye and smiled. "Don't let her frighten you."

Not certain how to respond, Tam continued chopping tubers and roots.

"My name's Poll. What's yours?"

"Tam," she whispered back, her eyes darting to Linna.

The girl's friendly demeanor made Tam feel a little less alone, and she returned Poll's smile.

Linna descended on them, but not about their chattering. "Poll, I have to go to the keep kitchen. The Laird is expecting guests, and a special meal must be made. You are in charge here."

The large woman left without waiting for an answer. As soon as she was through the doorway, the scullions let out an almost unanimous, audible sigh. One giggled.

"We love when there are guests," Poll said, "because it means she is in the keep much of the time. Usually most meals are prepared here, since this kitchen feeds the staff and guards."

Was this information Tam needed to know? An ignorant girl from the mountains would likely ask silly questions—wouldn't she? "Who lives in the keep, besides the Laird?"

"His son, the Atheling. But he isn't here. He left for North Port some time ago. So it's only been the old man to cook for over there, much the worse on us."

"So no one eats in th' grand hall shining with gold but one old man?" Tam asked, her eyes wide.

Poll laughed and so did several of the other girls.

One paused in her chopping to glance at Tam, lip curled. "And what would you know of grand halls shining with gold, mountain girl?"

"I heard stories from me Fa about the shining walls here. I never thought I'd see such meself."

"And how'd you come to be out of your mountains?" Poll asked, not unkindly.

"Me Fa died, and I was alone. The Thane himself came across our cabin and said I shouldn't be alone, so he brought me away." Her eyes roamed the ceiling and walls, taking in all of Laird Hall by implication. "I never thought he'd bring me to such a place as this!"

"Not that you'll ever see the finery of it," the scornful girl said, her knife poised in the air. "We only get to see the drudge parts."

"Work while you grumble, Salinn," Poll said. "Linna or no, we have work to do."

After a few moments silence, Tam asked, "Who are the guests? Is it fine lords, d'you think?"

"Most likely." Poll gasped and Tam lifted her head to see a guard taking a pot from her. The scullion began to laugh. "Tavnol, you sneak."

The guard carried the pot to the hearth oven with a grin. "Linna's not here. So I thought I'd stop to see if you needed help."

Poll gave him a very strange, silly-looking smile. "And aren't you going to get in trouble, being in here?"

He leaned over Poll as if to whisper, but his voice was loud. "Only if you tell that I came in here on my rounds."

The girls all tittered, and Poll turned red, but she tipped her head and planted her fists on her hips. "How did you know Linna wasn't here?"

"I'm a guard. We are always on alert for the slightest happenings, you know."

They all laughed, then he said in a more serious tone, "Lords Batrig and Cardhal arrived, so I knew she'd go over to the keep. The better for me to cadge a snack." Tavnol kissed Poll's nose, snatched a piece of tuber from the edge of the table, winked at the blonde girl, and headed for the door, whistling.

After he left, the girls all broke out in chatter and laughter, with talk of how tall and straight Tavnol was, and how handsome—and how fortunate Poll was. Tam was uncertain what they meant, but she could sense Poll was both embarrassed and pleased.

However, at least Tam learned one thing: the names of the guests.

That evening, Linna came in as the girls cleaned and made preparations for the next day's meals. She looked more out of sorts than when Vitran first brought Tam in. One hand on her hip, and the other brushing stray wisps of hair out of her face, she said, "Poll, you and another girl come over to the keep. With the lords here—and their sons, I need more help."

The blonde nodded as Linna stormed out and looked around. Her eyes rested on Tam and she smiled. "You wanted to see the fancy keep.

Come along. If you don't mind Linna's yelling."

Tam trotted after Poll across the torchlit bailey. "What sort of men are these lords?"

"Same as other men, I suppose. Mostly hands—especially Lord Cardhal's sons."

"What do you mean?"

Poll stopped and turned to face Tam. "How many years do you have, girl?"

"Fifteen."

Poll studied Tam's face. "And living in the mountains..." she murmured, her brow furrowing. "You stay close to me when you can. Or the other girls—I'll tell them to look out for you. But you'll find out soon enough, I'm sure."

Tam wasn't sure why Poll seemed worried, but her care was genuine; the warmth and concern in her eyes bespeaking the feelings radiating from her.

The keep kitchen was as expansive as the range kitchen. Hearths lined the one wall, and many work tables dotted the floor. Linna glowered. "Took enough time getting over here. Dally dally—and things getting more behind here. Poll, finish the syrup for that confection." Linna's voice became even more snide. "Milord Batrig must have his sweeting. You girl, come here—what was your name?"

She continued without waiting for Tam to answer. "Stir this pot. Don't let it burn now, or I'll use this spoon on your back."

Tam approached Linna at the central hearth. The cook grabbed her arm and pulled her roughly to her side. "Stir like this." She put a hand over Tam's on the spoon, squeezing almost to pain, and scraped the sides of the pot and along the bottom. "Understand? Don't just with play the spoon in the center of the sauce, keep drawing it away like this. When it starts to thicken, pull it away from the fire and call me. Can't have burnt food for the lords, they'd never stop complaining."

Linna watched Tam stir for a moment, nodded, then went to another hearth and began fussing over something in one of the wall ovens. Tam glanced up at Poll who smiled at her.

The sauce thickened, and Linna whisked it away to put over whatever she took out of the oven, calling over her shoulder, "Take the pots and dishes to the back kitchen and start washing."

The back kitchen, where the basins were, was cooler, a relief from the heat in the main chamber. Tam dutifully began scrubbing the pots, and Poll soon joined her in cleaning up. Afterwards, they rested in the scullions' chamber off the back kitchen. The fireplace radiated too much heat, yet Tam doubted not that the cold stone under her mat would penetrate her body before morning, and she would wake stiff.

She stared into the dark, musing what she had heard the Thane tell her father about the traitors: the lords of the near provinces were all suspect. So Lords Cardhal and Batrig might be here as part of their plans. But, how could she find out what those plans were?

~:~

Poll woke Tam before dawn to begin preparations for the lords' breakfasts. The lords required much for their early meal. Wine-soaked bread, sliced meats, small rounds of cheese, roasted redfruit, simmered pod seeds, halved keeberries, and three types of tea.

As she arranged the foods on the trays, Tam peeked over at Poll. "Who takes their trays to the lords?"

"Maids. We just need to prepare them." Poll leaned over the work table, her voice low. "And as soon as they go up, we may pinch a bit of what's left."

Tam's stomach rejoiced at the notion, having had nothing yet that morning, but her duty scolded her. "But I thought...perhaps to see th'lords."

Poll's nose wrinkled. "I'm sure you'll get the chance, and I hope it won't be Cardhal's sons. Better to stay here, my girl, in the kitchen, where it's safer."

Tam nodded, as it seemed to be what Poll expected, but she did not understand what danger there could be from the young lordlings, unless they found out who she was. She needed to find a way to spy upon these lords—something inside told her their visit was very important.

~:~

"Start preparing the Laird's afternooning now, Poll," Linna said to the two girls just after luncheon. "He's having a meeting with the lords and their sons, and afterwards will be dining with them, so I need to send up more elaborate trays."

Tam's heart beat faster as she chopped fat and set it in the pot for rendering. The Maker must be smiling on her! This meeting might be important, and if Tam could hide and overhear, she might discover something that could help Uncle. A simple call of nature should get her out of the kitchen.

~:~

Servants are invisible. Tam held her breath, her uncle's words echoing in her head as a guard approached. Would he notice her nervousness—reveal her as a spy? She kept walking, her eyes on the red and gold carpet lining the white stone floor of the hallway. The guard passed her without a break in stride, and Tam let her breath out in relief.

She glanced at the gold-tasseled tapestries along the corridor while looking for the door to the council chamber. There—flanked by banners. One with the seal of the Teldheri people, and one white and purple, the colors of Viltara, the Laird's clan.

Tam opened the door and froze, her heart racing. A woman holding a dusting rag bent over a long table.

She saw Tam and straightened. "What are you doing here?"

Chapter Seven

Tam swallowed, thinking fast. "I—Linna thought perhaps the lords would want a pot of hot tea during the meeting."

The woman frowned. Tam forced herself to be still under the woman's scrutiny. Had Tam erred that the ill-tempered cook might send a scullion to ask about tea?

The woman's eyebrows rose and she slowly nodded. "Not a bad idea. They do drag on sometimes. Go tell Linna to send up the tea."

"Yes, mim." Tam tried to curtsey as she had seen other servants do, and left the room. Stars, how was she to get back in there? She chewed her lip as she slowly retraced her steps down the hall. She could not merely return to the kitchen. She peeked over her shoulder several times and saw the woman exit the room.

Tam flattened against the wall and slid sideways into a nearby alcove. Would the woman notice her as she went by? She turned and fluffed the cushion on the seat, her heart threatening to drum through her ribcage. *I do not like being spy, Uncle.*

The woman passed without comment. Tam kept watch until she disappeared through the door into the servants' staircase, then ran back down the hall to the council chamber. Once inside, she closed her eyes and took long breaths to slow her heart rate.

Tam opened her eyes and turned, searching for any place she could hide. A huge table and chairs dominated the chamber, and tapestries and portraits graced the walls between the blazing sconces. Embers glowed in the fireplace along the side wall. Tam would have thought the weather too warm but the stone Hall did seem to have a chill throughout. She walked around the table, frantic for an idea that would allow her to eavesdrop at this meeting.

As she continued around the table, she saw a door on the side wall across from her. She ran to it and lifted the latch. With a slight squeak, the door opened into a smaller chamber. Only a few sconces lit this room, but Tam could see cushioned chairs and several round tables. She entered and pushed the door almost shut, hoping the nobles would not notice it remained slightly ajar.

A glance about the inner chamber revealed no other doors. Her only way out passed through the council chamber. She fingered the rough material of her skirt in absent agitation. The nobles would have swords, and perhaps knives as well, and she had no weapons to hand.

She wandered the furnished chamber, a hand brushing the brocaded cushions on the chairs, listening for the lords to arrive. Before long she heard voices in the hall. Tam crept to the door and put her ear to it. She could hear the council door open.

"If this meeting is about shipping concerns," asked a deep, rumbling voice, "why are Lords Tadhrol and Rildhran not attending?"

Tam peeked through the narrow opening and saw a noble, nose hooked like a bird of prey, enter and walk along the far side of the table. He wore a surcoat of red and black, colors of Nelatan, making him, presumably, the lord of that province. Cardhal was his name then, although in Tam's mind "Hook-nose" was a better appellation.

Nelatan's lord stopped just at the edge of Tam's vision. A man in a white surcoat and long grey hair faced him. She stared in awe: only the Laird and his heir wore full-white surcoats! On their other side, facing her, were two young men who looked quite a bit like Hook-nose, their surcoats trimmed with Nelatan's colors. Tam didn't move and barely dared to breathe; if either young man's gaze left the Laird's face, they might see her in the crack of the door. Fortunately, they focused on the elderly man.

"We had not time for them to arrive, since their provinces are so distant, Your Grace. And 'tis mostly concerning the northern route, which is so dangerous," someone—not Hook-nose—said. Who was the other voice, and how many others were with them? Tam wondered if she dared crack the door to see more. No—not wise as then she would most certainly be discovered.

"Ah, I see. Vitran said Lord Krendhal has arrived and will join us momentarily. We can make ourselves comfortable while we wait." The Laird lifted one arm indicating the chamber where Tam hid. She held her breath, her gaze fixed on his craggy profile.

Hook-nose raised a hand. "We did have one other concern, Your Grace, which we wished to bring to you."

"Aye?"

Tam breathed a sigh when the Laird stood still.

Hook-nose straightened, licking his lips with a smirk. "Rule has stagnated. It is time for a change."

"Change?" The Laird snorted. "Would that our Thane could hear you."

"Thane." The unseen man's voice was disdainful and commanding. The Laird turned toward him as the scornful voice continued, "I think he would not approve of the changes we will implement. It is time for the provinces to rule themselves without oversight."

The Laird barked out a laugh. "Your jesting is too heavy."

"'Tis no jest, Your Grace."

Silence reigned. Tam bit her lip. She needed to know more—needed to sense these men's emotions. Her father had forbidden it, ordering her to block at all times, but the Thane had never said a word on those occasions she slipped. Would these men sense her as well? She must take the chance. Tam swallowed and stopped blocking.

Excitement, arrogance, and malice churned within these nobles. Tam clutched her stomach at the onslaught. It did, however, give her a headcount: eight men.

"So," the Laird said, his voice hard, "the Thane's warnings that my ministers begin to grow bold were not groundless after all." He controlled his anger, but Tam felt the rage shaking his body. "Even if I truly agreed, the Rangers would never allow it."

"The Rangers," the other man sneered. "After the ambushes we have planned for today, the Rangers will be lacking their Thane and all of their chiefs. The next Thane will back us. He eagerly awaits his new position."

Tam squeezed her eyes shut. Oh, Maker! Ambushes? They planned on killing her father, her uncle, her cousins! And treason had wormed its way into her clan if a Ranger would help these traitors. She must escape to warn them. But how?

"Your cooperation will guarantee your life and your clan's rule of this province. So you see, Your Grace," Hook-nose said, "it is in your best interest to capitulate."

"You cannot think such threats will force me to declare—"

"We—hold—the—Atheling," the other man said slowly, enunciating each word, triumph in his voice. "And if you do not wish your son dead, you will turn rule over to us."

Tam sucked in a quick breath at not only the threat but the glee the man felt. Hateful. Cruel. Unable to bear the intensity of his dark emotions, she blocked, shuddering.

"Whatever vow you give me, if you wish rule abdicated to you, then you will not let my son live. As my heir, he would be a threat to your plans." The Laird's voice broke. He lifted his chin. "I will not do as you say."

"We had hoped you would see reason, Your Grace," Hook-nose said. "But 'tis obvious you will not listen."

The Laird spun to face him, jaw set. Hook-nose's eyes flicked aside, and he gave a slight nod.

A blade flashed and drove into the Laird's back with a meaty *thunk*.

Tam's hands flew to her mouth as the Laird jerked straight and gasped. Mouth open and face registering shock, he fell forward. The dagger protruded from his back, his white surcoat darkening to red. Oh, she should have stopped them! She should have known! Why had she blocked again?

"Quick work, my Lord Batrig," Hook-nose said with a bow. "Now to wait for Krendhal so he can join his Laird."

So the disdainful voice did indeed belong to Lord Batrig. And they were going to kill Krendhal. Stars.

"Aye. Strange how he knew we would not release his son. I would not have thought him that discerning." Batrig chuckled, an evil sound. "My messenger stands ready to send word to kill the Atheling. All we need wait for is news of the ambushes. Things go well."

"But what if Lord Krendhal sees the body as he enters the chamber and calls for a guard?" asked a younger voice—one of the sons, no doubt.

"You have a point," Batrig said. "Drag the body in there."

Tam took a step back, her eyes widening, her skirts balled in her fists. They could only mean in her chamber.

~:~

Alcandhor walked across the bailey of Lairdton's Ranger Hold, his mind on his niece. How did she fare at Laird Hall? Most likely they had her scrubbing floors or doing scullery work. Putting her in such a dangerous position stabbed his heart, but he must know who the traitors were inside that hall. He slowed as he overheard Rangers discussing Tam and propped his shoulder against a tree, rubbing the pommel of his sword.

"So Loch'alan contested this lass? How did she fare against my daunting brother?" asked Marcalan, his eyes twinkling.

Several Rangers interrupted each other to give details. Marcalan's face filled with glee as the overlapped details gave an embellished view of Tam's victory.

Finally, Marcalan held up his hands. "Wait, wait! She ended the contest how?"

"By spinning and catching him with the back of her fist dead in the temple." Haladhon slapped his fist into his hand. "He fell like a sack of grain."

Marcalan doubled over laughing. "Oh, stars, what a time to be roaming. I would have given my sword to see that cockerel humbled!"

Several other Rangers snickered and murmured agreement.

Alcandhor wished he could continue to listen to their banter, but he had no time. He pushed away from the tree and approached the Rangers.

"'Twas sweet," Haladhon said, chuckling. He winked at Alcandhor.

Marcalan spun, his grey cloak flaring out, and swept into an elaborate bow. "My Thane. Had you known Valdhor had a daughter?"

Marcalan's question, although lightly delivered, returned the stony dread to Alcandhor's stomach. By the Bells, would someone call Question on Tam's birth record? He answered with his face and voice neutral. "Nay."

"Why did he train her?" Marcalan asked. "There is no precedent for it."

Alcandhor resisted the urge to sigh in relief at the conversation turning away from Tam's birth as Haladhon gave his cousin a playful shove. "Why ask you the Thane? Ask Valdhor if you see him."

Marcalan grinned. "I will." He turned back to Alcandhor. "When can we meet Valdhor's Ranger-daughter?"

"She is on a mission, vagabond. And I am, too." Alcandhor nodded at Haladhon. "I am to meet our scouts. I wish you to join me."

Marcalan stepped close, whispering, "Valdhor is one of them, is he not?"

Alcandhor expelled his breath in irritation. How did that rascal always seem to know such information?

Haladhon whisked the stray lock of hair off his forehead with a frown. "Stars, cousin. Is there aught that escapes your ken?"

As Marcalan chuckled, Alcandhor glanced over the group of Rangers. He had best disperse them before they heard something they should not. "Are you all to join the others at the perimeter?"

"Aye, Thane," said one as the others nodded.

"Best be moving out then. You can discuss Tam later."

The Rangers bowed and started for the tall gates flanked by the silver and blue banners of their clan. Alcandhor and Haladhon headed out, too. Marcalan came alongside Alcandhor, his boots scuffing the grass with jaunty side-steps.

"Thane, may I attend?"

Alcandhor stopped and turned to Marcalan, annoyance and affection for his fun-loving cousin warring inside. "Why? Is it because of Valdhor? You have not seen him since you were small."

"Nay, I saw him once as a stripling." Marcalan put a hand on Alcandhor's shoulder. "Thane, he has such great affection for me, I cannot deny him the pleasure of seeing me again."

Haladhon groaned as Alcandhor closed his eyes, muttering, "Bells and stars, deliver me."

Marcalan waited, eyebrows raised in innocence.

Alcandhor chewed the inside of his cheek. "If you promise not to provoke Valdhor, then aye, you may go with us."

"Stars, 'Candhor, this is Marcalan." Haladhon waved a hand at their cousin. "His presence alone will provoke Valdhor."

"Valdhor needs no provoking," Marcalan said, his voice lilting. "He is provoked by nature."

"I will regret this," murmured Alcandhor, shaking his head as they walked out the gate.

~:~

The scouts had gathered by a copse of neena trees. Wild keeberry vines tangled through the sharp-leaved trees, further twisting their already crooked branches and stunting their growth.

As Alcandhor and his two cousins approached, one of the scouts lifted a hand in greeting. Valdhor's grey eyes narrowed, and Alcandhor wished he had not agreed to let Marcalan come along. The rascal said nothing, but Valdhor's lip curled.

"What business does this rogue have here?"

"Ah, I, too, am pleased to see you again after all these years, Valdhor." Marcalan gave a deep bow.

Valdhor took a step forward, and Alcandhor lifted a hand. "Enough. What say you? What have you found?"

Valdhor glanced over the assembled men and nodded toward nearby verga shrubs, indicating he wished to speak alone to his Thane. Frowning, Alcandhor walked to the side with him.

"They have the Atheling," Valdhor hissed. "He is being held in the Enaisi's structure in the mountain of the Forbidden Peninsula. From what I overheard, I believe they plan on sending a message today to have him killed."

"Where did you hear this?" Alcandhor asked, his stomach tightening. The lad not only would be the next Laird, but Randhal had been his pupil, and he loved him as a son.

"Cardhal and Batrig had words as they journeyed here together from Polli." Valdhor's nostrils flared as he leaned close, his breath warming Alcandhor's cheek. "They cannot allow him to live long. We must act."

Alcandhor ground his teeth. "Think you a rescue can be made?"

"You always studied the places of the Enaisi. Know you the layout?"

"Aye. And Father took me there. I have walked through it."

Valdhor stiffened, but since he blocked his emotions, Alcandhor could not sense why. Was he jealous their father had taken the younger son there but not the elder, or did he disapprove that they had entered the Forbidden Peninsula?

"Then you know the place? Does the key work there as well?" His eyes darted toward Alcandhor's neck. The Enaisi's key hung on a chain hidden under his leather jerkin and shirt.

Alcandhor rubbed his chin beard, shaking his head, then he remembered the maintenance levels and the ventilation shafts. "Not for most things, but aye, I think I know an advantage. Return with me to the hold. I wish your advice."

Valdhor hesitated, frowning, and inclined his head. They rejoined the others. The remaining scouts gave their reports but none had news as dire as Valdhor's.

The scouts disappeared into the woods, and Alcandhor and his men started back to the hold.

Marcalan gestured to their right. "We are near enough the road. Why not take it instead of twisting about past overgrown thickets?"

"Always the easy way for you, enh?" Valdhor sneered.

"I need not prove how toughened I am by taking the most rugged path," Marcalan said with a chortle.

"Marcalan," Alcandhor said in a reproving tone, holding up a hand to Valdhor with a warning look. Those two would come to blows before the day ended. The woods here held no wild roughness, being near Lairdton. Children played in them daily. Why did Marcalan have to antagonize the hardened fighter? Had he no sense?

Haladhon nudged him with a grin and shake of the head. Alcandhor rolled his eyes. He knew Marcalan's presence would cause trouble. Why had he given in to the rascal?

Movement past the trees to his right caught Alcandhor's attention. A small band of Rangers journeyed on the road. "Let us join them."

They approached the road and Haladhon lifted a hand. "They are from Nelatan province. I know them." Haladhon hailed the Rangers, calling their names.

The traveling Rangers stopped to wait, and when they saw Alcandhor, they bowed.

"Thane," one Ranger said. "Well met. We are on our way to Lairdton's hold."

"Easy journey?" Alcandhor asked, as they stepped out of the shade of the trees. The warmth of the sun on his back felt good, easing the tension in his shoulders.

"Aye. But men watch the roads."

Alcandhor nodded. "Aye. So other reports have said as well."

They walked on, raising a slight dust on the dry, rutted road.

The Rangers talked among themselves as Alcandhor pondered his scheme to rescue the Atheling. A chill foreboding coursed down his spine as emotions drifted to him from ahead. He halted just as Valdhor threw his arm across Alcandhor's path, and they exchanged glances. Marcalan watched with a somber face.

The other Rangers stopped with questioning looks.

"What is it, Thane?" Haladhon asked.

"Men wait ahead. Let us cut across the woods instead of going to the crossroads."

Valdhor pointed to five Rangers. "You are Thane's guard."

The men murmured assent and, along with Valdhor, positioned themselves around Alcandhor. They entered the wood, hands on sword hilts.

They had not gone far when a score of Rangers approached from the direction of Lairdton, led by Lamadhel. He bowed. "Thane, Zandhral claimed sight and warned of danger to you. I took it upon myself to gather Rangers from the perimeter and come hence."

"Stars, if only we had more with Enaisi blood," Haladhon said. "The Thane and Valdhor both warned us away from the road."

Lamadhel nodded. "Let us hurry our Thane to the safety of the stronghold."

Before they had gone twenty paces, men crashed through the trees with shouts, swords raised. Alcandhor drew his blade and charged with his Rangers even as he took a quick tally of the enemy. Three score men at least—nay, more swarmed from the woods, joining their comrades.

Alcandhor slashed, ducked, thrust, and parried against several men at once. One man fell. And another. Five more charged, but the Thane's guard, Haladhon, and Valdhor ran at them. Assailants came from behind. Alcandhor shouted warning. Valdhor whirled and struck down one. Alcandhor continued fighting, only vaguely aware of his kin fighting at his back.

An attacker screamed—a deep gash in his arm. He broke and ran. Another dropped to his knees, a slash of red across his belly. Two more fell. Rangers pressed harder, and the ambushers began to fall back. Bodies fell, but those remaining fought grimly.

The Thane's guard encircled Alcandhor while the rest of the Rangers, led by Haladhon, slowly drove the attackers away from their Thane. Alcandhor ground his teeth but stayed within the circle of protection, as was custom.

The sounds of the fighting grew distant. But despite the silence now about them, Alcandhor sensed a menace still present. Valdhor peered into the trees, a scowl on his face—he must feel it too. "Alcandhor..."

The sounds of arrows hitting near made Alcandhor spin. Two Rangers gasped and fell. Someone dove into Alcandhor, knocking him face first into the mould. He glanced up to see Rangers shooting arrows at their attackers.

Alcandhor struggled to rise but Valdhor's voice in his ear said, "Stay down."

"Get off," Alcandhor growled. "Let me up to fight!"

"Nay, you are Thane, 'tis my duty to protect—"

"Get off!"

Men bore down on them with swords, giving Valdhor no choice. He leapt to his feet. Alcandhor joined him, his blade at ready.

A Ranger leaped in front of Alcandhor, taking an arrow meant for his Thane. He slammed back against Alcandhor's chest. Alcandhor lost his sword as he stumbled back. He jumped over the fallen Ranger, ducked the lunge of the swordsman facing him, then dove into him. The two men rolled, exchanging blows. They regained their footing, and Alcandhor caught him with a thrusting kick to the sternum. The man thudded to the ground and lay still.

Another swordsman ran at him. Alcandhor sidestepped, avoiding the sword-strike, and kicked him in the face.

Pain shot through his back and side from blows. Hands grabbed his arms before he could turn. A large, well-muscled man grinned, approaching. Fists slammed into his body, and Alcandhor clenched his teeth against crashing heat in his ribs and abdomen. The one he had kicked in the face scrabbled on the ground for his weapon, yelling, "Kill him! Kill him!"

Alcandhor kicked the hammer-handed man in the chest and used his heel to smash the knee of the one man holding him. Sharp fire knifed his side as he twisted and broke the other man's arm. He dove for his sword. Despite the pain, he rose as more men closed in with blades.

A flick of his eyes told Alcandhor that bowmen still stood in the trees, waiting for a clear shot. He stood back to back with Valdhor—all the other Rangers lay sprawled on the bloody ground.

Even as he thrust at one of his attackers, a cold knot in his stomach told him this fight could not be won.

Chapter Eight

The door swung open, and a young man, surcoat edged in green and white, gaped at Tam. His blue eyes narrowed to an icy glare. Before she could move, he yanked her by the wrist into the council chamber.

"What is going on here?" a new voice thundered.

Over her shoulder, Tam glimpsed a tall man with purple and white noble's robes standing in the hallway door. The new voice distracted the lordling, and she twisted her arm out of the young man's grasp. She then kicked him in the gut, bending him double.

"Krendhal!" someone yelled.

"Seize him!" Hook-nose ordered.

Two of the men—by surcoat colors, one was Nelatan, the other in green and white was Estan—grabbed the tall noble's arms. Krendhal struggled to pull free.

Before Tam could turn, her head snapped back, her hair snatched from behind. A blade gleamed near her face. Tam pivoted, lifting her arms over her assailant's and down, trapping his arms under hers. She brought her knee up into the man's ribs. His dagger dropped. Her fists smashed down on the back of his head. As he sank to his knees, groaning, she aimed a kick at his face. He fell to his side with gasp, hands covering his bloody nose and mouth, his heavy body on top of his weapon, effectively keeping Tam from retrieving it. *No weapon, no space, too many men! I must take the fight to a better place! But how? Where?*

She stepped away from the noble on the floor, assessing the room in the space of a breath. On the other side of the table, two men—Hook-nose and one of his sons—stared at her with open mouths. Krendhal still fought his attackers at the door-end of the table. The men scrambled around the fireplace-side of the table, Hook-nose growling almost like an animal.

The blue-eyed Estan lordling straightened with a choking sound, reaching for her. Without thinking, Tam shot her palm into the sternum of Blue-eyes and jumped over the fallen noble—Batrig of Estan her mind supplied, even as she ducked past the two struggling to hold on to Krendhal and raced out the door. She tore down the hallway toward the servant stairs, sounds and shouts of pursuit behind her.

76

She jumped several steps at a time, but her smooth-soled sandals could gain no purchase on the shimmerstone. Gritting her teeth, she held the rail as she slid and leaped down. Above her, the men yelled for her to stop.

She reached the bottom. Where should she go? Guards were everywhere and once the men behind her gave call, she would be stopped. The only place she knew was the kitchens.

She raced down narrow halls and through the wide doorway, skidding to a halt by the hearth. Linna and Poll both turned, mouths hanging open. The men piled into the kitchen, brandishing swords or knives.

Poll screamed, and Linna began yelling for calm while begging the lords' pardon and what did they want, her red face turning white.

"Grab her!" snarled Batrig, his lip now split and swollen, blood smearing his face. The men swarmed around him, closing in on Tam.

No knives were close to hand, but the small rendering pot hung near the hearth. *Aye, that would work!* She grabbed the handle by its padded covering and, protecting her other hand with a fold of her skirt, hurled the contents of the pot at them. Two screamed in pain, one falling to the floor, the other doubled over, arms wrapped over his head. Poll shrieked.

Batrig stepped forward. He grinned at her, flourishing his sword. *Is he trying to intimidate me?*

Tam grabbed the hearth poker and held it as a sword.

"Put the poker down, and I will not hurt you, lass."

"If you would stab the Laird in the back, you would harm a lass."

His face contorted. "Wench!"

He lunged at her, but she sidestepped, smacking his blade aside. Both slid in the grease, and backed off to catch their balance. Batrig thrust and Tam parried, again slipping on the slick floor. As she scrabbled for footing, he grinned and came in with an overhead strike. Once more, she sidestepped, circled the poker, and struck downward on his sword arm. He dropped the blade. She swung in to his belly, doubling him over, and brought the poker crashing down on his head.

Tam stared at the still body, suppressing a shiver. She'd just taken a life.

"No!" the Estan lordling cried, shaking her out of the moment.

The lordling, Hook-nose, and one of his sons drew their swords and maneuvered through the grease around the hearth on either side of her. Tam froze. How could she fight in two directions at the same time?

"Cardhal!" Krendhal stood in the doorway, sword in hand. Hook-nose turned with a snarl and charged the noble.

By the Maker's mercy, one less! She swiped at the remaining two with the poker and jumped back. They seemed to sense her dismay and widened their distance from each other, flanking her.

She ducked to her left, and scrambled backwards around a work table. *Uncle, how do I fight thus? Father! You never taught me to fight more than one man!*

Her breath came in pants, her heart pounding as the two closed in on her again, their faces smug, knowing her fear, knowing they could best her.

Krendhal ran up behind the one on her right, his sword hilt striking the man's skull. He fell like a sack. Her ally turned to the other, and Tam, recovering, knocked down the villain's sword arm. Krendhal's sword fell in a fatal blow.

He took a breath and stood sword in hand, frowning at Tam.

She gulped for air as she returned his stare. Bruises marred the lord's strong, regal face. Blood trickled from his forehead down the side of his left eye.

"Who are you, lass? You fight well for a woman."

"I am a Ranger. Tamissa, daughter of Valdhor, milord." Tam paused and added the traditional Ranger response. "I am honored to serve."

"A Ranger?" Wide-set eyes under arching eyebrows looked her over, surprise and disbelief wafting from him. "Well, *Ranger*, I am Krendhal, First Minister to the Laird and Lord of Viltara Province."

"Lord." She bowed. "I must warn the Rangers of the ambush these traitors have planned—and tell the Thane they have abducted the Atheling and planned to send a messenger to order him killed."

"Indeed." Krendhal glanced about. "I will go with you. If we have such traitors, I need to take counsel with the Thane."

Linna and Poll emerged from the corner where they had taken refuge. One man still writhed on the floor from his oil burns, alternately screaming and crying for help. Tam ground her teeth, unwilling to let herself regret her actions. If she had not acted, she would be dead. She would be dead...

Krendhal turned to the servants. "Are you loyal to the Laird?"

"Of course we are," Linna answered.

"These men are all traitors," Krendhal said. "They killed the Laird. Hold them."

"Do not call for guards yet," Tam added. "Give us time to leave and warn the Thane."

Hands over her mouth, Poll nodded. Linna just stared.

Krendhal stopped at the door of the chamber. "Go ahead of me, lass. A servant walking with me would look too unusual. And drop the poker. You cannot go out carrying that."

Tam pointed at his bloody forehead. "You should wipe your face, milord."

"Aye." He took a cloth from under his sash and pressed it to the side of his face. "Go on, lass. I shall meet with you on the road past the gates."

Tam took a deep breath and turned to the outside door of the kitchen. She hurried across the bailey. Though her heart pounded whenever anyone drew near, Tam hoped she kept her face emotionless. She swallowed as she approached the inner gatehouse, but the guards paid no attention. She passed through the outer gatehouse, and one of the guards called to her.

"Aren't you the girl the Thane brought here yesterday?"

Tam's heart thudded its way up her throat, but she strove to appear calm. "Aye—I am," she slurred the affirmative into the pronoun, hoping he did not notice the slip in her dialect.

The guard took a step toward her. "And what are you going into Lairdton for in the middle of the day?"

"Do Linna's scullions answer to you?" Tam asked.

The guard blinked as his partner on the other side of the gate laughed.

"Go about your task, girl. Don't pay attention to him. He chases anything in a skirt."

As the guards began bantering with each other, Tam turned away. Her eyes closed for a moment in relief, then she continued on the road across the field. If she could just get to the safety of the woods and Lairdton...

Tam heard one of the guards behind her hailing Krendhal. Was the guard loyal? Should she turn and see? Without weapons, what could she do?

She kept going—her one thought to get to her father and uncle. Where was this ambush to take place? She knew not the area, only the road to Ranger Hold. The success of a mass ambush depended upon knowing when many Rangers would be gathered together. Where might they gather besides at the hold, which would be too defensible? A shiver crawled over her as a picture flashed in her mind—the crossroads beyond Lairdton!

She walked faster to reach the woods where it would be safe to run. An arrow whistled past. She glanced back. Krendhal raced along the road toward her. She broke into a run.

He caught up with her as they hit the woods' edge. Tam, without breaking stride, managed to say, "Follow me, lord."

They did not go through Lairdton but stayed in the strip of woods between the town and the main road. They could hear no more arrows or sounds of chase. Tam wondered why, but only gave thought to keeping pace with Krendhal, who had long legs and moved surprisingly fast. Her sandals made her slip and stumble, blistering her feet, but she gritted her teeth and fought to keep steady. Her apron and skirt caught on bushes and brambles, and she ruthlessly snatched at the material.

Tam passed the lane to Ranger Hold. Not long after that the clashing of swords could be heard nearby, and she dashed toward the sound. "Father! Uncle!"

"Wait!" Krendhal called out.

Tam crashed through the underbrush to see a bowman taking aim at Rangers. She shouted and he turned. Diving into him head-first, she knocked him to the ground. She punched his face to stun him. Using her palm, she gave a sharp upward strike to the nose.

As she stood, she saw her father. He parried an attack, swung in hard, and his opponent fell. He looked up and yelled, "'Candhor!"

Her uncle swung around. An arrow struck him. He halted, gasping, and fell back against a tree. Her father's knife flew, embedding in the bowman's throat. Another bowman's arrow hit Valdhor square in the chest, and he froze, mouth agape.

A scream ripped from Tam's throat as she closed the short distance and dove at the assassin. She beat his face until he quit moving, and she sensed his life drain away from him. She stood, looking around for a weapon. She took her father's knife from the body of the nearby bowman and ran up behind the man fighting her uncle. Alcandhor stood, arrow in his shoulder, red blood bright against the brown of his leather jerkin and left arm hanging useless, wielding his long sword with only his right hand. She buried her father's blade in the man's back, yanking it out again as he fell.

"Tam!" Alcandhor shouted.

She whirled, but Krendhal drove his sword into the bowman who was taking aim at her. Tam looked around, knife ready, but the battle seemed to be over.

She dropped to her knees by Valdhor, her sweat-dampened hair falling about her face, tears blurring her vision. Alcandhor knelt next to her.

"Father!"

Frothy blood came from the arrow wound and from his mouth and nose, his breaths in shallow gasps. He looked up at his brother for a long moment. His gaze moved to Tam with confusion, but his face relaxed with an expression of comprehension, and a warmth drifted over Tam. He exhaled sharply, almost as if in a laugh, but the sound changed into a cough. Tam's hand flew to her mouth to stop a sob as more blood ran from his mouth. With an effort, her father managed a thick, gurgled whisper. "You look like your mother." His eyes went blank.

A cold void grew in Tam as she sensed her father's presence leave—drift away, deserting her for some place afar off. Her insides knotted, and she could not move. She gasped, mouth open, taking breaths over and over, but could not feel air getting to her lungs. Tears blinded her.

From out of a mist, the faraway voice of Krendhal said, "Thane, they killed the Laird and have the Atheling hostage. We must rescue him. They mean to kill him, too."

"Aye. I know." Her uncle's hand touched her back. "Tam," he whispered, "we must go."

She did not move. How could she? Why would he want her to?

"Tam..."

"Nay!"

"You cannot help him now. You are a Ranger, and you have duties."

"I cannot leave him!"

"We must. We must leave all of them."

She shook her head, still gasping for air.

"What would your father tell you to do?"

Tam collapsed on her father's chest, shaking with sobs.

"Lord Krendhal, help me," Alcandhor said.

Hands lifted her, held her up. She twisted free and dropped again by her father. Timidly, she touched his face and caressed it gently with her hand.

"Thane, we do not have time for this," Krendhal said.

Tam boldly leaned over and kissed her father's cheek. She rested her face against his. Stubble sanded her skin, and she breathed in his special smell. How many times had she wished to touch him, hug him— but dared not. Never had she felt his arms around her.

Once more hands lifted her, more firmly this time. She started to twist away again, but Alcandhor put his one hand on her jaw and forced her to look at him. His face glistened with tears.

She saw the arrow still in his shoulder and gasped—shocked back to *now*. "We must take care of you!"

"Nay. We must get to the young Laird before he is murdered. Come, let us hurry to the hold."

"Thane, let me break off that arrow," Krendhal said.

"Quickly," Alcandhor said.

Tam glanced away. She heard a sharp snap and almost inaudible grunt.

"Now, hurry," Alcandhor said.

As they walked past the bodies, Tam saw other Rangers among the dead and closed her eyes. She did not want to know if any of the cousins she had recently met had fallen with her father.

Alcandhor began to slow before they got to the hold. Krendhal put an arm around him to help him. Tam could not assist; she could not make herself approach his left side for the wound. Helpless and worried, she sensed him as he struggled to keep pace. Pain wracked his body, not just the fiery pain of his shoulder—he must have unseen injuries.

The Rangers guarding the gate started toward them, but the Thane commanded, "Stay at your posts." They obeyed, although doubt and worry churned in them.

Sherel, the hold-keeper, ran toward them with a cry as they entered the foreroom.

"Get a healer," Krendhal ordered.

Sherel ran out. Krendhal helped Alcandhor down the hall to a chamber with bookshelves, a large table, and chairs. The Thane dropped into the nearest seat and pointed to several scrolls propped in the corner. "The large one, Tam. Bring it here."

She and Krendhal spread the map out on the table and used candlesticks to hold it down.

"A messenger was to be sent today with word to kill our young Laird. I am sending you after him, Tam. You must be swift."

"Know you where he is, Thane?" Krendhal asked.

Before Alcandhor could answer, Tanadhon rushed into the chamber. "Thane! What happened?"

"Ambush. We are sorely hurt. Was the perimeter set?"

"Aye, Thane, it was," Tanadhon said. "After Zandhral's warning, Eladhrel and Andhrel both thought I should return here. Eladhrel is in charge at wood's edge."

"Good. Drum a message that Laird Hall is besieged. We need to stop anyone from leaving that place." He frowned, his breathing labored. "The other Rangers who are routing some of the ambushers will return soon. I will send them to the perimeter."

Tanadhon ran out.

Alcandhor gazed up at Krendhal. "Milord...I need to speak with Tam in private."

"You should lie down and wait for the healer, Thane," Krendhal said.

"My duty is to our young Laird. After I have briefed this Ranger, I will rest."

Krendhal wavered, but after a moment's hesitation left, one eyebrow arched high as he shut the door.

Alcandhor's finger jabbed a spot on the map—a peninsula due east, by the coast. He spoke in a low voice. "Here is where they are keeping the young Laird."

Tam stifled a gasp. Her uncle named it not, but Tam's father had drawn crude maps to teach her the geography of their planet and its history. The Forbidden Peninsula. What men would dare go that area? And the Thane willed her to journey there?

"He is in an edifice of the Enaisi tunneled into this mountain near the sea. One entrance on the east side. However—" He paused, reaching under his shirt with a grimace, and pulled out a chain with a small object dangling from it. "There is a secret way in."

Entering that peninsula and also a place of the Enaisi? Tam suppressed a shudder and brought her mind back to the Thane's instructions.

"If you climb up from the southwest, you will see an unnatural formation—a smooth, rounded shape called a dome. Just under that is small platform, protected by a thick grate with an entrance on the south side. Once underneath it will seem a small cave. On the back wall is an opening to a ventilation shaft."

He winced as he took the chain from around his neck. "This will open both the entrance and the locked ventilation cover. The shaft is big enough to crawl into. You can sneak in that way and out with the young Laird. If you are stealthy enough, no one will know he is gone until it is too late, and you both will be safely away." His hand closed over hers, his grey eyes earnest. "Keep that key safe and hidden, Tam. It is part of our oldest duty, and the only way we have into the Enaisi's structures."

She put the chain around her neck and tucked the key inside her shirt, both awed and fearful that he gave her something that had belonged to the Enaisi.

"The Laird will not trust you at first. Tell him I sent you. Ask him who besides me would know of the Enaisi's ventilation shafts from studying their records, even if I know not the reason they built such a place. And tell him if he does not come with you, I will box his ears so they ring until the Enaisi return. Remember you all of this?"

"Aye, sir."

"Repeat it," he said, grimacing in pain.

She did so, while watching his ashen face, worry constricting her stomach.

He nodded. "Good. And Tam, the Laird's safety is of uttermost importance. Nothing else matters."

"Aye, sir."

"Now, as to how to find him in these shafts. They would probably keep him in a back-most room, which means as you travel forward in the shaft, search straight ahead, especially the ones nearer you and to your left before searching to your right."

"Aye, sir."

"Now repeat it all to me again. How to get there, how to find the secret opening, what you will tell him—all of it."

She repeated it twice before he seemed satisfied. He gave a weak nod. "Good. Now, go into my chamber across the hall and get dressed and have Sherel pack provisions. You must leave as soon as possible."

Tam ran across the hall. She shut the door and stared at her father's knife still clutched in her hand. Choking back a sob, she wiped it clean on the rags of her skirt and with reverence laid it on the small table. She shed the rough-woven garments and kicked them into the corner. Her grey trous and dark green tunic felt good against her skin after that dratted dress. She had never worn skirts before and hoped she need never wear any again.

Tam could hear conversation across the hallway, due to the large gap at the bottom of the stout wooden door. Krendhal gave an account of what happened in Laird Hall. Afterwards he asked, "Thane, how think you that you can besiege the hall? 'Tis folly to try. You will only lose more men."

"We have ways, Lord Krendhal. I would advise you to stay here for safety until we know who is to be trusted." She could tell her uncle grimaced in pain as he spoke. Sensing all his wounds made her ache for him and frightened her as well—how badly was he injured? Would he die too? She blocked. She dared not break down; she was a Ranger, after all.

"Nay, Thane. If you wish to throw your men's lives away with this siege, I will do the same. I wield a sword well."

"Are you a bowman, Lord Krendhal?"

"Aye, but I have not practiced in some time."

"You will have practice now."

"And what of this lass? You truly mean to send her after our young Laird?"

"I do. She has much wild-sense and moves quickly."

At that moment, Sherel's voice said, "He's in there."

Tam heard shuffling footsteps in the hall. It must be the healer. The conversation between Krendhal and the Thane stopped.

She donned her weapons, save her staff; the length of tough lorzwood would hinder speed. She picked up her father's knife and opened the door.

Krendhal stood in the hall, his eyebrows lifting as his gaze raked over Tam's attire. A short, bent man with grey hair supported Alcandhor out of the chamber, and Tam backed away as they crossed the hallway.

Sherel muttered, "Careful, Santran. Be careful with him."

"Leave me be, woman," he grumbled. "I know my work."

Tam turned to Sherel, holding up her father's blade. "I need a sheath for this. And the Thane asks you to pack journey provisions. Twenty days, perhaps more. And two waterskins." She paused. The weather was cooling. Would the boy who lived in that fine hall be used to the chill of the wild? Her mind returned to the dead Laird, red on his white surcoat; the son would also wear white outer garments—white would be no good for journeying in secret. "Have you a spare cloak I can take?"

Nodding, Sherel led her down the hall to a large armory chamber. Tam found a back sheath that fit the knife and strapped it on, adjusting it as she strode out.

She stood in the bedchamber doorway, watching Santran cutting Alcandhor's bloody shirt away, barely able to breathe for fear he might die. She blinked hard to keep tears away.

Sherel brought Tam the food and a cloak. Tam had to remove her spare Ranger clothes to make room for the extra food and cloak. Sherel took them with a terse nod. Tam still had her own pouch of dried meat as well. She slung the two waterskins over her head and shoulder and pulled her hood free of the straps.

Tam looked again in the bedchamber at her uncle lying still, his face pale. She tiptoed close. Because she could not hug him, she put a hand on his cheek and kissed him on the forehead. "Be well, Uncle."

He opened his eyes for a moment and lifted a hand to give a weak wave toward the door. "Go."

Tam hesitated and then ran out.

Chapter Nine

"Vitran."

The steward stopped in his trek across the bailey of Laird Hall as he saw the head cook, Linna, crossing toward him, her broad face pale. He sighed in irritation; he didn't have time for a menial's gossip.

"Is it true what the guards are saying?" she asked, her apron knotted in her fists. "That we are besieged?"

"Yes."

"But why?"

"Lord Krendhal killed the Laird and escaped the Hall. And it appears the Rangers are involved in the conspiracy. They will shoot anyone who approaches the woods."

Linna frowned. "Lord Krendhal said that Lord Batrig killed the Laird. And I cannot believe the Rangers would help traitors."

"It's all part of Krendhal's plan to take over. And it appears the Rangers have been scheming with him. Otherwise, why should the Thane set a siege against this Hall? For what purpose?" He leaned close as if sharing a secret. "To stop those who would tell the truth."

Vitran put a hand over his heart with a sorrowful expression before she could say anything. "I thought he was my friend. But look at what he's done. He isn't the man I thought he was."

Linna's lips thinned. "The Rangers uphold the law."

How easily could Vitran undermine that belief? Trapping innocent people in this siege would work to his advantage. The Rangers would come out as villains; he would see to it. "If you don't believe me, walk out the gate. Ranger arrows will make you a target before you reach the woods."

Linna shook her head, but dropped her gaze. Good. He had planted doubt. Raising his chin, he said, "Don't worry, though, Linna. I have plans—"

"I hope so," she said sharply, crossing her arms, "because we don't have a large store of food. The tribute caravans haven't arrived yet. Much is brought several times a lunation or even daily at this time of—"

"I'm the steward," he yelled, waving an arm at the fat cook. "You think I don't know that?" He rubbed his bald head. "If we can't break the siege soon, how long can we expect the food to last?"

"Even at half the amount I usually cook for this hall, we won't last a lunation. And I only say that long because there are some stores of grain and seed pods, as well as fruits and vegetables in the gardens and some salted meat. You'll be tired of the rations before long. And don't forget about cooking the food. We have to be careful with our supply of wood."

Linna pursed her lips, spun on her heel, and returned to the kitchens. Vitran ground his teeth and hurried to the Master of the Guards chamber. Talrig sat in the work chair, his arm swathed in bandages, and his face splotched red with burns. His eyes were glazed, but from the pain itself or herbs and drink to dull it, Vitran could not be certain.

"What in bloody Bells happened?"

"You speak to a lord thus?" Talrig said, his words slurring slightly.

Vitran leaned on the table, teeth gritted. "You claim all of us in the conspiracy are equals, and yet you want deference due your rank? Hypocrite! Tell me what happened."

Talrig glared but slumped in the chair. "It was that cursed girl and Krendhal. They killed everyone but me."

"No, Jandhal was found alive in the council chamber." *Alas.* "His wounds are being tended."

Landhal had also been alive. With the healer out of the Hall, Vitran easily made certain the dose of panvarin given the lordling would not just ease pain of his horrific oil burns and cause sleep, but assure he never awoke.

"I thought everyone had been killed except me. Are you sure the Laird is dead?"

Vitran fingered his knife pommel, wishing he had been the one to deal the killing blow. "I have personally verified his death. I would like to know who that girl really was. Alcandhor brought her. He said she was an orphan he found."

"A lie! She was a spy. I heard her. She claimed to be a Ranger. If I ever get my hands on her—"

"We have to figure out what we're going to do," Vitran said, interrupting the noble's useless tirade. "We're besieged."

Talrig blinked. "Know you how much food there is?"

"Not much. I just talked with the cook."

Talrig pounded his fist on the table. "It is that cursed Alcandhor. How did he know?"

"He knows too much. He must have more spies than that girl. Perhaps one of us."

"No! What would such a betrayal gain any of us?"

"Who knows?" Vitran closed his eyes, running a hand over his smooth head. "But how else would he always seem to know just when we are moving?"

"You have a point. Of those of us in on the planning, Jandhal and we two are the only ones left inside these walls. How many in this hall are loyal to us?"

"I cannot give exact count but enough that I believe we have the majority. Guards and servants on our side are spreading word that those loyal to Viltara and the Rangers are the traitors. Doubt is keeping the rest in line for now." Vitran took a breath and leaned against the table. "I have already had Galran, Master of the Guards, seized and put into a cell so he cannot stop us. Some guards rebelled immediately and are also in cells. I would have killed Galran, but he is too highly respected, and his martyrdom could turn many guards to his cause. We don't need a revolt."

"What is our plan then?"

"We follow the original story that Krendhal killed the Laird. But some of the ambushes must have failed for the Rangers to besiege us. And the message was never sent to kill the Atheling."

Talrig barked a short laugh. "Nay, a messenger was dispatched yesterday morning."

"What?"

"My father did not agree with that cloddy Cardhal that we needed the boy alive as a pawn. So we sent our own man with word to kill him. He headed out from Polli, dressed as a commoner. No one will pay attention to him as he journeys east."

Vitran blew his breath out slowly. "Then that is one thing in our favor. But for now, we must concentrate on a way to end this siege."

"Have you plans toward that end?"

"I have the guards trying to maintain calm for now. Tonight we are going to try two plans. The first is an attack on the drum tower. Rangers are still in there."

Talrig's eyes widened. "What? Have they sent messages?"

"Only one. I can't understand all their codes, but they sent an 'All's well' and one was sent in return from the small tower at Ranger Hold. There's been silence ever since."

"We have to get them out of there."

"We will. And we are going to try the tunnel tonight too."

"Tunnel?"

"There is a secret tunnel that goes deep and far and into the woods. Few know about it."

"Think you the Rangers know not of it?"

Vitran curled his upper lip at the tight-laced, primping noble's fancy talk.

Talrig glowered at him and, with an exaggerated commoner accent, asked, "What? Yuh can't understand?" He continued more slowly as if speaking to a dull-wit: "Don't you think the Rangers know about the tunnel?"

Vitran glared until the noble looked away. "I don't know. I don't think so. Perhaps Alcandhor would. That inbred by-blow has been privy to too much in the hall. But hopefully he is dead."

"If that plan has not gone wrong too," Talrig grumbled.

"Not everything could have."

Talrig cradled his burned arm in his other. "I would not count on it. Did you not say the Ranger Hold drummed 'All's well'?"

"That could be a lie so we wouldn't know their losses."

"Possible. Have you thought of an attack on the Rangers to stop the siege?"

Vitran sighed at the naïveté these nobles sometimes displayed. How did they manage to rule provinces when they understood so little? "They have this whole hall surrounded. They are hidden in the woods so we cannot see them, and we have no idea how many there are. What should I do, have all my guards charge forth across a clear field and see how many get shot before they even find a target?"

Talrig muttered imprecations at the Rangers. "There has to be something we can do."

"I told you what we have planned. And if all else fails, remember, we do have allies outside. They could be plotting against the Rangers at this moment. Now, why don't you go rest and get some food while there is still food to be had."

A vicious smile played on Vitran's lips as Talrig left—that one could be manipulated with such ease. Jandhal would be the one to watch. If he lived. Drink and women would keep that one distracted though.

Swaggering insects. Power and control should be for those who could take it and hold it, not because one happened to be born to a particular clan. Vitran would survive this siege and become a living testimony of the Rangers' cruelty. His chin lifted—he would show through his self-sacrificing leadership and strength that clan meant nothing and new ways should be embraced. Perhaps he, himself, would sit in the Great Hall in the Laird's chair one day.

~:~

The icy grip on Haladhon's heart did not ease as he and his band of Rangers came through the gate at Ranger Hold.

"Haladhon! Lamadhel!" Tanadhon ran to them, his face flushed. "Dire news! The Laird is dead, and the Thane is wounded. We have begun the siege of Laird Hall. The Thane ordered that when these Rangers returned we send them to the perimeter to help with the siege."

Haladhon exhaled in relief, gripping Tanadhon's shoulder. "He is alive then." Turmoil and dread had seized him when they returned to find Valdhor and the Thane's guard all slain and Alcandhor missing. Not only because he feared for his Thane, but the man was his best friend, close as a brother.

Haladhon turned, his fist over his heart, as his men brought in their dead. All the Rangers not carrying the bodies lined up, likewise saluting, as their fallen kin were borne to the crypt in the southwest part of the bailey. There they would sleep until preparations for proper interment in their home provinces took place.

As the bodies passed, Haladhon called their names, as was custom. "Lindhor, Lasdhran, Jandhor, Vadalan, Alardhor, Valdhor."

Silence reigned until the Rangers passed. Haladhon then turned to Tanadhon, the worried expression on his friend's face echoing his own. "When I saw that Alcandhor was not among the bodies, I knew not what to think." He swung to face his men. "Any wounded stay here, the rest to the perimeter." As the Rangers turned toward the gate he called out, "Marcalan, you are wounded. You stay."

"'Tis but a scratch, Haladhon."

"Stay."

"Aye. Sir." With grudging tone and manner, the wounded Ranger trudged toward the hold.

Lamadhel clasped Haladhon's shoulder as he asked Tanadhon, "How is the Thane?"

"He is in an herb-induced sleep to help him heal of his wounds." Tanadhon's voice softened. "It does not bode well."

Lamadhel nodded, his jaw set. The lines around the older Ranger's eyes seemed deeper with worry. He looked at Haladhon. "Do you wish me to stay here or join the others at the perimeter?"

Haladhon sorely wanted his uncle with him but only for personal assurance. He took a deep breath. "Take charge at the perimeter for now. We need to set two watches."

Lamadhel squeezed Haladhon's shoulder and joined the men heading out. Haladhon strode into the foreroom, Tanadhon trailing.

"I wish to see Alcandhor. Then we will discuss—" Haladhon stopped. Krendhal stood in the hallway, his purple surcoat torn and dirty, dried blood on his forehead.

"Lord Krendhal helped defend the Thane and bring him in from the ambush," Tanadhon said.

"Milord." Haladhon bowed deeply. "Thank you for your assistance.

Have your injuries been tended yet?"

"Nay, Ranger Chief. They are not serious, but this treason is. Set your mind at ease about your Thane," he nodded toward the bedchamber door, "then we can give you our reports."

Haladhon licked his lips, staring at the door before opening it slightly to see his cousin and his Thane. Alcandhor lay, face wan and dark hair tossed on the pillow, his shoulder swathed in bandages.

Santran, the Laird's own healer, sat with him. How was it he was not in Laird Hall? The elderly man turned, frowning, and gestured for Haladhon to close the door. Haladhon obeyed, his chest tight with worry, then turned to Tanadhon and Krendhal. "What happened?"

"Arrow." Dark lines etched Krendhal's face.

Haladhon groaned. Marcalan stood nearby, looking somber, blood seeping through the piece of shirt he had tied around his arm. The others had crowded into the foreroom. His men—they needed care. Haladhon asked, "Where is Sherel?"

The hold-keeper stepped forward from the dining chamber door, her eyes red-rimmed. "Here, Haladhon."

"Ah, good. I would not ask Santran to leave the Thane. I need another healer for my men and some refreshment for them."

"If they are not badly wounded, I can tend them," Sherel said.

"I will leave it to you, then."

He nodded for his men to follow Sherel. As they filed past, he noted with relief that though some were pale or limping, none looked seriously wounded. Stars, what a bloody fight, though.

He inclined his head toward the meeting chamber, and followed Tanadhon and the First Minister inside. A map had been spread on the table. Haladhon eyed it as he sat. Marcalan shut the door and pulled out a chair.

"You are injured and should rest, Marcalan."

"I am fine." Marcalan raised his voice above Haladhon's protest. "I cannot rest not knowing what is happening!"

Haladhon leaned on the table with his fists and glared into Marcalan's eyes. Finally he straightened with a sigh and sat down, accepting Marcalan's presence. That cheeky young Ranger always got his way.

"Now, I want to know exactly what has happened this day." He gazed at Tanadhon, calling him by his title as commander of the hold. "Steward, your report."

"My part is short, sir." Tanadhon splayed his hands on the table. "The Thane told me to set a perimeter in the edge of the woods around Laird Hall. I returned here at Andhrel and Eladhrel's insistence to find the Thane in here, wounded, with Lord Krendhal and a young lass. He told me there was an ambush and to drum that Laird Hall was officially besieged. I did so."

Haladhon nodded. He had heard the drum message. "After this meeting, drum for them to deliver the message that we will allow those in Laird Hall to exit, one by one, unarmed."

Tanadhon nodded.

"How can they deliver such a message, Ranger?" Krendhal frowned, leaning forward. "Guards and servants would not know drum code."

"They will write it and wrap the paper around arrows to be shot into the bailey. Word should spread."

"Ah." Krendhal sat back.

Haladhon turned back to Tanadhon. "Any more news?"

"Nay. Other than that Lord Krendhal told me the Laird is dead."

Haladhon set his jaw as he turned to the noble. "Lord Krendhal?"

Arching an eyebrow, Krendhal gave a concise summary of the betrayal of Lords Batrig and Cardhal and their sons, the death of the Laird, his encounter with Tam, and how they escaped from Laird Hall with guards chasing and shooting arrows after them. He shook his head. "I knew not why the guards quit the chase, but now I suspect it was your Rangers at the woods' edge."

He gazed at Tanadhon, who nodded. "I am impressed, Ranger Tanadhon, as I saw nothing of your men. They were well hidden."

Tanadhon gave a seated bow.

"Please, lord, continue," Haladhon said.

Krendhal inclined his head. He told of the ambush, helping the Thane back to Ranger Hold and how Tam had been sent out to find and bring back our new young Laird before he was killed. He spread his hands. "I cannot believe he would send such a young lass on a most important mission."

"Did you not just tell us, Lord Krendhal, of her deeds?"

"Aye, but—"

"She has been Confirmed and Presented, Lord Krendhal. We judge a person by his—or her—actions. She has proven herself."

"I cannot wait to meet this young Ranger." Marcalan said with a lilt in his voice, his eyes twinkling.

"Indeed, Marcalan." Haladhon tried to keep a stoic expression. "But remember that with her training she would know to do more than slap your face."

Marcalan turned red. "And you would know this from experience?"

Tanadhon snickered as Haladhon grinned.

Krendhal clenched his fists. "We have serious matters to discuss, Ranger Chief Haladhon."

Haladhon turned to him, smile gone. "Indeed, Lord Krendhal. First of which is, how do we keep those vermin from crawling out of their holes in Laird Hall in the dark? On a clear night with either moon up or even just the nebula's glow, we should see even one man skulking toward the perimeter, but what about an overcast night? 'Twould be peace to my mind if that gate were closed, although they could still come over the walls with enough rope." Haladhon pursed his lips, thinking of the many discussions the chiefs had held about how to conduct the siege.

"Lamadhel, ever the engineer, wanted to build trebuchets, but Alcandhor knew they would likely not harm the other-worldly shimmer-stone of Laird Hall. Not to mention it would be difficult to build such things in secret, much less transport them here without word spreading."

Krendhal fell back in his chair, eyebrows lifted. "Thane Alcandhor knew this was coming?"

"Aye," Haladhon said. "He is farsighted, as was his father."

"Not farsighted enough to keep from being ambushed," the lord said, his voice edged with bitterness.

"I said farsighted, not infallible, Lord Krendhal."

Krendhal inclined his head. "My apologies, Haladhon. I meant no disrespect. It distresses me how many Rangers were lost today, not to mention the Laird." He looked down, his clasped hands before him on the table, the creases on his forehead and around his eyes deepening. "Would that I could have been clear-sighted enough to see what was happening. I did not suspect any of the lords could be capable of such treason."

"We have no time for self-reproach, Lord Krendhal. It drains mind and body, and we have too much at stake to waste time and thoughts in such a manner." Haladhon rubbed his neck. "What worries me is that the siege has not trapped all the treasonous lords as Alcandhor planned. Only Cardhal and Batrig and their sons were present. Now the others will be forewarned. Which is just what the Thane wished to avoid." He leaned back. "We can do nothing about that now. Our focus must be to hold this siege and to help Tam. We need to make certain no messenger leaves so as to give Tam a lead in finding the Laird and getting him away from his captors. We cannot guarantee a messenger has not left already."

"I do not believe one has, Haladhon. At least, not since we set the perimeter this morning," Tanadhon said.

"We know not when the messenger might have been sent. One might have been sent out early this morning and be a half day—or more—ahead of Tam." He exhaled slowly, worrying over Tam despite himself. He nodded toward both the noble and his impertinent cousin. "Lord Krendhal, you should rest and have that wound tended, as should you, Marcalan. If we have need, we can speak again later. And Tanadhon, get that message drummed out. Perhaps we can end this siege quickly."

~:~

Haladhon barely tasted the stew he had for afternooning. He went back to the bedchamber where Alcandhor lay and tapped lightly on the door.

Santran opened it, a scowl on his face.

"I need to see him. Please. Just for a moment."

Sighing, Santran opened the door a bit wider. "Look from here."

Haladhon peered past Santran at his cousin, lying still as death. "How is he truly?"

"He has Elders' blood, doesn't he?"

Haladhon noted the slip into commoner contractions. A sign Santran, who had picked up the nobles' way of speaking in his many years as Laird Hall's healer, was worried.

"Aye."

Santran nodded. "That may make a difference."

Haladhon swallowed and gazed at his cousin again. He inhaled as realization struck him—only the marriage necklet lay about Alcandhor's neck. No key. "Santran," he whispered. "Was there anything else about his throat?"

"Anything else? What would there be besides his necklet?"

What, indeed. "Was there?"

"No. Now, you have seen him, go away, and let him rest."

Haladhon stared at the wood grain of the door after Santran closed it in his face.

"Any closer and you can kiss that door," came a lilting voice. "Beware of splinters, cousin."

Haladhon turned to glare at Marcalan and gestured across the hall to the meeting chamber. Once inside, Haladhon said, "He is so pale. Santran asked about his Enaisi blood."

"Enaisi blood? Why does he ask about that?"

"Those who are Children of the Enaisi often have a better capacity to heal."

"Really? I knew that not."

Haladhon dropped into a chair. "You should have paid more attention in your studies."

"This from you?" Marcalan sat on the corner of the table, his expression turning serious. "What can I do to help, cousin?"

Haladhon scrubbed his face with his hands. "I know not. I have so many questions, and Alcandhor may never awaken to answer them."

"Such as?"

Haladhon sighed. "The Rangers in the drum tower."

"They drummed all is well."

"Aye, but they are besieged within a siege."

"Stars. Did the Thane not discuss that with you?"

"Nay. 'Tis not like him to overlook such things, but he did not discuss the tower. I hope he did not forget about them. Hang it, for all his planning, he did not foresee he would be wounded." Haladhon slammed a hand on the table. "Curse that ambush! Five good Rangers plus a chief lost. And perhaps our Thane too. They knew our strategy. They knew, Marcalan!"

"Aye," Marcalan whispered. "Disturbing, that."

Haladhon flicked the lock of hair off his forehead as his thoughts wandered to his young cousin with large eyes the color of clear gold. "I also worry for Tam. I know not where Alcandhor sent her. I cannot imagine anything but a heavy guard around the Atheling. How does Alcandhor think she can free him?"

"You think he was addled with pain when he gave her orders?"

"I know not." Haladhon peered hard at his cousin. "You know what you hear in this chamber is to go no further?"

Marcalan crossed his arms. "I am no fool."

Haladhon leaned back with a snort.

"So how can I help?" Marcalan asked.

Haladhon nodded at his cousin's arm. "How is that wound?"

"'Tis but a scratch, as I said. I am fit to join watch at the perimeter."

Haladhon shook his head. "Nay. I need men I truly trust to go to Cardhal's and Batrig's provinces to take charge and bring order."

"I will take Estan. I have roamed there and know the locals."

Haladhon rubbed his eyes. "I thought you said you were not a fool."

"Why?" Marcalan asked with a chuckle. "Merely because it is the most troublesome of all the provinces? I relish a challenge."

Haladhon shot him a wry look. "Until we know who can be trusted within the nobles' families, we will take charge of administration of those provinces, either keeping Rangers directly in control or implementing an interim government. I will leave it to your discretion what to do in Estan."

Marcalan inclined his head. "I shall prepare to leave." He stood. "Do not forget you do have Lamadhel to help."

Haladhon exhaled as the door shut. He needed not Marcalan to give him advice. He knew what needed to be done. At the moment, that meant checking the hold's defenses in the event of an attack and heading out to the perimeter.

He rose, straightening his shoulders. He must hold this siege. He must.

~:~

Dusk deepened, and Tam barely slowed. She tripped over a gnarled root but kept on. She must arrive before a messenger brought a sentence of death for the young Laird.

Woods gave way to fields, and Tam hurried across them, guided by the moons' light. What sort of place was this fortress of the Enaisi? Uncle had said it was tunneled into a mountain. The Enaisi must like building underground. Zaidhron had been built to guard the Enaisi's portal, housed deep in the mountain behind it. But—if the Enaisi had a dwelling on the Forbidden Peninsula, they must have lived on this planet before her people came here. Would Uncle know more about that?

Tam hissed as her foot dropped into a hole. The opening to a field viper's nest perhaps? More likely to a sorpah's tunnel. Hang those little crop-eating creatures! Tam could not see clearly at night and a serious injury would be disastrous to her mission. Perhaps she should stop until dawn.

Tam went on a short way, careful of where she stepped, and soon saw a clump of neena trees. She clambered over twisted trunks into the center of the copse and wrapped her cloak around herself as she settled between two tall roots. A pleasant, flavorsome odor wafted to her. Wild sheena must be growing nearby, she thought as she dropped off.

~:~

Vitran found little sleep that night.

Some of the guards refused to attack the Rangers in the drum tower even upon threat of pain or death. Fighting broke out among them but his men prevailed, and he had the ones loyal to the Rangers locked in cells with those previously imprisoned, hoping the conditions and the lack of food would change their minds. But that reduced his manpower.

Their attempt to storm the drum tower failed dismally. Any guard mounting the spiral stairs met with a sword or arrow. After losing several guards this way, Vitran ordered a bolt installed on the lower door and guards stationed to keep the Rangers trapped within the tall structure.

But that was Vitran's only "victory."

Soon after, cries came from the west wall. A guard screamed as he tumbled off the wall, down the roof, and onto the ground. The Rangers in the drum tower had begun shooting at the men on the walls, especially concentrating on those guarding the inner and outer gates, in the gate towers, and the outer bailey.

With the glow from the moons silhouetting the lofty drum tower, the guards could see no target in the dark windows, yet the Rangers did not have the same trouble. Vitran yelled to remove all guards from the west and north sections of the walls and the bailey to keep them safe from the Rangers' arrows. Being a steward not a warrior, he did not know their range but would take no chances. Dead guards would not help him maintain control.

A message drummed in an unfamiliar code. Great Bells, what did the Rangers have planned now? No time to concern himself with that as guards ran up.

"Vitran! You had us withdraw men from guarding the northeast gardens because of the Rangers' arrows, and now people are starting to steal food!"

"Send men with longbows to stand along the borders of the gardens outside the range of the drum tower. Give a warning, then shoot if they don't obey. That food must be rationed, or we'll all starve!"

His men saluted and ran off. He stared up at the forbidding edifice, wishing its foundation would crumble, and a spark of thought lit and grew. Vitran ran over to nearby guards. Snatching their arms, he pointed up at the menace. "Set fire to arrows! Shoot fire into the tower!"

With lively shouts, his men ran to obey. Soon they returned and one of them, Tavnol, said, "Vitran, of the guards not in cells, most of us are more trained for sword, and there are not many who can draw a longbow. Those who can are watching over the gardens."

Snatching handfuls of Tavnol's doublet, Vitran screamed, "Get them shooting at those blighted Rangers in that bloody tower!"

Hidden in the black shadows cast by the keep, the bowmen fired their tar-dipped shafts as soon as they were lit by the small firepot, and scurried away before Rangers could rain death down on them.

Arrows streaked upward like shooting stars into the night sky. Most spat off the tower and fell dizzily as though drunken flames.

"Can't you aim?" Vitran grabbed one of the bowmen. "Shoot them!"

"You try landing an arrow in those dark windows with the moons high behind the tower," the bowman flung back.

"He's no warrior, that's certain," came a mumble.

"Neither are we," another replied with a dour chuckle.

Vitran spun to the bowmen, fists clenched, his gaze raking across their faces, not certain who made the remark. "No, I'm not, you cursed fools. But unless you have any better ideas, you'd best do as I say. We're in danger as long as those inbred by-blows sit up there shooting at us."

The bowmen muttered among themselves but resumed their assault. What arrows made it through the windows caused no fires. They must have water to douse them. But how? Did they have water stored? Curse them! Vitran comforted himself with two thoughts. One, that they must run out of arrows sooner or later. Two, they were besieged as well. Being trapped in the drum tower, they would die of thirst and hunger if nothing else, and sooner than the rest of them.

Shouts came from the southwest tower. A guard ran over to deliver their news. "Rangers are crossing the field and heading for the gates!"

"Shoot them!" Vitran screamed.

"We can't! They're on the north side, above the road, where the drum tower is, and our guard towers nearby are deserted. And the Rangers in the drum tower can take aim on us if we go near the gates!"

"Send men to shut the gates, then!"

"But Vitran, the Rangers—"

"Just do it!" Vitran's fists flailed the air as his voice hit a new high and broke. Before he could rage more, two guards ran to him, covered with dirt, sweat, and blood. They leaned on each other, breathing heavily.

"They know of the tunnel, Vitran. We are the only ones who made it back alive. We can't get out that way."

Vitran pounded his temples with his fists. "Block off the tunnel then. I don't want Rangers sneaking into this hall through it."

As his men ran off, Vitran ground his teeth. An attack force was impossible—he did not have enough men against all the Rangers that had to be out there. With no clouds to cover the moons or nebula, he could not think of sneaking men out the gate, even if he dared open them again. He scowled up at the night sky. Did even the heavens help these accursed Rangers?

Vitran strode to the Great Hall muttering maledictions. All his plans had failed, but he had one hidden advantage—their confederates outside the walls. Help would soon arrive. He would best the Rangers yet.

~:~

Grey mists covered the ground like a damp blanket as Tam pushed up, blinking. Dawn-singers announced the day, and several other birds added happy morning noises, as well.

Tam stifled a yawn and stood, pulling the food sack out of her pack. She opened it and stared. The journey rations would not be enough. Why had Sherel given her so little? She closed her eyes with a quiet moan—the blame was her own. She had not told Sherel food for two. She closed the sack and reached for her own small pouch of dried meat. She must save the food for the young Laird.

How many other ways would she fail? The Laird had died. And her father. His words as he argued with her uncle over using her as a spy echoed in her head. *You are relying on a girl-child for such an important task. 'Tis folly. You have no regard for the danger to the Laird!*

Her uncle had trusted her, and she had fallen short. Her father had been right.

Chapter Ten

Searing pain—his shoulder—his sides.

Though already shut, Alcandhor squeezed his eyes tighter and clenched his teeth. He took a breath. Blazing spears drove through his ribs and chest. He almost choked, unable to gasp in pain.

Trying to avoid motion that would cause the burning agony again, Alcandhor opened his eyes. Shadows danced about the room from embers in the fireplace.

Ranger Hold. This was Ranger Hold in Lairdton. But why was he here? Memories flooded back. Valdhor's body falling, a scream that pierced his heart, echoing his own pain.

Alcandhor closed his eyes. Nay, Valdhor could not die. Yet, he had. He had not blocked his feelings at the end. Alcandhor felt Valdhor's pain, physical and emotional, and sensed his spirit leave his body. Traveling away...beyond...

And Tam. The emptiness and sorrow in her eyes would haunt him for a long time. A hard taskmaster and unfeeling man, aye, but still Tam loved her father. He had been the center of her world for fifteen years.

How would he proceed with Tam? Alcandhor tossed his head on the pillow but froze at a sharp pain in his shoulder. He had forced the chiefs' conclave to accept her as a Ranger without law or precedent to back him up. Or rather, Haladhon had, although he knew not if the man had canny insight or merely wanted to irritate Valdhor.

But dare he reopen the issue of her as possible heir to Thane? It could force some in the clan to call Question on her birth record. Or on the fact he never pursued the rumor of Valdhor's child. As Thane, he was considered the embodiment of the law and paid full penalty for any infraction he committed. If Question were called, Alcandhor could lose all—he would be clanless: no family, no home.

~:~

Sherel came into the meeting chamber, hands on her hips, and Haladhon looked up in irritation.

"Do you realize how many Rangers are here now? They are sleeping on the grounds in the bailey. And more arrive every day.

Cooking for hundreds is not like cooking for a score of men. I need to hire help."

Haladhon put down the quill and rubbed his eyes. "Most of the Rangers are camped by the open-air kitchens established at points around the perimeter."

"Yes,"—Sherel crossed her arms—"but that still leaves many here at the hold, and you don't have any idea of all the extra work."

"I will not trust anyone from the town. The Thane gave us all warning about the trustworthiness of those in and near Laird Hall."

"But Haladhon—"

"Conscript help from the Rangers. We all are taught to clean and cook for ourselves."

Sherel sniffed. "Can't tell it by how the lot of you act. Like babies at times."

She stamped out before Haladhon could retort. Someone in the hallway murmured to her. Sherel said, "Go on in."

Nandhal appeared at the door. "You wished to see me?"

"Aye. You have not given report, Ranger, and I need numbers on our weapons. I especially need to know how things fare in stocks of arrows and extra bows."

"Additional supplies arrived before the siege started." Nandhal frowned, crossing his arms. "And more have come since then. I reported that to Tanadhon."

Haladhon pointed a finger at Nandhal. "Your duty as armory warden is to report to me, not Tanadhon, during this siege. In writing. Is that understood?"

Nandhal straightened. Anger flitted over his face, but he dropped his gaze as his shoulders slumped. "Aye. I apologize." His brow creased as he raised his head. "How is the Thane truly?"

Haladhon lifted his eyebrows, not expecting that question from the surly Nandhal. "He mends."

Nandhal's lips twitched in a slight smile, though his eyes bespoke his disquiet. "Good. I did not know whether to trust the news that has flown about the bailey."

"I shall tell him of your concern. Now,"—he wagged a finger at Nandhal—"go get that report written."

Nandhal's smile grew. "Aye, sir."

Haladhon shook his head at the younger Ranger as the door shut. Perhaps being assigned to this post had helped Nandhal mature. A little.

Haladhon picked up the quill. These letters, to be sent to Rangers and provincial lords, must be assertive. The provinces must understand that despite the siege, Rangers watched and would enforce the law.

Sedition would not be tolerated, nor would outlawry from those who thought to take opportunity. The lords should be vigilant as well to guard and undergird the law.

Lordless Estan and Nelatan provinces—they knew not their lords had died, but thought them only besieged as traitors—received a special letter reiterating that the temporary councils must be obeyed until each of their provinces appointed a new lord.

Haladhon finished the letters and pushed them aside. He would review them later; his muddied mind needed respite. Had Maradhor been tapped for duty during the siege, or did the Ranger stay at Zaidhron to instruct journeymen scribes? He would look at the roster. Haladhon would fain have their best scribe write the final drafts.

He spread the map that he had found on the table the day Tam left to find the young Laird. Where had she gone? His gaze kept straying to the Forbidden Peninsula, but he knew not why. The last report had the Atheling in North Port in Estan Province, just south of that dreaded land. That must be where Alcandhor had sent her.

He stifled a yawn and blinked, his eyes burning from lack of sleep. As he rubbed them, he heard a throat clear and looked up to see Tanadhon standing in the doorway.

"Lord Krendhal wishes to see you, Haladhon."

Haladhon stood, nodding, and Tanadhon backed up a step to allow Krendhal to enter. The noble swept into the chamber and paused, glancing over his shoulder. Tanadhon hesitated, bowing, then shut the door.

"Haladhon," Krendhal began, "how is the Thane?"

"Santran said he was going to lessen the dosage of herb, so perhaps Alcandhor will wake today, milord."

"Then he has passed out of danger?"

"I know not. Santran told me that if it were not for his Enaisi blood, he should have been dead."

"We have to hold to hope."

"I try." Haladhon changed the subject to something less likely to cause him to display his emotions. "How are you faring, Lord Krendhal? Our accommodations are not quite what you are accustomed to."

A wry smile pursed Krendhal lips. "Indeed. However, I think I could not be in safer surroundings. And your Rangers have been an inspiration to improve my bowman skills. But what of you? You do not seem well. Have you slept at all?"

Haladhon waved his hand over the reports stacked on the table. "I have too much to do, milord."

"Sit, before you fall over. You do us no service if you fall ill from exhaustion."

Haladhon slowly reseated himself. "How may I help you, lord?"

Krendhal sat and bowed his head, looking at Haladhon from beneath his eyebrows, his expression grave. "Ranger, I wished to talk to you. My clan is almost gone. If the Laird is not brought back safely..." He kneaded his hands together. "I am too old to find another wife and sire children to keep our clan alive. I still grieve for Berniss's death and my family as well. Would that I had died of the fever too." He stared at the table, then took a deep breath and looked up. "What would happen if my clan dies?"

"I know not. The Thane has studied these matters much more than I have, perhaps he would know. I only know that we still have two of you. You are well protected, as you have pointed out, and hopefully Tam will be able to complete her mission." He paused, a smile spreading. "And, milord, you are not as old as you would have me believe. Why not marry again? I have heard it is very pleasant."

Krendhal shot him an amused look. "Then why have you not tried it yourself?"

Haladhon raised his eyebrows in surprise that the lord would jest with him. A knock interrupted his reply.

Sherel came in, curtseying to Krendhal. "Your pardon, milord, but Santran has called you, Haladhon."

Both men hurried out. The healer stood in the hallway, smiling. "He is awake and asking for you."

Haladhon shut the door and leaned against it in relief to see Alcandhor conscious. He brought a chair over by the bed.

"What news?" Alcandhor asked, his voice a hoarse whisper and his breathing labored.

How weak his cousin sounded, and still so wan. "The siege holds."

"How long has it been?"

"The siege began five days ago."

Alcandhor frowned. "That long? I need to be up."

"From what Santran says, you should be kept quiet and in bed for many more days. If you do not behave, he will give you more herbs to keep you asleep."

Alcandhor moaned.

"How do you feel?" Haladhon asked.

"How do you think?" the Thane retorted with halts every few words to take small breaths. "All this trouble, and I am stuck here."

"You are here to advise me, Thane, if I need it. I am carrying out your orders. Trust me."

Alcandhor swallowed. "I do. 'Tis just difficult to lie here. So much is happening."

"I know, cousin. I understand." Haladhon hesitated; should he ask those questions that burned in him? Despite Alcandhor's stoic expression, Haladhon knew him well enough to see the pain he hid. His alert, restless eyes pleaded for news. Haladhon knew he would go mad in that same situation if kept ignorant. But he did not have to share all his concerns, only the most urgent. "Thane, I have several worries, but I hesitate to trouble you."

"What are they?"

Haladhon rubbed his neck. "Not all the nobles were in Laird Hall when the siege began."

Alcandhor's eyes widened, and he lifted his head exclaiming, "What?" With a grimace, he lay back.

Haladhon winced in sympathy. "Only Cardhal, Batrig, and their sons were there for the meeting. Paltor and Lorwith are journeying toward Lantral. Presumably to meet with Zantith, who is still at his hall."

"How could this happen? Why were we not told?"

Haladhon let out his breath in a slow exhale. "From what I can gather, the reports were gathered and put on Tanadhon's table, but somehow got tucked under other reports, already read. So both you and he missed them."

Alcandhor rolled his head on the pillow. "Nay. I read and ordered every report on that table."

"So Tanadhon says as well. Yet I found the reports that evening." Haladhon hesitated, not wanting to doubt his—and Alcandhor's—childhood friend. "Think you Tanadhon might not be trusted?"

"'Tis hard to believe. I would not unduly cast a shadow. That room is open and unguarded."

"Aye. 'Tis true. We should have—" Haladhon stopped; this was not the time for bemoaning oversights. "But still, we have treachery close to our hearts," Haladhon said in a hushed voice. "The ambush within an ambush."

Alcandhor remained silent, staring at the ceiling. Haladhon saw the flit of doubt, anxiety, and anger on his cousin's face. "Aye. And it could be anyone—a Ranger, including Tanadhon. Or Sherel. Even Santran."

Haladhon's mouth fell open. It had seemed fortuitous that Sherel found the Laird's own healer in town the day of the ambush—he had been visiting his daughter's family. And he seemed genuinely enraged at the Laird's death. "Stars. Santran? You suspect him? Yet he has been all but living here to tend you."

"Aye. I think he has proven his loyalty, else I would not be alive. I merely point out we cannot overlook anyone. Whoever it is will be very careful and very correct right now. Send word to Zandhral to report to me. I will have him sense for anything amiss."

"Aye, his ability might net us a traitor."

"Perhaps. But those of us with Enaisi blood are weak—our abilities are not reliable as generations ago. If they were, I could have identified the traitor among us." Alcandhor frowned, staring at the ceiling for some time. Finally he said, "Tell me your other concerns."

"Our Rangers in the drum tower. I worry for them."

"They are not our regularly stationed drummers. I ordered a change over a lunation ago. The Rangers in there are Bardhal, Madhrel, Vardhon, and Sandhral."

Haladhon chuckled. "Four of our best bowmen? Alcandhor, you are a devious rascal."

Alcandhor managed a weak grin. "My thanks. And aye, they have provisions and arrows to last them a long time."

"That is a worry off my mind. I had wondered how they were going to survive the siege. There is no way to access the tower's well, is there—except from within the tower itself?"

"Nay. That well is a Ranger secret and 'twas built that way purposely. In a conflict, Rangers could be perceived as adversaries within Laird Hall."

"The Enaisi thought of everything. But why did you never mention the change to me?"

"I thought I—aye, you are right. I gave the order while you were out of the city, then the day you returned I left to find Valdhor." A shadow of grief passed over Alcandhor's face. "Have the bodies been properly interred?"

"Aye. Kin of each man is here, and Lamadhel stood in your place for Valdhor. You can visit the crypt to give your Loosening when you are healed."

Alcandhor cleared his throat. "Six good men, cousin."

"I know..."

Santran opened the door. "That is enough visiting."

Alcandhor looked despondent.

Flashing a smile and a wink, Haladhon rose. "I will visit again later."

The healer eyed Haladhon as he passed and turned to look at Alcandhor. "You have not been letting him wear you out, I hope, Thane?"

Haladhon grinned at Alcandhor over Santran's shoulder. His Thane's eyes shone with mischief. Despite his Thane's injuries, obvious pain, and inability to say more than a few words without a halt to breathe, Haladhon found himself reassured by that twinkle.

"On the contrary, my dear Santran. Haladhon has answered questions that have set my mind at ease."

The healer sniffed in disbelief and shot a reproachful look at Haladhon as he shut the door.

~:~

Zantith stood as his guests, Lord Paltor and Lord Lorwith, entered his solar. His gaze swept the rich tapestries and plush furnishings of his private living chamber with pride. Despite the circumstances, the chance to display his excellent taste and costly furnishings pleased him.

He indicated a small table with gilded edges and carved with delicate designs. "Wine?"

"You think of wine at a time like this?" snarled Paltor, lumbering toward the table.

"I would like some." Lorwith tossed his fair hair over his shoulders, his blue eyes flitting sideways at Paltor.

Zantith seated himself with a shrug. "Serve yourselves."

Lorwith filled his goblet and held the decanter up.

Zantith nodded and watched the pale lord pour the wine. "How came you here so quickly, Lord Lorwith? Have you wings?"

"I–I had a dispute to settle concerning surcharges on goods being delivered to my province and had gone to Lord Paltor about it, so was to hand when the message came about the siege. We traveled together."

Zantith smiled. Lorwith cared not about his people to involve himself if they were being overtaxed in buying out of province. And what might Lorwith need badly enough to deal with Paltor and wrestle over that lord's outrageous boundary fees? Nothing. Zantith would bet on it.

Lorwith's fears had been a plague to them all. He would not be in a meeting with anyone except the provincial lords. No guards or servants—he would not even allow the sons of the other lords to be present. Any message he received he burned after reading, and he sent no messages, but would either remain silent or—ah, if he had been to Paltor's hall, he wished to discuss their plots. Did these two conspire behind his back then? He would watch, but best let them think him deceived.

He lifted his glass to toast Paltor. "Still giving your overseers freedom in the depths of their pockets, or do all the added surcharges go into your coffers?"

Paltor's eyes snapped with anger, his face flushed. "We did not come all this way to discuss boundary trade fees. What do you know about this siege?"

Zantith sipped his wine to hide his smile at Paltor's discomfiture but sobered as he brought his mind to the current crisis. "'Tis true. Our confederates are all trapped within Laird Hall, and word is the Laird is dead."

"When did this happen? How?" Paltor dropped into a chair.

Zantith winced. The chair matched the table and had not been made for a massive frame, much less for the attack of a dead load.

"The siege started five days ago. I know not what happened except that there was either a skirmish or an ambush of the Ranger chiefs. One chief was killed."

"Aye, so I heard. And it was not Alcandhor." Paltor's fleshy fist smashed on the table. "Bloody, cursed Rangers, I wish them all dead!"

Zantith steadied the two goblets that shook with the assault. He picked his up and swirled the dark red wine. "Softly, softly."

Paltor scowled at him.

Lorwith spread his hands on the table. "We had it all in hand. We were readying to move only a few more days. I do not understand what went wrong."

Paltor's thick lips curled at Lorwith in contempt, as he leaned forward, arms on the table. "Alcandhor is what went wrong! That cursed, inbred by-blow is the threat. He has undermined the dissension we have been sowing with his Rangers' arbitrations and talk of changes to our traditions and how we have strayed from the Laws of the Enaisi. And all for his own gain." He rasped in a breath. "If we want independent control of our provinces, we need to stop him. Get rid of him."

"Stars!" Zantith sat back with a weary groan. "I wager you would blame sea storm surges and ground tremors on the man." And likely had. Zantith often wondered if Paltor was mad. He had never liked the precocious son of Thane Saldhor from the time the boy first became involved in council matters. Alcandhor had an incredible knowledge of the law in the most minute details and had often corrected Paltor, who considered himself an expert.

Zantith also suspected something involving that wench Aleta, who married Alcandhor. Paltor had been panting over her before her marriage. But whatever the reasons, Paltor's hatred of the Thane had been festering for years, and it now consumed him.

"Save your wagers, Zantith. You have so much debt from gambling now, I cannot see how you manage to keep control of your province."

Zantith's back stiffened and his fists clenched. "At least I am not so consumed by hatred that I cannot see clearly."

"Enough!" Lorwith looked stunned at his own outburst and flushed.

Zantith gazed over at the thin, pale lord in amusement. How could such a weak man govern a province?

Paltor's lips drew back in a mirthless grin. "Does our spineless partner have something to say?"

Lorwith dropped his gaze. "There is a difference between cowardice and caution."

"Indeed." Paltor gave a condescending bow of his head. "And when you learn that difference, you will no doubt let us know, will you not?"

"This bickering is getting us nowhere." Zantith fingered his goblet. "We have important matters to discuss. Such as what to do now. Our confederates are besieged, and we need to know why." He raised a hand. "And do not say on about Rangers, Paltor. We need to consider what happened, not just point blind blame."

Paltor snorted. "And what think you happened?"

"I think..." Zantith paused and leaned back. "I think that Cardhal and Batrig stabbed us in the back by going to the Laird with the ultimatum on their own. And used their own men to plan the ambush of the chiefs."

Paltor and Lorwith exchanged glances, and at length, both nodded. Did they not both come to the same conclusion themselves before this, or did their silence agreement refer to something known only to themselves?

"Aye. It makes sense," Lorwith muttered.

"Batrig is a greedy fool." Paltor's chair creaked as he sat back with a sigh. "And Cardhal more so. I think you have the right of it."

"So what do we do?" Lorwith asked.

Paltor smirked. "We will go to Lairdton to see what is truly happening. Once there, we must kill the Thane. With all that is happening, he may be pushed to make Claim."

Zantith pursed his lips at such an audacious idea. *Alcandhor* take power?

Lorwith's head snapped up, his eyes wide. "What do you mean *we*?"

Zantith set his goblet down and leaned forward. "Even if Alcandhor made Claim—and I do not think he has the character for it—the chiefs would not back it."

"His humility is but an act. He would fain make Claim and have all provincial lords reduced to nothing. You know him not as I do."

"But the chiefs—"

"The chiefs have little will of their own." Paltor fingered the edge of his robe. "Haladhon is only interested in himself. Lamadhel and his sons bow to Alcandhor. Valdhor hides away as a hermit and gave up his chance at the Claim long ago. Our *dear* Thane—"

Lorwith half-stood, leaning over the table. "What do you mean *we*?"

Zantith glared at the pale, wide-eyed noble, as did Paltor.

"*We* lords," Paltor sneered over the table at their partner, "have heard about the insidious attack on the Laird, and how the Rangers had to besiege the hall, and are coming to offer our support and assistance, my dear Lorwith."

"Are you mad?" Lorwith's querulous voice cracked. He sank back into his chair, his palms rubbing its arms. "The Rangers must know who we are if they have besieged the others in Laird Hall. You would walk in the door of their stronghold now?"

The wood of those chairs held a high polish—Zantith glared at Lorwith's sweaty hands. The fretful lord straightened, his fists sliding into his lap as Paltor explained.

"They know nothing. How do you talk to people besieged? And Cardhal and Batrig acted on their own. If Batrig or the others did say anything before the siege, we can claim we have been wrongly implicated—as we did to Krendhal."

Lorwith's eyes widened. "Great Bells! What of Krendhal? Is he caught in the siege?"

"Word is he is at Ranger Hold." Zantith shrugged. "We know nothing else. He may be their guest or their prisoner." He had heard no more than that from his own source, which bothered him, but he would not share that with his peers.

Paltor's eyes narrowed. "Now, back to Alcandhor—"

Zantith groaned. Not again. "Back to our plans. Or what is left of them after this debacle."

"Alcandhor is our plan. Or rather, killing him." Paltor's eyes shone with malicious glee. "I have send word to my assassins. They are journeying to Lairdton as well. The Thane will soon be dead."

"Assassins?" Lorwith squeaked.

Zantith turned away from him and faced Paltor. "You never deviate from your course, do you? Tell me, how does one openly assassinate the Thane and live to tell it? Who would be foolish enough to attack him when he has Rangers about him all the time?"

Paltor's small eyes glinted in feverish delight. "You cannot think it through? Who else but Rangers themselves—or rather, former Rangers."

"Rogues?" Lorwith whispered, his eyes wide.

Amazement and fear gripped Zantith's insides. He had never seen any of those outlaws himself, but his mind supplied a vivid picture—tall, strong men, foreheads branded with a broken sword as a warning to others to beware of them. "How found you such renegades?"

"I have dealings with them to our mutual benefit. They do tasks for me, and I hide them when Rangers are on search for them. This band's leader is a man named Uardhel and he hates the Thane almost as much as I do." Paltor leaned back with a smirk. "They are journeying to Lairdton from my province—"

"How did you communicate with them?"

"I contacted them as I left for your Hall. I knew the Thane had survived an attack, and I determined I would change that." Paltor's teeth showed viciously in what was for him a smile. "I want Alcandhor dead. And one day soon I will see it done." His eyes darted at Lorwith and over at Zantith. "We shall see it done."

"I refuse to go." Lorwith raised his hands with a shake of his head. "I will not knowingly put my head in a noose."

"Coward! Zantith, what say you?"

Zantith took a deep breath. "Our stakes are too high not to play this through. But you are forgetting one thing—the Atheling."

"What about him?" asked Paltor.

"He is still our prisoner and is a hindrance to our plans. As long as he—and Krendhal—are alive, our plan to rid ourselves of oversight are forestalled. If we wish autonomy over our provinces, the Atheling must die."

Paltor rubbed his heavy cheeks. "You are right. We need to send word to kill him."

"Aye. But even starting now, a messenger would take time to get there, and what if he were to run into Rangers?"

"What are you saying?"

Zantith suppressed a sigh. Did Paltor understand nothing? "We should send the message not by a single messenger but by a group, to guard against the Rangers."

"One runner can make better time," Paltor said.

"One runner would be easily stopped by Rangers." Zantith jabbed the table with his finger in emphasis. "Do you want speed or a guarantee the task will be accomplished? Look at the odds."

Keladar's lord gazed at Zantith, his thick lips pursed in contemplation. "How quickly can a group be assembled?"

"I could have perhaps six to eight well-trained fighters with wild-sense ready by morning."

"Six to eight? Will that be enough?" Paltor asked. "Rangers usually travel in groups of two or three and I would send more than eight men against three Rangers. They train their whole lives. Fighting is all they know."

"Have either of you brought men that would be able to fight Rangers?" Zantith glanced from one noble to the other.

"Look not to me for such men," Lorwith said. "I am well out of this."

Paltor raised his hands. "I need all my guards with me."

Zantith believed that—Paltor ever feared betrayal, even by his own sons. "Then departure is delayed. Think you ten will be sufficient?"

"At the least, ten men," Paltor said.

"I will see how quickly I can find more men and dispatch them."

"Do it, Zantith."

Chapter Eleven

Tam woke, blinking, her cloak still wrapped about her. She stretched, inhaling the earthy scents of moist dirt and dewy grass. The crested nightsingers had stopped their din, but other creatures continued their noise as dawn broke. Some of them Tam had not seen or heard before; they must be native to the low marshes.

The flatlands and their forests were different from the high mountains where Tam had been raised, but skirting the marshes yesterday had been a new and unpleasant experience. Now she faced a fresh challenge: the Forbidden Peninsula. That mysterious land lay beyond the fens, fetid odor, and swamp gnats she had left behind. Tam did not know which she dreaded more.

Her father would never tell her why the peninsula had been shunned.

From Uncle's map she knew that the north, east, and south coastlines were high, sheer cliffs. Tam readied herself and hoisted her pack, facing east. Today she would discover what this dire land looked like. With a deep breath, Tam set out.

Later in the day Tam stopped at a stream to wet her face and fill her waterskin. The warm sun on her back cast long shadows before her. She took a strip of smoked meat from her pouch as her meager afternooning. Her stomach ever gnawed, but the Laird would need food for the journey back. She had no time to hunt or gather food except to snag a few berries in passing.

As she chewed, Tam glanced up at the sloping, forested hills on each side of this valley that ran east to west on the peninsula. If she had not known she headed toward the ocean, she would have thought she traveled in foothills.

After one last drink, Tam rose and assessed her surroundings, wondering about that messenger. As yet she had neither seen nor sensed anyone. She had tried in vain to journey inside the edge of the forest on the southern side of the valley, hoping to hide from unfriendly eyes. However the wild undergrowth in this lonely place tangled and choked the way, making it nearly impossible to travel among the trees.

Tam began walking again, her pace quick. Blind ferocity scraped along her spine—no sense of thought or meaning, just a wild viciousness. She drew her knife. A distinctive growl made her arm hair stand on end. A ballan. They attacked for no reason, and despite their small size, were unafraid of any other predator. Their jaws could crush bones.

She whirled to face the ballan as it launched itself from under a bush. She jumped back, her blade slashing at its throat. Her strike went awry. The creature flopped to the ground, blood mingling with saliva as the ballan worked its wounded mouth. She sheathed her knife, drew her sword, and beheaded it.

A snarl came from above. She spun. Claws out and teeth bared, the mate sprang from a branch. She swung her sword hilt up, catching the ballan on the side of the head, but a claw sliced her forearm. She clenched her jaw against the pain and struck at the ballan. It darted to the side and leapt at her. With a desperate swing, she smacked it with the flat of her blade. While it lay dazed, she swept her sword back in and killed it.

She inhaled deeply to regain control of both breath and heart and stared at the carcasses of the ferocious little creatures. Such soft fur belied their nasty disposition.

Tam pulled the tatters of her dark green silk shirt away from her arm. Blood dripped freely. She unslung her pack, grinding her teeth against the pain and loss of time.

Before long she had a fire started and set a little pan of water to heat. She rummaged in her pack and stopped with a groan. She chided herself for not remembering to retrieve the salve she had lent her uncle and began to search for herbs.

Freyala and ch'illeya soon sat in a small pile. Tam cleansed the slashes with the warmed water. She chewed the herbs, applied them to her arm, and wrapped the wound with a clean cloth from her healing sack.

She eyed the dead animals. Food for the taking, and she needed strength. More time lost. She skinned one of the ballan, trying to ignore the ache as she worked with her wounded arm. The sun sank low by the time the meat had roasted. The delay soured her stomach so that she had little appetite. She would have to go on in the dark. She must make up the distance. She must arrive before any messengers.

~:~

Despite the bright sun, singing birds, and bustle, which he normally enjoyed, Haladhon walked back from the perimeter through Lairdton with a briskness he did not feel. A merchant left the doorway of his shop and bowed, wiping his hands on his apron. Haladhon halted, waiting for the inevitable question.

"Sir, how is the Thane?"

"He heals well. I thank you for asking."

"I'm glad he is recovering. We all worry about him."

"Thank you."

Haladhon continued along the street. A young woman curtsied to him, her brown hair glinting gold in the sun, and her cheeks slightly flushed. Hang the clothing styles of the more affluent clans—her overdress hid what appeared to be a comely figure. He stopped, his gaze dipping to the neckline of her linen chemise and back to her face as he smiled.

"If you please," she said, holding out flowers. "Would you be able to give these to the Thane?"

He took the flowers and bowed over her hand, enjoying the darker blush that rose to her cheeks. "What is your name, lass?"

She hesitated.

"So I can tell the Thane who gave them to him."

"I–it does not matter. He knows not who I am."

Was she that intelligent or that shy? Despite his exhaustion and worries, he just had to find out. He gave her his most charming grin. "I would not mind knowing."

She blushed again and murmured, "Tarinn."

"Tarinn," he repeated. "A pretty name. Perhaps you could walk with me to Ranger Hold? I would fain have the company."

Her eyes widened. "I–I do not think I should."

"And why is that?" Haladhon leaned forward slightly to share the secret.

She bit her lip with a shy smile, squinting slightly in the sunlight. "I have chores to do."

"Perhaps tomorrow then?"

She nodded, curtsied, and ran off.

Ah, if not for the dire circumstances, he could enjoy a few walks through the town. Amazing what the face of a pretty girl could do.

His lightened heart diminished as he proceeded to the hold, however. Bearing all these responsibilities, worrying that Alcandhor still wavered near death, and above all, hiding his fears and appearing strong in front of all his kin, had taken its toll.

Opening the door to the meeting chamber, he stopped in surprise. A Ranger sat in the Thane's chair, his feet crossed on the table. A great weight lifted from Haladhon. "Marcalan!"

"About time you got back. I was getting bored."

Haladhon shut the door and strode over before Marcalan could rise. He grabbed him by the neck, hauled him to his feet, and pounded him on the back.

Marcalan gasped, laughing. "Stars, man, you break my bones!" He pushed Haladhon back and looked at him, his smile fading. "Great Bells, cousin! You look like you died some days ago and have not had the good grace to lie down yet."

"I feel I did die, Marcalan, when the Thane almost did. This is my worst nightmare."

Marcalan snorted. "And I thought I had that honor."

Haladhon managed a smile. Marcalan spotted the flowers in Haladhon's hand, and his eyes sparkled as he remarked in his lilting voice, "For me? How thoughtful, but really, you should not have gone to such trouble."

Haladhon tossed the flowers on the table. "I am losing my touch, Marcalan. A pretty lass wants to give flowers to a sick, married man, but will not even take a walk with me."

"Sounds like she has intelligence to me. Good taste, too."

Before Haladhon could retort, Marcalan asked, "What is her name?"

"Think you I know her name?"

Marcalan grinned. "Cousin. I know you. What is her name?"

With a smirk, Haladhon replied, "Tarinn."

"Tarinn," Marcalan repeated but his smile dimmed as he eyed Haladhon. "Have you slept in the last five or six days?"

"Not much."

"You need to sleep."

"How can I?" Haladhon fell into a chair. "How are you back so quickly from Estan? Give me a brief report."

Marcalan crossed his arms, his expression sober. "Estan Province is in turmoil, which is no surprise. The people have been stirred up by Batrig's men and blame the Laird, Rangers, and the law for their sorrows. Now that he and his sons are not there, it is almost anarchy. The Esteni Rangers have their hands full. I used my authority to set up a temporary council of locals to govern—all highly respected men, and the Rangers will work with them to administrate and arbitrate matters."

"That will not work for long."

Marcalan lifted his shoulders while shaking his head. "'Tis not an ideal situation, but it seems to have mollified those people somewhat. Normally I would have stayed to help with the organization and oversight, but Estan ill favors outside interference, so I reluctantly bowed to their request and left the council in charge. We can only hope it keeps order for now. We have names of all of Batrig's extended family that could be considered when their clan decides who to appoint lord. Some of them bear watching." He pointed to papers on the table. "I have the details all written out to submit for the records."

"Good work, Marcalan. Thank you." Haladhon rubbed his face with both hands.

Marcalan crossed his arms again. "Have you eaten?"

"Nay."

"Neither have I. Be right back."

"I have not the time for food," he said as Marcalan left the room, then louder— "I have to report to the Thane." Hang it, had Marcalan even heard? He rose and walked across the hall as Zandhral exited and closed the bedchamber door.

"Well met, cousin," Zandhral said with a smile.

"Anything?" Haladhon asked.

Zandhral's smile faded. "Nay. I spend part of each day walking the grounds, talking to men here and on the perimeter. I have felt nothing amiss, and have had no sight in the matter. Keep on guard. We know not who we can trust."

Haladhon nodded, clasping his cousin's shoulder, even as the fleeting thought that Zandhral could be the traitor passed through his mind.

Zandhral grinned. "I have let the Thane sense me, all guards down. No blocking. I must have passed muster, or he would not have me on this assignment."

Had the moment of doubt been apparent on Haladhon's face, or had Zandhral felt it that easily? "Bells, you are as bad as the Thane."

"So I am told."

They chuckled, and Haladhon nodded toward the bedchamber. "And how is he?"

"You know him. Growling to be up. Go on in."

Haladhon lightly tapped on the door as Zandhral strode off.

"Come in, please," the Thane's voice begged.

Haladhon closed the door, relieved to see his cousin propped up now instead of lying flat.

"What news?" Alcandhor asked, eyes eager.

Haladhon pitied him—to be shut up in this bedchamber day and night when he loved being outdoors, and worse, to be injured so that he could not move around.

"The perimeter is fine. Marcalan returned from Estan Province. I have not yet read his report, but he tells me that he set a temporary council to rule for now, and it seems to have eased the fears of the people."

116

"Think you we need to send more Rangers to help?"

"I know not. I will discuss it with him."

"Perhaps he could talk to me about it himself."

"If Santran allows it."

Alcandhor made a face and rolled his eyes. "Have there been more drum messages while I slept?"

"None since we received the one from Taladar yesterday."

"A faithful province. Lord Tadhrol has had some difficulty, bordering Estan."

"Aye, but he weathers it well. Speaking of provinces, more Rangers from all over have arrived. All swear enough Rangers are left in their bounds to keep peace."

"I hope so. Now would be a ripe time for sedition with attention focused on Laird Hall. Make certain I speak to Marcalan this afternoon about Estan. I wish to know the climate in that province." Alcandhor slowly pulled up on the pillows with a grimace. "No change in the siege?"

"None. We received an all's well from the drum tower. Nothing more."

"No more attempts to sneak out by ropes over the walls?"

"Nay. I think they have discovered that the Bells alone shed too much light for them to sneak by us at night," Haladhon said. "And when even one moon is up, it is more useless."

Alcandhor nodded and narrowed his eyes with a too-knowing look. "You give me complete details of all those things you do report, but I know there are matters you leave out."

Haladhon shook his head in resignation at his cousin's ability to hit the mark. As usual. "How do you always know?"

"Am I not Thane?"

"Do not try that smug line on me, cousin-who-is-closer-than-brother. I am not some stranger."

"Think you it does not work both ways?"

Haladhon raised his hands, conceding the point.

"So tell me what you have been holding back."

Haladhon shrugged, rubbing the back of his neck. "Concerns, questions..."

"Ha, I thank you. That tells me quite a bit."

"Sarcasm from the Thane? That will not do."

"Evasions in answering the Thane? That will not do." Alcandhor grinned. "Come, talk to me. 'Tis my body that needs healing, not my mind. I am much more at ease when I know than when I am blind."

Haladhon sighed, crossing his arms. "There are...a couple of worries."

"And they are?"

"One is, where has Tam headed to find the Laird, and how does she intend on rescuing him alone?"

"Is that all? You knew I sent her, did you not?"

"Aye, but I had no knowledge of where and no idea if I should send more Rangers after her." *Nor did I know if you were addle-headed and knew not what you were doing.*

"You listen to Santran too much. How would your questions add to my worries? You are not thinking, man." Alcandhor paused. "Valdhor found out they had taken Randhal to the Enaisi's broken stronghold on the Forbidden Peninsula. There are ventilation shafts. Tam can sneak him out without the guards knowing. I gave her my key so she can access the shafts."

Haladhon closed his eyes for a moment in relief. "That answers another concern. I knew the key was missing, but..."

Alcandhor smiled. "If you had only asked, my dear cousin, instead of carrying the burdens yourself for fear of overwhelming me."

Haladhon made a wry face.

A knock came at the door. Sherel opened it without waiting for permission. "Your luncheon, Thane."

Haladhon stood. "I will let you eat, Thane. We can discuss matters later."

"I count on it."

Haladhon went back to the meeting chamber. He sat with a thud and pulled that cursed map toward him. Exhausted and frustrated, he rubbed the back of his neck as he stared at it. How could anyone, even traitors, dare enter the Forbidden Peninsula, much less take the young Laird hence? And Tam headed there? Haladhon shuddered.

Marcalan entered, carefully balancing a tray, and kicked the door shut behind him. He slid the map aside. Haladhon made a grab for it, but Marcalan shoved it further out of his reach with a grin and set the tray down.

"What is this?" Haladhon asked.

"Luncheon, of course." Marcalan bent in a dramatic bow. "Delivered by your faithful servant." He set out cups and bowls and sat down, his eyebrows raised in expectation.

Haladhon did not trust him. Marcalan looked too innocent. Always the first clue he was up to something. But what? He remembered the questions of when he had eaten last and slept and eyed the cups.

Haladhon picked up the spoon and took a mouthful of stew. Oh, stars, it tasted wonderful. How long since he had eaten? Sherel had quit pestering him about meals since he gave her a snarling command to leave him alone. He winced at the memory.

Marcalan ate, but Haladhon saw his cousin take notice when he picked up his cup. As he suspected. He had already seen Marcalan take a drink, so without saying a word he switched cups. Marcalan's eyebrows went up in shock at being accused of such a thing.

Haladhon finished the stew and the tea. He pushed back the bowl with a groan, his eyelids heavy. As his head slowly sank down, he saw Marcalan's smug smile and heard his voice as if from a distance.

"You have indeed exceeded your limits, my dear cousin, if I could fool you so easily."

Chapter Twelve

Haladhon awoke disoriented. He blinked, staring lost at the ceiling. *Of course.* The upper story of Ranger Hold. He sat up, looking about him at sleeping Rangers in their cots. With a frown, he tried to remember coming upstairs—the events with Marcalan all rushed back to him.

He threw the blanket off, sprang to his feet, and bounded down the stairs like a hungry ka'gua after prey. He grabbed the first Ranger he saw—Tanadhon. "Where is Marcalan?"

"I know not, Haladhon."

"Find him."

A worried yet confused expression crossed Tanadhon's face, but he answered, "Aye, sir," and ran off.

Haladhon strode to the meeting chamber. Empty. Reports stacked on the table awaited his perusal. He paced, his thoughts focused on laying hold of his cousin. When the prankster entered the chamber, Haladhon whirled and grabbed him by his jerkin. "Give me one good reason why I should not thrash you!"

"It would hurt," Marcalan said with calm earnestness. He cocked his head. "Think you I require a thrashing? In that case, we should take it outside. I thought you would settle for merely knocking me topside down."

Haladhon held him up for a moment, considering whether to give in to his anger, and finally threw him back. Marcalan gasped as he hit the door. Haladhon pointed a finger at him. "If ever again you do such a thing to me, I swear to you a thrashing would seem a mercy by comparison!"

Marcalan let his breath out and adjusted his jerkin with a smile, his voice light. "Well, I got off easy."

Haladhon opened his mouth to continue his rant but Marcalan pointed back at him. "You needed the sleep, so leave off! Do you know what your trouble is?"

Haladhon whipped the stray short lock off his forehead. "I am certain you are going to tell me."

Marcalan leaned back against the door, crossing his arms. "You are a great Ranger and a great leader. Anyone who has ever served a mission with you will testify to this. You are doing well in keeping up with all the problems and missions that are going on right now during the Thane's recovery. Lord Krendhal and the chiefs all have confidence in you. They have said thus."

Marcalan pointed again. "If the Thane had said, 'Haladhon, I am leaving on an important mission and need to you take charge,' you would have simply done so with your usual flair and humor, which are sorely lacking, by the way. But because he is in that chamber"—he jerked his thumb over his shoulder—"and you fear both his dying and the burden of your becoming Thane if that happens, you have lost all perspective."

Haladhon's stomach twisted; Marcalan had seen through his façade, knew his fears. Did all the Rangers? He drew his anger as a cloak to hide his doubts and leaned forward with gritted teeth. "Are you through?"

"For now. I will leave you to think on that. Perhaps it will sink into that stone head of yours. If not, and you do not start finding a balance for yourself, I might have to put panvarin in your stew again."

Haladhon shook his head, sighing. "The stew. Of course."

"My point. I should never have been able to trick you that easily. You were so sleep deprived you could not think. Now you have had a good night and day's rest."

"Night and day? How long did I sleep?"

"It was about this time yesterday I arrived."

Haladhon groaned. "I have much to do."

"Such as? Lamadhel wrote his report for you this morning, as did Tanadhon. Capalan returned from his mission, and his report is here as well. More Rangers have arrived. Their names and provinces are duly recorded, and we now have enough Rangers to besiege Laird Hall twice round and still have two full watches. 'Tis your discretion whether the watches should be shortened. Since you were indisposed with other duties, I went out to the perimeter in your place today. By the way, Tarinn is very pretty."

Haladhon glared at the cocky, smirking Ranger.

"I thanked her on the Thane's behalf for the flowers and told her how they cheered him," Marcalan continued.

"You did not tell her the danger he is in?"

Marcalan straightened with a mock frown. "Think you I look like a fool? Several townsfolk asked how he fares, and I replied he is healing well."

Haladhon let his breath out in relief but realized something. "You lied to her."

"I what?"

"I never gave him the flowers. I forgot about them."

"But I did not." Marcalan gave a self-satisfied grin. "I fetched a glass, put them in water, and took them to him. They had wilted but perked up nicely once in the water. He did say they cheered him. She sent more today." He cocked his head with a pleased expression. "I helped her pick them."

"Did you actually flirt with her?"

"Bells, no."

Haladhon snorted; his cousin mystified him.

"By the way, my dear Haladhon, have you eaten yet today?"

"Think you I would eat any food you brought me?"

Marcalan chuckled. "Think you I would do the same thing twice?"

"Nay. But neither will I eat anything you serve."

"Then you had best go to the dining hall, and you can serve yourself if you wish. But you might go wash up first and get your boots on. You look like you just tumbled out of bed. And you will want to appear an upstanding Ranger when Santran arrives after luncheon to examine the Thane."

~:~

Alcandhor watched as the healer undressed the wound. "Will you allow me walks yet?"

Santran's lips thinned. "Thane, must you bring it up at each visit?"

Alcandhor sighed and decided to be honest, or at least, partially honest. "I walk about this chamber all day, staring at the walls. Why can I not walk without?"

Santran sat back, staring. "You walk?"

"Aye."

Santran frowned. "How do you get up?"

"A slow roll. Let me go on walks. I swear to you, I will go mad if I cannot get away from Sherel. How much harm could there be in allowing me to walk around the bailey, or to the town?"

"You have not the strength for such long walks yet."

The healer examined and redressed the wound, then palpated his abdomen. Alcandhor focused on the cursed ceiling that had been his companion all these days while trying not to wince.

"You heal, but slowly," Santran said.

"Short walks. Please."

"We will see."

Alcandhor groaned and rolled his head on the pillow.

"You have not your strength yet. You lost much blood. I know you think I am over cautious, but," Santran lifted a finger, "we cannot lose you. You are too important to us."

"I am only a man."

"You are our symbol. People look to you. To Alcandhor. The town is in uproar, and folk are very frightened. I am asked constantly how you are healing. Knowing you survived an attack and are still taking care of matters is giving them a sense of peace and hope."

"I may still be Thane, but I am not taking care of matters."

"They do not know this. Haladhon gives orders in your name. It is known you were injured. I could not hide that fact, but you are healing well and are still Thane."

"You are a scoundrel."

"That may be."

"But you know..." Alcandhor paused and grinned. "Your story would be more convincing if people saw me taking walks."

Santran looked at him in irritation and wagged his head. "Who is the scoundrel?"

Alcandhor met his ponderous gaze with a pleading one.

The healer's shoulders slumped. "I will allow short walks in the bailey—from here to the bench under the tree out front. You must be accompanied, and you must let them know if you become tired. You must also tell me if any pain worsens, if you pass blood, or if you experience trouble with—"

Alcandhor waved his hand. "I know, Santran. You tell me every day. I know. I will. I promise it."

Santran eyed the Thane with a disbelieving grimace. He held up a finger. "If you obey me, and I see you are not wearing yourself out, I will see about allowing longer walks."

Alcandhor smiled, relieved. "May I see Haladhon now?"

"I'll have him found and sent in."

~:~

Haladhon—and Sherel, wringing her hands—waited for the healer to come out of the Thane's bedchamber. Rangers gathered in the foreroom, their faces grave and concerned.

Haladhon straightened as Santran exited the bedchamber. The healer caught his eye, inclining his head toward the meeting chamber.

Once inside, Haladhon closed the door. "Is he healing well?"

"He heals slowly, even for one with Enaisi blood. He was badly wounded. Broken ribs, internal injuries. How he bested so many men..." He shook his head.

Haladhon squared his shoulders, pride swelling in him. "Even the arrow did not stop him. He ran out of opponents."

"You Rangers push yourselves too hard."

Haladhon refused to get into an argument with Santran about the abuse the healer felt Rangers inflicted upon themselves with their rigid training. He asked again, "Is he healing?"

Santran hesitated. "He heals." He squinted up at Haladhon. "We need him. His confounded idealism holds him in good with both commoners and nobles."

"I realize this."

"He nearly died. He..." Santran rubbed his eyes with his fingers. "He still could. He wishes to take walks, and I have decided to allow it."

Haladhon's mouth fell open. "What? He is still on his back!"

Santran snorted. "Not he. He told me today he has been walking in his chamber."

Despite his worry, Haladhon chuckled. Aye, that was his cousin.

Santran scowled at him. "It's no laughing matter. He has internal injuries that could still kill him."

Haladhon sobered and gave full heed as the man continued, "He may walk from here to that tree in the front of the bailey. The one with the bench. No more than twice a day. He is to be accompanied on these walks. If he seems too weak, loses color, or shows any sign he is in pain or distress, you have me called immediately."

"I will."

"He wishes to see you—no doubt to crow that he is able to be up. Keep the visit lighthearted, and do not trouble him. I will stay here until he has finished this first walk to be sure he will be all right."

"Thank you."

Haladhon crossed the hall and entered the chamber to see Alcandhor sitting up, grinning. "Santran says I may go on walks."

"He has told me what he has allowed. But I think we had best get you properly dressed first."

"Stars, aye!"

Haladhon pulled clothes from the chest, eyeing his Thane as Alcandhor threw back the coverlet and began to slowly roll onto his hands.

"You are certain of this, cousin? You seem so weak."

"I am not as weak as you think. Nor as Santran thinks."

"You are also not as strong as you believe. Santran did not wish to allow you up at all. I think he would not, save you have Enaisi blood. If you have a setback, what will that do to all of us?"

The Thane set his jaw, turning his head away. Some things Alcandhor did share with his late brother—like that expression. Haladhon got the clothes and began helping his cousin dress, which did not please the Thane at all.

"Thane of the Rangers, and I cannot even pull up my own trous," he grumbled.

Haladhon hid his grin. "A secret I will keep to my grave, my Thane."

Eyes narrowed, Alcandhor asked, "With that look in your eye? What will it cost me?"

Haladhon chuckled. "I will have to consider that."

"'Tis good to see you laugh. You have looked so worried and tired."

"I am fine." Haladhon avoided Alcandhor's eyes. "Now, let us see how carefully I can get your arm out of that sling and get a shirt on you."

Despite Haladhon's attempts to be gentle, barely perceptible winces flitted across Alcandhor's stoic face. He got the jerkin on his Thane and the sling back on his arm. Lastly, the boots.

"My knife," Alcandhor said.

Haladhon crossed his arms. "I know not if Santran would wish you to have that sheath-strap going around your ribs."

"A Ranger may be without sword, staff, or bow, but never his knife."

"I will risk it not."

"You would disobey your Thane?"

"I would. And you can crawl back into that bed before I let you put anything constricting around your ribs without Santran's permission."

"Get Santran in here then."

Haladhon resisted the urge to slam the door as he left the bedchamber. Santran looked up from the table as Haladhon entered the meeting chamber.

"He says he will not go out without his knife. Is it all right to strap his sheath around his ribs?"

"That man! Tell me, are all you Rangers so stubborn?"

Haladhon found himself grinning. "Healer, must you ask?"

Santran grunted. "I will let nothing go about his ribs. Pressure could send a cracked rib into a lung."

Haladhon rubbed his neck as he echoed his Thane's words. "A Ranger is never without his knife..."

Santran shrugged. "Use a leg sheath."

Haladhon exhaled in a short laugh. "Of course." He strode down to the armory. Nandhal leaned against the door.

"Have you a leg sheath to spare? For the Thane's knife."

Nandhal's eyebrows rose, and Haladhon followed him inside. The young Ranger looked over several sheaths and took one down. "This one appears to have the same length and shape, it should work."

"My thanks."

Nandhal nodded. "Haladhon..." He paused, his brow furrowed. "He truly heals?"

His question echoed that of all the Rangers. Haladhon hoped Alcandhor's walk would set their hearts at ease. He met Nandhal's anxious gaze evenly. "Aye. Worry not."

Keeping his step jaunty to belie his own concerns, Haladhon returned to the Thane's chamber. He held up the strap with an incline of his head. "A leg sheath, my Thane. You can have your knife and keep your ribs safe."

Alcandhor shot him a wry glare. Haladhon chuckled, but it faded when Alcandhor finally stood, one hand against the wall.

Haladhon licked his dry lips and swallowed. Was this a good idea?

Chapter Thirteen

Could the unsteadiness Alcandhor felt be seen? He had to do this; his men needed to see their Thane. He pulled himself up straight, head erect, and lifted the latch. Sherel jumped back, gasping. Alcandhor stifled a smile that she had been caught with her ear to the door. She stepped farther away and curtseyed.

He hoped his steps, although slower than usual, seemed firm. Rangers crowded in the foreroom. They gaped at him as he walked toward them, their astonishment giving way to smiles and grins. Some clouted each other on the back. As he halted in the archway to the foreroom, they all stood to attention and bowed, pride and affection surging from them. He smiled as he put his fist to his heart.

Haladhon swept his arm out in a gesture for him to continue, and the Rangers shuffled back, clearing a path for him.

He stepped outside, and a deafening cheer arose.

Alcandhor's mouth dropped open. He knew from Haladhon's reports that many hundreds of Rangers had arrived, but seeing the packed bailey made the words a reality. The Rangers continued to cheer, and he could not help but grin.

The sun's warmth cheered him as well; he had missed being out of doors. He kept slow pace to the appointed tree, Rangers bowing or saluting as he passed. He sat on the bench with careful deliberation and leaned back, hopefully giving the appearance of casually resting, not trying to recover the strength he had drained with the short walk. He took as deep a breath as his ribs allowed, enjoying the tangy crispness in the air that presaged autumn.

His men did not approach him, which told him they comprehended the seriousness of his injuries, but their moods indicated relief, exhilaration, pride.

"They needed this, Haladhon," he murmured as his cousin sat down next to him.

"Aye."

"Now, give me your report."

Haladhon opened his mouth, hesitated, and licked his lips. He cleared his throat. "Things are well."

Alcandhor frowned. "What do you mean, *things are well?* Report

127

man!"

Haladhon swallowed, his face flushing. "I...I cannot, Thane."

"What do you mean you cannot?"

Haladhon fidgeted and rubbed his neck. "I am sorry. I have failed you, Thane."

"How? What has happened? Has the siege been broken?"

"Nay," he said quickly. "Everything is fine."

"If 'everything is fine' then how have you failed?"

"I...I have neglected my duties, Thane."

"How so?"

"I...Marcalan thought that I—"

"Marcalan? Hold, cousin." Alcandhor looked around. Rangers everywhere but no sign of the rascal. His ribs would not allow him to shout. With a grimace at his own limitations, he said, "Summon him, Second at Table."

"Marcalan," Haladhon bellowed. "Report to the Thane!"

Rangers turned to stare. Soon Marcalan came running toward him. He went down on one knee in front of his Thane, his head bowed.

"Save that for when I find out what you have done now."

Marcalan raised his head. "What I have done, Thane?"

"Haladhon is unable to relay this morning's reports and is reluctant to tell me why. However, since your name was mentioned, I assume you can enlighten me?"

A wide grin spread over Marcalan's face. "Gladly, my Thane."

"Good. Sit and tell me."

Marcalan sat at Alcandhor's feet. "I returned yesterday from Estan Province, as you know, and I found our dear cousin here, looking like he had not slept since I left, which was probably the case. When I suggested he rest, he refused. So, I persuaded him by use of a little panvarin in his stew." He cocked his head, looking smug. "He slept almost an entire day."

Alcandhor glanced over at Haladhon who sat forward, elbows on his knees and hands folded, looking down at the grass.

"I told Lamadhel last evening what I had done, and he instructed me to gather all the reports for Haladhon to read through when he awoke. That is why he cannot report, my dear Thane, because he has not been awake long enough to read them."

Alcandhor leaned back against the tree, snickering, despite the agony to his ribs. "He got you, Haladhon. At least I know now why you did not come to see me yesterday afternoon. Serves you right for not taking care of yourself. You know better."

"Thane—"

"Not another word. Proper sleep and proper meals, Ranger Chief. That is an order. If you do not, I will see it is told to me." *And Sherel would gladly play informer.*

"Aye, sir."

He wished he could clout Haladhon on the back but he could not. Hang that arrow. And the sling. He prodded Haladhon's foot with his own instead. "Now that I am allowed to be awake and get up, it will not be so burdensome for you. You will still have to be my eyes and ears and report all to me, of course."

"Aye, sir."

"Oh, come, do not look so glum. I am certain Marcalan already is up to something. Why do you not go with him for awhile and create a little mayhem? You have been atypically somber, cousin."

Marcalan slapped Haladhon's leg in happy agreement, but Haladhon shook his head. "I need to stay with you, Thane. Santran's orders. You are to be accompanied on your walks. And then I still need to read those reports."

"Stars, man, you are starting to sound positively grim," Marcalan exclaimed. "Almost as bad as our Thane."

Alcandhor shot his cousin a dark look. "Anyone can accompany me on these walks. I can easily call one of a hundred Rangers over. The reports will be there later. Take a little time for yourself. Not seeing you jesting or up to something, especially with Marcalan around, will cause me great worry."

Marcalan slapped Haladhon's leg again, and said in a feigned whisper, "We could walk to the perimeter. And perhaps see about picking some flowers."

Haladhon straightened, a twinkle returning to his eyes.

Alcandhor glanced at the two, puzzled. "Picking flowers? Why would you two wish to pick—" he stopped. "The lass, of course. What was her name?"

"Tarinn," they both said at the same time.

Alcandhor rolled his eyes. Those two were forged on the same anvil. "You two just remember. Not everyone in the town is to be trusted. Regardless of their claims, many do not like Rangers. You behave while there and," he stopped and met each of their gazes, continuing in a measured tone, "that goes doubly for that girl. Do you understand?"

Marcalan rose to his feet, but Haladhon still hesitated.

"Go."

Haladhon stood and looked down at Alcandhor. "You are certain, Thane? I feel I am neglecting my duty."

"Get out of here, you vagabond. It will ease my mind to know you are relaxing for time."

The two bowed and headed for the gate. Marcalan walked sideways next to Haladhon, hopped ahead to back step in front of him, circling from one side to the other, laughing and taunting. Haladhon swatted at Marcalan, who skittered out of his way. He broke into a run, chasing his cousin. Alcandhor could still hear Marcalan's mocking laugh after they passed the gate.

He shook his head, smiling. Their jesting and good humor always lifted his spirits when nothing else could. He had missed that in Haladhon these last few days. He seemed dragged down and overburdened. Most likely worried over Alcandhor's injuries. Perhaps now Haladhon would relax and go back to being Haladhon.

A bird sang in the branches above. He leaned back against the rough bark and closed his eyes, listening.

Footsteps approached, stopping near the tree. Alcandhor easily sensed the strong personality. "Hear you that bird, Lord Krendhal?" he asked. "Amid all our woes and worries, the birds still sing."

"How knew you it was me, Thane?"

Alcandhor opened his eyes to smile at the tall lord. "Sit with me, lord, if you will."

"I am honored." Krendhal swiped the bench of a few leaves and a spinner's net and adjusted his purple surcoat before sitting.

Alcandhor forced himself erect, ignoring the pain in his back and sides. "How are you faring in Ranger Hold?"

"Well," he responded and gestured at Alcandhor. "'Tis good to see you up, Thane. Although I would suspect you are not as recovered as you would wish us all to believe."

"You are astute, lord."

Krendhal looked away for a moment. "We have never been friends, you and I. But you are a good man, Thane, and you are needed. Do not risk your recovery."

"Men need not be friends, Lord Krendhal, to be allies. And I remember your assistance and concern for me the day I received my wound. My thanks."

Krendhal gave a curt nod. "What are your plans, Thane? When siege is broken and our Laird, hopefully, back here with us?"

"Think you I have it all planned out already?"

"I doubt it not. I have seen what you had prepared for the siege. You are farsighted, as Haladhon has said."

"I may have plans, Lord Krendhal, but what direction they take will depend on many variables. Whether Tam does succeed in her mission, how many traitors are still out there, unknown, working against us, when will they move next and where, how long the siege lasts—these are but a few things I must consider."

"It is much. But see you now why I oppose changes? This is the result of attempting to alter our ways."

"Nay, milord. The other lords talked of change because they had their own motives—change offered them a cloak under which to move. Granted they have sown much dissension, but the discontent has been there. From my father's time and before. And I speak not of change for its own sake, but to return to our laws. We have strayed from them and become hidebound and comfortable in our traditions."

"So you have no personal motives or agenda?"

He shot a piercing look at Krendhal, sensing him, but the noble's face matched his emotions. He asked the question with honest intention, not in suspicion. "We all have motives and agendas. But what think you, milord? What do I gain in this matter?"

"It has been said you have great personal ambition to power."

Alcandhor bowed his head, smiling. Krendhal, as most nobles, could not bring himself to even speak the words *make Claim*. Did they think the unmentioned was unknown or forgotten? But no matter how many times reassurances were given, few understood that making Claim was not a bid for power or to overthrow their government, replacing it with a monarchy. Claim could only be made in emergencies only, a temporary suspension of civil rule, and for only a limited duration; a stratocracy.

The current crisis could have fallen into that category. Alcandhor wondered how many worried that he might still make Claim. Did Krendhal? Is that what he was really hinting at? He looked up at the noble. "Think you there is truth in that?"

"I know not. You seem very straightforward and truly concerned for all our people." Krendhal leaned back, staring into the distance, his voice contemplative. "I have been shown lately that I am not as good a judge of character as I thought. Perhaps if I was so mistaken about those murderous nobles, I was mistaken about you, too. I will attempt to keep a more open mind in our discussions."

"I would fain explain why I feel changes are necessary. Perhaps we can come to more of an understanding."

The noble shrugged, and Alcandhor knew the lord had reached his limit in conciliatory discussion on that matter.

"There is one point, however, that I still disagree most strongly about."

"Tell me, milord."

"This young lass you sent to rescue our Laird. I do not think she should have been the one selected for that mission."

Tam, Tam. Where are you, child? Are you safe? Alcandhor swallowed, setting his jaw. Worry would not help her, and Krendhal must not see his fears or doubts. "That point is immaterial. 'Tis done. She is seven days' journey out and soon will enter the Forbidden Peninsula. In three, she will reach the Enaisi's broken stronghold near the east cliffs."

Krendhal straightened at the mention of the Forbidden Peninsula. "They dared go there? And with the young Laird?"

"It makes sense. Who would think to go to a place shunned and avoided? A perfect place to hide. And if they did kill him, who would ever find the body?"

Krendhal shuddered. Alcandhor wondered if it was over concern for his cousin and Laird, or over the traitors breaking tradition by going to that dreaded peninsula.

Finally Krendhal spoke. "Three days more and ten back. We will find out who is right within this lunation. And I do hope, for once, that I am mistaken."

"I would not have sent her if I did not think she could accomplish the task, milord. I grant you she is young, but she is Valdhor's daughter and better Trained than many Rangers who are already of Age."

Krendhal stared straight ahead, not answering. After a time he cleared his throat. "There is one more thing I have wanted to talk to you about, Thane. But it is Ranger business, and I am not certain you will discuss it with me."

"Aye?"

"That ambush. How could it happen? You Rangers seem to have an ability to anticipate. How did you get caught off guard?"

The Thane sagged against the tree with the weight of that matter. Aye, though Ranger business, this man could be trusted despite their differences—he felt it. "Few there are these days that have such ability. Things would have gone much worse if Valdhor and I had not been there. They attacked in haste as we had called a halt to our group and changed our course when we both felt something amiss."

"You both have—" Krendhal grimaced and continued, "had the ability?"

"Aye. Not strongly, but the strongest that there has been in several generations. Yet, it was not enough..." His voice trailed off and he frowned, remembering Valdhor's death. He inhaled sharply, denying the ache in his heart, and brought himself back to the conversation. "Back to your question, I think there is only one way the ambush could have successfully been planned."

"Treachery?" whispered Krendhal. "Within your clan?"

"Aye. I know not who. Not yet. 'Tis a terrible thing to contemplate, but I see no other answer."

Chapter Fourteen

"So did you really mean to visit Tarinn?" Haladhon asked as they headed into the town. He alone knew Marcalan did not deserve the reputation of rake.

"Cousin, tell me, how do two men call on a lass at the same time?" Marcalan held up his hands in a gesture of generosity. "You do the visiting. I shall go to the perimeter and harry Andhrel."

Haladhon rubbed his neck, remembering Alcandhor's warning. The Thane's words held special bite considering the siege and unknown loyalties. "Perhaps 'tis best to avoid temptation. Even on proper behavior, who knows her father's leanings, and accusations might be made."

The prankster put a hand on Haladhon's shoulder, his twinkling eyes belying his solemn face. "'Tis a hard decision you make, cousin. I am awed at your sacrifice."

Haladhon slapped at Marcalan, but he jumped back, laughing. "To the perimeter, then?"

"Aye."

Once there, they gave an account of the Thane's walk, and the Rangers' morale lifted. Soon, word would spread around the perimeter—a welcome bit of news. They jested with the Rangers a little, but started back toward the town before Andhrel became too irritated with them.

They agreed to stop for an ale and turned in at their favorite tavern, the Copper Kettle. Haladhon blinked not only at the darkness of the place after the bright sun but also in amazement. The place had always been clean and filled with happy patrons, but now the tang of smoke hung in the stale air. Rushes had been thrown on the floor in lieu of a good scrubbing. All tables save one were empty, and the four men there glared at the Rangers. He shot a questioning glance at Marcalan who shrugged.

Haladhon approached the counter, throwing his most winsome grin and a wink at the serving girl. Her lack of a returning smile did not dismay him; he had time enough to thaw her. As a matter of fact, the challenge of drawing her attention was the perfect antidote to all his stress.

He ordered two tankards of ale, brought them to the table, and sat on the corner from his cousin, giving both a view of their glowering, fellow patrons. Both Rangers took long draughts and sat back.

"You have been here for a full day. What have you been up to?" Haladhon asked.

"Sherel," Marcalan said, blinking, "has had a time trying to find some of her spices and herbs in the kitchen. They do not seem to be where they ought."

Haladhon chuckled. "She has not sorted it out yet?"

"Nay." Marcalan snickered. "She is running in circles trying to discover why she cannot find them. She blames having to use Rangers as scullions. I will leave off for a day or two then start again. I wish to see how long it takes before she realizes what I am doing."

"You are a rascal," Haladhon said and took a long pull.

"My thanks."

"You do realize she will box your ears when she finds out?"

"Of course."

"Do you enjoy pain so much?"

"I am a Ranger, am I not? I am used to pain."

Haladhon snorted. "What else have you been up to? I saw no evidence of anyone chasing you or charging about trying to find you, and you do not look thrashed."

Marcalan cocked his head to one side. "You forget that you were charging about this morning trying to find me."

Haladhon rolled his eyes at the memory. "There is that. But I cannot have been your only victim."

"You will have to wait and see, cousin." With a wink, Marcalan lifted his tankard and downed his ale in one long draught.

"Stars, Mar! Slow down. I want not to carry you home."

Marcalan straightened, looking indignant. "Carry me? When has that ever happened, cousin?"

"My apologies." Haladhon took another swig, then pointed the tankard at his cousin. "But the Thane asked us to be careful, and you cannot be careful if you have tipped too many back."

"Then what are we doing here?"

"A point." Haladhon glanced to the table of men, hunched over and whispering among themselves. "What say you? Shall we stay or leave?"

Marcalan scratched his chin beard. "Just another ale or two."

Haladhon grinned. "You will receive no argument from me." He rose and returned to the counter for more drinks. The serving girl did not notice his approach, for her gaze was on Marcalan. Haladhon twisted to see his cousin staring at his tankard with keen interest and fought a smile.

The innkeeper—not old Contel but a stranger—cleared his throat. "Since it's slow in here, my girl can just bring the drinks to you,

Ranger." His voice, thick with the soft, non-gutturals of Estan province, bespoke his origins.

Haladhon's eyebrows raised. "You are new, enh? A novel idea. Is that a common practice in Estan?"

The man shook his head. "Just trying to show courtesy."

Haladhon smiled and shrugged. "My thanks."

As he sat back down, Haladhon whispered, "A new custom. They will serve us our ale."

Marcalan's gaze flicked toward the counter, then he continued to study his tankard.

Haladhon grinned. "I am amazed that you keep your reputation when you avoid flirting."

"I have not tried to maintain the farce." Marcalan let out a soft sigh, his thumb tracing the pattern on the drinking vessel. "Yet my lies have followed me."

Haladhon leaned back, staring at his cousin. How rare for Marcalan to show his serious side. "Why does this bother you all of a sudden?"

"I fear my attempts to impress you all those years ago may snap back like a whip and strike me in the face."

"Aye, a woman might have a harder time believing a commitment to faithfulness with such a reputation." Haladhon grinned. "Are you considering marriage?"

"Stars, no!" Marcalan exclaimed but leaned back as the girl arrived with their ales. She lingered, smiling at Marcalan, but he never looked up as he muttered thanks. He lifted the fresh tankard and took a deep draught. Haladhon tried to catch her eye without success. With a disappointed frown, the lass walked away.

Haladhon smiled; this provided a perfect opportunity to rankle his cousin. He tapped the table with his knuckles. "So what say you? When are you going to marry?"

"When I fall in love."

Haladhon groaned. "Stars, what a radical! You sound like Alcandhor. He married for love and look at the result. Find a girl who is fairly pretty and understands being the wife of a Ranger. Then marry her."

"You have a sad view of marriage, cousin."

"Aye, and I have my reasons, as you well know." Haladhon lifted his tankard and drained it—the more to keep his mind from bitter turnings.

Marcalan's knowing look quickly switched to a humorous one. "Did you not just caution me about drinking too fast? Shall we order food to offset the ale?"

"Nay." Haladhon took a deep breath and matched his cousin's grin. "One more ale. I will drink it more slowly. We cannot go back yet."

"True. Our dear Thane will expect we have caused trouble and will want to hear all about it when we get back, then moan and complain about what rascals we are."

Haladhon snickered. "I think he enjoys the trouble we incite, despite his grumbling. He would probably be here with us were he not Thane." He turned, caught the innkeeper's eye, and raised two fingers.

"I think you are right. Becoming Thane sobered him much, yet in moments he is as much fun as he used to be."

"Perhaps when this is all over, we can get him to come with us and forget his rank for one night."

"A worthy thought." Marcalan downed his ale then said, "Have to keep up, you know."

The serving girl approached with their drinks. What a delicious sprinkling of freckles on her nose and cheeks! This time he would catch her eye. He tossed her a rakish smile. "Thank you, lass. What is your name?"

She smiled but her gaze strayed to Marcalan as she set their full tankards alongside their empty ones. "Colinn."

"'Tis fairly empty for a tavern." Haladhon's gaze swept the room again. The four men still murmured amongst themselves, glances cast toward the two Rangers.

"Yes. Even in the evening it's still too empty."

The girl was much more pleasant to look at than the sullen men. He widened his smile. "Think you it would cause you trouble to sit with us for a few moments, since there are not many patrons?"

She flicked an apprehensive glance at the innkeeper. "Perhaps not." She assumed a flirting smile, and sat down. "It's been quiet since the siege and not much work for me. Lonely, too." Her eyes lingered on Marcalan, but he gave her a blank stare. Haladhon swallowed a laugh as she turned to him. "Aren't you the one who walks to the perimeter for the Thane and reports to him?"

"Aye."

"He is a chief of the Rangers." Marcalan's eyes laughed over the rim of his tankard. Haladhon glared at him.

"You are!" She gave full attention to Haladhon now.

"And the only chief who is unmarried."

Haladhon hoped it wasn't obvious that his grin was truly only clenched teeth. He would thrash Marcalan for that!

The innkeeper called Colinn at that moment. She gave Haladhon a seductive smile before walking away.

"You are going to die, you scoundrel." Haladhon grabbed Marcalan's jerkin, pulling him half out of his chair.

"If she had an eye, she should have known your rank by the Thane's crest on your jerkin. And if she had any knowledge of our clan traditions, your commitment status by lack of a necklet. But it did take her interest away from me."

Haladhon let go with a shove, and Marcalan fell back into his chair, chortling.

"It would be nice to find one woman who could at least decide she likes me before discovering my rank."

"Why would you care if you do not wish a commitment?"

"It would be nice to be noticed for me, not my rank."

"I have not that problem, cousin, so I cannot give much sympathy."

Colinn returned. She leaned over and picked up the empty tankards, giving Haladhon the chance to admire her cleavage. "Sorry. I forgot to take these away."

Marcalan kicked Haladhon under the table, grinning at him. Haladhon brushed the back of his hand up Colinn's arm. "Care to sit a few more moments?"

"As soon as I finish up I can be back." She lingered a moment, leaning toward him with a smile. Oh, stars, the woman knew what she was doing. Her hips swayed as she headed back to the kitchen, and Haladhon let his breath out in a slow exhale. He met Marcalan's gaze with a smirk. "See what you are missing?"

Marcalan shrugged, his face reddening. He downed his drink, and stood. "Priv."

Haladhon frowned, concerned, as he saw the slight weave in Marcalan's walk. His cousin's earlier boast was not vain. He had never seen Marcalan unsteady, regardless of how much he drank.

He was still musing this strange aberrance when Colinn came back to the table, her eyes alight. Haladhon dismissed Marcalan from his thoughts as he slipped a hand around her waist and pulled her toward him. She did not resist as he lowered her to his lap, and her arms slid up to his shoulders. He drew her toward him for a kiss, but at that moment Marcalan thudded into his chair, and Colinn jumped.

With a knowing smile, his cousin asked, "Think you I should return to the hold without waiting for you?" His voice slurred, and Haladhon peered hard at him in disbelief.

Colinn twisted to look at Marcalan. "Later, perhaps." She smiled at Haladhon, pushing away slightly. "I'm still serving for awhile."

Haladhon sighed with regret and allowed her up.

Marcalan lifted his tankard as she walked away. "To you, cousin.

You never cease to amaze me."

Haladhon laughed, and they both drank deeply.

Marcalan set his tankard down with a satisfied *ahh*. "'Tis good to see you relax. You looked like a stranger yesterday."

"There have been so many worries." Haladhon flicked the lock of hair off his forehead, frowning. Tension bunched in his shoulders anew. "Although now I report to the Thane, still there are many details I carry myself. Things I am concerned about that I do not wish to ask him for answers on so as not to burden him too greatly."

"Such as?"

Haladhon shook his head. "Not here."

Marcalan nodded, mumbling, "Foolish of me."

"My turn," Haladhon muttered, rising. He paused to clear his head of ale.

"Do not get lost," Marcalan said over his shoulder.

The walls in the narrow corridor seemed to move on their own, and Haladhon almost walked into them. While in the priv he could barely stand and had to balance with one hand against the wall. *Stars, this is not right.*

As he readied to leave the priv, light footfalls and whispers gave away the presence of men outside the door. A chill swept over Haladhon—he had been snared in a trap. One hand on the door latch, the other gripping his sword hilt, he shook his head, desperate to clear his mind of the benumbing fog.

Chapter Fifteen

Three men brandishing swords awaited Haladhon outside the priv in the narrow back hallway. Dull-witted from drink, Haladhon had not the ability to be elegant or careful. He cut down all three in a flashing blur. A scream rent the air, and he staggered to the common room as quickly as he could. A man lay in a pool of blood near Marcalan with a second just thudding to the floor. A woman's wail echoed in his head. Colinn fell by one of the men, weeping.

Marcalan slowly sank to his knees, eyes glassy, sword still gripped in his hands, tip touching the floor.

Haladhon waded over, slapped his cousin's face, and tried pulling him to his feet. "Mar? Marcalan?"

"Haladhon?"

"Did they injure you?"

"What happened?" Marcalan asked.

"Let us leave. Now."

Haladhon barely found the floor with his feet and almost toppled trying to help Marcalan rise, but somehow, they managed to help each other to the door. The sun glowed just above the horizon. They had to hurry before darkness fell.

Marcalan groaned and asked again, "What happened?"

"Attacked. We must get to the hold." Haladhon's tongue felt thick and numb in his mouth.

"You hurt?"

"Nay."

They struggled to keep walking. Rangers at the edge of the town grabbed the two weak men and tried to steady them.

"Attacked at the Copper Kettle," Haladhon managed to mumble. "Go. See if any are alive."

The Rangers ran on to the town. Haladhon forced himself to keep on, although his body did not want to obey. He felt wrapped in a thick blanket and could not even see clearly.

Many hands grabbed him before all went dark.

~:~

"It is my fault!" Alcandhor ranted to his uncle as he paced back and forth, despite the hot pain to his ribs. "I did not see! I was not thinking! I knew there were a good amount of people in Lairdton not to be trusted, yet I allowed them to go into that town. What kind of fool am I?"

"Ask a question that is not ridiculous so I can answer," Lamadhel said, arms crossed. "And sit down. You have little strength yet."

"What if I lose them both?" Alcandhor dropped onto his bed, hissing at the shooting fire that lanced his side.

"You have not, and they are both strong—and too ornery to die. What time have you for *what ifs*? Or blame? We struck a solid blow, Thane. Five traitors are dead."

Alcandhor combed a hand through his hair. "The innkeeper was one of the traitors?"

"Aye. He had recently purchased the tavern." Lamadhel paused. "He is from Estan," he said, his voice softer and full of meaning.

Alcandhor let his breath out, nodding. More trouble from that province. Nothing new. "So the Copper Kettle is closed then?"

"Nay. His son is running it. He seems so afraid of reprisal that he is all but groveling at our feet."

Alcandhor rubbed his shoulder with absent agitation. "He is to be watched. Fear will fade—if it is genuine and not a trick. And if he is of his father's mind, he will begin to think of ways to achieve retribution for his father's death."

"Aye, Thane."

"What of the serving girl?"

"The innkeeper's daughter. She claims she had no knowledge of her father's plan to attack Haladhon and Marcalan. We have no proof otherwise, so she is free."

"She is to be watched as well." Alcandhor rubbed his eyes. "No one is to leave these grounds alone. I want Rangers stationed in pairs throughout the town, not just at the edges of it, both as guard and to keep watch on activities."

Lamadhel bowed and left.

Alcandhor dropped his head into his good hand, his worry over his two dearest friends keen, piercing his heart. He rose with care and walked out to the end of the hallway. A young Ranger sat on the stairs that ran to the barracks above, ready to run errands for Sherel.

"Any news, Baidhrol?"

"They are still sleeping, Thane."

"Send me word when they wake."

"Aye, Thane."

Alcandhor slowly made his way to the meeting chamber. He eased into the chair at the study table and pulled a report from the stack. Rubbing his shoulder, he began to read. By the end of the page, he groaned. *How can the eyes read, yet the mind not comprehend?* With a sigh, he began again.

~:~

From the corner of the small, dimly lit chamber, Vitran gazed at the men dipping their hands into the small pot and rubbing charcoal onto their faces and any other exposed skin. They all wore black.

One of the men looked up, the whites of his eyes shining. "You're certain the Rangers won't see us?"

This had been discussed before, but to set the men at ease, Vitran went over it again. "Tonight is the perfect time. It's heavily overcast and black as a Keladar mineshaft. The Rangers are encircling the entire woods' edge, which is about a five-hour march. They cannot have that many Rangers to set their men more closely than one hundred paces apart. You men have good wild sense. Creep slowly in the tall grass, and you should be able to pass the Rangers. After that, make your way to the Copper Kettle. A friend owns it and will hide you. Give him the messages for our noble friends, letting them know how desperate things are here. They must move soon."

To get the men's minds off the fear of being caught, he grinned at them. "In a few hours, you will be treated as heroes in the Copper Kettle, dining well. Think on that."

White smiles shone from the black-smudged faces.

Ropes hung from crenels so the men could descend. Vitran watched from the parapet as they swung over the side of the outer curtain wall, holding his breath.

"Fortune's best," he called softly over the edge.

~:~

The Ranger-scribe Maradhor shrugged and rotated his shoulders in an effort get out the stiffness. Stars. He had never stood a watch as miserable as tonight on perimeter. Thick clouds obscured the sky so it seemed draped in a black cloak.

The night sky usually gave them enough illumination, but not so this night. Someone suggested using torches but that had disadvantages, such as backlighting them for any enemy and causing fire-blindness. Besides, to cover the woods' edge they would need over four thousand. So instead they peered into the dark, even more at attention than usual.

Or they were supposed to be. Maradhor could not keep his mind on his watch. Stars. He was a Ranger. He was disciplined. Why did the blackness distract him so?

The weather had grown unusually muggy and warm as night fell, increasing the *cri-cri-cri* from the crested nightsingers. Those insects set his teeth on edge anyway, but he pledged that tonight they tried to vex him personally. He wiped the sweat off his forehead, wishing he had put his hair back in a thong. Strands stuck to his skin, damp and itchy. Another irritation.

How long he had been on watch he knew not as the low clouds obscured all—the night as black as the ink he used in scribing.

Scribing. Stars, he wished he were scribing now instead of listening and watching the darkness in these woods and across the field. He thought back to his last scribing assignment before coming to Lairdton for the siege—the chiefs' conclave to introduce Valdhor's heir. Even after seeing her best Loch'alan, he felt astonished that such a slight lass could be a Ranger.

But Maradhor would wonder more about her when and if she returned from her mysterious mission. For the moment, he had to keep his eyes and ears trained for the almost impossible chance that someone might try to break siege.

The hair on his arms and neck stiffened, and he came to alert. Something had changed but he could not hit the mark. Wait—the nightsingers had stopped their raucous din. Behind him and around him they still gave their maddening song, but, in the open field ahead, they had ceased.

Drawing his knife, Maradhor pursed his lips and gave a soft, mournful call. Almost the cry of a bearded tarl, a nocturnal, predatory bird, this was subtly distinct, a warning to his fellow Rangers. The nightsingers to his left quieted. Using instinct rather than sight, he dove, and before the man could shout, Maradhor had him pinned, face shoved into the thick carpet of leaves and mould to keep him silent until any companions should be captured.

~:~

"Thane!"

Alcandhor's head snapped up. He blinked. Bells, he had fallen asleep at the table. He stood, his stomach lurching in fear at the look on Lamadhel's face. "Is it Haladhon? Marcalan?"

"Nay, they are both fine, to my knowledge. But we have news. Six men were caught trying to sneak past the perimeter in the dark. They are being held in cells."

"Have they talked?"

"Only to say they were trying to escape the hall. They will not give any other information, but tomorrow will be questioned further. Their dismay at being caught eased when they were fed."

Alcandhor closed his eyes in anguish. "Stars, innocent or not, I abhor what is happening to the people in there."

"Unless we attack, which will certainly cause a great loss of life for both sides, we have to wait it out."

Alcandhor rubbed his eyes. "I know."

Lamadhel's lips thinned. "You should be sleeping."

The Thane swept a hand over the table with a wry grin. "I was." Lamadhel did not smile, and Alcandhor sighed at the tacit chastisement. "I shall retire."

"Now."

Alcandhor left for his bedchamber, leaving Lamadhel to tidy the table and blow out the candles.

~:~

Haladhon lay propped up, drinking broth from a bowl, as was Marcalan. He had awakened first and had already given account to Alcandhor. Now he rested, sipping the stock, glad to finally keep something down. He had thought his insides had heaved out. Whatever they dosed the ale with must have been powerful.

Sherel had hovered over them for a whole day as they lay helplessly on cots, unable to do anything but sleep and retch.

Now the headache and eye pain had gone, and he could sit up without feeling nauseous. The horrible bone-jarring shaking had left too. He hoped the broth would give him strength enough to get on his feet today. His cousin grinned at him, and he winked in return.

"Where did they attack you?" Marcalan asked.

"Priv."

"How many?"

"Three. When I came back to the common room, I saw you fighting two of them, but you bested them before I could get to you. I thought I would fall over trying to get you to your feet."

Marcalan slumped down. "I have no memory of the fight."

"I think the next time we decide to stay at a tavern until we have gotten into trouble, we should reconsider, cousin."

"I think I will just stay away from taverns for awhile." Marcalan grimaced, but the look spread into a grin as he pointed at his cousin.

"You missed your chance with that girl."

Haladhon shook his head in disdain. "Her father was one of the attackers—she is likely of the same mind. What have I told you? Women cannot be trusted. See you why I have never married?"

"One day you will."

"Never."

"Be careful saying that, cousin. The Maker has a sense of humor."

"Ha! And how know you this?"

"Why, just look at me," Marcalan said with an insufferable smirk.

~:~

The mountain loomed ahead of Tam, a dark silhouette in the predawn sky. She let her breath out in a slow exhale, relieved to be near the end of her journey.

As the sun rose higher, unfamiliar feelings wafted to her. Not a storm of emotions as when she first sensed the Thane but—someone was close.

Could it be the messenger? Stars, she must get to him before he reached the mountain! Tam broke into a run but halted. What should she do, slay him without warning? How could she? What if this man was not a traitor? She chewed her lip. If he were not, he should have no qualms about meeting a Ranger. She would know by his reaction to her. Decision made, she rushed ahead, her course parallel to his.

At the base of the mountain, the sparse woods gave way to rocky terrain where little grew. Not far ahead her quarry trotted along. She left the safety of her cover in the trees as she caught up with him and stepped into his path.

Shock and confusion crossed his face as he halted. "What business brings a girl—and one dressed as a Ranger—to the Forbidden Peninsula?"

"What business brings you to it?" Tam asked.

"That is not your concern. Stand aside."

Tam widened her stance slightly, keeping her face hard and hopefully impassive although her heart raced.

The man frowned, his hand straying to his sword hilt. "You don't wish to play games with me."

"I play no games."

She drew her sword as he did. He stepped in with a down-strike. Tam deflected it and countered. He jumped back, surprised.

"You think you can fight?"

Staying in mid-guard, Tam twisted one hand around her hilt. "Do you fight or talk?"

"Trous-donning bawd! Wait till I get that sword out of your hands!" He lunged forward with a thrust. Sidestepping, Tam aimed a down-cut to his neck. He fell back, narrowly avoiding the strike. His blade slashed up. Tam gritted her teeth as his sword slid along the flat of hers, jarring to a halt against her crossguard.

He flexed his arms but before he could shove her back, she leaped to the side with a cross-strike. He recovered his balance and jumped back, but not far enough. He grunted as her sword slashed into his body. Stumbling to his knees, he stared at her in disbelief before slumping to the ground.

Tam took a step backward, repressing a shudder that she had killed again. She gulped in deep breaths, grimacing, and swallowed convulsively. She cleaned her sword and sheathed it with shaking hands. Her mission. She must concentrate on that. Blinking to clear her vision, she continued on.

~:~

Tam flexed her fingers as she pulled the gloves tight, squinting up at the forbidding mountain. She took a deep breath and began to climb, hoping she could easily find the landmark her uncle had described.

Sweat soon ran down her face and body, not only from exertion, but the hot sun beating down. Her angle was correct, ascending from the southwest, so the strange, round-topped formation should come in sight when she had climbed high enough. She hoped.

When she finally spied the landmark above her, to her right, perhaps half hour's climb away, she moaned in relief. The dome was not as large as she had expected.

Tam paused. With the site so near, she ought to be more careful. Any patrolling guards might see her. Her gaze flitted about as she sensed for anyone near, and finally, she continued on.

She drew near, squinting as the sun shone off the metal of the grate that enclosed the area underneath the dome. Awed and a little fearful of something of the Enaisi, she touched the barrier. How many years old was this place? Hundreds? More? Yet the grating was shiny and not rusted at all. Hinges marked one side of a section that must be the entrance Uncle mentioned. She peered through the grate. A soft breeze brushed Tam's hair back over her shoulders and cooled her face. She hooked her fingers through the grating of the metal gate and shook it. Solid.

She pulled the chain out from under her shirt and held out the odd piece of crystal her uncle had given her. It was narrow at the top, where it was inexplicably attached to the chain, and larger and round at the bottom. *But how do I use this "key?"*

One point married the smooth metal: a small circular indentation. Biting her lip, she touched the crystal to the spot. The gate swung inward. Steps allowed Tam to walk down and stand inside. The hair on her arms straightened and her skin prickled from the coolness in this sheltered area after the hot sun, and she shivered. She blinked to adjust her eyes to the comparative darkness. Sand and dirt collected in small piles along the walls, but no animals could get in through the grate. A large, round hole in the rock face of the far wall was the source of the wind. She walked toward it, her hair blowing back, and tentatively crawled inside.

The crystal hanging from her neck now glowed with a soft white fire in the increasing darkness. Tam had no time to consider this new oddity as she crept forward toward another grated barrier. She saw an indentation and set the glowing crystal against it. The gate swung open, and keeping the key in her hand as a light, she continued to crawl down the tunnel. Before long she stopped in horror: rocks barricaded her way for as far down as the key shone. A cave-in had partially blocked the shaft. The Thane's plan would not work! *Oh, Maker, how will I get the Laird out?*

Chapter Sixteen

Tam bit her lip. She had only one choice. If she could not sneak the Laird out, she had to break him out. But how? One Ranger against an unknown number of guards? And a young, untried Ranger at that.

Think. Do not feel, her father's voice echoed in her head.

What would her father do? What would the Thane want her to do? *Maker, guide me.*

First, Tam must roam the area. If perimeter guards patrolled, she must discover where. And who knows—perhaps she might find a weakness that would help her.

She climbed out of the dome and began to creep across the mountainside. The grade gentled, sloping more easily as she continued east.

She crouched behind boulders, peering for guards. At this height, the terrain had no trees to interfere with her view, although the huge, sharp rocks could hide an army. A guard stood watch a little below her and to her left.

She flitted from boulder to boulder as she descended the mountainside, hoping she could find all the guards before they caught sight of her. Trees grew among the rocks a bit lower, and Tam used them for cover to circle east and around to the north. She found three guards, one south, one east—at the woods' edge, and one on the northern side.

The entrance, set into the rock, faced east and guards flanked its open, metal door.

Five guards in all. She would start on the north and work east and back around to the south. Tam took a long, slow breath, eyeing the nearby guard. She took off her bow and nocked an arrow. She tried to think of him as a target, not a person. She had faced these qualms before when her father taught her to hunt. Killing animals so she could eat and live had been hard, especially if she did not block, as she would sense their deaths. This was no animal though, but a man. He had a soul.

She took a deep breath. *I am a Ranger. I must do this.* But still her fingertips would not loose the bowstring.

She swallowed, eye on her target, as her mind turned to the young Laird locked inside somewhere, his father dead, though he knew it not. His home besieged. Her own father—and other good Rangers—dead.

Her uncle lying wounded. Those thoughts hardened her, and she let the arrow fly. The guard collapsed with a strangled moan and lay still.

Tam almost tiptoed to the body. She wanted not to see it, to see the face of the man she had just killed, but she needed to retrieve her arrow. Her gaze flicked to his face, and she let herself sense for a moment to be certain he was dead, then she placed one foot on the corpse, gripped the shaft as close to the body as she could, and yanked the arrow straight out.

With a long, slow exhale she rose. She must do this again. And again. *I do not like being a Ranger! I want not to do this!* She had no choice. Duty. She must do her duty: to her kin, her Uncle, the Laird. She set her jaw and moved on.

The east guard died without a sound. Tam crept to the south. The third guard yelled as he tumbled downhill over several rocks. The guards by the door drew their swords and ran in her direction. She took aim on one guard, let the arrow fly, nocked the next arrow, and released it as well. The first guard fell on his face. The second stumbled with a cry and continued on. She shot again. The man took a step and another, his face contorting with pain and shock. The taste of acid bile nauseated Tam but she made herself continue to watch. The guard stumbled and sprawled on his side. He rolled down the mountain until his body wedged under a boulder.

Tam licked her dry lips, her heart thudding against her ribcage. This would not do. She must think of her mission, not the killing. Dutifully, she checked the bodies and retrieved her arrows, then peeked uphill.

The first guard had fallen near the door and could be seen if anyone came outside. Tam stared at the body. Dare she try to get that arrow back?

A motion in the rocky shadows caught her eye. A ka'gua. Drawing up on its hind legs, it hissed through its sharp teeth, tongue darting out, the frills along its neck and back flapping. Blood. It smelled the warm blood of the body. Tam shuddered and stole away to a safer distance. She would not go near those reptiles. Although only the length of Tam's forearm, an adult ka'gua could kill a grown man.

A second ka'gua crept out and joined the first at the body. Another soon joined the feast, followed by young ones. A nest must be nearby. Tam avoided the scene by keeping her gaze on the door. What could she do? To approach the door meant risking attack. She must wait until the ka'gua finished eating and slunk back into their nest in the rocks.

Tam noticed a crude bolt installed in the rock next to the door. She recalled the covers that opened with her key. Perhaps if they had not such a key, they could not lock the door. That would explain the bolt. Would Tam's key lock that door? And even if so, could she find the small spot for her key in the dark? That bolt might be useful.

The sun sank low, creating long shadows with its yellow, westerly rays when five men stepped outside and began looking about, calling for their companions. One shouted, and they all ran toward the partially consumed carcass. Tam's hands flew to her mouth. Spitting, hissing ka'gua leapt, and the men screamed.

One man pulled a knife. Fool—he should run! He attacked the ka'gua on his friend's face. The creature spit and launched at him. He jumped back too late and shrieked with pain, writhing as he fell to the ground, sharp teeth ripping out his throat.

Three men rushed out the door, swords drawn.

"Where are they?"

"I don't know. But I tell you I heard yelling."

"There!"

Tam chewed her lip. Better to kill them than watch the ka'gua do it. She shot one man. He dropped, and she blinked fiercely. Her next arrow found its target as well. The third fell with a horrified scream before Tam could nock another arrow.

Soon quiet fell. Tam shook, not from the chill of the evening air, but from what she had witnessed. The ka'gua would soon return to the rocks to sleep, their bellies full. Tam must then be ready to go inside.

If the Thane had been correct, the Laird would be locked away in a chamber toward the south, and maybe to the west. But how many chambers did this place have, and how many men remained inside?

The sun set. Tam could not see if the ka'gua had left. Unwilling to take a chance, she stopped blocking to sense for them. The creatures had gone. Tam lifted her face toward the door, eyes wide. By the Maker, she could sense men inside! Of course. Her father would have sneered at her for being so dense. Now if only they did not sense her...

Tam approached the door, detecting no one to hand. Still, she peeped around the doorframe, her heart beating rapidly. No guards. She stopped, staring—the wide, illuminated corridor did not use fire as a source. Angled corners between the greyish-white walls and ceiling glowed with a bright, white light.

Stars, what magic did the Enaisi have?

Fear of discovery hit Tam's stomach, making her heart thud even faster. She swallowed her awe and drew her leg-knife. Her leather soles padded softly on the grey-white floor, her hand brushing along the cold surface of the polished stone wall.

The faint presence of someone near crept over Tam, and she paused. Asleep. Two or three persons slept close by. Tam continued walking, trying to separate the wispy feelings of several people not far away.

Irritation and frustration mixed with a trickle of fear rippled from the southwest and farther off.

Tam reached the end of the main hallway. She pressed against the wall and peeked around the corner. Clear. She hurried along that passage.

A door swung open ahead of her. She froze, her throat constricting. The guard jumped in alarm, yelling, "Intruder!"

She ran forward. Her dagger sank into his chest before he could unsheathe his sword. As she pulled her weapon out with a quick jerk, two others crowded out the door.

The second man grabbed her knife wrist. Tam drove forward with her shoulder, knocking the second man into the third. The two men grunted, but the second did not release her wrist. She punched his face— and again. His hold loosened and she thrust her blade into his chest.

The third snarled, sword in hand. Tam stepped back, drawing her own, her eyes flicking at the close walls. No room to maneuver. His weapon in high-guard, the man jumped over his companions' bodies with a straight thrust. Tam deflected with the flat of her blade. As she shifted weight to her back leg, she brought her blade to high shoulder and into a quick downward cut. He leaped back with a grunt, avoiding the strike.

"Wench!" Teeth bared, he came at her with an overhead down-cut. She hopped aside, deflecting, and rotated her sword into a down-stroke, partially severing his sword arm. With a strangled cry, he fell to his knees, weapon clanging to the floor. Tam thrust her sword into his heart and out again, needing only a slight saccade to wrench it free.

Dazed and nauseous, Tam fell back against the cold wall. *Oh, Father, why Trained you me thus? Uncle, dearest Uncle, I cannot go on. I cannot.*

Her uncle's voice echoed in her mind. *The Laird's safety is of uttermost importance. Nothing else matters.*

Tam pushed away from the wall, swallowing hard. She retrieved her dagger from the one corpse and using the dead man's clothes, Tam cleaned her sword and knife, berating herself for having trembling hands—no, her whole body was shaking! Her father would scorn such weakness. She breathed in again, forcing herself to be calm and sense about. Nothing near. No wakeful awareness ahead.

Her sword at ready, she continued down the passage and into the next corridor, drawing closer to the strong emotions. The last door on her left contained the source of the anxieties.

She sheathed her sword while taking a deep breath, slid the bolt back, and opened the door.

"My heart!" A young man stood from a small cot. He tugged at the collar of the white, sleeveless surcoat, straightening the garment over black trous, purple shirt, and black waist sash. Long, pale gold hair fell over his shoulders. The traditional small braids pulled his hair back at the temples, and several other small braids overlaid his hair as well.

Tam bowed. "Your Grace. I am honored to serve."

Square-shouldered and tall, the Laird had almost her uncle's height, but with a gangly look. His blue eyes, round as moons, scrutinized her in curiosity and astonishment. "Who, by the Enaisi, are you, lass?"

"I am a Ranger, Your Grace. We must leave. Guards are still about."

"A lass as a Ranger? Your ignorance gives away your playacting, girl. I am not 'Your Grace.'"

Tam frowned. His clothes, his manner all bespoke he was the Laird. She hesitated, then asked, "You are not Randhal of Viltara?"

"I am." His lips crooked in a small, arrogant smile.

"Then why—oh!" The realization hit her—he would not know! And she must be the one to tell him. She swallowed. "I am sorry, Your Grace, but you are." She lifted her chin slightly. "And I am *too* a Ranger, and am sent from the Thane himself to rescue you."

"Your jesting is too dark," he hissed.

"'Tis no jest, I assure you. The Thane knew you would require proof to trust me, and that it would be hard to provide it so he bade me ask you this—who besides the Thane would study the Enaisi's books and ways, and know of this place, even if he knew not the reason the Enaisi built it?"

The Laird's lips twitched in a smile, but his eyes glittered like ice. "Not many. But that is not conclusive. Lord Paltor often complains of the Thane's obsession with the law, history, and the Enaisi."

Tam sighed, glancing down the dark hall. "He also bids me tell you that he will box your ears so they will ring until the Enaisi return if you do not come with me."

The Laird's face softened slightly—only slightly. "If you are truly a Ranger, then who in the clan are you?"

"I am the Thane's niece and sit as Second at Table, Your Grace."

"Indeed." The Laird's eyes narrowed. "I knew not females were Trained as Rangers."

"I am the first. I was Trained in secret by my father, Valdhor."

"Valdhor is your father? Yet you sit as Second at Table?"

"He was, and aye I do, Your Grace."

"Was!"

Tam winced, holding up her hands to quiet him. They both glanced down the corridor then he leaned forward, his eyes locked on hers. "Tell me, then, if you are Valdhor's daughter, why he was not Thane."

Again Tam paused, this time to shove down her own hurt. "I know not his reasons. I only know he renounced Thaneship and let his younger brother become Thane when their father died. My father never talked of family." *Not even to tell me who they were.*

The Laird rubbed his fingers on his forehead. Bells and stars above, why was he so distrustful? *The key! Would he know of it?* Tam drew out the glowing crystal and let it dangle. "Does this convince you?"

The Laird gasped. "Aye." He swallowed, staring at it. "I trust you now."

She took the key in her fist and put it back inside her shirt as she let her breath out in a slow exhale.

"But if you are—you called me 'Your Grace.' Do you tell me my father is dead?"

"Aye, Your Grace. I am sorry."

His face contorted with sorrow and he fell back against the wall. "No!" He sank down to the ground, hands over his face. Tam knelt on one knee in front of him as he sobbed.

"Quiet, Your Grace! Please! I understand your grief, but we will be heard and found. Please."

"How can you understand?" he cried. "My father is dead!"

"My father died the same day," she whispered. "I watched as the arrow struck him. I saw him fall. I knelt next to him as he drew his last breath. I left him lying there to begin this journey on the orders of my uncle to save your life. We—have—no—time—for—grief!" Each word of the last sentence she spat out in quick urgency.

He looked up, his face wet and filled with heartache. She met his blue eyes, wishing she could hold back the tears that coursed down her own face as she stared at him in determination, willing him to get up. To *move.*

He finally averted his eyes, taking a ragged breath. "By the moons, if a lass can, I can." He stood and swallowed, his lips a thin, set line.

She nodded at his garments. "Take off your surcoat, Your Grace. 'Tis white and can be seen in the dark."

With a nervous glance up the passage, he did so, still sniffling and wiping his eyes, while she unslung her pack. She removed the dark cloak and handed it to him as he offered the surcoat. She folded and packed it, sensing for any approach, but so far the corridor remained clear.

Tam drew her leg knife and offered it to him. "I know not if you will need this ere we are gone from here, but best be prepared."

His hand clasped the dagger, and he stared at it for a moment. He drew his shoulders back with a deep inhale. "What is your plan?"

"I noticed a bolt installed on the entrance. We could trap them all inside. That way we need not worry about being followed."

"Excellent."

Tam bit her lip. "It is getting to the door that is my concern. I cannot be front and back for you, Your Grace."

He hefted the knife. "I have not your training, but I have some small skill in wielding blades."

"Good. I will lead. You watch our back and yell if you see guards."

The corners of his mouth twitched and a slight arrogance belied his bow. "Aye, Ranger."

They ran to the end of the Laird's corridor and into the next. As they reached the guards lying on the floor of the second corridor, the Laird gasped.

"They came out, and I had to fight them." She stepped over them, her gaze averted as much as possible yet trying not to tread in the blood.

The horror that radiated from the Laird melted into awe.

She came to the archway that opened to the main corridor. Hearing voices and laughter, Tam peeped around it. Two men walked toward the entrance, their backs to her. If they ventured outside they would see the dead bodies!

Tam leaned against the wall, her heart pounding, trying to think. She ran to the nearest door in their corridor and, hearing and sensing nothing within, cautiously opened it—dark and empty. "Your Grace, let us hide in this chamber."

Once inside, she held the door closed, her ear at the opening, listening.

Before long, yells echoed and she heard running. The men passed their door and shouted in alarm at the bodies in the corridor. One called, "Check that cursed boy!"

More sounds of running and men asking, "What's happening?"

"The outside guards are dead. And these men, too. Tantil has gone to make sure the boy is still locked up."

"Alone? What if he runs into whoever did this?"

"Bloody Bells, you're right. Let's go!"

The sounds receded. Tam opened the door and peeked around despite feeling no one. Clear. She glanced back at the Laird. "Come!"

They ran along the main hall to the entrance. As they reached the door, shouts behind them made Tam jump. Guards raced toward them. The Laird almost pushed her aside rushing through the doorway. He slammed the door shut and tried to slide the bolt. "It will not move!"

The men shoved against the door. Tam drove her shoulder against the door to add her weight to the Laird's, her feet braced against the ground, but the door inched outward.

Chapter Seventeen

"Give me the knife." Tam snatched the weapon from the Laird's outstretched hand and stabbed around the doorway with the dagger. She hit flesh. Curses issued through the crack. She jabbed again and heard a cry of pain, then hammered on the bolt with the pommel. It moved a bit. "Now!" she screamed, and they threw themselves at the door. It shut. She scrabbled at the bolt and slid the metal rod forward.

They leaned against the door, breathing heavily. Tam's heart pounded in her throat and ears.

"It seems wrong to leave them to starve but we have no choice," she said when she got her breath.

"They will not. This place has fresh air, is well stocked with food, and has a water and waste system that is beyond anything I have ever seen. They will survive until we send someone back to take them prisoner."

"That is good." She inhaled deeply again. "Ready, Your Grace?"

"Aye, I believe so."

Tam sheathed her knife. "Come."

The Laird followed her across the rocks. He tried to talk once but she quieted him, telling him to save his breath and strength for now. She had to go slowly, as he could not climb and scramble over the rocky terrain with ease as she could.

"I cannot go on," he finally said, panting.

The ground had leveled out somewhat, and they had reached a sparse wood, giving them some cover. Tam peered between the branches of the trees at the position of the larger moon. An hour or so before the middle of night's thirteen. With the clear sky, Tarnal would give them light to continue for some time.

The Laird leaned against a tree, breathing heavily. With a sigh of regret, she unslung her pack and dropped it. "We will rest here for awhile."

He sank to the ground, groaning, and propped his back against the trunk. She handed him one of her waterskins. After taking a long drink, he let it drop to his lap. His eyes closed.

Tam rested against a tree and kept watch as he slept. The moons made slow flight in their orbits as night passed.

The Laird shifted in his sleep, sliding down from leaning against the tree to a position on the ground, so exhausted she doubted he realized where he was. She studied him in the light from Tarnal. He had what seemed to be a strong, good face. What age had he? At most he had one or two years on her, but regardless, he was not of Age either.

A ten-day journey lay ahead of them and the food, although she had gone lightly with it, would not be enough. And this young man was not hardened to journeying. Travel would be slow.

If somehow those guards broke through that bolted door, the Laird would be in grave jeopardy. And might they meet other men sent by the traitors? Could she keep him safe and deliver him alive and unharmed?

~:~

As the sky began to turn grey, Tam called the Laird. He did not move. She bent closer, but dared not shake him—one did not touch the Laird. "Your Grace? Your Grace! We must move on."

He groaned, starting to roll over. His eyes flew open, wild and disoriented. He gazed about at the hard ground with grass and the scattered leaves under him and sat up, blinking and holding his arms. "It is cold!"

"You will warm up as we journey."

He groaned again and stretched. "What about breakfast?"

She offered him journey rations. "Drink sparingly until we come to a stream, Your Grace."

He began eating while eyeing her. "How do you Rangers do this?"

"Do what?"

"This!" He threw out his arms. "Live like this. It amazes me."

Tam shrugged and thought of the little she saw of Laird Hall. What seemed a normal part of life to her would seem very different to one raised in such a place.

The Laird began picking leaves and twigs out of his hair while chewing. Oh, stars, they needed to move on! She stood, gritting her teeth, and looked around, getting a feel for the coming day and of the land. She let herself sense, but no one was near.

"How can you do that?" he asked.

She turned. "What?"

"Get up so easily after sleeping on the ground. My bones feel sore."

"I did not sleep."

"You did not sleep?" He frowned. "Why?"

"I had to keep watch."

"But how can you go on without rest?"

"'One does what one must,'" Tam said, quoting her father. Hoping her voice did not betray her irritation, she added, "Please, Your Grace, eat quickly. We must begin."

He ate in earnest and soon finished. As she shouldered her pack, he said, "I–I need a few moments for privacy."

She gestured toward a few trees clumped together nearby. With an embarrassed smile, he disappeared behind them.

She scattered leaves where they had rested. Rangers would not be fooled, but if some of these traitors that seemed not to have much wild-sense came after them, they should not notice this resting spot.

The Laird soon returned. "I am ready."

She began walking.

"Can we talk now?" he asked.

"If you walk next to me and talk softly. I wish to be able to hear not only if there is pursuit but also in case we approach others."

"That is not likely, is it?"

"Rangers do not go on assumptions. We do not take chances."

"Well, of course, but I mean, you took care of the guards behind us, and this area is not lived in."

She stopped and turned, sighing. "Your Grace, I know not if the men trapped inside might be able to get that door open. We could meet others in this area who have been sent with messages to your captors, or who are bringing supplies. I am overly young to have been given this mission. My uncle had few Rangers to hand after the battle that claimed many lives and with most of the Rangers besieging the traitors in Laird Hall—"

"Besieging? Laird Hall is besieged?"

"Aye, Your Grace. So when my uncle learned the danger you were in, I was sent to rescue and protect our Laird and bring him back safely. And I will do that," she said with fierceness to belie her own doubts.

The Laird grew quiet, perhaps dwelling on his own grief, the news of the siege, or the fear of pursuers—or possibly all three. Whatever his thoughts, he kept up with her pace as they traveled on, the rising sun and cheery dawn-singers at odds with the sadness Tam felt, not only for her own loss but the Laird's. He followed a step or two behind her, head down, occasionally wiping his face with a piece of linen he kept tucked under his sash. Tam could not tell if he wiped tears, sweat, or both.

They stopped at a stream to drink and fill their waterskins. Strange hollow cries came from above—birds in formation were flying south. They must be shore birds, as she had never seen such in the mountains. She watched them until she was squinting in the sun and could see them no more before turning back to the Laird. He dripped with perspiration.

"Take that cloth from your sash and wash it out in the stream, Your Grace. It will not stay wet long, but while it does, you can use it to cool your face."

"Thank you. I would not have thought of that."

He bathed his face and neck in the stream, then rose to his feet with a quiet moan. "I am ready." He squeezed out the cloth.

She nodded and turned to continue. He came alongside her. "I know not your name, Ranger."

"Tamissa, Your Grace. But I go by Tam."

"Tam," he murmured but said no more.

The sun had risen high when the Laird asked, "When will we stop to eat?"

She opened the pouch slung on her side with her waterskin and handed him a piece of smoked meat. "You can eat this as we walk, Your Grace."

With a sigh, he stared at it for a moment, bit off a piece, and began to chew. "Are you not going to eat?"

"Not until we stop for the night, unless I find food."

"Find food?"

"There is plenty of food in the wild if you know what it is and where to look."

He glanced with skepticism at the flora about them and at the strip of meat in his hand. "I think I will just eat this."

Tam had her own doubts about finding food here. This place seemed somewhat barren, quite unlike the region she knew, filled with food for the digging or picking. She would have to endure hunger for now. Within a day, though, the land would become more fruitful.

"Tam?"

"Aye, Your Grace?"

"Know you how my father died?"

She hesitated. "Aye, Your Grace."

"Tell me."

"It was a dagger," she murmured. "And it was quick."

He walked in silence for awhile. "I wish I knew more. Exactly how it happened..."

"I will tell you, Your Grace, if you think you can bear it."

"I...I need to know. Tell me."

She grimaced at the memory as she began. "I was in a side chamber, listening—"

"You? You were actually there?"

"Aye, Your Grace. My uncle had me in Laird Hall as a spy. He needed someone he could trust to try to find out who was behind the treason."

"I see. Please continue."

She had no trouble giving him a quick summary of what happened. She had reviewed the events of that day in her mind endlessly. She paused after telling how she had seen his father on the floor, a dagger in the back. The young Laird breathed heavily, tears in his eyes.

"What of Lord Krendhal?" he asked after awhile. "Did they kill him, too?"

"Nay, Your Grace. He and I both escaped the hall to warn the Rangers of a planned ambush." She stopped talking, the memories threatening to choke her.

"Then what happened?"

"I...I was not in time," she managed to whisper.

"That is when your father died?"

"Aye. And the Thane was wounded very badly. I know not if he lives."

The Laird put a hand over his heart, tears welling in his eyes. "By both moons and the Bells, not him, too!" He took a deep breath. "He cannot die. I—we need him. Our world needs him."

He blinked and drew his sleeve across his face. "We must continue. He would chide us, would he not, for stopping to talk of him? He would tell us we must do our duty." His lips tipped up in a hesitant smile.

She nodded. The depth of his feeling for her uncle gave Tam a sense of companionship with him.

~:~

Alcandhor chewed his cheek as the sense of foreboding grew. He rose and paced his bedchamber and, finally, went searching for Haladhon. He found him in the dining hall, having his afternooning, and sat next to his cousin.

"I am disquieted about Tam and the Laird," Alcandhor whispered.

"Think you there might be trouble?" Haladhon asked in a soft voice.

"I know not, but send some Rangers to the peninsula, just in case."

"How many think you we should send?"

"Three, perhaps."

"I will choose and send them out immediately."

~:~

Alcandhor heard excited voices in the foreroom and hallway. Haladhon opened the door, a glint in his eyes. "Thane, you will not believe what our scouts have seen approaching."

Alcandhor closed his book, laid it on the table, and leaned back, waiting.

"Nobles are on their way here: Paltor and his sons, and Zantith. They are accompanied by several score of guards."

Alcandhor exhaled slowly. "Aye. To display their allegiance while in reality spying on us, no doubt. How far away are these nobles?"

"Less than a day."

"Lorwith is not with them?"

"Nay."

Alcandhor nodded. Not surprising. Lorwith would have others do what he would not. A nervous creature, driven by fears and ambition, but he had a cunning best not underestimated.

"If they come as allies, what do we do, Thane?"

"Be friendly and do not let them know we suspect them, but they are not to pass the gate. Tell them we have no room for them here. They can find accommodations in the town or camp in the woods. We can arrange a place to confer nearby."

His lips twisted in a wry smile as Haladhon rubbed the back of his neck. "'Twould be easier if they did not come as allies."

~:~

"Can we not light a fire?" The Laird fell to the ground, groaning. A chill wind swept through the copse sheltering them and not much light from Tarnal or the Bells came through the thick branches of the trees.

Tam hesitated, weighing the risks. A fire might discourage a ballan from attacking—though not necessarily stop one in a foul mood, but it could draw another, two-legged danger. "Nay. We do not know that it might not attract unwelcome visitors."

"More dried meat?" he asked.

"And dried fruit and journeybread."

He looked doubtfully at the food she gave him. After swallowing a bite of the dry bread, he asked, "Not much flavor to it, is there?"

She shook her head, chewing. Her eyes burned from exhaustion. How was she going to keep awake to guard? She felt her head nod and snapped it up with fierce determination.

"Tam? You have not slept at all. Can I not watch for a few hours? I will wake you if I hear anything."

She looked over at him in surprise, not expecting assistance from a pampered noble. The dim light shadowed his face, but still she could see concern written on his features.

She needed the rest, yet she worried he would fall asleep or be taken unaware. "It would help me, Your Grace, but you must wake me if you start to feel drowsy or hear the slightest noise."

"I will," he said with a faint smile. "Now sleep, Ranger."

"Thank you, Your Grace," she murmured, lying down.

~:~

Tam sat up as she felt a touch on her shoulder and heard her name called. She blinked the sleep from her eyes, shuddering at the blackness that disturbed her dreams.

"I am sorry. I started to doze off despite my best efforts. I thought it best to wake you."

"You did right." She looked up to see the position of the moons. Tarnal had passed meridian, clouds scudding across it. The Laird had watched a good while.

As he lay down, she rubbed her eyes to wake. 'Twas long hours until dawn.

~:~

Alcandhor looked up from the letter he was writing and put down the quill. "They arrived?"

"Aye, Thane. And they offer any assistance that we might need in dealing with the treason and rebellion."

"I am impressed!" Alcandhor slapped a hand to his chest in mock astonishment.

Haladhon grinned. "They are going to stay in the town, and since it is so late in the day, we will meet with them for a conference tomorrow afternoon." He shook his head. "I still do not like the idea that we will meet in Lairdton. 'Tis a long walk for you, and you are less guarded there. What if they wish to finish the task started by their confederates? You could be in danger—and Lord Krendhal as well. Especially with the distraction of the equinox festivities in town. 'Twould be a perfect trap."

"I will have you next to me, and we are taking many Rangers with us."

Haladhon crossed his arms with a skeptical expression. "And what if you cannot make the walk?"

"I will be fine, Haladhon."

Haladhon nodded toward the table, his voice mocking. "You should not be working on reports."

Alcandhor snorted. "'Tis a letter to my children. I am missing equinox with them...again."

"Ah." The mocking expression faded into a tight-lipped smile. "I will leave you to write it, then." He closed the door.

Alcandhor picked up the quill, dipped it in the inkhorn with a sigh, and resumed writing.

~:~

Tam called the Laird as the sky turned grey-blue. He started to groan but stopped and sat up with a sigh. He accepted the meat and journeybread she offered with a grimace, saying, "This gets tiresome."

"I will pick if I find anything. Perhaps we can add greens, roots, or tubers to our meal this evening. But they will have to be eaten raw. I will not chance a fire by day or night."

He sighed again and shook his head. "I would fain chance a fire. I am chilled to the bone."

"Then let us continue. You will wish for a cool breeze before this day is out, I wager. And be prepared, we will enter the marshes by day's end or early tomorrow. 'Tis not pleasant, but once we clear that foul place we shall be off the peninsula."

The Laird grimaced and disappeared behind some trees.

"Do you have a comb, Tam?" he asked as he returned, loosening his braids. She rummaged in her pack and handed him hers. He smiled and as they began walking, he combed his blond hair.

"When I was a lad, I used to wish I could be a Ranger," he said. "It seemed an exciting life. I would watch the Rangers come and go with their swords and bows and was awed by them. Your uncle was amused by my admiration and taught me a little about how to use a bow, sword, and staff. But in spite of his tales, I had no idea of this side of your life. I know now what he meant that it is a hard life."

"Not to one Trained to it, Your Grace. I think the hardness of it is in the grief. It is rare a Ranger lives to an old age," she said, repeating what her uncle had told her. "My father died only days ago. I saw other Rangers, kin all, lying dead near my father. Empty places at Zaidhron, family who will never again see fathers, brothers, sons..."

"I never thought of that. I am sorry for your loss, Tam."

"And I, yours, Your Grace. You carry a heavy load now. Not only your grief, but also the weight of the decisions you will be required to make as Laird. And to start thus with treason in your home..."

"I feel at a loss to understand all of it—treason, a siege, murder." He gave a grim shake of his head. "We both are now laden with heavy burdens at a young age."

The Laird busied himself putting braids back into his hair. Unable to control her curiosity, Tam asked, "Why bother you with the braids, Your Grace?"

His round, blue eyes stared at her. "Habit, I suppose. Since I was young, I have always had them in my hair, as do most nobles." He chuckled. "I was proud that I taught myself to do braids after being brought to the peninsula. I had no servant to do my hair then."

He claimed pride of so small an accomplishment as braiding? Tam shook her head and kept walking.

As they ate luncheon rations late that morning, the Laird nodded at her. "Tell me about yourself."

Tam stared as she chewed. After swallowing, she said, "I...I know not what to tell."

"What was your childhood like?"

"Being Trained by my father." Her father's forbidding, displeased expression flitted in her mind. Her stomach tightened—she had never succeeded at meeting her father's expectations. Appetite now gone, she put the piece of dried meat she had been eating back in the pouch.

"Aye. But I mean, what else?"

Tam shrugged. "That is all. Except tending my garden."

The Laird frowned at her.

Tam wished she knew how to speak with people. Her father had never talked with her except to give orders or teach. Conversations were uncomfortable. "I am sorry, Your Grace. I know not what you wish to know."

After a short silence, the Laird asked, "Where did you live? I never knew where your father's bounds were, save in Pashelon province."

"Aye, 'twas remote. His bounds were high in the mountains, with only a few small villages and some herders and mountain folk. But I rarely met them. I tended camp when I did not stay at home."

"Zaidhron must have been very different for you."

"Aye."

"How does your clan feel about a Ranger-lass?"

Tam shook her head. "I think most are not pleased." Tam stopped before mentioning the chiefs' conclave. Was record of that meeting private? Best not to say on.

"You sit as Second at Table, you said?"

"Aye. I have that status, but hold not the rank."

"So you are not in line to become Thane?"

"Stars, nay! Uncle mentioned it—" Tam shut her mouth. More conclave business.

"The Thane mentioned what?"

Tam swallowed. "Being a lass, I am not my father's heir to Thane."

The Laird nodded, and they continued on in silence.

By late afternoon, the smell of rotten eggs grew strong.

"By the moons," the Laird exclaimed, wrinkling his nose. "What is that odor?"

"We near the marsh, Your Grace."

The Laird grumbled, swatting at the biting swamp gnats swarming about them. Tam shook her head and walked faster. What would he complain about when past the marsh? Moments later, the Laird cried out and Tam ran back. He gripped his forearm, blood welling between his fingers.

She ripped his sleeve to see the wound and hissed. No bramble caused such a deep gash, and 'twas already swelling. Nay, let it not be! She peered at the bushes and saw sharp spines thrusting from under the whorled leaves. Aye, a ch'iltar plant—known for its baneful thorns. Her stomach knotted. Stars, all the worry over protecting him from traitors and he might die of poison?

Chapter Eighteen

On his walk into the town, Krendhal at his side, Alcandhor paid close attention to his surroundings. Not necessarily for safety's sake—that task was Haladhon's and his men, but to gauge perceptions of the townsfolk.

In the distance, procession bells large and small, held aloft in frames, chimed and clanged dissonantly amid the sing-song chanting of those making their way to the festivities in the market square several streets north. But despite the autumnal equinox celebrations, people lined the street here, bowing as they walked by, their eyes fixed on the Thane.

"What think you of that, Thane?" Krendhal asked with quiet amusement.

Alcandhor nodded pleasantly at the crowd, noting inwardly that although some truly felt respect, others...did not. "I think quite a few people wear two faces, lord."

"The fact that your men fought well despite being poisoned has made a rather deep impression on the town. There is a deeper respect from what I have observed." The noble's eyes met Alcandhor's with concern. "How are you faring?"

"I will be able to make it without falling over, I think."

"You do well for a man who was almost dead less than half a lunation ago."

"We Rangers are vigorous, lord." His tone remained light although he only kept pace by strength of will.

The conference would take place in a private meeting room of the Copper Kettle. Alcandhor did not insist on another tavern as he wanted to establish that Rangers retreated from nothing.

Haladhon's eyes darted about constantly, his jaw set. He had personally organized the Rangers used as guards for this task, knowing the potential danger. As far as the nobles knew, only the Thane and Krendhal stood between them and their goals. As Haladhon had said, this would be a perfect trap.

Haladhon shot a worried look at Alcandhor as they approached the tavern's meeting room. His tall cousin opened the door, and he and several other Rangers went inside. He emerged, nodding, and the two leaders entered.

165

The other nobles had already arrived and stood at the table with their men posted around the room. Rangers stationed themselves between the guards. The Thane, Krendhal, and the other two nobles all bowed. Haladhon held a chair for the Thane to sit, and also for Krendhal, as he had no second or attendant.

Alcandhor noted as he sat that Paltor's girth had grown. Zantith's piercing blue eyes were as wary as ever.

"'Tis good to see you healing well after that abominable attack, Thane," Paltor said, seating himself.

"I thank you, Lord Paltor," Alcandhor said, wondering if he had the energy to play the verbal sparring game. "Especially since we both know you hold not the Rangers in highest esteem."

"My opinion of the too-broad powers you wield is well known. But it does not mean I would condone such an attack or rejoice at your injuries."

"It is good to know that despite our disagreements we can be conciliatory."

Paltor inclined his head. "What is the situation? And how may we be of service?"

Alcandhor leaned back in the high-backed chair and gestured for Krendhal to proceed.

"I was summoned for a meeting with Lord Batrig and Lord Cardhal. When I arrived, the Laird lay dead on the floor, a dagger in his back." He stopped as Zantith jumped up with a gasp, looking horrified at the news.

After a moment, Krendhal continued. "The lords turned and attacked me, and I fought them. Just then, there was a commotion concerning a servant girl who was caught listening. As they chased the girl, I was able to break free and, in the following confusion, escaped Laird Hall. I arrived at Ranger Hold just as the Thane was brought in from the ambush and the Rangers declared the siege."

Alcandhor kept his face impassive but wanted to burst into laughter. Krendhal did well. No one outside the Rangers knew any more than that, and even among the Rangers only the chiefs, Marcalan, and Tanadhon knew the entire story.

Zantith reseated himself, gaping. "How insidious! I cannot imagine such evil doings. It is indeed fortunate that you were able to escape."

"Despicable." Paltor's jowls swayed as he shook his head. "Imagine Batrig—and Cardhal—capable of murder." His gaze slid between Alcandhor and Krendhal. "What of the boy, the Atheling?"

The Thane shifted in his chair, adjusting the sling. "The *Laird* was not in North Port, as had been reported. We have no idea where they are keeping him, which has us worried."

"I have given it much thought, as has the Thane," Krendhal said, his hands palm up on the table, his tone dark with desperation, "but we have had no success locating him. Do either of you have any ideas?"

Paltor rubbed his fleshy face while Zantith sat with his eyes narrowed in thought.

"You have checked through Estan Province?" Paltor asked. "In Estan Hall? Lord Batrig is fond of hiding places and secret tunnels, you know."

"Aye, his hall and province have already been scoured, milord," Alcandhor said.

"So you have also searched throughout Lord Cardhal's province, I take it?" Zantith asked.

"Aye," Alcandhor said. "We have, Lord Zantith."

He shook his head. "I am at a loss, then."

"I fear he is probably already dead," Paltor said. "If they already had him captive and if those holding him heard of the siege, they probably would kill him then."

"Not necessarily. They might think to use him to bargain with to end the siege," the Thane said.

"A good point," Zantith said. "Perhaps there is hope."

"So we are trying to find him while waiting in case they contact us to bargain for his life," Alcandhor said.

"And what would you do if they did contact you?" Paltor asked.

Alcandhor feigned amazement at the question. "I would bargain, or course. The Laird's life is of the utmost importance."

Zantith and Paltor exchanged glances. Surprise surged from them although their faces revealed little. Alcandhor wished he had not only empathy but also telepathy—he would give his sword to know what both men thought of his statement.

"I do think one thing we can do is put our minds to the question and see if we can think of any place they might use to hold him captive," Zantith said. "As the Thane says, his life is most important."

"Aye, agreed," Paltor said. "But tell me. Why do you speak as if he is now Laird? He is not yet of Age. Lord Krendhal should be interim Laird, at the least."

"Despite his age," Krendhal said, "I wish to establish his right to be Laird by declaring him now. With treason and uprisings, we need one person as a steady hand over the provinces."

"Who would listen to a boy?" Paltor asked.

Krendhal drew himself up, his voice low and commanding. "The lords will heed the Laird."

Zantith frowned, the confusion swirling in him easy for Alcandhor

167

to detect. Anger simmered in Paltor as he licked his thick lips and stared at the table. He swallowed and looked up. "Is there any way we can render assistance?"

The Thane shook his head. "I think not at this time. Rangers oversee the siege and we are at a standstill until that is ended. But your support is invaluable. 'Tis good to know who our allies are."

"What will you do with the traitors inside Laird Hall once the siege is broken?" Paltor asked.

"There will be a trial, of course," Krendhal said.

Paltor's chair creaked as he stirred in it. "And who will preside?"

"If the Laird is not found, that duty will fall on me," Krendhal said. "But surely, Lord Paltor, you must know that."

"With all this upheaval I am not certain of anything anymore."

"We follow the Enaisi's Laws as always," Krendhal stated.

"Of course."

"What of Estan and Nelatan provinces?" Zantith asked. "With their lords besieged and accused of treason, who rules now?"

Alcandhor had waited for this question. "Cardhal's cousin Perdhal has taken temporary rule of Nelatan. Estan was stickier—the factions of Batrig's clan cannot agree on a successor. Rangers set up a governing body as an interim."

Paltor's face suffused, and he growled through his teeth, "Rangers control Estan?"

Keeping his countenance all innocence, Alcandhor replied, "Nay, of course not. A council of local authorities, made up of arbiters, wardens, and law-keepers have taken governance."

Paltor grimaced, glaring at the Thane. Alcandhor waited, hoping the lord would overstep, say overmuch, give away something, but Zantith cleared his throat, breaking the tense moment. "I think that we have discussed all that can be discussed for the moment. The Thane is still recovering, and I would not tax his energy. Why do we not adjourn and go to the common room for afternooning? I understand the Copper Kettle is known for its cooking and fine ale, although," he glanced about, his lip curling, "the atmosphere and furnishings are quite untoward."

"I am honored, Lord Zantith, but unfortunately, I still have the day's reports to finish, and Santran ever rails at me for not resting enough." Alcandhor stood. "If I hear word of anything concerning the Laird or news about the siege, I will inform you immediately."

Krendhal rose as well.

"What about you, Lord Krendhal?" Paltor asked. "Will you join us?"

"Thank you, nay. Not today."

"Tell me." Paltor rose, eyeing the First Minister as he lumbered in their direction. "Why is it there is room for you at Ranger Hold?"

Krendhal's eyes crinkled with amusement. "I was kept there when the siege started for my own safety. I have no guards of my hall here to protect me as you brought with you."

"Why do you not send for your guards then? Your hall is not far away. Or you could return home."

"It was lack of foresight. I did not think the siege would last long. Sending for guards seemed unnecessary." He paused. "It later came to me that it might be prudent to keep as many around my hall as is possible at the moment. So I decided that I would be safer where I was, barracked with Rangers."

"How are you getting along with the Thane?" Zantith's eyes flicked back and forth between the two men.

Krendhal looked over at the Thane with a slightly haughty and displeased expression. "We have had the chance to discuss our differences."

"And?"

"We still disagree on most everything."

Everyone in the room smiled or snickered at that expected response.

"You are a stubborn man, Lord Krendhal," Paltor said.

"Indeed. So is the Thane." Krendhal sounded aggrieved.

The Thane and the lords all bowed. A Ranger opened the door. Haladhon left first and signaled it was safe for the Thane and Krendhal.

They both stepped into the sunshine, and the tall noble leaned close. "What say you, Thane?"

"Wait."

They began the walk back toward Ranger Hold, Haladhon and his men still vigilant. Again, people lined the street to see them. Alcandhor noticed a young woman standing among the crowd, holding flowers. She stepped forward and stopped, glancing uncertainly at the Rangers surrounding the Thane. He smiled and gestured for her to come. She curtsied.

"You must be Tarinn."

Her eyes widened. "Yes, sir. These are for you, sir, to not only wish you a full recovery but also bountiful blessings this equinox celebration."

"I thank you, Tarinn. You are both thoughtful and kind. Your flowers have brightened my days."

"I am glad, sir."

Haladhon winked at her, and she blushed. As they walked on, Alcandhor glanced over at his cousin. "I hope you have behaved yourself with that young woman."

"I am always a perfect gentleman, Thane."

Krendhal raised his eyebrows, and the Thane waited in amusement and expectation. Haladhon looked at them both and grinned. "When ordered to be."

Krendhal sniffed with an expression of disbelief.

"I am delighted," the Thane said. "Because the families here—"

"Believe me, Thane, I understand." Haladhon rolled his eyes. "I know when to keep my trous laced."

Alcandhor closed his eyes with a silent groan. He would say thus before a lord? "Subtlety has never been the way with you, has it?"

Haladhon chuckled. "Personality will out, my dear Thane."

"Vagabond," Alcandhor murmured and fell silent, struggling to keep from showing weakness.

"Are you all right, Thane?" Krendhal quietly asked as they left the town.

"Aye, milord." Alcandhor hoped his voice sounded light.

"You held up well."

"'Tis the walking, not the talking, that is taxing, lord. But I thought you did very well at the meeting. I was hard put to keep a straight face at your dissembling."

"Yours as well, Thane. The Rangers are men of action, 'tis said, yet you ever handle yourself well in a war of words."

"These nobles dissemble just as well. I wanted to laugh at Zantith's displays. I do believe we were successful in our effort to give them the impression we knew not where the Laird was."

"Aye, and that was the crucial point."

Alcandhor gave a brief nod. *One of them, at least.*

They walked in silence for a few seconds, then Krendhal asked, "Think you your Rangers will find this Ranger-lass of yours and the Laird to safely escort them in?"

"They will find them. We know not that any traitors might be lying in wait on that peninsula, but in case, I would rather have a guard of Rangers bring in the Laird than one."

"I agree. However Thane, think you it was wise to send Marcalan out on this mission when he is just recovering from being poisoned? Haladhon seems to have a strong constitution, yet he is still weak."

Haladhon looked insulted, but his twinkling eyes gave him away. Alcandhor grinned. "Marcalan seemed well and insisted on going. I think he feels a need to redeem himself for being caught off guard. Besides, he is an Elite and has an uncanny knack in the wild." Alcandhor hesitated, glancing at the lord. "Lord Krendhal, I would not presume to give you orders, but I would advise against going out from the grounds of Ranger

Hold until further notice. I would fear for you."

"I fear I must agree. I do not trust these nobles and their guards."

"Careful, milord. Let not word spread that we have agreed on two things."

Krendhal actually laughed.

~:~

Zantith entered Paltor's bedchamber in the Copper Kettle, his eyes sliding over the plain, commoner décor, pleased to find it no finer than his chamber. He wrinkled his nose. The limp curtains riffled but the slight breeze did not rid the room of a closed, stale air.

Paltor sat on the bed, which sagged beneath his weight.

"So what thought you of the meeting?" Zantith asked.

Paltor snorted. "He postures as much as ever. Did you see him pretend to defer to Krendhal?"

"My heart," Zantith said with a groan. "I asked about the meeting not for you to begin ranting about the Thane again." He pulled a chair from the drab table and rocked it to check its stability. He grimaced as he sat—not even a cushion. "I think they are full worried about that boy. Alcandhor always doted—"

"Aye. Doted. Fawned over him, feigning he cared for him. Another noble swayed to his side when grown."

"If you cannot discuss this situation without turning every facet into a diatribe against the Thane, I will leave and keep my own counsel."

Paltor glowered. "Say on, then."

"Their concern over the boy tells me they are not certain of what to do. Krendhal is the last of his line. No other member of his clan is in a position to become Laird. If only Krendhal could be influenced, we could have autonomous control of our provinces. But he is, unfortunately, too hidebound."

"Then he should die." Paltor shifted his weight, and the bed creaked. "After Alcandhor, of course."

"Conceded." Zantith stood and walked to the window to see laundry flapping on lines below him. Paltor did not have a view of the main street. He turned to look at his partner. "So why are your Rogues not here yet?"

"Think it through. They must be slow and cautious to avoid detection, and with so many Rangers concentrated in this province right now, it may take time. But they already know their orders. Kill the Thane. If they can accomplish murdering Krendhal and the chiefs as well, then it is a boon. But Alcandhor will soon be dead."

Chapter Nineteen

Alcandhor looked up from the reports as Haladhon and Zandhral entered the meeting chamber.

"Stars, Thane," Haladhon said. "We can gain no sign of who might have been behind the ambush."

Alcandhor met Zandhral's gaze. "You have felt nothing?"

"Nay."

"Nor have I." Alcandhor combed his hand through his hair. "And direct examination would reveal nothing. Our men are too well Trained."

"Is there another with Enaisi blood we could use?"

Alcandhor snorted. "Nandhal is also a Child of the Enaisi, but he has never been known to have sight or other abilities beyond making a key glow. He barely senses emotions." He chewed the inside of his cheek, realizing he only had the ill-natured Ranger's word for that. "Or so he says."

Haladhon straightened, frowning. "Stars, 'Candhor. He ever had an attitude. Why did we not think of him?"

"An arrogant personality does not a traitor make. Think of Valdhor. But he does bear closer watching, I think."

"Could one with Enaisi blood go so far astray?" Haladhon asked.

"You forget Uardhel," Zandhral said. "He went Rogue, remember?"

Haladhon nodded with a quiet groan. "Could Nandhal not be sensed, as Alcandhor did to you?"

"Not without his knowledge." Zandhral crossed his arms. "'Tis hard to explain. The probe Alcandhor did to me is one that goes deep."

"It can only be done with mutual cooperation," Alcandhor said. "'Tis a type of bond."

Zandhral chuckled. "I can state with assurance that our Thane is not the traitor."

Haladhon laughed. "'Tis good to know that Alcandhor did not plan the ambush that nearly killed him."

Alcandhor shot a wry look at his grinning cousins.

"So you cannot merely sense Nandhal?" Haladhon asked.

"'Merely?' Nay," Zandhral said. "Our ancestors who had strong Enaisi blood could easily do such things."

"Aye. What we sense is surface emotions," Alcandhor added.

172

"So can you not ask Nandhal to allow this deep probing of his emotions?"

Zandhral's eyes mirrored Alcandhor's own aversion to that suggestion. Alcandhor shook his head. "I would not."

"Nor I." Zandhral said.

"Why?"

"It is mutual. And intensely personal. One could almost say spiritual." Zandhral grinned. "Would you like to share your heart—and soul—with Nandhal?"

Haladhon held up both hands with an exaggerated expression of horror. "Nay."

Alcandhor sniffed in mock vindication and grew sober. "Keep eye on Nandhal. Tell the chiefs all to keep eye. You as well, Zandhral—try to sense him. I know not if he is the one, but 'tis a possibility."

Zandhral bowed and left but Haladhon hesitated. "Did you ever share with your brother or sister thus?"

"Not consciously, but Sarinna and I share a familial bond. In most families it is a natural occurrence as children have more open hearts." Alcandhor averted his gaze, staring at the table and shaking his head. "But Valdhor would not allow closeness. Not even with family."

~:~

Her heart thudding, Tam fell onto her hands and knees and crawled, looking for a crown plant, which, by the Maker's wisdom, always grew near ch'iltar in the wild. If only she had the salve back she had given to the Thane. She had a short time before it would be too late to apply the plant.

"What are you doing?" His voice cracked but, though the fire from ch'iltar thorns burned with vengeance, he did not scream or cry out. He had more self-discipline than Tam thought.

"Sit you down, Your Grace, and wait a moment." *There!* She snatched a large leaf and backed out of the bushes, holding it up. "Chew this and put it on the wound."

"What? Why?" the Laird asked, leaning against a tree.

"It will help. And please, sit down."

Still grimacing with pain and clutching his arm tightly, he sat, staring with doubt at her outstretched hand.

Tam shoved the leaf at him. "We have not much time."

"How can I chew a piece of leaf?"

She rolled her eyes, not caring if he took offense at her disdain and put the leaf in her mouth. After chewing it thoroughly, she took it out and applied it to the wound. "The swelling should stop and before long you will find the pain fading, Your Grace."

He stared at the green mess. "As you say, Ranger."

Tam cut crown leaves to wrap around the arm and sat back, biting her lip. He needed more care and should not move for awhile. That had to take precedence over continuing their journey.

She used a few rocks and large stones to make a ring, started a fire, and set a pot of water to boil. "That poultice will do for now, but I need to make a better one. We will stay here, and for once, I will chance a fire."

Tam boiled leaves, cooled them, and squeezed out the water to make a proper poultice. She applied it to the wound and gazed up into his pale face. Some hot food would help his strength.

The Laird rested, propped against a tree, feebly swatting swamp gnats. Tam gathered herbs and several kinds of edible roots and tubers. Something white caught her eye by the roots of a tree.

"Ah!" She ran over and knelt in the moss by the trunk.

"What is it?" he called,

"Tree brackets!"

"Pardon?"

She removed feathery, shelf-like protrusions from the lower part of the old tree trunk. "You have complained about journey rations." She rose, holding up the white fungus. "This will be a tasty addition to a soup."

The Laird raised an eyebrow. "As you say, Ranger."

"Have you not had them before?"

"Only groundcaps. I care not for them much. You are certain these are not poisonous?"

"My father taught me young which ones should be avoided."

Tam set to work. After filling her little pan with water and setting it on the fire again, she washed and cut the roots, tubers, and brackets.

Tam crushed the fragrant hadra bulblets she found and tossed them, the vegetables, and the herbs into the pan. She added some of the dried meat as well.

Her stomach growled at the wonderful aroma, but she ignored it. She watched and sensed around them, not letting her guard down, as she kept an eye on the roots, testing them periodically with her knife. Finally, they were done.

Using her cloak to protect her from the hot handle, she put the pan on small stones near the Laird. She took out her little travel mugs and dipped broth out with one and speared a large piece of root on her knife. She bowed, offering them to him. "Eat, Your Grace."

"Thank you, Tam."

She used the other mug to dip out some broth. Oh, stars, after all this time of limiting her portion of the journey rations, hot soup seemed the most delicious thing she had ever eaten!

Tam eyed him as the evening wore on. His color did not return; his eyes seemed dark against his pale skin. Tam reviewed herbs in her mind but could think of nothing more to be done for ch'iltar poison.

And of all places to have to camp—although she had skirted the marshy lands, the stench of the swamp and the biting insects would not make rest easy.

The Laird kept rubbing his arm although he said he did not feel weak and that the pain had subsided. Tam changed the poultice every few hours all night.

He blinked and woke just before dawn as she examined the wound.

"I did not mean to wake you, Your Grace."

"I thank you, Tam," he murmured as she wrapped the arm again. "How came you by such knowledge?"

"The Maker gives us what we need." Tam shrugged. "If we learn it."

"Aye, so it says in the Laws of the Maker, but I thought that was just a reference to food."

"For our healing, also."

"No wonder 'tis said that Rangers have the wisdom of the Enaisi."

"I cannot speak to that. I have only the knowledge set down by those before me. However I do not claim to have wisdom—from the Enaisi or anyone else."

Tam sat back and gazed closely at the Laird's face in the dawn light. Still pale. She had already touched his arm many times, but dared not do more without his permission. She held her hand over his. "May I?"

He frowned and nodded. She picked up his hand and said, "Squeeze. Tightly." His feeble attempt made her stomach churn. If some of the poison had weakened his arm, it might slowly be traveling through his body. *Oh, Maker, what can I do?*

Chapter Twenty

Tam stared at the Laird's hand. "Harder!"

"I do not wish to hurt you."

"You must. Please, Your Grace!" She stared into his blue eyes, willing him, urging him, wishing she dared tell him the danger he could be in from this poison. How afraid she was that she had not drawn it out in time.

His grip tightened. Her fingers bunched and her knuckles felt crushed together. She squeezed back—a contest. His lips parted with effort, and Tam gritted her teeth against the pain. At the same moment they released, and he shook his hand, grinning. "By the Bells, girl, you are strong!"

Tam sat back, relief flooding over her. "Let us eat, and continue our journey." She eyed his still pale face. *Albeit, a little more slowly.*

~:~

A shiver prickled up Tam's spine late in the afternoon and strong emotions flooded over her. Stifling her dread of having to kill again, she halted the Laird, and they hid behind some trees. Soon they could see three men in the distance, heading in their direction.

The Laird gasped, ready to jump out when he saw the Ranger garb, but Tam ordered they backtrack a little. Drawing her sword, she advanced with caution, staying hidden behind thick bramble bushes, the Laird keeping back a dozen paces or more at her orders.

One of the men put his arms out, stopping his companions, and stepped forward, grinning, staring straight at Tam, despite her hiding in the shadows of the wood.

"What is this? Trying to slyly come upon Rangers? What impudence!" His voice had a saucy lilt to it. He walked toward her so she came out to meet him, her sword at ready. He had thick, dark hair hanging loose, laughing blue eyes, and as many Rangers did, wore a short chin beard and moustache. Merriment bubbled in him and something else she could not describe except that it warmed her, curling her stomach, and drew her to him in a strange, unsettling way. She hardened herself, blocking. She must not assume she could trust him, even if she was drawn to him, wanted to like him.

"A lass dressed as Ranger! How comely! Come now, need you brandish a weapon on your own kin?"

She returned his gaze with a cool stare. "You are dressed in Ranger colors, but that need not mean you are Rangers."

He laughed, eyeing her with a nod. "You are right, young Tam. Haladhon was not lacking in his assessment of you."

She did not move, and his smile faded a little but his eyes remained merry. "What need I do to prove to you I am a Ranger?" he asked in jaunty challenge.

"You could contest her, Marcalan," one of the other men said with a chuckle.

Was this truly Marcalan? The one her uncle had spoken of who loved jesting even more than Haladhon?

Marcalan put a hand to his heart in mockery. "Oh, Tandhral, you cannot be serious! After what she did to Loch'alan?" He looked her over slowly and began to smile. "Then again, it might be worth something to try." He winked at her.

Tandhral snickered. "Might be worth a broken bone."

"What think you, Tam?" Marcalan asked with a hopeful, teasing grin. "A match?"

"If I had time for such foolishness I would fain give you a thrashing." *Or try.* If she could only best a cockerel Ranger by chance, how would she fare against a seasoned one?

"Oh, come, Marcalan," the third man said. "She has not the humor you do and does not know us. Be you serious for a moment?"

Marcalan sighed with a wry face and sobered. "What would you consider proof? Haladhon sent us to meet you." The roguish grin that so easily came to his face was already spreading again. "We know all about you, cousin Tam," he said with a dramatic flourish, emphasizing especially the *cousin Tam*, saying it slowly with a slightly mocking tone. "We know about Loch'alan contesting you when you were Presented as Ranger-Trained, and that you soundly defeated him. What more proof do you wish?"

He cocked his head, his eyebrows raised as he gave her a playful, daring smile.

Soundly defeated? Oh, stars! She looked him in the eye, hesitating not only because of her doubts of him, but of herself.

Should that contest be enough proof? Only those in Zaidhron would know about it. "What was the blow that ended the contest?"

Marcalan chuckled. "You spun and caught him in the temple with the back of your fist. And I wish I had been there to see it!"

She slowly lowered her sword, hoping she was not being too easily fooled. She sensed nothing to warrant not believing him, and besides, she did so want to like this mischievous scoundrel. He seemed even more a rascal than Haladhon, as her uncle had said.

"Bring our Laird out of hiding, cousin, so we can begin the journey home."

Her guard rose a little at the mention of the Laird, but who but a Ranger would know she had been sent to find him?

Still wary, she stepped back a few paces, looking at Marcalan, at the one he called Tandhral, who was taller and dark, and finally at the third one, with round eyes and light, thin hair. She returned to where the Laird waited.

"Trust you they are Rangers?" he asked.

"I believe they are. One matches name and description given by my uncle, and they know things that happened in Zaidhron."

"Then let us go down and join them."

Tam's heart pounded with trepidation, her sword still in her hand. She half expected one to be taking aim with arrows to shoot the Laird, or to find all three with their swords drawn. But they remained as she had left them.

They bowed to the Laird.

"Your Grace. Haladhon sent us to accompany you and our cousin," the rascal said. "I am Marcalan, this is Tandhral and Capalan."

"You say Haladhon sent you. What of the Thane?"

"He is being driven mad by the attentions of our dear Sherel. She hovers over him solicitously to the point he has convinced the healer to allow him walks to get away from her." He gave a melodramatic wave of his hand. "Never fear! Our dear Lord Krendhal or Haladhon accompany him at least, and there are always Rangers close to hand." Marcalan grinned. "As much as he wants to take back full leadership, I think he is enjoying watching Haladhon have to deal with all those weighty matters," he said the last two words slowly with mocking emphasis, his one hand to his head dramatizing a headache.

Tam bit back a smile.

"Ah! I caught you! You can smile, after all. Come, admit it." She averted her face, and Marcalan squatted almost to the ground to try to peek at her. Despite herself, his antics made her smile wider.

"Ha! A beautiful smile it is, too. You really should try it more often."

Capalan snorted. "With you as jester, there is no doubt we all have plenty to smile about. May we begin our journey now?"

Tam found it quite different traveling with Rangers. Or was it just that Marcalan always found something outrageous to say or point out? The Laird laughed with them, which eased her heart. She had felt him holding his grief too heavily.

Her thoughts went to her own father, and her heart dragged. She would never see him again. Over and over, she saw the arrow hit his chest and the look on his face. She still could not believe he was dead.

Marcalan moved close to her. She avoided his gaze. She did not want him to try to make her laugh.

"What is it, cousin?" he whispered.

She hesitated, afraid he would mock her grief or her father's death. "Where have they laid my father?"

"He is at rest," Marcalan said, his voice quiet and respectful. "In a place of honor."

Her chin quivered, tears smarting her eyes. Marcalan walked next to her in silence, his sympathy as a warm cloak about her.

~:~

"Blessed camp!" Marcalan fell to the ground with a dramatic sigh and lay as though dead. Tam stared at him in disbelief; he could not be that tired.

Capalan started digging a firepit while Tandhral gathered wood.

"Come, you lazy vagabond." Tandhral nudged Marcalan with his foot. "Get up and help."

"You are going to risk a fire?" Tam glanced doubtfully at Capalan.

He shrugged. "There are four of us."

The Laird sat near Capalan, watching him dig the firepit. Though she knew he would be safe, Tam hesitated before going off to gather kindling.

As Tam stacked wood in a pile, the Laird smiled at her. "Hot food, Tam!"

"I am sorry, Your Grace, that we had to subsist on journey rations as we did."

"Do not apologize. You cared for me very well. And gave me some valuable lessons, too."

"What lessons can our cousin teach, Your Grace?" asked Marcalan.

"She taught me just how rugged you Rangers are, and that there is much more to your life than what we of other clans see of you."

"Indeed? Such as?"

Marcalan eyed Tam, and she raised an eyebrow at him, her lips pressed together. Why did he always stare at her?

"Such as the grief you endure. The dangers you put yourselves in willingly for the sake of the rest of us."

Tandhral gave Tam a searching look. She forced herself to meet his gaze, but stars, she did not like such scrutiny.

"Curious that such lessons would come from such a young Ranger." His tone did not seem mocking.

"Our dear Thane did tell on you, cousin," Marcalan said. "I understand you have a blend of tea that is marvelous."

"He likes it, aye."

"Have you any with you?"

"I do."

"Wonderful."

The Rangers had brought ample supplies with them, and she had helped Tandhral dig wild bata roots, which they set to roast at the edge of the fire. They ate the sweet roots as a dessert after finishing their meal. Tam allowed herself to eat all she wanted for the first time since leaving Ranger Hold, and it felt so good to be rid of that gnawing in her stomach.

If only I could bathe. Even in long journeys with her father, she had never gone so long without bathing or having clean clothes. Her hair felt greasy, and her head itched. She was surprised Marcalan would sit next to her.

They requested Tam brew tea. The men sat back sipping it, exclaiming it was very good, but she just hugged her knees and stared at the fire. Thoughts of her father haunted her and the killing she had seen and done as well. Why did she feel it all so heavily now? It must be because she no longer had to keep her every thought concentrated on protecting the Laird, being only one of four Rangers guarding him.

"You and Tam astonish me, Your Grace," Capalan said. "We did not expect to find you so close to home."

"Indeed," Tandhral said. "We expected it would be another day or two at least before we might find you."

"She urged me on," the Laird said.

Marcalan threw a taunting look at Tam. "Is she merciless then?"

"Nay, but I was determined a 'mere lass' was not going to do anything I could not do."

The Rangers burst out laughing.

"You found she is no 'mere lass,' I take it?" Marcalan asked, still chuckling.

"Indeed."

"How many days have you been journeying, Your Grace?" Capalan asked.

"Six days," the Laird said.

Capalan frowned. "But that is only average journeying time. We are but four days out from the hold. It has been but fourteen days since Tam was sent out and it is ten days there and ten back." He stared at Tam, incredulous. "Have you wings, girl? Did you journey there in only eight days?"

"I travel fast," she murmured, picking at the torn knees of her trous. Could they not just leave her to her thoughts? Why must they talk so much?

The Laird began laughing, and when they all looked at him, he threw up his hands. "The jest is on me! I thought I was being so pushed to go on, and was handling it so well, and I find it is what is considered 'average'? You Rangers are cut from a stout cloth!"

"Even our women," Tandhral said, "as Loch'alan found out."

Marcalan giggled. "Would that I could have been there to see my younger brother thrashed."

Tam's head snapped up, and she stared at Marcalan. Loch'alan was his brother? Aye, their looks were somewhat similar, although Marcalan had darker hair and firmer features.

The Laird looked from Tam to Marcalan. "What—? What is this you say?"

"When Tam was Presented, Loch'alan contested her," Tandhral said.

"And she bested him, I take it?"

"Knocked him topside down." Tandhral laughed. "Haladhon said 'twas a sight to behold."

"I would still fain have a match," Marcalan said. After a silence he asked, "Tam?"

She looked up from the fire with a frown. They all thought she bested Loch'alan. She should jump up and tell them the truth. But...she could not; her uncle wanted her accepted. She had to maintain the illusion he created.

"I would fain have a match with you," he repeated with a defiant grin. "Think you that you can thrash me as you did my brother?"

Her doubts of herself warred with her irritation with Marcalan. The latter won out. "That would depend on whether or not your fighting abilities are as honed as your wit."

Marcalan and Tandhral both roared with laughter, falling back on the ground. Capalan chuckled while the Laird grinned.

Tam blinked. What did she say that was so humorous?

Marcalan recovered enough to sit up, gasping to get his breath. He put both hands over his heart. "I am in love!"

"Watch yourself, Marcalan. This one would not just slap your face but could break your neck." Tandhral's eyes twinkled.

Marcalan threw his hands out in a gesture of innocence. "You are the second person to caution me of that."

"Perhaps we need to caution Tam," Tandhral said.

Marcalan turned to Tam, all innocence. "My dear cousin, think you that you need to be cautioned against me?"

Feeling untutored and foolish, she hesitated before saying, "I do not understand your jesting."

"You do not—?" Marcalan stopped, staring at her. "Are you in earnest?"

"I think she is very earnest, Marcalan." Capalan peered across the fire at her. "Tam, do not be afraid to tell this brash Ranger to leave off if his teasing bothers you."

She glanced at Capalan to acknowledge what he said before returning her gaze to the fire again. Somehow their chatter grated on her as she battled against her doubts. Why had they brought up the match with Loch'alan? And why, why did she feel the weight of her father's death so strongly now?

The Laird cleared his throat. "Tell me of the siege. How does it go?"

"I do not think it will be long until they surrender, Your Grace," Capalan said. "They must not have many provisions. Starved bellies will out, I deem."

Tam had not thought before...Poll—and Linna—trapped, perhaps starving. Stars.

"Strange, is it not?" Tandhral murmured. "Such a fortress, built for defense yet unable to sustain against a siege?"

"There were no preparations." Capalan shrugged. "A siege against Laird Hall is unprecedented, so why would great stores be necessary?"

"The traitors never considered that they might have to endure a siege inside the hall," Marcalan said. "'Twas no thought of their plans going awry."

The Laird gave a grim smile. "I believe they underestimated the Rangers."

"Especially our cousin Tam." Marcalan nudged her shoulder with his own.

"Aye, you did seem to be the hinge that swung events in our favor, Tam," Capalan said.

Tam fidgeted, her gloomy thoughts switching from Poll to her own failures. "I was just doing what my Thane ordered."

Capalan gawked at her. "What he ordered? Taking on Batrig and his traitors?"

Tam glared at him. "I was sent to spy and got caught. I only fought them because I had no choice. I did nothing to be proud of."

"Nothing to be proud of?" Tandhral snorted in amusement. "You killed Batrig and probably most of the other leaders as well!"

"Only Batrig—I only killed Batrig." She glared around at them. "Is killing something to be proud of?"

"It is something that we do when we must, Tam," Tandhral said.

Tam looked away. 'Must' or not, she hated spilling blood. And she despised that they seemed proud of her for doing thus.

The Laird frowned, gazing at her. "I think Tam gave me an incomplete account of what happened in Laird Hall. Tam, tell me what you did to Lord Batrig and the others?"

"I simply did what I had to. Lord Krendhal and I fought the lords and escaped the hall."

"Marcalan tells us that you killed Batrig. That you sword-fought him wielding but a hearth poker," Capalan said.

"Aye, I did fight him with the poker. It was the only weapon to hand. I did what I had to do. Must I discuss it again?" Her voice cracked and she dropped her head in shame.

"I think," Marcalan said softly, "that we are forgetting what it was like when we were young. When the first realization of what we sometimes must do did hit us in the face and left us staring into the dark. Forgive us, Tam."

The others muttered apologies. Tam's gaze went back to the fire. She must not cry.

The silence seemed to grow loud, but no one broke it for some time. Finally, Capalan began humming a tune. Tandhral joined him and soon all three Rangers began singing:

When e'er the soft twilight doth fall
And we dwell not in cot or hall
Then rest we 'neath the Bells on high
Which overspread our starry sky.

Our hearts do long for hearth and home,
But destined e'er are we to roam,
So guide us Bells, O most belov'd,
'Til we return to those we love.

The song trailed off. Tandhral grabbed a stick and poked the fire, sparks showering upward.

The Laird rubbed his face with a rueful smile. "You Rangers have razors with you, do you not?"

Marcalan grinned back at him. "Your Grace, your beard is so fine

183

and blond, why bother?"

Tam looked over in shock. "Marcalan, that is no way to talk to the Laird!"

The Laird chuckled. "I am not offended, Tam. 'Tis true. But still, Ranger," he scratched his chin, "it itches."

"You may borrow mine, Your Grace," Tandhral said, inclining his head.

"My thanks."

Marcalan stretched. "Who will take first watch?"

"I will," Tam said.

"You have been out half a lunation without help. Let us take watch tonight and you get a good night's rest," Marcalan said.

"Nay. I will do my portion of the watch."

Marcalan looked over at the other two Rangers. "Will you two tell her to be reasonable?"

"Marcalan." Tandhral lifted his hand. "You never tell a woman to be reasonable. Have you not learned that by now?"

"And if you think we are foolish enough to want her angry with us, you are quite mad," Capalan said.

"I have been told I am mad before," Marcalan said. "But I do not think I am foolish enough to actively invite pain."

"What a lie, Marcalan! You boldly acknowledge every prank you pull and take whatever punishment is dealt you if your victim does not appreciate your sense of humor," Capalan said.

"I am proud of my accomplishments. What is wrong with that? If I do not admit the prank is mine I am a coward."

"What a thing to be proud of," mumbled Capalan.

"What sort of pranks have you pulled, Marcalan?" asked the Laird.

"Beware, Your Grace," Tandhral said. "You will probably be a victim before we reach home."

Tam looked up, again shocked. "You would not truly pull a prank on the Laird?"

"Why should he not?" asked the Laird.

"But you are the Laird!"

"Indeed," he said with a chuckle, and Tam frowned, puzzled.

Tandhral leaned forward with a grin. "My Laird, I believe you have just invited yourself to be a victim."

Chapter Twenty-one

The innocent look on Marcalan's face set Tandhral and Capalan both groaning, and the Laird smiled.

Why did they think it funny to play tricks on someone? Even the Laird appeared not to care if he were victim. But it did not seem funny. Tam set more wood on the fire and poked at the smoking pieces with a stick until flames licked around their sides.

The Laird held his hands toward the fire in the silence.

Marcalan stretched. "We never settled the watch."

Tam looked up to see her prankster cousin watching her. "I said I will take first watch."

"You look so tired, Tam," Marcalan said. "Why not let me take first watch? I am not a bit sleepy. I would only be awake with you anyway."

"Oh, please, Tam! If he is going to stay up anyway let him have first watch. Otherwise he will never shut up, and none of us will get any sleep," Capalan said.

Marcalan chuckled, and Tam sighed. "All right."

"Take fourth watch, Tam," Marcalan said. "That way you would get some uninterrupted sleep, and I am sure you would not mind that."

She shrugged, and Marcalan grinned. "Good! All settled then. Capalan, you take second watch, and Tandhral, third."

They nodded assent. Tam wrapped herself in her cloak and stretched out. Sleep came quickly.

~:~

Tam felt someone shake her shoulder. She blinked, trying to dispel the haunting blackness from her dream out of her mind. She sat up, saw the sky a light grey, and looked around. The others were all eating. *What?*

"Good morning, Tam," Marcalan said, smiling.

She scrambled up, the fog of sleep dissipating into irritation that she had not done her watch. Not been treated as a Ranger. "You did not wake me for my watch, Tandhral?"

"I ordered him not to, Tam." Marcalan sipped his tea. "You needed the rest."

Tam's aggravation rose to ire. "I will decide what I need! It was not fair to not wake me!"

"I stood your watch for you." Marcalan shrugged. "I did not mind it. Who was it not fair to, then?"

"Me! I pull my share. I am a Ranger. I will not have you treat me as a child or a lass!"

"Ranger or not, Tam, you are still both," Marcalan said.

Tam stomped her foot. "I am not. I had to prove that to your brother, and I will fain prove it to you as well!"

"A match?" Marcalan put his mug down and stood, an eager look on his face.

Capalan groaned. "We have no time for this."

"Come, Tam!" Marcalan said, grinning. "Match!"

She inhaled and straightened, her eyes narrowing. "Why? You keep asking me for a match. And now you have tried to provoke me to fight you. Why?"

Marcalan smiled, all innocence. "Why not?"

"You are angry because I bested your brother in that contest, is that it?"

Marcalan laughed. "If he was fool enough to contest you, he deserved what he got."

"Yet you provoke me. Why?"

"I got you, Tam. And you cared not for my prank. If you wish to try to thrash me because of it, here I am."

She stared at his grinning face. His face bespoke the eagerness radiating from him. Why did he want a match so badly? But...not giving him what he wanted might be the best way to get even. "It would not be fair to you. You had to stand two watches last night. I would not take advantage of a tired Ranger."

Marcalan stood with his mouth open, and Tandhral hooted as she strode away for privacy. Admiration from Marcalan drifted after her, confusing her. What an enigma the man was!

~:~

The sun had not risen high enough from the grey mists to dispel the chill of the morning when Tam's spine tingled. She stopped. Marcalan turned to look at her, a questioning frown on his face, and she said, "Someone approaches."

Marcalan stared at her as he listened, then grinned. "Aye. Long-eared are you?" He gave the signal for them to hide.

Tam checked that the Laird had safely hidden behind a large clump

186

of bushes before taking off her bow and crouching in preparation.

Could these men possibly not be in league with the traitors? Might she not have to fight and kill again? She closed her eyes for a moment in dread, but the sounds of men to their left brought her mind back.

Peeking through leaves, Tam spied a dozen men traveling northeast. They would cross the Rangers' course slightly to their west. Tam nocked an arrow, licking her lips.

It seemed the men would pass by the Rangers without noticing them, but one strayed from his companions. He skirted a bush near Tandhral. With a jump he shouted, "Rangers!" while drawing his sword but stopped, gasping, as an arrow struck his chest.

The rest shouted, drawing either sword or bow. In quick succession four of them fell. Before she could nock another arrow, a heavily muscled man fell upon her with a sword. She dropped the bow and retreated a few paces, drawing her blade.

He swung downward, and she sidestepped. A second man closed on her left. She froze in panic. Backstepping without thinking, she evaded his cross-strike. Deflecting the first's next attack, she aimed a kick at the second's knee. He stumbled, crying out. She stepped left, outside a diagonal strike by the first man, and swung in to his midsection.

He jumped back. Her blade barely missed his stomach but caught his forearm in a neat shallow slice along the length of it. He growled and came in with a down-strike, but Tam hopped to the right, dropping to fool-guard stance, sword pointing down.

The second man came in with a cross-strike. Tam ducked. She stepped back, but the men flanked her. She froze—just as she had in Laird Hall. *Father! How do I fight two men?*

They brought their swords down at the same time. Tam dove and rolled. She rose and turned to face them as they ran forward, again coming on each side of her.

A fighting cry rent the air. The man to her left arched, eyes bulging—struck from behind. Tam spun to the other and circled her sword in, nearly making two of him.

Her throat clenched shut in horror as she whirled back to the first one. Marcalan stood over the body, sword red. Another man ran up behind her cousin, weapon high. Tam yelled, "Marcalan!"

He spun and parried with the flat of his blade. The new fighter danced back from Marcalan, brandishing his sword with a cocky grin. Why did her stomach knot in worry for Marcalan? He was a Ranger and well able to defend himself.

Marcalan did not give chase but stood ready, that maddening smirk on his face. He stepped back and dropped his sword point to the ground, in an almost-lazy fool-guard. His expression and stance bespoke boredom, his eyebrows lifting in what Tam recognized already as innocence masking mischief. His attacker jumped forward, a surge of anger radiating from him, blade swinging downward. Sidestepping, Marcalan's sword flashed up in a deep, fatal stroke. The traitor gave a strangled cry as he fell face-first into the grass.

Tam let out her breath in a quiet *whoosh* of relief that Marcalan was unhurt. As much as he irritated her, why did she care so much?

"Stars," the Laird said as he came up next to her, his blue eyes round. "Four Rangers besting a dozen men."

Tandhral shook his head. "We had Tam's forewarning and took some down with arrows, or it may not have gone so easily."

"Come," Marcalan said, glancing about. "We need to keep moving."

A dark cloud loomed over Tam's mind and heart all day. But why? Was it her dismay that she panicked for a moment during the fight when facing two opponents or that she had had to kill again? Should she even be a Ranger? These men did not seem bothered by killing. She could not stop thinking about it.

Marcalan asked once what dispirited her, but she shook her head and did not answer. After that, he left her alone.

~:~

"I will take first watch tonight," Tam said that night as they ate, glaring at Marcalan across the fire.

He grinned. "I think I will not argue with you."

The men jested and talked, but she remained quiet. Why had she become so morose? Perhaps the lack of restful sleep on top of the grief and memories she kept trying to avoid. The dreams of a blackness that she had endured since a child grew worse lately.

The Rangers finally all went to sleep but Tam.

She woke Tandhral for his watch, wrapped herself in her cloak, and stretched out. Amidst her dreams, the blackness called to her once more. It pulled at her, and she began to fall toward it. She struggled, fighting against it—and sat up, gasping for air, her heart pounding, hair plastered to her face with sweat.

"Stars, Tam, are you all right?"

Still trying to catch her breath, she could only manage a nod to Marcalan, who had watch.

"What is it?" Capalan asked, sitting up.

She gulped for breath, unable to answer. She had never had to fight the blackness with that much strength before.

"Tam?" Marcalan scrambled over to her, concern written on his face.

She took a few more deep breaths, her heart rate slowing somewhat. "I am fine," she mumbled.

He took her by the shoulders, staring at her with a worried expression. "What is wrong?"

"A–a dream. I think. I am sorry I disturbed you both."

Capalan shook his head. "Are you certain you are all right?"

She nodded, her eyes averted in abashment. Marcalan hesitated before letting go of her shoulders and going back to where he had been sitting.

"Quite solicitous of that Ranger, are we?" Tam heard Capalan ask, as she rolled herself in her cloak.

"Shut up," Marcalan shot back.

~:~

Tam felt a touch on her shoulder and opened her eyes to see that dawn had come. She sat up, looking over at Marcalan who had awakened her.

He chuckled, shaking his head. "How can you be so awake and alert at a moment's notice? You never moan or complain about being tired. How do you do it?"

She shrugged. "Is it not thus for all of you? It is how I was Trained. If I complained or did not get up at once when called, my father would thrash me."

Why did the grave look Marcalan gave her unsettle her so? She rose, avoiding his eyes, and walked off for privacy. Laughter erupted just as she returned to camp. The Laird yawned, looking at them all, puzzled. Bright blue and purple tunista flowers had been braided into his long, blond hair.

Tam gasped, aghast. "Marcalan, how dare you!" She strode over to him with narrowed eyes.

"What is wrong?" the Laird asked.

"Oh, Your Grace," Tandhral said, breathless with laughter. "He got you!"

Capalan wagged his head, trying to keep a straight face.

Tam grabbed Marcalan by his jerkin and hauled him around, trying to get him to stop laughing. "It is not funny!"

"What did he do?" The Laird looked down at his clothing. He burst into laughter, lifting a flower-bedecked braid.

Tam let go of Marcalan, confused. It seemed an affront to jest so with the Laird, but he did not mind?

"How did you do it and not wake me, Ranger?" the Laird asked.

"I have many years of experience in the stealthy ways of being a Ranger, my Laird," Marcalan said with a formal bow.

"You have many years of experience in stealthily executing pranks, you mean," Tandhral said, still chortling.

"Is there a difference?" Marcalan asked with a grin.

"In your case, nay."

Tam knelt to check her pack, frowning with bewilderment.

"What is wrong, Tam?" the Laird asked.

Tam did not lift her head to answer. "I just do not understand."

"Why? It was merely a prank. What harm is done?"

"It is an affront to the dignity of your office."

The Laird let out a slow breath. "'Tis hard for you to understand, but I have lived my whole life having to be dignified. I have never been allowed to just be me." He slapped a hand to his chest. "For this scoundrel of a Ranger," he waved a hand toward Marcalan, who had the most infuriating, cocky grin, "to treat me as a person means much."

"But the Laird is—"

"Still just a person, Tam, who would fain have friends rather than dignity. The latter is cold and lonely."

Marcalan lifted a hand. "Hear! Hear!"

The Laird pointed at him, the smile twitching on his lips belying his menacing expression. "However, since you braided them in, you can get them out. And you had best not pull out my hair along with them."

"So be it," Marcalan said with a bow.

~:~

Looking up from the cauldron of soup, Linna saw one of the guards, Tavnol, standing in the door, his eyes darting about. A strong, handsome young fellow, he had been in service at the hall for only a few lunations but had made friends with many guards and servants. He hung about her kitchens pestering her until she would chase him out with a spoon or knife. Linna would never admit she enjoyed his light-hearted teasing, sorely wanted and sadly lacking now, in such dire circumstances.

She put her hands on her hips. "What do you want?"

He walked close. "You have been here a long time."

Linna eyed him. "Yes. So?"

"I..." He licked his lips. "Is it wrong to be a coward?"

Linna frowned. "A coward?"

He nodded and whispered, "I don't agree with Vitran, but am too afraid to say so. Look at all the guards in the cells. But I'm afraid of what will happen to us if the siege holds. Vitran won't give in."

Linna hesitated before giving a slight nod. She did not want to jeopardize herself in case Vitran was testing her. Bad enough he had guards watching her cook the food and carry all items from stores to keep her honest in how much she used.

Tavnol chewed his lip for a moment. "Linna..." He swallowed, his fear obvious. "Please...if you have any notion that Vitran is wrong, I...think we could do something to end this."

Tavnol jumped as a voice bellowed from the door.

"What's going on in here?"

Linna snatched the spoon from the soup she was stirring and waved it with menacing intent in Tavnol's white face. "You quit asking for favors! There's not enough food for all of us, and I'm not handing out one spare morsel! Now get out!"

Tavnol spun and ran for the door. The guard at the door, Karnin, grabbed Tavnol's doublet. "I think we should give you a taste of the whip or stocks, you sneaking cur!"

Linna's stomach churned. What had she done? She must do something to help him. "I have a better idea." She walked slowly toward them, her mind in a furor to think of something.

"Like what?"

Linna crossed her arms as a thought came to her. "Give him duty here."

"What?" Karnin asked as he and Tavnol both stared at her.

"He will smell the food but get no more than anyone else. That should be punishment for his grumbling stomach."

Karnin grinned. "Yes, it's hard being assigned here with our stomachs all scraping against our backbones. I think I'll talk to Vitran about a change in duty roster. But meantime, you come with me."

The stricken expression on Tavnol's face pierced Linna's heart. He was just a scared young man, trying to survive. Why had he come to Linna? Why had he trusted her? She could easily have just turned him over as traitor. Should she still?

Linna was torn. She had not liked the Laird. He had been a cold man, and it did not bother her much he was dead. Word was the Atheling was dead too. She did feel sorry about that. He had seemed a nice-spoken boy despite being ignored by his father and spoiled by his rank.

But she did not take at all to these lords, Jandhal and Talrig. She had seen their arrogance and cruelty. And they said the Rangers were the traitors and the murderers. Something deep inside her told her this was not true. Not Rangers

Look at the ones in the drum tower—they never shot anyone but the guards. And she herself had seen the notice, delivered by an arrow, stating that anyone who wished to leave the hall could do so. One by one, unharmed.

Vitran had raved when she asked about the paper, begging him to let her girls leave at least. He claimed the Rangers lied and would kill anyone who ventured near the gates or outside the walls. To protect everyone—he said—he refused to let anyone try.

Linna knew nothing of politics. She was just a cook trapped in a siege. She looked at her scullions, huddled by the fire, hungry and frightened, thinner by the day.

She thought back to Tavnol's fearful face and his words. *Vitran won't give in.* She knew it was true.

~:~

In a jovial mood, Marcalan entertained them that evening with stories about mishaps and pranks. He sat across the fire from Tam, his comic expressions and lilting voice amusing her and lifting her dark mood a little. His pranks seemed only intended to hurt pride, not cause injury, and she saw how some might be humorous.

Marcalan's eyes lit up as he began to tell of an occasion from years ago. He and Haladhon had gone to collect buckets of mud by the lake behind Zaidhron in preparation for a prank, but the mire proved deeper and more slippery than they realized.

"We both landed flat on our backs in the mud." He threw out his arms in demonstration. "Alcandhor was prowling about that day—remember how he used to patrol and roam before he became Thane?" he asked Capalan and Tandhral. They nodded.

"Anyway, he saw us wallowing in it, and you should have heard him laugh, the scoundrel! He did not even try to come and give a hand."

"You would have pulled him in, I am sure."

"Would I do something like that, Capalan?"

"Only if you were still breathing."

They all laughed and even Tam smiled.

"He called us mudworms for a long time after." Marcalan shook his head. "I never did think we would get all the mud out of everything. We washed our clothes over and over and still the water would be dirty. My boots were a mess." He giggled, winking. "Not to mention where else I found it."

Tandhral leaned forward, his eyes twinkling. "And where else did you find it?"

Marcalan's eyebrows raised in innocence. "In my ears."

Tandhral groaned and he tossed a clod of dirt at Marcalan, who snickered. Tam stared at the fire as they laughed. She understood not their humor. Would she ever feel as if she belonged?

"Did you ever pull the prank with the mud?" the Laird asked.

"Not at the time, Your Grace, but aye, we did."

"Oh? What was it and who was it on?"

"Thane Saldhor."

Tam lifted her head in shock.

The Laird sat up. "Oh, stars! What did you do to him?"

Marcalan's eyes lit up. "It was one of my finest achievements, if I do say so myself. Not that as a prank it was all that spectacular or brilliant, but the execution had to be done so carefully."

"To avoid being executed?" asked Tandhral.

Marcalan laughed, waving a hand. "You see, Haladhon and I had a long, wide, shallow tray and we filled it with the mud and carried it to the Thane's chamber and hid it under the bed." He cocked his head to the side, too innocent. "Good thing for the cooler weather and long coverlets. Anyway, that night after the Thane and Taniss had both gone to bed, I crept into his room—"

"Great Bells, he did not wake?" Capalan asked.

"That is where it was an achievement. We made sure the hinges were well oiled to avoid squeaks, and the sconces in the hallway put out, then I crept in ever so slowly and inched along the floor. It seemed like it took hours to get under the bed. Then I had to push the tray out next to where he had his boots, and it was an effort, let me tell you. It dare not make even a scraping sound so I had to move it by the slightest fractions."

He acted out being under the bed and pushing out the tray with such comical, animated expressions that Tam found herself smiling.

"I finally got it in place, after a few frights when he or Taniss would roll over or something. Then I had to slowly back out and get out of the chamber without him or Taniss waking as well."

"What happened the next morning?" asked the Laird.

"Oh, 'twas glorious! He stepped smack into the mud with both feet. When we were hauled in, the floor was splattered with it, and the coverlet, and we were told later that he had Taniss scrub his feet before even getting out of bed. Can you just imagine?" Marcalan stuck his feet in the air in demonstration.

Tandhral roared, and the Laird and staid Capalan both laughed too. Even Tam giggled at Marcalan's comic display.

"What happened to the two of you?" the Laird asked when his

laughter subsided.

Marcalan shrugged, still grinning. "You mean *after* scrubbing his bedchamber and bedcovers? I was a scullion for five days. Apron and all. Haladhon was given kitchen duty as well, even though he was Confirmed."

That set them into laughter again.

"Why do you do such things when you know it will cause you trouble?" Capalan asked.

Marcalan grinned, shrugging. "Life would be awfully dull without a little fun."

"I would think you could find better ways of amusing yourself than pranks."

Tam thought so too, but said nothing.

Chapter Twenty-two

Dusk fell to night as they approached Ranger Hold. They slogged through rain the day before and had a wet, sleepless night. A bright sun made the day unseasonably warm, and Tam, still sticky with sweat, detested how filthy and rank she was.

Rangers saw them in the woods north of Lairdton and word of their arrival went ahead of them. Haladhon came striding toward them before they even got to the gate, followed by Rangers carrying torches. He bowed to the Laird with a jaunty grin. "Good to see you safe and well, my Laird."

"And you, Haladhon."

Haladhon and Marcalan clasped shoulders, eyeing each other with wide smiles for a long moment. Then her tall cousin looked down at Tam. "You have done very well." He hung an arm around her shoulders and pulled her tight, not seeming to care how dirty she was. "Let us go inside. You will all want—"

"A bath!" Marcalan cried.

"You need one," Tandhral said with mock terseness.

"Oh, how the guilty talk!"

The men laughed and jested as they walked toward the gate. Krendhal met them inside the walls, greeted the Laird with a bow, and walked next to him back to the hold, talking softly.

As they entered the torch-lit bailey, Tam inhaled with astonishment at the number of Rangers crowded around. They all bowed as the Laird passed.

Tam saw Alcandhor standing in the doorway, smiling, and her heart seemed to stop. He held out his right arm to her. Tam did not care who saw, or what anyone thought of her acting like a lass instead of a Ranger. She broke from Haladhon's arm and strode across the bailey to her uncle.

He pulled her into a tight hug, and she clung to him, careful of the sling on his left arm. She had no father, but she still had him! As the others got to the door, she felt him incline his head in a slight bow. Remembering how filthy she was, she tried to push away but he gave a slight squeeze instead of relinquishing his hold.

"Your Grace," Alcandhor said. "Sherel has prepared baths for all of you. Food will be waiting when you are through."

They all passed in, and he looked down at her, smiling, his eyes as kind as ever. He kissed her forehead and murmured, "I am glad you are back safe, Tam."

"I am glad you are healing, Uncle."

"I am improving. You have done well. I am proud of you." He gave her a quick, tight hug. "Now, go, wash up."

Sherel met her inside, led her back to the side corridor, and opened a door. It would be so good to wash. Tam entered the room and stopped to see one huge chamber with recessed tubs as at Zaidhron. Only a curtain separated the tub at her end from the rest. She heard splashing and Marcalan moaning in delight.

"Oh, blessed, blessed bath!" he cried.

"We've only the one room," Sherel said. "Rather than have anyone wait, we curtained off this last tub. I'm staying to guarantee the curtain is respected. They will use the other door that goes out to the main hall." Sherel sat down in a chair by the wall, staring at her. "Go on, girl."

Tam hesitated, feeling her face grow warm. Sherel frowned and, pursing her lips and crossing her arms, turned her head away.

Tam dropped her pack, took off her weapons, and undressed with uncertain glances at Sherel and at the curtain. She eased into the hot water, glad to find it deep enough that she could slouch down and be modestly covered.

From the other side of the curtain, she could hear Marcalan give a dramatic sigh. "I am ecstatic there are enough tubs for us all to bathe at once. I could not have borne waiting a turn, and I know it would have gone by rank."

"Are you implying anything, Marcalan?" the Laird asked.

One of the men hooted. Probably Tandhral.

"No offense, Your Grace," Marcalan said. "But whether by Rank or by rank, you would have had a turn at a bath before me."

The Laird laughed.

Tam doused her head and began soaping her hair.

"One of you vagabonds scrub my back," Marcalan said.

"I am too busy scrubbing my own," Tandhral said.

"Oh, come! I will make it worth your while."

"What have you got that would interest me?"

"I will think of something."

"I am certain you will. Just remember you still owe me two desserts for that match."

"On the contrary, you said we would make it two out of three."

"You said that, I never agreed to it. Two desserts."

"Two out of three. Come, Tandhral, be a sport."

"Two desserts."

Tam ducked under the water to rinse her hair and came up blinking water out of her eyes. She glanced again at Sherel, but the woman continued to stare at the curtain. Tam had no choice; she turned away and concentrated on getting clean. The bantering on the other side of the curtain continued and soon erupted into a splashing war between Marcalan and Tandhral. Capalan howled for them to stop. Tam listened in disbelief as she scrubbed.

After a while Sherel sighed. In a loud, firm voice she called, "You men are going to clean up your mess in there."

Silence.

"Sherel, will you come scrub my back?" Marcalan asked in a plaintive whine.

"I'll scrub your hide raw, you worthless scamp."

"Is that a promise, my dear Sherel?"

"It's a threat."

The men chuckled.

"You are worse than little boys," Sherel said. "I would think you would behave at least to show respect for the Laird."

"I have journeyed with them four days, Sherel," the Laird said. "I know what to expect of them."

"Oh, mercy, Your Grace!"

Laughter burst forth followed by sounds of someone getting out of a tub.

"Through already, Capalan?" Marcalan asked.

"The quicker the bath, the quicker to the food," Capalan said.

"Why did I not think of that?"

"Too much effort, Marcalan," Tandhral said. "Your brain is atrophied from lack of use."

The splashing began again. Did their silliness ever stop? She finished washing, but did not want to get out of the tub in front of Sherel. As she wondered how to delay, the curtain swayed and a shadow moved next to it. Tam froze.

"Keep away from the curtain," Sherel ordered.

"I am just getting out of the tub," Marcalan said.

"Your foolishness does not extend to that curtain, Marcalan."

"My apologies, Sherel. And Tam."

Tam's face grew warm. They had to know she was there, but hearing it acknowledged aloud made it a reality.

"I really was just getting out of the tub," Marcalan said, his voice contrite.

Soon she heard the sounds of the others getting out of their tubs too.

How long could she stall? Sherel met her eyes, and her lips thinned. With almost a sulky thump, the woman turned the chair more toward the wall.

Tam hurried out, grabbing the drying cloth on the shelf behind the tub. Before even getting dressed, she put the key back around her neck. She must remember to give that to the Thane the first moment she saw him alone.

She donned the clothes set on the bench and used the drying cloth on her still dripping hair again before combing it out. Sherel turned and watched with a disapproving expression as Tam slung and strapped her weapons back on.

Tam gestured to her dirty clothes piled on the floor. "Where may I wash them?"

"Later. The Thane awaits you at table."

Tam followed Sherel to the dining hall. The Laird sat at the head of a table, in borrowed Ranger trous and shirt. Capalan and Tandhral on a bench to his right, but with room for two between them and the Laird.

He stood as she entered, and he gestured to his right. She took her place, with a longing gaze at the food heaped in bowls and on platters.

"Must we wait for Marcalan?" Capalan asked Sherel.

"No need," Marcalan said from the door. He sat down between Tam and Capalan, tossing a grin at Tam. His long hair still dripped.

Tam enjoyed the food. And the quiet; the men did little talking as they ate. Tam refused ale and just had water.

Sherel soon came in with Tam's pack. "The Thane insists on some of your tea."

Tam wrinkled her nose as she dug inside the filthy pack. She would have to clean it tomorrow and her jerkin and boots as well. She pulled out the Laird's white surcoat and handed it to the Laird, who inclined his head with a smile. She rummaged further, found the pouch, and gave it to Sherel.

Before long she could smell the tea. Sherel brought in a large pot and mugs on a tray. The Thane followed behind her with Haladhon.

The Rangers all rose to move down, but Alcandhor waved at them to stay seated. "Worry not. This is informal. I just wished to sit and enjoy some tea."

"You do not require a report, Thane?" the Laird asked after swallowing a mouthful of food.

"Nay, my Laird, you are exhausted. After the meal, you shall all rest." He walked around the table to the far bench.

"Is that prudent?"

"If it were Rangers on a mission to uncover information, I would require an immediate report, Your Grace. The object of this mission, however, was to rescue you. That was accomplished." The Thane smiled at Tam. "After you have rested, we can discuss matters."

The Laird inclined his head. "Where is Lord Krendhal?"

"He is checking that your sleeping arrangements are suitable. Actually, I fear he thinks they are not. He has endured sleeping barracked with Rangers since the siege began and although he has borne it well, he is not elated about you doing the same."

"Thane, I have been sleeping on the hard, cold ground for many nights. Barracking on a cot with Rangers will seem like luxury."

"That should reassure him," Marcalan muttered.

Sherel poured tea for the Thane and left. Alcandhor took a sip and sighed, closing his eyes. "You have a special assignment, Tam. One of grave importance." Her uncle leaned forward, his eyes earnest. "It is your first duty after you rest."

Tam straightened. So soon? "Aye, sir?"

Alcandhor tapped the pot of tea. "You are to write this recipe down and give it to Sherel."

Haladhon rolled his eyes. "Aye, please do, Tam. Before our Thane drives Sherel mad. He has had her trying to come up with this blend almost since he awoke from his injuries."

"I can easily do it now," she said.

Alcandhor shook his head, setting down his mug. "You need sleep first."

"Do not be in too much of a hurry, Tam," Marcalan said, leaning close and speaking in the slow, lilting, melodramatic voice he used when being a rascal. "I want to see who drives whom mad first."

Tam frowned at him, not understanding.

"Our dear Sherel has been driving our Thane mad trying to mother him, and he has been driving her mad for your tea. An interesting experiment." He gave an innocent blink to the Thane. "Who will win, do you think?"

"You need a spanking, Marcalan," Sherel's voice said from behind him in the doorway.

"Aye, 'mother,'" Marcalan replied over his shoulder, winking at Tam. She found herself smiling at the twinkle in his blue eyes.

Haladhon chuckled, and the Thane shook his head.

The Laird stood and they all followed suit.

"I think I will follow the Thane's wise advice and retire. You Rangers may be hardened to journeying, but I am not. Night's rest, gentlemen and lady."

He smiled at Tam and walked out.

"Night's rest, Your Grace," they called after him.

Sherel walked toward the table, hands on hips. "When you are finished, you Rangers will clean the mess you made in the bathing room."

The men murmured assent. Tam stood, but Alcandhor shook his head. "Not Tam."

"But the bathing room—"

"Not this time. She has been out on a hard mission and looks ready to fall over. Show her to her chamber."

Aye, Tam felt exhausted, so much so that her eyes burned, however she did not want to be treated differently than the rest of the Rangers. "But, Rangers take care of their own chores."

"Not always." Alcandhor pointed a finger at her, stopping her before she could complain. "Especially following an arduous mission. Now, go. It is an order from your Thane."

Tam hesitated, but her uncle's stern face defied opposition. She followed Sherel down the hallway toward the front of the hold, seething quietly. Rangers did not sleep when there was still work to be done, no matter how tired.

"I had your bow and quiver set in here already," Sherel said, opening a door.

Tam frowned. "This is the Thane's chamber."

"It is yours now."

"It is his. I cannot sleep in there. Where will he sleep?"

"We have no other place for a woman to sleep. We moved him across the hallway into the meeting chamber."

"I will not."

Sherel crossed her arms. "I will not argue with you, girl. This is where you are sleeping."

Tam stiffened and set her jaw. "I will not."

Sherel stepped back, eyeing Tam with a frown, and strode down the hallway. Tam stood, unmoving. She heard Sherel's voice as she returned. "...sounds just like her father."

Tam squared her shoulders as the Thane and Haladhon came out of the dining hall with Sherel.

"Tam—" her uncle began.

"I will not sleep in your bedchamber. It is for the Thane."

"It is for the steward of the hold, actually," Haladhon interjected.

Tam glared at her cousin. "Uncle is injured. He needs a good bed. I can sleep anywhere."

Alcandhor sighed. "Come with me, Tam." He opened the door into the meeting chamber. Several candles on the table gave warm light, and an open book lay face down on it. He closed the door, and his arm swept the room. "This has already been turned into a bedchamber for me. I can read and study when I am restless and yet not exert myself. Look around. 'Tis very comfortable."

"But I cannot take your room!"

He sat on the bed set at one end of the chamber in front of a bookcase. "Tam, I am not the one to try to explain things to you which should have been explained long ago. Believe me when I say that there are certain proprieties, which must be followed. Can you understand?"

"Nay."

He sighed. "How uncomfortable would it be to not have privacy for sleeping?"

"But I slept among Rangers while we journeyed. Why can I not sleep barracked with Rangers now?"

"That is the wild, where it is unavoidable. This is a hold. Women do not sleep in the same chambers as men."

"Where does Sherel sleep? Why can I not sleep with her?"

"Sherel normally does not sleep here. She has a cottage at the edge of town. We are keeping her here for her safety at the moment and have set a corner of the back kitchen with a cot and curtain. And before you ask, there is no room for you there. She and I have discussed this matter and have agreed you need the privacy of your own bedchamber."

"I can sleep anywhere. In a corner. Fully dressed."

He stood, his eyes dark. "Not in my hold, you will not!" As he strode over to her, he reminded her of her father. "You will sleep where your Thane tells you to sleep. Do you understand?"

She met his eyes with defiance, her jaw muscles working as she wondered if she could press him to give in. A glimmer of her father sparked in his eyes, and she thought about this man's stubbornness and how even her father had yielded to him when he had not wanted to. She swallowed hard, not wanting to give in, to lose. "Aye, sir."

He relaxed. Her pride not satisfied, she took a step back toward the door. "With your permission, Thane?"

He nodded, looking tired, and regret filled her. "I am sorry, Uncle."

He smiled. "You are overtired. Go rest."

Tam bit her lip as she opened the door, wishing she dared hug him but—would he rebuff her because of her attitude? Ignoring Haladhon and Sherel with a lift of her chin, she crossed the hallway and entered the Thane's bedchamber.

Embers glowed in the small fireplace, and a candle sat on the small table, now bare of his personal effects. Her anger rose again. She slammed into the chair to take off her boots. It was not right. She hurled her right boot across the floor. *Thud!* Her father had never treated her as a lass. He treated her as a Ranger. Left boot. *Thud!* And she was a Ranger. Why did they now treat her as a lass?

She unbelted her sword and her leg-knife and threw them onto the pegs. Taking off her father's knife, she stared at it, blinking back tears as his death flashed before her yet again. No. She would not cry. She unlaced the jerkin and snatched it off. What a weak fool! Rangers do not cry.

She started to unlace the top of her shirt when her fingers touched the key. She gasped. Without thinking, she jerked the door open and rushed across the hallway, knocking on her uncle's door, the key clasped tightly in her other fist through the shirt. Haladhon opened it. Her uncle sat on the bed. "Aye, Tam?"

"I–I need to, to..." What should she say? He said to keep the key hidden. Did Haladhon know about it? As a chief, he should, but..."May I see you alone for a moment, Uncle?"

Alcandhor gestured for her to enter.

"I have bid you night's rest, Thane. I bid it to you as well, Tam." Haladhon bowed and closed the door behind him.

"What is it, Tam?" her uncle asked.

She took the key from around her neck and held it out, its glow illuminating the dim chamber. Alcandhor struggled to his feet, holding his side and shouting, "Haladhon!" And, after a moment, louder, "Haladhon!"

Light spilled in as the door opened.

"What is it?"

"Get in here and close that door."

The latch clicked and Haladhon gasped. Tam looked from one to the other in confusion.

"Tam, hold the key in your hand, please," the Thane said.

She did so and the key glowed even brighter.

"By all the Bells in the heavens and the two moons," Haladhon whispered with reverence.

"What does it mean, Uncle? What is wrong?"

Alcandhor sighed with a relieved smile, sitting back down on his bed. "Nothing is wrong. Nothing." A burden seemed lifted from him. Haladhon clasped his cousin's shoulder and sank down next to him.

"I do not understand," Tam said.

"Give me the key, Tam." The Thane held out his hand. She did so and the light diminished.

"It is barely glowing at all!"

"Back away, Tam," Haladhon whispered.

She did as he said.

"Now blow out the candles."

Again, she obeyed. Hardly any light came from the key.

"It was the same with Valdhor, was it not?" Haladhon asked.

"Aye. It glowed for him as for me, very dimly. You hold the key, Haladhon."

"No light at all, Thane," Haladhon said, his tone blithesome. "Further proof I should never become Thane."

"Hush. Now, Tam, slowly walk toward us."

As Tam came to stand before Haladhon, the key began to glow slightly.

"By all the Bells and stars," Haladhon murmured.

"Now hold the key again, Tam," the Thane said.

She took it and the glow became bright—brighter than many candles. Tam trembled. *What caused this?*

"Have you ever seen that?"

"I have only read about it. How long has it been, Haladhon?"

"You are more well read than I am, Thane. You know not?"

"Please, Uncle, tell me what is happening."

"'Tis too long to explain in one night," the Thane said. "When this crisis is over and we are back at Zaidhron, we must begin your studies of the Enaisi and eventually go to the Enaisi's Portal Complex nearby."

"But what does this mean?"

"It means, my dear cousin,"—Haladhon leaned forward, elbows on his knees, his eyes shining—"that you have the blood of the Enaisi in you."

Chapter Twenty-three

Fear gripped Tam's insides as she stared, frozen, at her uncle and cousin, clearly seen by the light of the key.

"I...what?" she whispered.

"Valdhor taught her little of the Enaisi, I think, Haladhon," Alcandhor said. "Tam, do not be alarmed. 'Tis a rare thing these last years to find a Child of the Enaisi—someone who can cause a key to glow."

"But, how does this happen?"

"Oh, stars, Tam, it is too complicated to explain. Keys, like this one, were created by the Enaisi—they called them bio-crystals. They react to the bio-electromagnetic field of an Enaisi, or of one who has certain of their genes. Know you how we came here?"

"Only that the Enaisi brought us here."

"Aye. They saved us when our world was dying. Some of them stayed here and lived among us. And married into our clan. 'Tis what makes Ch'shalna clan unique, separate from all other Teldheri clans."

Tam swayed, light-headed. Haladhon pulled out a chair and pushed her into it, telling her to breathe deeply. She could not. Her breath came in quick puffs. Haladhon took her by the shoulders and stared into her eyes. "Breathe slowly, Tam. Control."

Her father's word. Control. She closed her eyes and fought to master her body with slow, deep breaths until the light-headedness left.

"We need to tell the Laird," Haladhon said.

"I do not wish to overwhelm Tam. This is too much shock for her already."

"He needs to know."

Tam opened her eyes. "I am fine now, Uncle."

Alcandhor chewed the inside of his cheek. "Go. Wake him."

Haladhon left, and Tam just sat, looking at the strange, alien thing shining in her hand. After what seemed an eternity she whispered, "What does it mean, Uncle? Why is this important?"

"'Tis a symbol and a sign, Tam. For those reasons alone it is important. I have hope it may mean more, but I will not speculate yet."

Tam remained quiet, thinking of all her uncle had told her. "Uncle, what are genes?"

Alcandhor rubbed his chin beard. "'Tis what causes traits to be passed from parent to child, such as eye or hair color, for instance." He let out his breath slowly as he took her hand. "You need to learn so much. Will you study with me, and come with me to the Enaisi's structures?"

Her heart thudded with dread, but she ached at his pleading expression—she did so want to please him. "Aye, Uncle. I will."

Haladhon and the Laird entered the chamber.

"What is so important, Thane? Haladhon would not give explanation." The Laird laughed as he continued, "Bells, that key gives off a light in her hand! I was astonished when she first showed it to me."

Tam lowered her head, self-conscious and half afraid to move.

"You...you knew she could make it glow thus?" Alcandhor asked.

"Of course. You gave it to her to convince me, did you not?"

"It is the Elders' key. Few know of it, but I had shown it to you. If she had it, you should know she was truly sent by me."

"I thought you had given it to her so I would know by its glow that she was Ranger clan."

Alcandhor chuckled. "Nay, but regardless of the misunderstanding, the key did its work: you are here safe." Her uncle sighed. "Now, I must decide what is best to do with regard to her abilities. I think we have an augury of hope."

"I think I must agree, Thane," the Laird murmured. "I had not thought of it that way. When was the last such Ranger able to do thus?"

"It has been many years since any Ranger has had more than the feeble glow such I have. I know not the last who could have lit a room with the crystal."

Silence reigned as they all continued to gaze at the key. Tam wished she could fidget, or rise and leave, but what could she do with all of them staring at that thing in her hand?

"I have never kissed a Ranger before," the Laird said. "But for such a sign, I will this one time." He bent and touched his lips to Tam's cheek. "Thank you. I can sleep now, I think, with a breath of hope. And perhaps it is a sign that, in my time, I will have the wisdom and courage to do those things that need to be done." He strode to the door. "Night's rest," he said to them before he went out.

"Well, not that I think I can sleep now, but I had best try," Alcandhor said. "Tomorrow is a long day."

"And if you do not rest, Sherel will—"

The Thane groaned. "Do not remind me."

Haladhon chuckled.

"Go to bed, Tam," her uncle said. "You need rest."

She held out the key to him. He hesitated, then whispered, "Keep it."

Haladhon stiffened. "Thane..."

"Let it stay with her for now. It is safe."

"You are aware of the implications of her keeping it?"

"This key is still mine. If I choose to allow the Second at Table to hold it safe for me..." He shrugged, allowing the sentence to trail off.

"So be it, Thane," Haladhon said as he bowed, his voice not unhappy.

Alcandhor turned to her. "Put it away."

Tam put the chain back around her neck and tucked the crystal inside her shirt as she rose.

"Now get some sleep, niece."

"Aye, sir," she murmured, rising, grasping the key through the material.

"Night's rest, Tam." Haladhon opened the door for her.

"Night's rest." She stood in the hallway for a moment, after the door closed, still stunned. She did not understand any of it. But it seemed to make them—what? Happy? Nay. Pleased. Aye, pleased. And relieved. But why? She would study with her uncle so that she could understand what it all meant.

"Tam?"

She shook out of her reverie to see Marcalan walking toward her, a peculiar glint in his blue eyes.

"Is everything all right?"

She did not know, but thought it was. "I suppose so. Aye," she said with a slight smile. "I think everything is all right."

Marcalan returned her smile with a puzzled frown. "It must be, if you are smiling, cousin. Night's rest."

"Night's rest," she said yet again and entered her chamber.

Tam sat on the cot, trembling, and pulled out the key. She stared at the crystal, knowing it glowed because of her. She felt strange, almost alien to herself.

Enaisi blood. The Enaisi had seemed a legend, a myth from centuries ago. But now they seemed less nebulous, yet more fearsome. What abilities did those beings possess? Yet, something of them lived in her.

Tam stared at the key for a long time. Despite her exhaustion, sleep did not come easily.

~:~

Alcandhor sat at the table in his study, a steaming cup of Tam's tea next to him. The morning sun warmed his back while he read a book, waiting for his two mischievous cousins to answer his summons. When they entered, he closed the book and set it aside, eyeing them. "I wanted to talk to the both of you."

Marcalan blinked. "But we have not done anything yet."

Haladhon nudged his arm with a warning frown. Alcandhor closed his eyes, shaking his head with a woeful expression, but inwardly, he smiled.

He gestured to the two chairs on his side of the table. "What think you both of your cousin?" he asked as they sat.

Hands clasped between his legs, Marcalan's eyebrows raised in innocent puzzlement. "Which one?"

Haladhon leaned forward, elbow on his knee, favoring Marcalan with a look of frank disbelief. The Thane glared until Marcalan raised his hands in defeat. "All right! She is adorable."

Haladhon stared in amazement. "Adorable?"

"Aye. Adorable. Beautiful. Sweet. Innocent. Pick a word."

"You traveled with her for four days, saw her fight, and you say she is sweet, adorable, and innocent?"

"All right. Sweet, innocent, and deadly. Better?"

Haladhon opened his mouth to retort, but Alcandhor cleared his throat. "May I continue?"

Marcalan inclined his head in compliance, while Haladhon swept his arm out in exaggerated permission.

Alcandhor exhaled in annoyance. "I would like to remind you both that Tam was raised alone by Valdhor."

"And what is that supposed to signify, Thane?" Marcalan asked.

Alcandhor's lips tightened.

Haladhon turned to his cousin. "You should not need be told about Valdhor, Marcalan. Do you not remember the beating he gave you when you were barely off the teat? Imagine what it was like being raised by him!"

Alcandhor held up his hand to regain their attention. "As Haladhon said, Valdhor was a hard taskmaster. Tam has never known anything but his harsh criticism. He did not love her and was brutal and cruel to her. He even told her she had no family."

Marcalan turned pale and dropped his head.

"I am telling you both that she is not to be teased or tormented by either of you. And no pranks." He relaxed, smiling at Marcalan. "I understand you obeyed my order last night in the bath and made no mention of her presence. I want to thank you for that."

"I would never wish to hurt her," Marcalan said with fervent tone and expression.

"I hope you mean it. As her nearest kin, she is now my responsibility, and I am as her father. You would both do well to remember that."

In the silence, Marcalan's eyes began to sparkle. "So are you saying we cannot even try to get her to laugh? I was going to make that my lifelong project. To try to get a true laugh out of her."

Alcandhor rolled his eyes. "I have saved you the trouble, my good Marcalan. I have already achieved that."

"What?"

Haladhon perked up. "You did? How?"

Alcandhor leaned back, feigning a rueful sigh. "All it took was my complete embarrassment and humiliation."

"You have to tell us," Haladhon said.

The Thane raised his good arm in capitulation. "She and I were traveling here, and we stopped so she could change into clothes such as a mountain girl would wear. She, uh, she did not know what some of the garments were."

Marcalan's head tipped in curiosity. "What do you mean?"

"Valdhor raised her as a lad, not a lass. She had only ever wore a lad's clothing and—"

"Wait a moment!" Haladhon lifted both hands. "Do you mean to tell me she has no idea what an underbodice is?"

"I am certain if you had been there, you would have had no trouble explaining it," Alcandhor said dryly. "But I have not your, hmm, open attitude, shall we say?"

Marcalan sat forward, his eyes twinkling. "How did you explain it to her?"

Alcandhor shrugged, holding his one good hand up as if showing a garment in front of his chest. "I held it up in front of me to try to show her where it goes..."

Haladhon threw his head back laughing while Marcalan doubled over.

"Strange," Alcandhor said, affecting an injured air. "That was her reaction too..."

Marcalan fell out of his chair, laughing uncontrollably. "Our very virtuous and missish cousin," he finally managed between howls of laughter.

Alcandhor watched him with amusement for a moment before prodding him with his foot. "Get up, scoundrel."

"So," Haladhon asked, wiping his eyes. "Did she figure out how to put the garment on from your help?"

Alcandhor frowned, puzzled. "Nay."

He joined them as they both burst out laughing again. When they quieted, he asked, "Need I tell you not to embarrass her by mentioning this?"

"I would fain embarrass you with it, Thane, but not her," Marcalan said.

"I thank you."

"So was this what you wanted to talk to us about?" Haladhon drew his sleeve across his eyes again.

"Aye. And I hope I was in time, or have you already some prank set in motion?"

"Not for Tam," Marcalan said.

Alcandhor rolled his eyes, groaning. "Think you that this is the time for such things?"

"Aye, 'tis perfect, Thane," Marcalan said. "One needs some levity for a balance in such grim times. 'Tis a burden, but I try to bear up under it."

"Your noble motives and sacrifice are most laudable, cousin," Alcandhor said, striving to keep a straight face.

"Why, thank you, Thane."

"And your dissembling is remarkable." Haladhon poked his cousin in the ribs.

They exchanged grins, and Alcandhor said, "Oh, get out, you vagabonds. Get reports on the siege. Find out if the Laird and Tam are available to discuss their journey with me. Lamadhel has not reported yet this morning, see if you can find him. And get Sherel to bring more tea."

The two men left. Marcalan stuck his head back in the door. "Lamadhel is waiting to see you. And the healer is here as well."

Alcandhor made a face. "Send him in."

"Which one?"

"Santran, you scoundrel!"

Alcandhor took a nervous sip of tea. Were his injuries permanent? Santran had been closed-mouthed so far. Would he give any answers today? Alcandhor must know, and soon, because disability could cost him Thaneship, even being a Ranger.

Chapter Twenty-four

Alcandhor endured the probing and flexing of his shoulder and arm. Santran squinted up at him. "You are not overusing it, are you?"

"With Sherel and all my Rangers to babble on me? I do the exercises you tell me, but I do not overdo it."

Santran snorted. "If you are like most of your Rangers you do not know what 'overdo' means."

"I want full use of my arm and full strength back, Santran. How long will that take?"

"The damage was bad, as I've told you, Thane. The best that happened was that there was no infection. But it will take awhile yet for you to heal. Do you feel pain in your side or in your back? Do you still tire easily?"

"I would be fine if it were not for the shoulder."

"So you say. But that wasn't your only injury. You were battered badly. Your kidneys sustained injury, as did several other organs. You may not feel pain from them, but they are not fully healed. Not to mention your cracked ribs. You are most fortunate you did not puncture a lung."

Alcandhor suppressed a sigh. "You tell me this every day."

"I will tell you until I make you understand!" Santran paused, continuing in a more gentle voice. "Now go lie down, and let me see what I can tell."

With reluctance, Alcandhor obeyed. He felt torn between allowing the healer to know where it hurt when he palpated his abdomen and obeying his training, which told him to show no sign of pain. Santran continued to ask questions—the same ones he always asked: any cramping, passing blood, black stools, chest pain? Alcandhor shook his head, muttering, "Nay" over and over.

Santran finally seemed satisfied and straightened. "How go your walks?"

"Fine."

"How far?"

"The same as yesterday," Alcandhor said in a weary voice. "Through the town and back."

Santran cleared his throat. "Sit up and let me see you show me the exercises again."

Alcandhor sighed but obeyed.

"You still have trouble getting full rotation, do you? Now squeeze my hand. Harder. How much feeling do you have in your hand and arm now?"

"A little more, I think. How long until it is healed?"

"Hmm. Hard to say. Keep exercising and I'll see you tomorrow, Thane. Do not overdo it."

Alcandhor stood after the healer left and paced back and forth. Hang the man! He asked questions and carried on about how fortunate Alcandhor was to be alive and how careful he should be, but never, never one word about how he was healing! He kicked a chair.

"Careful, my Thane," Lamadhel said, from the doorway. "Some might accuse you of cruelty if they saw you attack an innocent piece of furniture."

"I am so frustrated, Lamadhel! The healer will not—"

Sherel bustled in with a pot of tea and cups on a tray. "I thought I would bring a pot since you will likely have several meetings this morning. What did Santran say?"

"That I am healing well, Sherel. My thanks for the tea."

She raised an eyebrow at him, but he turned to Lamadhel, saying, "Any news from the perimeter?"

She took the hint, as he knew she would, and he waited for the inevitable door slam to punctuate her displeasure at her dismissal. He and Lamadhel exchanged grimaces, and Alcandhor shrugged, resigned. "Any news?"

"No changes. How are you? What did the healer really say?"

"It is what he will not say. He avoids any answer on my arm being fully healed. What happens if—" He dropped his head, unable to say it.

Lamadhel grasped Alcandhor by the nape of the neck and gently shook him. Lamadhel had not done that to him in years. Not since he was a youth.

"You will heal. Some things heal quickly, others do not. It has not even been one lunation. We nearly lost you, boy."

"Then I did nearly die?"

"Aye. Has not Santran told you?"

"He says nothing."

"For two days that healer stayed at your side constantly, fearing he would not be able to keep you alive. You had severe internal injuries. The shoulder and regaining use of your arm might seem most important to you, but to Santran, it is secondary."

Alcandhor dropped into a chair. Secondary? A permanent injury could cost him rank and status as a Ranger! How was that of secondary importance?

"Although it is a horrible thing, the siege, for you, is a blessing," Lamadhel said.

"Why say you that?"

"You had prepared in case of siege well in advance. Your men already knew what they would need to do. When the time came, Iladhon simply carried out the plans you had organized. All you need do during the entire siege is sit right where you are."

"At least that is one thing I am allowed to do."

Lamadhel smiled at him. Alcandhor found himself returning it. He poured himself a cup of tea from the pot Sherel had left. "Would you like to try some tea?"

"Is this the famous tea of Tam's you have raved about?"

"Aye."

"Then I must try it."

Lamadhel made no fuss that Alcandhor wished to do something as simple as pour a cup of tea with his good arm. Sherel's nagging at every turn tired him.

"Tam brought the young Laird back safely, I hear."

"Aye."

"Amazing girl."

"More amazing than you know," Alcandhor murmured.

"Oh?"

"Lamadhel..." He leaned forward, his excitement growing as he thought of what he saw last night. "Uncle, she can make a key glow."

"So do you, Thane."

"Nay—"

"You do. I have seen it."

"It but faintly glows for me. It is brighter than candles in her hand."

"Great stars, I have never seen that. I wondered if it were but an exaggeration."

"Nay, 'tis no exaggeration. It is the most awe-inspiring thing I think I have ever seen."

"I would like to see it."

"You will."

Both men sipped the pleasant brew. Alcandhor's thoughts went to Tam's birth record. Dare he say anything to his uncle? He hesitated and inhaled deeply. "Uncle. What about her birth record? Or rather, lack of birth record?"

Lamadhel frowned, staring into the cup. "Leave that water undisturbed, Alcandhor."

"Someone will ask. And Valdhor is not alive to give an accounting of that breach of the law."

Lamadhel's head snapped up. "Leave it be. Your father knew what he was doing. All will turn out well."

"How can you know that?"

"Because your father and I discussed it in great detail. He had sight, and that is given weight as if law. You followed his orders."

"But—"

"Do what you need to do, Thane. I know what you intend."

Alcandhor's brows rose. "Do you indeed?"

"Aye." Lamadhel smiled. "I wonder at your wisdom, or lack of it, in this, but you will follow this path to its end, so my opinion will avail nothing. Perhaps your father saw this too. I know not." He exhaled slowly. "But I will back you, despite my reluctance."

With a hard stare, Alcandhor asked, "You truly think my father's sight will cover all?"

"I know it." His uncle straightened and took another sip of the tea, his eyes boring into Alcandhor's over the rim of the cup. "This is a good blend, Thane. Is she a good camp cook, too?"

His uncle would discuss no more. The dread stalking Alcandhor eased. Perhaps over time the remains of it, buried deep in the recesses of his heart, would fade away altogether. Perhaps.

He breathed out slowly and changed to his uncle's new topic. "Aye, better than most Rangers. 'Twas wasted on Valdhor, though. He cared nothing—" his throat closed up and he swallowed with a frown, recalling Valdhor's spirit passing beyond. "I cannot believe he is dead."

"He died well," Lamadhel said softly. "He died fighting, which is what he wanted."

The Thane nodded, remembering the look of joy on Valdhor's face any time he fought in a battle. Bittersweet memories that made Alcandhor miss him more. "I know. Of all the losses, I feel his most keenly. Yet, I had seen him not in years. Never got along with him..."

"He was your brother. 'Tis a close bond. I would be more concerned if you did not feel the loss deeply."

"Sometimes I wonder why we do it, Lamadhel. Our world seems not to care if we guard and protect it anymore. Why do we continue on, fighting and dying? Our blood spills and for what?"

His uncle did not reply, and he stared at his cup, regretting his outburst. "Will we survive this? Or will the traitors win out? I cannot see. I just cannot see."

"You see more clearly than you realize. I could not have planned all of this as you have. You have a gift. You just need to have a little more faith in yourself."

"You sound like Sarinna."

"Your sister is wise. Perhaps you should listen to her."

"I see my own faults, Uncle, as no one else can. My weaknesses."

"Yet you do not see your strengths. Balance, Canny," Lamadhel said, using Alcandhor's childhood nickname. "You must have balance."

He nodded to assuage his uncle. To avoid further lecture he brought the conversation back to the problems they faced. "Have any more supplies arrived?"

"Three more carts came yesterday, and more are due today. We will have plenty of food for those in the hall when the siege ends."

"If it does not end soon..."

"It will. Have you talked with the Laird yet?"

"Nay. That is next."

Lamadhel stood. "We will talk more later. When more carts come in I will send word."

Alcandhor rubbed his forehead. "You are keeping inventory of everything?"

"Andhrel is doing that."

"Perfect. Thank you, Lamadhel."

~:~

Linna glanced at Tavnol as he helped the other guard carry in supplies for the meal. She looked away, disgusted that her own fears kept her from doing something. Tavnol admitted he was afraid, but still wanted to try.

As the scullions began to chop the tubers and roots, her gaze swept over the guards. "Ease your stomachs' grumbling a little. Guard from outside the door so you don't smell the food so much. You see the food we have, and you have the keys to my storerooms." The guards hesitated and Linna pointed to Tavnol. "Except him. He can keep watch, since this duty was given to him as a punishment."

The guards filed out, and Tavnol stood near the door with a confused expression.

"Get closer so you can keep guard on us," Linna said. "We might sneak a bit of raw root, you know."

Tavnol approached, and Linna picked up a knife, grabbing some tubers. As she chopped she glanced up at him, wondering if he would dare say something.

He kept silent, but when she dumped the tubers in a pot he stepped in and lifted it for her. She followed him as he put it on a hook and swung it into the hearth, over the fire.

"Does it have enough water?" he asked.

Linna started to nod but saw his eyes pleading. "I think we could stand to have a few more pots of water handy," she said. "Come with me, you can carry a couple of pots back too."

They went into the back kitchen and began filling the pots with water.

In a low voice, Tavnol said, "You could slip an herb into the soup one night—panvarin, perhaps. Put them all to sleep. I could let the Rangers in the drum tower know and the siege would be over."

Linna stared at him. "How do I manage to get enough herb to do it? You guards watch me every time I enter the storerooms."

"If you keep Karnin distracted, I can grab the herb."

Linna's heart thudded. "You are mad," she hissed. "What if we are caught?"

"We're all soon dead anyway. I have never been brave, but my stomach tells me we must do something soon. And even a fool can see we are like mining powder waiting to be lit. Things are getting worse, and tempers and fears are rising. Please, Linna?"

A shiver swept over Linna and she rubbed her arms, unable to meet Tavnol's eyes. "Let me think about it."

~:~

Tam swirled her spoon in her porridge, dawdling over breakfast in the dining hall. What should she do when she finished eating? She had no assigned duty since completing the one allotted last night. She had written out the recipe before going to sleep. The activity took her mind off that glowing key for a little while. She had also cleaned her pack, jerkin, boots, and weapons.

The Laird came in while she sipped a second cup of tea, and she rose to bow. His eyes were still puffy from sleep, but his pale blond hair fell in neat braids at the temples.

"I am glad you are still here," he said, sitting down across from her with a smile.

"Your Grace." Sherel hurried over and curtsied. "What may I serve you for breakfast?"

"What did Tam have?"

"Ch'azsa. It's not what we usually serve, but there wasn't enough leftover bread for sop. But I'd be glad to bring you bread and wine—or ale if you prefer, or meats."

The Laird shook his head. "I shall have ch'azsa. And some tea, as well."

Sherel scurried to bring him his food.

He grinned at Tam. "No one else was offered a choice for breakfast, were they?"

"Not to my knowledge."

He chuckled.

"What is amusing, Your Grace?"

"Observing how people treat me. And 'tis not amusing at all, really. It is rather sad."

"Why? I would think it is good to know that people show you the respect due your rank."

"There is a difference between respect and fawning."

Tam frowned. "Fawning?"

"Aye. I imagine you have not been exposed to much of it, but you will. You sit as Second at Table. You will find you have many friends simply because of your status. They will not really care about you, but they will pretend that they do."

"Ah, I see. It sounds lonely. How would you know who your real friends are?"

"How, indeed."

She sipped her tea as the Laird ate. He had grown up as lonely as she had. Only now Tam had family, while he remained very much alone.

"What are you to do today?" he asked.

"I know not. I have not received any orders or duty except that we are to report to the Thane to tell of our journey."

"Aye, I received word he wishes to speak to me about that. And other things."

She watched his face as he took a drink of tea. He wore a slight frown, and she felt disquiet from him. "You are still concerned about being Laird, are you not?"

He raised his eyebrows. "You are very perceptive." He sighed. "Worried is closer to the mark, though, and perhaps even afraid."

"But fear is a good thing. The Thane says so. He says that fear held in check will keep you alert."

The Laird smiled at her and put his hand over hers for a second. "Thank you. I am glad I have one true friend."

She hesitantly smiled back.

He stood. "We had best see if your uncle is ready to receive us."

As they approached the door of the meeting chamber, Haladhon bowed.

"Is the Thane available, Haladhon?"

"Lamadhel is giving a report, Your Grace. He should be free in a few moments. If you wish, you could take a walk around the bailey, and I will call you when he is available."

"Considering all the walking Tam and I have done, I think a few more steps will not do my feet harm. What say you, Tam?"

"If you wish, Your Grace."

Tam squinted in the early morning sun as she followed the Laird outside. Rangers filled the bailey—sleeping near the walls, sitting in groups talking, matching and sparring—and diminished her enjoyment of being outdoors. She glanced up at the trees, glad that nothing stopped the dawn-singers' cheerful song.

"I would fain watch a match," the Laird said, leaning close. "Shall we?"

She nodded. A pair sparring with staves caught Tam's attention, and she and the Laird walked closer. Their advanced techniques fascinated her, and she studied them with keen interest, disappointed when the match soon ended. The two combatants saw the Laird standing near and bowed to him.

"Was it a good match, Your Grace?" asked a fair-haired Ranger, who stood to one side, arms crossed.

The Laird grinned. "I know too little to have an opinion. Tam?"

"They are both very good," she said.

"And you know this?" This Ranger could block his emotions well, but she needed not sense to know his attitude; his blue eyes dared her, mocked her.

"Believe me, Nandhal, she knows."

Recognizing the voice, Tam spun in happy surprise to the Ranger standing behind her and smiled up into his grinning face. "Loch'alan! I knew not you were here."

"I heard you returned yesterday, but I was on duty at the perimeter at the time." He bowed to the Laird.

"So you are Loch'alan?" the Laird asked with a knowing smile.

"Tam told you what happened, I surmise, Your Grace?"

"It was Marcalan."

Loch'alan rolled his eyes. "Of course."

Nandhal walked closer. His eyes still challenged as he stared at Tam, his head cocked at an angle that emphasized the fine features of his face. His posture indicated he thought well of himself. "So this is our famous cousin Tam."

Tam met Nandhal's eyes with a steady gaze. That was the difference with Marcalan and Haladhon; their mocking was in jest, not in arrogance.

"Nandhal.,." Loch'alan's voice held warning.

"Oh, let the fool get thrashed, brother," came Marcalan's flippant voice from behind Tam. She did not turn as Nandhal still locked eyes with her. She remembered her father and the Thane locking eyes as a contest, and she refused to look away from Nandhal. He broke first, his gaze sliding with disdain to Marcalan.

"Think you because she could thrash Loch'alan that she could take me as well?"

"Find out for yourself," Marcalan said with a shrug. "I would fain see your hide tanned."

"As would I," came another voice. The hold steward Tanadhon strode up, smiling. "But the thrashing will have to be postponed. The Thane awaits the Laird and our cousin Tam."

"Let us go, then," the Laird said.

Marcalan and Tanadhon walked with them back to the hold.

"Watch Nandhal, Tam." Marcalan leaned close, speaking in a furtive voice. "He fights dirty."

"What does it mean 'fights dirty?'"

"He does not fight fair."

"He does not follow rules of contest or of match?"

"Nay."

Tanadhon nodded, his blue eyes piercing. "Aye, cousin, I agree. If he wants to match you, be very careful."

Chapter Twenty-five

Tam entered the meeting chamber with the Laird. Curtains shaded the room from the sun streaming in the eastern windows. The Thane sat at the far side of the table, a book in his hand, a pot and cups in front of him. Tam smiled as he looked up.

He closed the book and stood. "Good morning, Your Grace, Tam. There is tea if you wish it."

"None for me, thank you," the Laird said, seating himself opposite Alcandhor.

"Nay, thank you," said Tam, sliding into the chair next to the Laird.

"So what news of your journey have you both to tell?"

"'Tis a long tale, Thane. But save watching Tam and the Rangers fight, not much is newsworthy, I fear," the Laird said. "My part consists of complaining about the hardship of traveling so hard and eating journey rations, only to later find that what I considered so harsh was average to a Ranger."

The Thane smiled.

"Tam did much to ease my worries. She has a good ear."

Tam's face grew warm at the Laird's praise.

"What worries, Your Grace?"

The Laird slouched in the chair, strangely out of character as he always had such correct posture. He seemed very vulnerable. "About being Laird," he whispered.

"Your father was elderly, and you knew the mantle would likely fall upon you at a young age."

"Aye, but without notice? And from murder? Bells, Thane, I am not yet of Age. I know not whether I can make the weighty decisions that will be demanded of me."

Alcandhor leaned forward with an earnest glint in his eyes. "That is good. A little doubt can benefit you as long as you do not let it make you indecisive." He straightened with a grin. "'Tis better than being a cocksure fool. And as you gain experience, your confidence will grow. Just one piece of advice. Be wary who you let see your doubts. You will need to appear strong and certain."

A smile flickered on the Laird's face. "I am glad I have you and Tam as counselors."

Alcandhor raised his eyebrows. "That is not the function of Rangers, my Laird."

"Is it not the function of friends?"

The Thane seemed surprised, a slow smile spreading. "Indeed. So"—he shifted in his seat—"that is all you can report of your rescue, my Laird? What of your captivity?"

"It was very boring and frustrating, but I knew not my danger. Not really."

"They did not mistreat you?"

"They did not treat me with respect, but nay, other than keeping me confined against my will, they did not harm me."

"That is good."

Alcandhor took a sip of tea. "And you, Tam. After luncheon I shall have you write out your report, but for now tell me of your mission."

"The journey out was uneventful, sir, until the day I arrived at the mountain. I met a messenger and had to fight him." She dropped her gaze for a moment and took a deep breath. "Then I found the entrance to the ventilation shaft just as you described it. But rock had fallen and blocked the way. I could not get the Laird out that way in secret as you had planned."

Alcandhor stiffened, staring at her. "Then how got you him out?"

"I killed all the men on guard outside and...a ka'gua nest was near. The scent of blood attracted them. As they feasted, more men came out, probably to relieve the ones on watch." Tam swallowed at the memory and whispered, "The ka'gua killed them, too." She took a breath. "After dark when they had returned to their nest, I felt it safe to approach the door."

Tam stopped, wondering if her uncle would chastise her for sensing and decided not to mention the matter. Better to skim over details anyway. She still saw the men's faces as they died by her hand.

"Once inside, I found the Laird. We hid from guards and made our way out, locking them all inside."

"That easy?"

"Not that easy." The Laird gave Tam a grim look. "You do not give a complete report, Ranger."

She studied the scars on her hands from years of sword fighting. "Is it necessary to review all the details?"

"When reporting to your superiors, aye, the details are necessary," the Laird said.

The Laird's censure gripped Tam's heart. How could she be a Ranger when she could not kill without anguish and could not bring herself to report the killing?

"What else happened?" the Thane asked.

Tam did not answer. Even if she had wanted to—which she did not, the memories still haunted her—she did not trust her voice.

The Laird answered for her. "On the way out we passed several bodies in one corridor. She said they discovered her and she had to kill them."

"How did you evade the rest of the men?"

The Laird told the Thane, concluding, "We were fearful at the entrance, as the bolt would not move at first, and they were on the other side, trying to push the door open. But we did get them locked in."

"You did well, Tam." Tam looked up to see the Thane gazing at her with pride. She dare not tell him of her hatred of killing. He would not think so well of her then.

"Is there a way to bring back captive those men, Thane? They have supplies to last them for quite awhile, from my understanding, but they need to be brought to trial."

"Indeed. Look you forward to that duty, Laird?"

"I do not. But it must be done."

"How many men estimate you are prisoner there?"

The Laird shook his head. "There were perhaps a score there when they brought me. I know not whether more came later. How many died, Tam?"

"Thirteen, in all," she said without a pause, closing her eyes to shut out each vivid remembrance. Her eyes flew open upon feeling a hand cover hers. The Laird's face showed concern and compassion, and she managed to smile as a thank you before he withdrew his hand.

"It is hard, I know," the Thane said. "There is no shame in regretting having to kill."

The ache in Tam's heart eased slightly. Did he, too, find it hard to kill? Surely not. Not the Thane.

"I will make arrangements for the prisoners to be brought back." Alcandhor pushed his book a little further to the side and took a sip from his cup. "Now, have you told me all?"

"There was the attack by those dozen men. Have you heard the other Rangers' reports on that, Thane?"

"Nay, Your Grace, I have not read their reports yet. What attack?"

The Laird gave an account, and when he finished the Thane nodded. "I am glad we sent those three to meet you two." He glanced between the two, shifting again in his seat. "Is that everything?"

Tam began to nod, but the Laird shook his head. She met his gaze with a frown.

"The ch'iltar thorn."

"Oh, aye." Tam gazed at his arm.

The Laird pushed back his sleeve to display the scar. "Tam made a poultice and tended me. The pain was fierce."

Alcandhor leaned forward, his face pale. "You have full use of the arm? There is no weakness?"

"Nay. She knew what to do."

The Thane's eyes bored into Tam's, and she resisted the urge to squirm. Had she done wrong?

"You have saved our Laird's life several times over, girl. Our world is deeply in your debt."

Heat crept into Tam's face. "I only did what was necessary. It is my duty and honor to serve."

The Laird sniffed. "You are too self-effacing, Ranger. But friend to friend, I thank you."

Tam returned his smile, and Alcandhor cleared his throat. "Now, we also must discuss plans for when the siege ends."

"Aye, please, Thane. Tell me what you intend to do."

"I doubt not that any guards faithful to you are either confined or more likely dead, Your Grace. Therefore, you have no one to guard your home when the siege ends. My suggestion is to use Rangers until you can secure more men and train them as guards."

"That is not a quick task, training guards."

"Indeed. But 'tis all we can do for now."

The siege—Poll! Tam's heart ached, despite not knowing the girl but for a short time. "Sir?" Tam ventured. "Is there no way to end the siege?"

The grimace on her uncle's face mirrored her own fears and pain for those inside. "Not without great loss of life to both sides. The gates are barred, we have no way over the walls, and they know of the secret tunnel—they have blocked it." He shook his head. "Nay, Tam, we must wait it out, for the best or the worst at the end."

Tam dropped her gaze to her lap. *Poll.*

"Wh-what do we do when the siege ends? I know the Rangers must go in and take care of the traitors but what else? My instruction was administrative and judicial, not in dealing with sieges, traitors, and murderers."

"We have carts with food and medicines to immediately care for any survivors. And we will, of course, secure the hall before allowing you to enter, for your safety. Also..." Alcandhor gazed at the Laird, hesitation and pain in his eyes. "Let us find and take care of all the dead before you enter the keep."

Tam's stomach plunged, remembering the body on the floor, dagger in the back, red blood staining the white surcoat. What had the traitors done with the bodies? Surely they would bury them!

The Laird's face turned pale. "I...I understand."

Neither man spoke. Tam wished to console the Laird but she dared not reach over and hold his hand for a moment as he had done for her. So she did something that seemed just as bold since her father had forbidden it, she quit blocking and sent him feelings of sympathy and peace. Her friend gave a deep sigh.

"Are you all right, Your Grace?" the Thane asked.

The Laird looked down at his hands, his voice a whisper. "Nay. But I suppose I will be."

Alcandhor leaned forward, his throbbing shoulder and aches echoing in Tam's body, now that she no longer blocked. She resisted wincing, wondering how he could sit so calmly in such pain.

"I am sorry for your loss, Your Grace, and that I did not anticipate them moving so quickly. I failed you."

The Laird looked up, frowning. "With all you have done, Thane, how shall I fault you? Did you not suffer loss as well? I would that I do as well as Laird as you have as Thane."

Tam watched her uncle's face, his misgivings strong. He doubted himself? She hoped she kept her face from showing surprise. Why should such a wise, good man doubt himself?

"Your Grace, I also need apprise you of another thing. Two nobles have arrived, Lord Paltor and Lord Zantith. We know they are in league with the traitors besieged in Laird Hall."

"Have you apprehended them?"

"Nay, Your Grace."

"Why? Do you lack proof?"

"For Lord Paltor and his sons, no. Rangers from within his province have been able to gather evidence. But for others, aye, and we wish to be sure of their identities before closing the net. Otherwise they will scatter and hide, including Zantith. We have nothing we can use as proof on him yet."

"I see."

"We are keeping your presence here a secret. They think you are still held hostage or dead."

The Laird's mouth twitched in a small smile. "You always seem one step ahead, Thane."

"So I am told, but it is not true. Unfortunately." Alcandhor cleared his throat. "When the siege ends, they will expect to be notified and accompany us to Laird Hall. That cannot be allowed. At that point, if they have any wits, they will know we at least suspect them of treason."

"What think you they will do then?"

Alcandhor sighed. "I know not. But we can discuss that later." He grimaced, leaning back. "Your Grace, I have to receive reports and discuss a few matters with my chiefs. If you wish, you can sit in, so you are aware of all that is going on."

"I am honored, Thane."

"Should I leave, then, sir?" Tam asked.

"Nay, Tam, I need you to stay."

Looking over at the Laird in puzzlement, she noticed Haladhon by the door. He had been in the chamber the whole time? Why was not he sitting here with them? And why did she not sense he was there? She willed her mind off her uncle's pain and became more aware of both Haladhon's and the Laird's moods. Strange that her uncle's presence was easier to sense; she wondered why. Feeling guilty for sensing, even though no one had said anything, she blocked once again.

One by one, Rangers came in to give their reports.

Marcalan, Tandhral, and Capalan each came in to orally give their reports of their mission to meet and escort the Laird and Tam.

Lamadhel gave a short and concise report. The siege held. No word or signal came from Laird Hall except the daily 'all is well' from the Rangers in the drum tower.

The Rangers keeping eye on the nobles, their attendants, and guards had little to report from the town. No suspicious activity could be seen.

No new reports came in from Rangers sent to the provinces. No drum messages.

The Thane sat back and lowered his head after the last one left. Tam stirred in her chair. "Uncle? What about those in the siege? Think you they are starving?"

"I know not, Tam. I worry for them, but what other choice have we?" Her uncle breathed out slowly. "One more bit of business." He nodded at Haladhon. The tall Ranger opened the door and Lamadhel, Eladhrel, Andhrel, and Maradhor, the scribe with the wide-set brown eyes who had been at the first conclave, entered. They bowed to the Laird.

"Your Grace, we wish you here for this conclave," the Thane said. He rose from the long side of the table, went to the head, and reseated himself.

The Laird stood, with an uncertain glance around. Haladhon gestured to the chair at the opposite end of the table.

Tam, at the corner, did not have to move. The other chiefs sat down. The scribe sat opposite Tam, on the Thane's left, flicking his sun-streaked hair over his broad shoulders and setting out his supplies.

Maradhor dipped his pen in the inkpot and nodded at the Thane. Alcandhor let a breath out slowly, glancing around the table. "I did not wish to do this so soon, but I feel it is necessary based on a discovery that has been made. Haladhon, if you please."

Her tall cousin rose, walked around the table, and pulled the heavy curtains across the windows, making the chamber quite dark.

"Tam, bring out the key," the Thane said.

Ducking her head to avoid stares, she grasped the chain and pulled it out from under her shirt. Gasps burst from the Rangers, and an ominous fluttering ran through Tam in the silence that followed.

"You may open the curtains now, Haladhon," the Thane finally said.

Haladhon did so and sat down next to Tam, putting an arm on the back of her chair with a grin and a wink.

The Thane looked at them all, one by one. "I call Question. I submit that the vow made by the conclave to Valdhor be honored since he provided a Trained Ranger that can claim ascendancy to Thane."

~:~

Zantith glanced up as Paltor thudded into a chair at his table in the tavern. He sighed, watching the wine slosh in his glass, and continued cutting his meat.

"They have the Laird," Paltor hissed.

"What?" Zantith stopped, knives in suspended in the air.

"Rangers arrived yesterday evening escorting the boy."

"How know you this?" *And why has my murmurer not reported to me?*

"I have ways of learning what goes on inside their hold."

Zantith set his knives on the table and leaned back. "A spy?" Revelation struck him. "Batrig's 'heir' to Thane—the traitor? You know who he is?"

"Aye. He reported to me today."

Zantith pursed his lips. Batrig's man would report to Paltor, would he? Yet Zantith heard nothing. He would see about this. He brought his mind back to the conversation as Paltor leaned forward. "*They* are close."

"Who?" Zantith tried to hold his irritation in check at being kept in the dark.

Paltor chuckled softly. "The Rogues." He sat back in his chair, which again creaked, a smug look on his face.

Zantith glared at Paltor in disbelief. "They are branded and must travel in stealth. They cannot be seen to send messages by drum or runner, how know you where they are?"

"Stealth is their way of life. 'Tis easy to secrete a letter in the bag of a runner while he sleeps at a journey station, or slip money and a note to be sent under a door of a drum tower. We have a code worked out so that a seemingly innocent message will have special meaning for us."

Zantith sniffed. "So when will they arrive?"

"Within three days, if all goes well." Paltor's eyes gleamed. "Soon Alcandhor will be dead—and perhaps the Laird too."

Chapter Twenty-six

In the silence that followed Alcandhor's declaration, Tam stared at the table, stunned, barely able to breathe.

"Tam is young," Alcandhor said. "She needs to study much and gain experience before she is ready to assume her role. I will mentor her until she comes of Age."

No—that was not right! Tam banged the table with her fist. "I cannot, Thane! I will not! I do not wish to be Thane. I wish you to be my Thane."

"It is not your decision, Tam," Alcandhor said. "It is your responsibility to our clan and to our world."

She shook her head, setting her chin.

The Thane gave her a wry look. "Unless you intend on taking the coward's way out as your father did."

She straightened, glaring at the Thane. "My father was no coward."

"What do you call someone who runs from his duties and responsibilities?" asked Haladhon, his voice slightly mocking.

Tam looked away. "I know not his reasons, and he is not here to ask so I will say no more but that he was not a coward." She gazed around the table at the chiefs with determination. "And I will not be Thane. Not now, not five years from now, not ever!" Her voice cracked on the last word.

Haladhon put his hand on her arm and Tam sat back, her face warming. She must learn to control herself.

"You will have quite a bit of convincing for the Rangers to accept a woman as Thane, Alcandhor," Lamadhel said softly.

"We are the only clan that has never been ruled by a matriarch, because in our clan, the Thane must be a Ranger. We now have, in direct line of ascendancy, a female Trained as Ranger. What in our law speaks against that?" Alcandhor looked over at the chief law-keeper of their clan. "Andhrel?"

Andhrel snorted. "Nothing, Thane, and you know it."

"Then what objections can they have? Especially if, in five years time, she has been mentored and readied for her position?"

"It will not be easy," Lamadhel said.

"True. But I think both Tam and I are up to the challenge."

227

"I have no say in this?" Tam asked.

Haladhon chuckled. "Not much, my young cousin. Especially considering that key."

"Aye. There is that," Andhrel said, awe in his voice.

Tam clenched her hands in frustration. "Why is that so important?"

"It is the symbol that we have the right to be the guardians and protectors of our world," Lamadhel said. "Only some few of Ranger clan can make a key glow. It is because we have the blood of the Enaisi in our clan. No other. But after all these years, that ability has greatly diminished. I have never seen a key glow as the one in your possession does, Tam. It means much. To our clan and to our world."

The Laird cleared his throat. "May I speak, Thane?"

"Most certainly, Your Grace."

"I can attest this is the truth. As the head of the administrative ruling body of this world, I will tell you that seeing that key glow meant more than I can put into words. I know you well enough to trust you, Tam, but if I did not, yet I saw that key glowing brightly in your hands, I would have much faith in you."

"I do not understand..."

The Thane put a hand over hers. "You have not been taught. When you have studied, you will understand."

"I wish to study. But I do not wish to be Thane."

The Thane chuckled. "I said that too, once, but look what happened to me."

Haladhon stifled a giggle. Tam glared up at her cousin, who returned an innocent stare.

She gave the Thane a hard long look. "You are going to give me no choice, are you?"

"Nay. I am not." He eyed the chiefs, determination on his face. "We are not."

No negation came from the other Rangers at the table. Tam licked her lips. "Can we not negotiate, then, at least?"

"Negotiate? How?"

"Continue to be Thane. Let me step up on your death. I do not wish to take Thaneship from you, and I think no Ranger would wish you to step down. I do not. You are loved and respected."

He looked down, his brow furrowed. The chiefs remained silent. At length he sat back and glanced around the table. "Let us simply agree today that Tam is in line for ascendancy and is Second at Table not just in status but in rank as well. Five years pass until she officially is of Age, and many things may change by then. Are we agreed?"

"Sir, I think Lamadhel brought up a valid point," Tam said. "I have already had a Ranger here all but contest me. I think he will contest me if the chance comes. There will be others, I am sure. If they cannot accept me as a Ranger, how will they ever accept me as Thane?"

"You will have five years to prove yourself to them before we face that."

"And what happens if...I–I deny the thought one thousand times, but, what if you die before that? Do I become Thane at that time?"

Her uncle smiled at her. "Not unless a new conclave voted to overturn this decision. The agreement I hope for today is simply that you are accepted into direct line of ascendancy as your father's heir. If you were male, had been raised in Zaidhron, had studied the Enaisi's Laws, and were known among the Rangers, still we would wait until you were of Age."

"Aye," Andhrel said. "Thaneship is usually held by the nearest adult to ascendancy until the heir is of Age, even if Confirmed as you are."

The Thane gazed about table. "So are we agreed, then?"

All the chiefs said, "Aye." Tam suspected they all knew beforehand what her uncle planned to acquiesce so quickly. She glowered at them.

The Thane looked at her. "Tam?"

"Sir? What if I am contested?"

"You were contested once already. What worries have you about that?"

"I mean, concerning today's conclave?"

"Ah, I see." The Thane lightly rapped his knuckles on the table. "To contest your rank, or heirship to Thane, a Ranger would have to demand a conclave be convened and at that conclave show proof in the law that you should not be in line for Thaneship." He shifted in his chair, grimacing and frowning slightly.

Tam bit her lip, knowing even though blocking the pain he must be feeling, but she had to continue her objections. "I have another question."

Haladhon snickered, and she cut her eyes at him in irritation before looking back at the Thane. "At the last conclave it was agreed that ascendancy has to go through the male line. Why has this changed?"

"She is good, Thane," Andhrel said.

"Wish you to answer this one, then, Andhrel?" asked her uncle.

"If you wish, Thane."

Alcandhor gestured assent, and Andhrel leaned forward. "At the last conclave, it was enough to set us topside down just accepting the idea of a female as Ranger. And it was overwhelming for you as well. The Thane was wise enough not to ask for too much too fast. Now, less than a lunation later you have proven yourself as a Ranger.

"We have talked to Lord Krendhal, Marcalan, Tandhral, and

Capalan, and although we have not had the chance to hear the report the Laird gave, I am sure it bears out the same as the others. You are well Trained. Also at that conclave, I claimed that heirs had to go through the male line. After the conclave, the Thane dared me to find the exact point in the law where that is said. I could not."

Tam's eyes widened as she turned to the Thane. "You planned this?" She straightened as realization hit her. "You have wished me to become Thane all along!"

Haladhon snickered. "Quick this one is, Thane. No one will ever pull much over on her."

The Thane smirked. "It is in her blood."

"But Thane," Tam said, not caring about blood, "heirs have always gone through the male line and females are considered part of the family they marry into, leaving their blood-family heritage."

"'Twas a conclave decision made long ago. We have many such decisions and traditions in our history. We are trying to purge ourselves of ones we feel are a hindrance."

"Why was such a decision made?"

"There were various reasons over the centuries." Alcandhor leaned back with an exhale. "The one most often given has been that many clans claimed Rangers gave special consideration to those families they married into and that our justice was biased because of that. The decision was made in an effort to reduce such bias."

"It is also one of the reasons we began marrying within the clan instead of out," Eladhrel said, tapping the table with a finger.

"True." Alcandhor inclined his head.

"But our clan structure is based on male heirship," Tam said.

"Also true, but again, that is tradition, not law." Alcandhor smiled wistfully. "Your father saw little, if any, distinction between the two, thus he would have taught you."

Tam frowned at the table.

"A question, Thane," said the Laird. "If I may be so bold as to intrude."

"Please, my Laird."

"If she became Thane, and married, what would her husband's rank become, and what of children?"

"Andhrel and I have discussed this and see no difference in how other clans handle a matriarch as thane. Heirship in general will still go through the male line. However, if a female is Ranger-Trained and has children who are also Ranger-Trained then she and they would follow heirship as if male. A husband would retain his own family rank. He would, of course, be given a chieftaincy as due a consort."

Tam's mind whirled. They had given this much thought, the schemers! She glared at the Thane and over at Andhrel, whose eyes were twinkling. If only she could thrash them both!

"Any more objections or questions?" asked Alcandhor.

She thought hard but could think of none. "I wish my father were here. He would not agree to this."

"On what grounds?" asked the Thane.

"He would have raised every objection brought up already."

"And we have discussed them. Conclave decisions are based on law, not opinions. And not on feelings."

"Then this decision should have been made at the first conclave."

Andhrel let his breath out in a low whistle. "She has you, Thane."

Alcandhor chuckled. "Aye, she has."

"I missed it." Eladhrel looked from his brother to his cousin in puzzlement.

"She is right," said Andhrel. "By law, this decision should have been made at the conclave at Zaidhron. But the Thane allowed it to pass in order not to arch too many backs."

Eladhrel sat back, nodding.

"Anything more, Tam, or do you vote?" the Thane asked again.

"Why bother with a vote if it is all based on law?" she asked, crossing her arms with a pout.

Andhrel leaned forward again. "Many times the law is not explicit, or we find, as we have in recent years as we diligently study the law, that what we have based our decisions on has been our tradition, not written law, and must be reviewed. Intent is often called into question as well. There are many reasons why a vote is necessary."

Alcandhor rubbed a hand on the table. "And so, if you have no more questions, will you give us your vote?"

Haladhon leaned close, speaking in a feigned whisper. "And no more trying to forestall, either."

Tam fidgeted, looking at each of them. Haladhon seemed amused, but that was Haladhon. Eladhrel's placid eyes met hers with expectation. Andhrel appeared smug. Of course. He had been conspiring with her uncle on this. Her uncle—he looked even more smug.

From the end of the table, the Laird gave her a slight smile. He must understand much of how she felt. Although not of Age yet, he was forced into his leadership position.

Maradhor scrutinized her with those wide, brown eyes. He did not seem either hostile or accepting. What did he think of this? She wished she could ask, but her father had taught her enough of conclaves and how they were conducted to know it was not proper for a scribe to speak when at his duty.

Lamadhel had a strange, pensive expression. What did he truly think of this? Should she stop blocking, sense his true feelings? But that would not stop the law from being law—would it?

"Do you agree because you must?" she asked her great-uncle. "Because the law gives no recourse?"

His eyebrows rose. "I have...reservations, lass. But my brother spoke of a sword's edge of change coming to our world. He knew not what, but warned us to beware of traditions that set us against the written law. His son"—Lamadhel nodded toward Alcandhor—"speaks the same. I give heed to Enaisi foresight. And trust my Thane." His lips twitched in a slight smile. "Young though he be."

Tam took a deep breath, not wanting to give in, but seeing no alternative. "I cannot fight the law."

"So be it." Alcandhor leaned back. "This conclave is ended."

Haladhon slumped back in his chair in relief. "That was easier than I anticipated. Is it time for luncheon yet?"

Alcandhor snorted. "If it were, Sherel would be pounding on the door, ordering me to eat to keep up my strength ere I succumb to my injuries and die."

The men all burst into laughter.

"So." Haladhon leaned close to Tam again. "Who is this Ranger you think will contest you?"

"His name is Nandhal. Marcalan and Tanadhon said to watch him because he fights dirty."

The luncheon gong sounded as Haladhon said, "Does he indeed? He cannot contest you, Tam, as he has never been Confirmed, but if he calls for a match, you be careful."

"If he wishes to match you, Tam, I will be called to watch," Alcandhor said.

"Aye, sir."

"Considering the situation, I think all the chiefs should be there," Lamadhel said, his eyebrows raised.

What situation? A loud knocking interrupted Tam's thoughts. Sherel's voice called through the door. "It's time for luncheon, Thane! You need to eat!"

"We are having conclave, woman!" bellowed Alcandhor.

Silence.

Haladhon fell back, chuckling. "Rascal," he whispered, pointing at Alcandhor.

The Thane's eyes sparkled as he whispered back, "Let us wait a few moments before leaving."

Eladhrel opened his mouth to say something, but the Thane put a finger to his lips and pointed to the door.

Haladhon had his face covered with his hand. Tam could not stop smiling as she watched Haladhon trying to keep from laughing aloud. Alcandhor reached over and slapped at Haladhon with his good arm. "Shu."

Haladhon almost convulsed trying to keep quiet. Everyone at the table fought laughter as they watched him.

"It certainly does not take much to amuse you," the Thane said softly.

Tam thought her cousin would fall out of his chair. Why did he find the whole thing so hysterically humorous?

"You do know, Thane," Lamadhel said, pointedly ignoring his nephew's antics. "That by telling Sherel we were having conclave, the entire hold will know by end of the meal."

"Think you she knows not by the fact all the chiefs are in this meeting chamber at one time with a scribe?" He shrugged. "And we will be making an announcement anyway." Alcandhor tapped Maradhor's arm, grinning. "Make yourself scarce, cousin, for she surely will be nagging you for details. Not knowing will drive her mad."

The scribe chuckled. "'Twill be enjoyment tormenting her with my lack of knowledge."

"You are evil." Haladhon wiped his eyes. "Both of you."

The men snickered.

Sherel seemed on such easy terms with the Rangers, ordering them about and taking charge. Tam eyed Alcandhor, her head tipped. "Who is Sherel, Uncle? Is she Ranger clan?"

"By marriage. She was raised in Thane Valley and married a Ranger. She came here when her husband was assigned to Ranger Hold. When he was killed, she stayed on as hold-keeper. She is a remarkable rock in a storm."

"And mothers all Rangers as her sons." Haladhon rolled his eyes.

"'Mothers?' Bullies is closer to the mark," Maradhor said.

"True. But we need such strength in a hold-keeper. Think you we have rankled Sherel enough?"

"Aye, Thane," Lamadhel said. "As is, she will likely rail you for this."

~:~

Tam rose from luncheon, and her uncle put a hand on her shoulder, his eyes sad. "I think you need to do something."

Tam frowned. "Sir?"

His grip tightened slightly. "I speak as your uncle, not Thane." He seemed to try to smile. "Come."

Tam followed him up the hall, through the foreroom, and outside, her eyes on his shoulders—solid and square, yet not the large, broad back of her father. A wave of sorrow swept her, and she blinked to stop tears.

They approached a small building in the corner of the bailey near the wall. Trees grew up around it, almost as sentinels, and ivy climbed up part of the one wall. Leaves crunched under her feet as she climbed the few steps.

Alcandhor stood by the door and inhaled with a grimace. "I know not if your father taught you of Loosening."

Tam nodded and stared at the building with understanding, her throat tight. She took a breath and whispered, "It is where one gives those who have died freedom from any ties here."

"Not exactly. It is not as if their souls are trapped by any feeling we have. Once dead, they are unfettered by this life. But it allows us a chance to put to rest what resides in our hearts." Her uncle's eyes probed hers with such depth that she wanted to fidget. "I know not that you are ready for Loosening, but I think you need to have some ritual to ease your heart."

Tam did not know what to say, so she stood, waiting, her heart thumping. Alcandhor lifted the latch and pushed the heavy wooden door open. Strong, heavy odors met her senses—she blinked and stifled a cough.

"Incense," her uncle said over his shoulder as he entered. "It is tended and renewed for a lunation to represent the prayers rising for the grief of loved ones left behind. Incense also masks undesirable smells, but our men are in sealed coffins awaiting departure for their home provinces, so that is not a great worry."

He took a torch from the wall and lit it from one of many candles set on small shelves along the walls. Shadows fled and grew as they walked across the columned chamber, their footsteps echoing.

They descended a stair to a landing, turned, and continued downward. The light of the torch revealed six long boxes of polished wood resting upon stone slabs in the lower chamber. Beyond that, the room remained a mystery, shrouded in darkness.

Tam glanced at the biers and over at her uncle. He put his arm around her shoulders and drew her closer to one. "This is where your father rests. You may speak to him if you wish."

Tam frowned at Alcandhor. "But he is not here."

"I know. But it is a way to bid him farewell. If you wish to speak your heart, I will withdraw."

Tam stared at the coffin and shook her head. "I do not feel him." She recalled how his presence rose, as if traveling away on the wind. Journeying to join the Maker. "I felt him leave when he died." She took a step backward. "There is no one here to talk to."

"It is a releasing of our hearts, not that the dead are actually here." His eyes met hers, expecting, urging. "If you could talk to him one last time is there anything you would wish to say?"

Chapter Twenty-seven

What did her uncle want? What could she say to—to what? A body that used to be Valdhor? That which was her father was gone. His cold dominance, his strength of spirit...gone. If he did indeed stand before her, what words could she find? She thought of his curled lip and narrowed eyes and shook her head again, hoping tears did not shame her. "Nay. I...I wish to leave."

Alcandhor hesitated and bowed his head. Wordlessly, they returned the way they came.

As they entered the hold, Haladhon stood in the hall, arms crossed. "If Santran discovers you are not resting after luncheon as ordered—"

"Bells above, Haladhon, you are as bad as Sherel."

"Be glad I found you before she did. You had best lie down." Alcandhor entered the meeting chamber with a wry face.

Haladhon turned to Tam, his twinkling eyes belying his serious expression. "And you, Second at Table, did not write the report of your journey. Since this is new to you, I shall assist if you wish." He gestured to the door the Thane had gone through with a sweeping bow.

Tam took a step back. "But, Uncle is to rest."

"He does not sleep, but endures lying down. Usually reading a book. Now, come."

As her cousin said, Alcandhor lay on his cot, propped on his good elbow, a book in front of him. He grinned as she sat at the table.

Haladhon made sure the report was thorough. He asked questions and went over points until, fingers aching from writing, Tam had a report he approved. Once set on the table for her uncle's perusal—although he quietly listened as she discussed and wrote of her journey—Tam was free of duty. She knew not what to do, so she wandered the bailey.

Rangers cast her baleful or curious looks, and some had strange but strong urgent feelings that made her uncomfortable.

One Ranger glared at her, his animosity apparent even without using her ability to sense. She willed herself not to hurry but relief washed over her as she headed to the back of the bailey, away from him.

Tam halted as she came across a large garden encircled by low walls. The herbs and vegetables seemed to call to her. She gave in to her yearning and ran to the kitchen.

Sherel stood in front of shelves, hands on hips as she muttered, "I know I left the pimin here. Nothing's ever where I leave it."

Tam cleared her throat, and Sherel turned. "What is it?"

"May I work in the garden?"

Sherel stared at her with a dumbfounded expression. "Work in the garden?"

"I like gardens. I had one at my cottage. May I, please?"

"Do what you wish, girl. My gardener likely won't mind if you wish to weed and work out there. But it seems a Ranger would have better things to be doing."

"Thank you, Sherel," she said, but the hold-keeper had already turned back to her work.

She wandered in the large, well-tended garden for a while, gazing about. One end of the garden wall had a small recess built into it with tools inside. She took a small hand shovel, and when she noticed some spots that needed a little weeding, she knelt down to work. It felt good to have her hands in the cool soil and feel the warmth of the sun on her back.

Before long, her stomach grumbled that it was time for afternooning. Tam came in to eat soup and bread and hurried back to the garden.

Her mind began to wander to the crypt. What had her uncle wanted of her? Her fingers dug into the dirt. *Deep root.* She plunged the shovel deeper into the soil. *What could I say to Father?* 'Why did you not tell me of my family?' Tam knew the answer. He had been ashamed of her. A mere girl-child.

Tam pulled on the weed, and it gave way. She tossed it on the pile of wilting greenery. 'Why did you Train me?' She would never know his reasoning for that.

She drove the shovel into the ground again and ripped out another weed. 'Who was my mother?' She shook her head. Another mystery never to be answered.

What would she say to him? Tam sat back on her heels and stared up at the darkening sky. 'I love you.' Silence. No reply. Valdhor never did say much, even when alive.

Biting her lip, she turned her mind back to the intruders among the vegetables and herbs.

"Strange duty for a Ranger," she heard the Laird say. He stood at the edge of the garden, smiling at her in the orange light of the setting sun.

She rubbed her hands together. "I have no duty for now. I enjoy gardening."

"Indeed? I have never paid much attention to gardens." He walked toward her on the path.

"I learned young. I had to help with the garden for our food, and when I was older, my father left its care to me. It is wonderful to be around growing things."

"It must be. Your eyes shine just talking about it."

Not certain how to answer, she resumed weeding.

"What are you doing?" He knelt next to her.

"Your Grace, you will get your surcoat dirty."

"It is washable. What are you doing?"

"These weeds will grow and crowd out the herbs and vegetables. They must be removed."

"I see."

"You truly have never been in a garden, Your Grace?"

"Nay. There are gardens within the bailey of Laird Hall, and I have passed by them, but never did I walk through them or pay attention to them. Not the ones with herbs and vegetables anyway. I have stopped to admire and smell the beautiful flowers. Tell me about some of these plants. What are they?"

Having an audience for her favorite subject, Tam began pointing out the herbs nearby and telling him their various culinary and medicinal uses. She told him of ragal, freyala, and sheena. She then stood and spread her arms to show off the tall, beautiful plant that was one of her favorites.

"Featherfronds are an annual, which readily self-sows. The seed of it is good for digestive problems. The leaves are often used in cooking." She pulled off a few of the thread-like feathery leaves and held them out to him. "Smell this, Your Grace."

He brushed them under his nose. "I think I recognize this as an herb sometimes used in soups at Laird Hall."

Tam nodded. "It is often used in soups."

"There are more of these plants in that plot." He pointed across the walkway.

"Nay. Those are sweetfronds. A perennial. Although often grown as a biennial." She rose and he followed her over to that area of the garden.

"These look like the ones we just left," the Laird said.

She pulled a few leaves off, and he sniffed them.

"Aye, they are different." He looked over his shoulder at the featherfronds with a confused frown. "Yet look so much the same."

"The leaves, aye, at a glance, but not the stalks. If you doubt which is which, smell the leaves. You will not be confused."

He grinned. "Will you turn me into a gardener?"

"I do not think there is a danger in that, Your Grace. You have many more important matters to keep your mind." She saw some weeds at her feet, sat, and began digging them out. He knelt next to her, watching.

She pulled one weed out by the root and a curled up, worm-like creature almost as wide as a Tam's pinky finger came up with it.

"Not good," she muttered. "Grubs."

"Grubs? What are they?" The Laird leaned close to see it.

"They eat the roots of the plants."

She held it aloft for him to see before smashing it between her fingers. The grub burst, its insides spraying the Laird's surcoat. He looked down, mouth agape.

She held her breath, stomach clenching, her hand flying to her mouth. "I am so sorry, Your Grace!"

The corners of the Laird's mouth twitched. "Tam, I journeyed for ten days with you. I slept on the hard, cold ground and walked under the hot sun, sweating more than I ever have. I got soaked through with rain and splashed and trudged through mud and swamps. I got dirty, nay," he lifted a hand, "I was filthy and stank, not to mention footsore, and more tired than I have ever been. But none of those experiences prepared me for being sprayed with grub guts."

"I am sorry, Your Grace. I truly am," she said again.

He shook his head with a mournful look at his surcoat, but began chuckling.

Tam relaxed that he truly was not angry and smiled, pointing at his surcoat. "You should change your surcoat, Your Grace."

"Perhaps I should, but this is the only white surcoat I have to wear. I shall have to go without while it is being cleaned. Show me more of the garden first."

They strolled through the garden, and she showed him various vegetables. When Rangers began to light the torches around the bailey, she said, "'Tis dark and evening meal will be soon, Your Grace."

"Aye. Let us walk toward the hold."

Crossing the bailey, Rangers bowed as the Laird passed.

He asked, "What think you that you are now heir to Thane?"

Tam wrinkled her nose and shook her head. "I do not like it, Your Grace. I will like it less when these Rangers know of it. I dread their reaction."

"You were born as heir, Tam, as was I." The Laird shrugged and clasped his hands behind his back. "You had the disadvantage to be raised not knowing of it, so it is a shock. In time you will adjust to the idea. But when you doubt, think of that key."

Tam threw out her hands. "Why is it so important? I still do not understand."

"If you had been raised hearing of the Rangers and their special abilities because of their link to the Enaisi—how the power of the Enaisi protects them, how they can see things others cannot, and how they can enter the places of the Enaisi..." He nodded toward her jerkin. "Keys such as the one you wear are the symbol of the rule of the Rangers. I know not if you are aware of it, but although the Laird is surrounded by more pomp and ceremony and is treated as being even above other nobles, in reality, the Thane has more power and more responsibilities."

Tam knew their history but had not thought—stars, if she became Thane then..."You frighten me, Your Grace."

He stopped, giving her a long look. "Tam, anyone who could do what I have seen you do need not be frightened of responsibility. You have time to grow accustomed to your role before being required to step into it. What did you tell me? Fear controlled is a good thing?"

She smiled. "Now you are the one I will call a true friend. I thank you, Your Grace."

He returned her smile, and they continued on to the front of the bailey and into the foreroom. Haladhon and Marcalan stood in the hallway by the doorway of the meeting chamber, talking with the Thane, who leaned against the doorjamb. Tam smiled at Marcalan.

Her mischievous cousin winked at her as the Thane said, "I had wished the entire first table here for the announcement, but with conclave only being held today there was no way to change the roster."

Tam sighed in disgust. The Thane was going to announce her again? The Laird shot her a sympathetic smile.

As they drew close, the three Rangers bowed while Haladhon said to the Thane, "Nay, many will not be here. I am certain word will make it around the perimeter before the next change of watch, though." He grinned at the Laird. "Did you have a pleasant afternoon, Your Grace?"

"Aye. At first." The Laird drew himself up, looking indignant, his lips thinned. "But I wish to report a despicable event. I was attacked by one of you."

Haladhon and Marcalan spoke at once:

"What!"

"Your Grace!"

Tam stared in shock. What was the Laird talking about?

Alcandhor straightened. "Who was it, Your Grace? Who would dare? Are you hurt?"

The gong sounded, but they all ignored it waiting for the Laird to answer. He turned to glare at Tam. "It was Tam."

She stared at the Laird, her heart thudding.

"Tam?" all three Rangers exclaimed at once.

"I have the proof here." He pointed to his white surcoat. "She attacked me with grub guts." On the last words, his stern face gave way, and he sniggered.

Tam let out her breath in relief as all three Rangers stared at the surcoat. Marcalan and Haladhon both burst into laughter. Alcandhor shook his head. "What happened?"

"She was showing me a grub before killing it. When she crushed it in her fingers, the insides—well, you can see what they did." He was chuckling now.

"I wish I could have seen her face. And yours, Your Grace," howled Marcalan. "Oh, how priceless!"

"Grub guts," Haladhon repeated, leaning against the wall weakly, still laughing. That set Marcalan off again, and he slid down the wall to the floor. Alcandhor nudged him with his foot despite his own laughter.

Tam could not help but giggle as well.

Sherel strode down the hallway. She stopped and curtsied to the Laird and looked at Alcandhor with disapproval. "Thane, it's time for evening meal. Do not make the others wait or let it get cold."

"Thank you, Sherel."

She whirled and stalked back down the hallway. Haladhon watched her and after she turned the corner, said, "Oh, dear Sherel. Like a bucket of cold water on a fire."

Marcalan got to his feet, snickering. "More ways than one."

Alcandhor held up a chastising finger to Marcalan and walked down the hall. Tam frowned in confusion. Would she ever learn what all the jesting meant?

"I think I have not the time to change into something clean," the Laird said.

Marcalan nudged Haladhon. "Think you anyone will dare say anything to the Laird about his appearance?"

"Think you the Laird should care what anyone thinks of his appearance?" Haladhon asked.

"I should wash my hands," the Laird said, "in case there are grub guts on them." He walked off with a wink and a grin.

"I should wash mine, too," Tam said.

Marcalan hung an arm over his tall cousin's shoulder. As Tam walked down the hallway, she heard him say, "You know, our dear Laird is really a fun fellow when not required to be a noble."

~:~

Tam washed her hands and almost ran into the Laird as he exited another washing room. They hurried together down the hallway toward the dining hall, and she bowed for him to enter first.

"I do not enter a chamber before a lady," he murmured.

"I am not a lady, Your Grace, but a Ranger," she whispered.

"You are both Lady and Ranger."

"Rangers are always deferential to the Laird."

"With all due respect, Your Grace," Alcandhor called from the head table, "can you two talk later?"

Tam ducked her head, chastised, and she and the Laird entered together.

The tables in this dining hall had not the length of the ones in Zaidhron. But then, this hold did not house large numbers of Rangers. The Thane, his chiefs, others of the first table, and those Rangers who normally barracked at Ranger Hold—such as Tanadhon, ate in the dining hall. The rest of the Rangers by necessity had to eat out of doors at either the camp in the bailey or one of the ones set up around the perimeter.

The Thane stood at place not by the end of the table, but where Tam should sit, Krendhal beside him. Tam would have to sit between the tall, dour lord and Haladhon. What marked opposites they were, and how tiny she felt next to them both.

The Laird hesitated. "You should sit at head of table in your own hall, Thane."

"You honor us by taking your rightful place at table as you now take it for our world. And you would honor me if you will stand with me as I announce Tam."

The Laird inclined his head, his eyes warm as he gazed at Tam. She felt her stomach churning. Quiet reigned as they all continued to stand in respect for the Laird who had not yet sat down.

The Thane held out his hand to Tam. She walked over, and he turned her around to face the hall, putting his good hand on her shoulder.

"For those of you who have not met her, this is Tamissa, daughter of my father's older son, Valdhor. Tam is Confirmed as Ranger-Trained and according to the vow the conclave made to Valdhor, his Trained heir is Second at Table and in line for ascendancy to Thane."

The Rangers gasped and murmured, just as at Zaidhron. The Thane stepped to the side, stood at attention, and put his fist over his heart. The rest of the men—some with hesitation—did likewise. Tam bowed. Hostility radiated from one and she looked over to the table next to hers to see the Ranger who had glared at her in the bailey earlier that day.

She returned to her place and waited. The Laird sat, and the Rangers all did as well.

Tam knew most of the Rangers at her table, including Marcalan and Capalan. Stars, that meant they all claimed close kinship with the Thane. And her.

Nandhal sat at the first table, too, on the end by Capalan. Tam did not like the idea of Nandhal as a close cousin. She would prefer him only a cousin by distant claim of being in the same clan.

Marcalan sat right across from Haladhon, which Tam thought would not be conducive to an uneventful meal. Marcalan kicked at her leg under the table to get her attention and gave her a mischievous grin. She smiled back, catching an odd look from the Ranger sitting on Marcalan's far side. He seemed pensive. He glanced at Marcalan and back at her, giving her a slight smile when he met her eyes.

Tam did not like the piercing look Nandhal gave her. What bothered her she knew not, save the gaze was not friendly. Trying to divert her mind from Nandhal, she turned to Haladhon. "Are you not sad to be displaced, cousin?"

Haladhon hesitated then grinned, shaking his head. "Nay. The farther I am from ever inheriting the headaches of that position, the better." His eyes sparkled at her. "I owe you a debt of gratitude."

Tam smiled. "I will remember that."

"Ha, Haladhon," Marcalan said as he ripped some bread from a loaf. "Watch her."

"What?" Eladhrel peered at Tam from the other side of Haladhon. "Watch what?"

"Tam said she will remember that Haladhon owes her a debt of gratitude," Marcalan said.

Andhrel chortled. "I agree with Marcalan. She has a shrewd mind, Haladhon, as you well know. She will call in that debt."

"You would not wish to be Thane?" asked Krendhal. "'Tis a most revered position, Haladhon."

"And I am the least reverential Ranger, milord."

"Ah!" Marcalan leaned on his elbow and pointed at Haladhon with his eating knife. "Second least reverential, perhaps, my dear cousin."

"I stand corrected. You took that honor away from me some time ago." Haladhon gave a mocking incline of his head.

Marcalan half stood to return the bow.

Krendhal looked down at Tam, his gaze somber. "I would advise you, Ranger Chief Tam, to take careful consideration of this gratitude your cousin owes you. You may be able to put it to good use at a most opportune time."

Despite his solemn demeanor, Tam could sense his amusement. The grim Lord Krendhal would take part in jesting?

"I am sure she will, too," Marcalan said, spearing a piece of meat with his eating knife. He drew it to his plate and picked up the table knife to cut it. "If she wishes, I shall endeavor to instruct her on making the most of such opportunities."

"I am sure there is no one more qualified in the giving of such instruction," the Laird said, straight-faced.

"Aye, 'tis the truth." Haladhon nodded to the Ranger next to Marcalan. "What say you, Lantalan?"

"Oh, stars, need I say on about this unrepentant rascal? He is the bane of my existence."

Marcalan slapped his hand over his heart. "'Tis heartwarming to know my father thinks so well of me."

As the Rangers chortled, Tam stared with interest at Lantalan. Marcalan had not much the look of his father, but Loch'alan did have his angular features.

"You truly must be loved by your father, Mar, or no doubt you would not have reached Age," Haladhon said.

"Nay, 'twas that he tagged after you and Alcandhor as a boy, making himself a pest to you both, and so kept out of my hair, that saved his life."

Haladhon snorted. "And helped set him on the road he is on, no doubt. He tried to emulate everything I did and then had to try to outdo me."

"A sickening case of hero-worship," Marcalan said. "Which I never realized at the time was totally unwarranted."

The men all burst into laughter again.

The jesting continued but turned to other topics as the meal continued. Tam listened as she ate.

Haladhon fumbled his table knife, and it fell to the floor. Tam retrieved it for him and continued eating. She picked up her mug, and the odor hit her nose before she took a sip. Ale. She glanced at Haladhon's mug but it was ale, not her tea. She eyed Marcalan with suspicion as she took his mug and sniffed it. Tea. She traded the mugs back with a dark look at her cousin. "Leave my mug alone, Marcalan."

"Look not at me," he said, glancing up from his plate.

Tam started to respond but noticed Haladhon sitting with his face in his hand, his eyes twinkling. She swatted his arm with the back of her hand, and he broke out in a snicker. "You have come a long way in less than a lunation, cousin."

"Behave, Haladhon," said Alcandhor.

"My apologies, Thane. It was an impulse of the moment."

Why had her uncle asked him to behave now when neither he nor Marcalan had behaved during the entire meal?

"Thane," the Laird asked, his eyes shining, "how keep you from going mad with those two both housed in Zaidhron?"

"We are often spared having them present at the same time, as Marcalan often roams. But when they are together at Zaidhron, we suffer."

Krendhal cleared his throat. "I would suggest, Your Grace, that if you lack entertainment at Laird Hall, you could send to Zaidhron for those two."

"It should perhaps be their main occupation." Nandhal slid his eyes to Marcalan with a sneer.

"Leave off, Nandhal. If you have any complaint, eat outside," Eladhrel said.

"They take jesting too far."

"I would fain take their jesting over your sour attitude," Eladhrel said.

Marcalan leaned forward, his eyes shining. He gestured toward Eladhrel with his eating knife, giggling. "This from the man who swore he would kill us by slow torture, Haladhon."

"I have not forgotten that, so take care," Eladhrel said.

"What did you two do to him?" Tam asked Haladhon.

Marcalan and Haladhon exchanged glances, and Eladhrel gave them both a menacing glare. Marcalan cleared his throat. "It is best not talked about."

"Why not?" Tam had never before seen those two reticent in boasting of a prank.

"There are some pranks that should not be talked about at table or in mixed company," Haladhon said.

"Mixed company?"

"It means men and women together, as we are," Capalan said, gesturing around their table with his knife.

She still did not understand but decided to say no more, especially since she could feel the flush of Eladhrel's embarrassment. She sipped her tea since she had finished eating.

Looking about at her kin, she wondered again about the close-around-the-throat necklaces some of the Rangers wore. The adornment could not be family or rank related, at least, not by any sense she could make of it.

She sighed inwardly. Her father had taught her much and taught her well, but some small things like this he had not mentioned. And why did he never teach her of the Enaisi? She would never know. She saw his face again in her mind as the arrow hit him in the chest. Why did the moment seem to happen so slowly? His body had jerked to a halt as the arrow struck, and he had looked shocked. She became aware of a voice, Marcalan's voice, calling her name and she shook herself, looking around.

"Excuse me?" she murmured, glancing at Marcalan.

"I said, you seem a world away."

Tam scanned the table, noticing they almost all looked at her. She gulped, her face growing warm. What could she say? "I–I was thinking."

"It must have been important."

"Nay. Not really." She seized her mug and pretended to drink although it was empty.

Marcalan began to say something else but the Laird stood, indicating the meal had ended. The Rangers all stood and bowed to him and began leaving the hall.

The Laird hurried to Tam. "Are you all right?"

"Aye, Your Grace. Why?"

"In ten days of travel I have become familiar with a few things about you, Ranger. I know the look that was on your face. You do not speak of it, but please know that if you wish to talk, I will listen. We do share the same grief."

She smiled at him, grateful for his friendship.

Marcalan came over. "Excuse us, Your Grace. Some of us are going to the foreroom for a while to relax, sing, and talk. Will you both join us?"

"What say you, Tam?" asked the Laird.

Sing and talk with strangers? Oh, stars. "I–I do not think so. I am a bit tired."

"But it is early," Marcalan said. "And some of the Rangers would like to meet you, Tam."

She gave the Laird a pleading look.

"She said she was tired, Marcalan. Forget you that she was eighteen days with little sleep and journeying hard and only one day back?" The Laird's tone of voice surprised Tam—it rang with authority.

"Aye. I did forget. But the Rangers will be disappointed."

"They will have plenty of time to learn of their new cousin. Your future Thane needs rest."

Marcalan bowed, eyes twinkling, and gestured for Tam to pass.

She entered her chamber and almost gasped at the heat. The fireplace had been stoked and seemed to pull the breath out of her. She snatched the poker and jabbed at the wood to separate it and let it die down. Through the door she could hear men laughing and singing from the foreroom, but her eyes stung from exhaustion. She would have no trouble sleeping.

~:~

A loud, desperate cry brought Alcandhor to his feet, pain shooting through his shoulder and chest. He rushed out to find Haladhon and Marcalan in the hallway, with many Rangers crowding behind them.

"Was that Tam?" Alcandhor asked.

"Aye, it was," Haladhon said, frowning with worry.

Alcandhor knocked on her door and entered as she answered. She was sitting up, soaking wet with sweat and gasping, the glowing key dangling in front of the coverlet she clutched to her throat. He pulled her bedclothes up, draped them over her bare shoulders, and sat down.

"What is it, Tam?"

"I know not. A dream."

"She had nightmares while journeying," Marcalan said from the doorway.

"What sort of dream?" Alcandhor asked Tam.

"It was blackness. I am not sure of more. I felt...called by the blackness."

"Stars," muttered Haladhon.

"Hush. Leave us," the Thane ordered over his shoulder. He got up and sat on her left side as the door closed. Pulling the child over onto his good shoulder, he leaned back against the wall. "Rest, Tam. Rest against me," he said in a soft, soothing voice. He willed her to relax, and finally, after she quit trembling, he said, "Tell me everything you remember, Tam."

"Just blackness."

"That is all?"

"That is all I remember."

"How long have you had such dreams of blackness?"

"I know not. Many years. But they happen more often now."

Alcandhor did not ask more, but just held her, as he would his little daughter, Amara, stroking her hair and sending her peaceful feelings. Truly, he had two daughters now. She snuggled against him and, slowly, relaxed.

"Think you that you can try to sleep again now?"

"I will try."

He kissed the top of her head and stood. "Sleep, then. We will talk of this tomorrow."

Haladhon and Marcalan still waited in the hallway. Naturally. Their curiosity played second only to their jesting. "What do you two vagabonds want?" he asked in feigned irritation.

"I saw the key, Thane," Marcalan whispered, wide-eyed. "She makes a key glow!"

"She dreams, does she not?" Haladhon asked.

Alcandhor sighed. How should he answer? What she experienced were not dreams, but should he share that yet? "Aye. But she remembers nothing."

"Think you she sees?" Marcalan asked.

Alcandhor rubbed his forehead, too tired to even think. "It will take some time to find out what she can do. Would that this siege were over and the traitors all found. I need to get her to Zaidhron."

"Hopefully this will be over soon, and we can return there with her," Haladhon said.

"I hope so, cousin," Alcandhor muttered as he opened the door to the meeting chamber.

"Night's rest," Haladhon said.

"I doubt it, but thank you." Alcandhor closed the door.

Chapter Twenty-eight

Tam did not sleep well. No more calls from the blackness afflicted her but she did dream of her father. He held her in his arms and told her he loved her. She awoke crying. Gasping back sobs, she wiped her face and struggled out of the bedcovers. Crossing the few steps to where her clothes draped on the chair felt like walking through soft, shifting sand.

She donned her trous and shirt by the light of the key and opened the door. Grey not black—not night, but the sun had not risen yet.

With bare feet she padded on the cold stone back past the bathing room to the washing rooms and privacy rooms. After she finished she tiptoed into the kitchen, not wanting to wake Sherel, but the woman had already begun the morning meal.

"Good morning, Sherel. May I help?"

Sherel turned. "You are Second at Table and would ask to do menial tasks? You have more important duties." She turned back to pots and kettles over the fire.

Tam sighed and walked to the foreroom. By the light coming in the windows, she knew sun-up would not be far off. She sat in a chair, watching the sky through the window becoming lighter and lighter and listening to the dawn birds beginning to sing.

If only she were at the small lake near the cottage. She loved to sit under one particular tree near the edge of the water and watch the sun rise.

Tam eyed the walls of the foreroom and stood. The room from the hall archway to the west seemed longer than it should be compared to her uncle's bedchamber. Oh, stars—the bedchamber had no windows! She stepped off the distance and afterwards ran on tiptoe down to the armory chamber, wincing as the door creaked. She peered at the walls in the dim light from the hall sconces. Aye. Much more distance as well. And this room had windows.

She heard a shuffling noise behind her and whirled around, almost smacking into a bare chest. A very tousled-looking Marcalan stood looking half-asleep and wearing only trous. She took a step back, her stomach tumbling as a warm shiver swept over her. She stopped blocking, wanting to feel Marcalan's warm, frothy presence. But he did not seem pleased or happy. He held himself in a strange reticence.

249

"What in the names of both moons are you doing, girl?"

"There is a discrepancy in the size of the rooms."

He rolled his eyes, groaning. "You are up at this tormentable hour to check the size of rooms? Bells, you make me tired."

"You are not going to try to tell me I woke you with all the noise I was making?"

"Nay, I had to use the priv and saw this door open."

Tam crossed her arms. "Then go back to bed until you have to get up."

"Why are you not sleeping?"

"I could not sleep."

"And so you creep around stealthily to measure the size of rooms?" Marcalan asked, with a sleepy smile. His warmth grew just a bit, and Tam relaxed.

"I was looking for the opening."

"If that is all, I can show that to you." He walked to the corner where she had been headed.

"What is it for?"

"A hiding place in case of attack, we are told, although that is not my personal opinion, as Rangers would not hide. Here is where a key would fit."

"Can we enter?"

"Bells, I know not the last time it would have been entered but I see no reason not to," he said with a yawn. "Not since you have the key."

"You know?"

"I saw it last night and..." he paused, his eyes flicking at her shirt and away. A tingle coursed through her from him. "In this darkened chamber it glows through your shirt."

"Oh." She glanced down and her face grew warm as she clutched the glowing crystal through the material. Stars, she had forgotten she was not wearing her jerkin. She drew the key out and placed it against the spot Marcalan indicated. A section of the wall swung back without a sound. Tam stood awed for a moment before taking a step forward. They both peered into the darkness. It should be fusty, being closed up, but Tam could feel a slight breeze, and the air did not smell stale.

"The key is bright enough to give us light, Marcalan. Shall we explore?"

He took a step back with a little intake of breath, and she asked, "Are we not allowed to?"

"I think there is little the Second at Table would not be allowed to do"—he nodded at her shirt again—"especially since the Thane has entrusted the key to her."

"Then why do you hesitate?"

He averted his eyes. She felt the tingle in him grow to a strong, warm roll of, of almost fear. Fear of her? She waited for an answer and when none came, she asked, "What is wrong? Why are you afraid?"

He shrugged, but his nonchalant gesture belied the strong emotions that coursed within him. "It is not being afraid. I just think it would be better if we waited and explored with more Rangers."

"Why? It would not be as much fun with lots of Rangers I do not know."

"We could at least ask Haladhon to join us."

She considered this while looking down the dark corridor. It beckoned her. "Nay. I want to explore now. Come, Marcalan."

He did not move.

"Please?"

He sighed, rubbing his face and eyes. She sensed a determination in him, but—

"What are you two doing in here?"

Tam turned at her uncle's voice to see him standing in the doorway, looking almost as sleepy as Marcalan although at least he was dressed. She ran past Marcalan to him.

"Uncle, I want to go exploring but Marcalan will not."

"Wait." He held up his hand. "How in the world did you find that? What are you both doing up anyway?"

"I could not sleep," she said, as Marcalan was explaining, "I had to use the priv and saw the door open—"

"I saw a discrepancy in the sizes of the rooms, Uncle, and Marcalan came in and showed me where the door was. We used the key to open it, and I want to explore it but Marcalan will not," she said in one breath.

Alcandhor blinked and combed his fingers through his hair, muttering, "'Tis too early for this." He sighed. "Later, Tam. I will show you around in there later if you wish. It will be time for breakfast soon, and you both need to get dressed."

Tam let out her breath, gazing at the opening in vast disappointment. "Aye, Uncle."

"Now, close that door, girl, and go get dressed, do you hear?" The smile in his eyes as he left belied his gruff voice.

"Aye, sir." She walked back to the hidden door and ran her fingers over the white stone—no handle or ring to pull. "How can we shut it?"

Marcalan shrugged. "I know not. Perhaps the key?"

She set the key to the spot on the wall, and the door slowly slid shut.

"Amazing," she whispered, smiling up at him.

He stepped back, his feelings again in a reserve. "Now we had better obey the Thane and get dressed. See you at breakfast, Tam." Marcalan darted out.

Tam frowned. Why did he wish to be away from her? With Marcalan, who could tell? She sighed and looked at that door again. She did not want to wait, but would not disobey her uncle. She tucked the key back inside her shirt and turned to leave.

Nandhal leaned against the doorjamb with an arrogant expression. She stopped, startled. Something in her did not like the way he scrutinized her, his gaze sliding from her feet up her body to her face. She blocked as her spine straightened and her neck prickled in danger— nay, not danger, but something repulsive.

"What are you doing in here?" he asked.

"Does the Second at Table answer to you?"

His eyebrows went up. "Like your taste of rank, do you?"

Even when contesting Tam, Loch'alan had not this hateful attitude. Not knowing how to respond, she decided to leave without answering. As she passed him in the doorway, he grabbed her arm, leaning close. His blue eyes glittered, and his smile was not friendly.

"I would say there is one thing that you are good for, girl, and it is not being a Ranger."

She did not understand him, but knew his meaning to be something unpleasant. "Let go of my arm, Nandhal."

"Or you will what, girl?"

She twisted her wrist around his, simultaneously breaking his grip and creating her own. Pulling his arm straight, her other hand pressed against his elbow, allowing her leverage and the ability to break his arm. Her point made, she eased pressure on his joint.

He bent his arm behind his back, trapping her hand, and dove into a shoulder roll. She followed through the dive with him. He leaped to his feet. Tam cross-cut his legs with hers and swept him onto his back. Her heel slammed down on his chest. He gasped for breath as she rolled away and rose.

"If you wish to match me, you do it the proper way." She spun around and stalked out.

~:~

The double doors to the dining hall straight across the hallway opened after Tam passed. Haladhon whistled softly through his teeth as he followed Alcandhor to the armory chamber. Tam had certainly cleaned the floor with Nandhal's face.

But his gut clenched at what he had seen and heard. Nandhal had not learned anything save to cover his attitude well when around the chiefs and those in authority over him.

"Have you a problem, Nandhal?" the Thane asked, his expression and tone forbidding.

The Ranger picked himself up slowly. "No problem, Thane," he said with a gasp.

"Good." Alcandhor grabbed a fistful of jerkin and hauled Nandhal's face close to his. "See you respect my foster-daughter and your future Thane, or the law will crash upon you with all force I can bring to bear." Nandhal's blue eyes rounded, seeming to glow in a face drained of color. The Thane dropped the cockerel, spun, and returned to the dining hall. Nandhal fell against the wall, his hands shaking.

Haladhon leaned over his cousin. "I begin to think there is one thing that you are good for, you young fool, and it is not being a Ranger." With a disgusted shake of his head, he strode away.

~:~

Tam again sat with Haladhon as the Thane heard all the reports. About mid-morning they finished. Tam stared up as her tall cousin stood and stretched. He grinned down at her. "Through for another morning."

"I will fain take a walk." Her uncle rose with a sigh. "I missed yesterday morning because of the conclave."

"How far are you walking now?" Tam asked.

He rubbed his bad shoulder for a moment and adjusted the necklace he wore. "Through the town to the perimeter. I rest there before returning as Andhrel and Lamadhel would fain report me to Santran, but I need not. My strength is returning."

Tam eyed her uncle's throat and decided to be bold. "Uncle, may I ask a question?"

"Certainly, Tam."

"Why do some Rangers wear a necklace as you do?"

Alcandhor and Haladhon both looked at her in surprise.

"You do not know?" Alcandhor asked.

"Nay."

"They are necklets and are given in commitment. At least in most clans, I think. Some seem to have abandoned the custom."

"Commitment?"

"Marriage. The woman braids some strands of her hair with the string used for the necklet, then adds beads of whatever colors she wishes. Blue and green for faithfulness and loyalty in love, silver for a peaceful life together, and so on. When the man accepts the necklet, they are considered to have entered a legal contract of marriage."

Staring at her uncle's necklet, Tam said, "My father never told me about that."

"He did overlook a few things. Be not afraid to ask any of us if you find you have questions."

"Thank you." Her morning excursion came to mind. "Uncle? When will we explore that chamber?"

"Chamber?" Haladhon asked, looking from one to the other.

"She saw the discrepancy in the room sizes. I promised her I would take her on a tour."

"I see." Haladhon grinned at her. "You do not miss much, do you, cousin?"

Tam shrugged. "I know not. If I missed something I would be unaware of that fact, would I not?"

Haladhon groaned. "Let not Andhrel tutor her, Alcandhor. He will turn her into another law-keeper."

"There is much about this young Ranger we do not know yet, cousin." Alcandhor gave an approving smile to Tam.

Warmth filled Tam at her uncle's favor but still she wanted to know about that hallway. "When can we explore, Uncle?" she asked again.

Haladhon rubbed the back of his neck, his lips twitching and amusement in his eyes as he gazed at Alcandhor. What did he find humorous?

"When I get some free time, Tam."

"This afternoon?" she asked, rising to her feet.

"Perhaps. Now you go on and take advantage of having some time free of duty."

"May I go on the walk with you?"

"If you wish. Or you could get some practice time in. How long since you have matched?"

She thought back to the grueling staff and hand-to-hand of her father's Training. "The morning of the day you arrived."

Her uncle shook his head with an amused grin. "Ah, you are mistaken. We matched while journeying."

She smiled at the happy memory. "You are right. I had forgotten that. But still, it has been some time since I have practiced. Perhaps I should go find a partner to match, since many offered last night, although I would rather walk with you."

"I walk every day. Twice a day if duties do not hinder it." He set his hand on her shoulder. "And we will be spending much time together from now on. You have an opportunity for as many matches as you could wish at the moment, with all these Rangers here. Take advantage of it. I wish I could."

Her eyes strayed to the sling.

He gave a dismissive wave with his good arm. "It will take time for it to heal. Worry not, though, niece. The day will come when we will match again."

Tam nodded but chewed her lip as she closed the door behind her. She felt the doubt behind his smile; her uncle worried also about his shoulder healing.

~:~

Linna turned to see one of her scullions, Tesill, in the doorway crying. Tavnol stood behind her, his face set and grim.

"Linna, have all your girls stay in here from now on."

The girl ran to a corner and collapsed in a heap, face in her skirt.

"What happened to her?"

Tavnol shook his head. "Keep them with you. Use this priv—don't go outside for any reason. Some of the guards aren't acting like guards, if you take my meaning. The servants in the keep have it worse. The nobles are...taking what they want. Vitran rants about it but does nothing." He leaned close and whispered, "We must act."

Linna glanced at Tesill, torn between rage and fear. She started to speak but Karnin walked in. The fear won. She drew back and turned away. What could a mere cook do to end a siege?

"The soup kettles will be prepared soon," she said over her shoulder. "Get the men ready to carry them."

Chapter Twenty-nine

As Tam stepped outside, the Laird saw her and came over, smiling. "Gardening again?"

"Nay, Your Grace. I seek match partners."

"I would fain watch."

"I am honored, Your Grace."

They walked to where several hand-to-hand matches took place. Tam studied the matches and saw some moves she had never seen before. She went over them in her mind.

Loch'alan sauntered over, grinning. "Match, cousin Tam? I would fain even the score."

She unstrapped her knife with a smile. The Laird reached for the weapon, and she bowed as she placed the blade in his hand.

She and her cousin put fists over their hearts and faced off. Loch'alan came in boldly, an edge to his sparring that Tam could sense had a bit of wounded pride to it. She fought back hard, using some of the techniques she had seen earlier. Both would remember the match by some nice bruises.

Finally, Loch'alan held up his hand to end the match, and she straightened. They held fists over their hearts in salute again.

"Stars, Tam, you fight hard," he said, breathing hard. "I am not used to such intensity in a match."

Tam frowned in confusion. "Is not that how one matches? It is how my father taught me." A crowd had gathered and a self-conscious warmth flooded Tam's face.

"Your father was a hard teacher, I am told." Loch'alan wiped his face on his sleeve.

"I have no comparison. He was my only teacher."

"A very good one, if one can judge by his pupil."

"I did try to learn what he taught." She remembered her father's disapproving looks and his scolding as they would match, doubting he would have found her efforts acceptable. She turned as the Laird held out her blade. "Thank you, Your Grace."

"Thank you." He bowed. "I enjoyed watching the match. Are you going to practice more?"

"If anyone will match me."

"If you will excuse me, Your Grace, and Tam, I am in need of a drink of water." Loch'alan bowed to the Laird and ambled off.

A Ranger with a round face, black hair, and deep laugh lines around his green eyes walked over, grinning. "Match, cousin Tam?"

"Going to assess her against your memory of her father, Cordhan?" asked the Ranger with him.

"Aye. Let us see if he was as good teacher as he was fighter." Cordhan smiled at Tam—cordially. "He was one of my match partners when we were striplings and cockerel Rangers. I would fain match his daughter."

Tam bowed.

Cordhan, being older, had much more experience and fought much harder than Loch'alan. She had to use much more skill against his strength than she had against her young cousin. But Tam's father had fought her thus. When the match was over, he grabbed her by the shoulders, grinning. "Thank you! I see your father when you fight. He was a good teacher, and you, a good pupil."

"You also remind me of my father when you fight," she said, trying to catch her breath. "I would fain match you often."

"I would be honored."

She had wondered if Nandhal would want to match her but did not see him. She wanted to give him a most thorough thrashing.

"Seek you another match?" Cordhan asked.

"Aye."

Cordhan peered about the bailey, eyes narrowed. "Hmm, Maradhor is not here. He must be on duty."

"I thought he was a scribe."

"Aye. And master swordsman as well. But he was one of your father's favorite match partners. Ah—I have the Ranger for you. Edhron! Come over!"

A short, lean Ranger turned from the match he was watching and jogged over to them. Grey streaked his wavy dark hair. This was the striplings' instructor who had called a greeting to her father in the training courtyard at Zaidhron. He bowed to the Laird and put his fist over his heart to Tam.

"Edhron, Tam is looking for a match. I thought you ideal."

The older Ranger lifted his eyebrows. "And why is that?"

"She was Trained solely by Valdhor."

"Ah, I see." He grinned, the lines deepening around his grey eyes. "I am honored."

The match taught Tam much. Edhron, being small and wiry, had to rely more on speed and agility in his fighting than a larger man would.

He caught her with moves she had never seen, and she used each one back at him as she saw the chance. He could best her easily, but instead of pressing his advantage, he allowed her to learn from him and try the moves, countering them once she had used them correctly. Never had she been in such a match; she was exhausted but exhilarated.

She tried one of the moves she had first seen earlier and used on Loch'alan in their match and caught Edhron with it. He hit the ground, kicked her in the back of the thigh, and grabbed at her as she fell. They wrestled as Tam tried to maneuver him into the hold she remembered the Thane using on her father—arm straight behind his back at an odd angle and wrist bent. Edhron somehow reversed it on her, and unable to break the hold, she called the match.

"Where did you learn that?" asked Edhron, as they both sat on the ground, sweating and breathing in heavy pants.

"Uncle used it on Father," she managed to gasp.

"Did he, now?" Edhron stood and held out his hand, his eyes shining. She took it, letting him help her to her feet. He clapped his hand to her right shoulder and she returned the gesture. "You are a quick study. I will fain match you any time, cousin Tam."

Tam warmed at the implied compliment. "Thank you, Edhron."

She stood with the Laird, Edhron, and Cordhan watching another match. They discussed various moves they saw and explained a few to the Laird. The luncheon gong sounded and Rangers scattered to eat.

~:~

As luncheon ended, the Thane leaned toward the Laird. "I must have a word with you, Your Grace."

The Laird nodded and they left the dining hall together. The Thane gestured to a chair as he closed the door to the meeting chamber. "Your Grace, I wished to speak with you concerning something unfortunate."

"What is it, Thane?"

Alcandhor set his elbow on the table and rested his chin in his hand, covering his mouth, trying to find the right words. "My Laird." He rubbed his hand over his face. "There has been talk about you and Tam."

The Laird's face revealed total puzzlement. "Talk? What kind of talk?"

"About the two of you."

"What about us?"

Could he possibly be as naïve as Tam? "Surely you must know what I am referring to, Your Grace."

Comprehension dawned on the Laird's face, and he blushed. "You cannot be serious!"

"I wish I was not."

"But why?" The Laird threw out his arms. "Who would make such an accusation?"

Alcandhor shook his head. "Some people enjoy creating trouble and would find shadows where none exist, but your journey alone with her was enough to set some tongues flapping."

The Laird rolled his eyes in disgust. "Between my grief and exhaustion, no thought entered my head. And her entire disposition is a barrier anyway. She is totally a Ranger and seems unaware she is female."

Alcandhor fought down a smile. "That is so."

"Is that the basis of the gossip?"

"Not entirely. You and she have spent quite a bit of time together since you have been back. And," he paused, "'tis said you held her hand at breakfast yesterday."

"I–I did no such thing!"

"It was seen by several people, Your Grace."

He shook his head, crossing his arms, then closed his eyes with a quiet groan. "I was telling her about my trepidation about being Laird, and she encouraged me. I did not hold her hand, Thane. I touched it for a moment. I was simply thanking her. She has given me friendship. I can talk to her. She is young, as am I, and understands feeling overwhelmed by responsibilities." His blue eyes pleaded with Alcandhor. "I was wrong to touch her hand, and I apologize. I can see how it was misunderstood. But I wanted to let her know how much I appreciated her friendship."

A grimace of pain crossed the Laird's face. "Do you know what it is like going through your life without being touched? To have people keep a 'respectful distance' from you so that you feel so isolated and alone?

"I remember when I was a child, and you were not yet Thane. We were Randhal and Alcandhor, pupil and tutor. I–I used to pretend you were my older brother, you know. You would pick me up over your shoulder like a sack of meal and carry me, then toss me on the grass and tickle me. Remember you that?"

"You were very young then." Alcandhor smiled at the memories.

"You were the only one who ever treated me as a boy instead of the Atheling." He stood and began to pace in frustration, his voice becoming shrill. "I will spend the rest of my life not being able to be close to anyone. And I try, one time, one time, to reach out to someone to thank her for being a friend, and that is misconstrued. I cannot be touched, and I cannot touch!"

He turned away from Alcandhor, his shoulders bowed.

The Thane rose, taking a deep breath. The Laird was just a boy still, overly young to have to take on such burdens. No family to turn to for love or affection. Alcandhor walked around the table to his Laird and put a hand on his shoulder. The Laird shook his head, his reply sarcastic. "That is not done, Thane."

"Will you stop me?"

He turned around with a wry smile. "I think I would not be wise to try."

Alcandhor grasped the Laird by the nape of the neck and gently shook him, as his uncle used to do to him. "You make your own choices now, my Laird. Whether you be touched, whether you allow close friends and kin to call you by name. Do not let traditions of the past cause you grief."

The young man's blue eyes lit up. "Aye! Aye, I can make those choices."

Alcandhor grinned and tapped his Laird's face in a mock slap as he used to, long ago. The Laird returned the grin but sobered. "But what about this gossip?"

"I am not worried about it now that I have talked to you and know there is nothing to it."

The Laird's face paled. "You thought there might be?"

"Your Grace, besides being her Thane, I am her closest kin now and foster-father. I had to be certain." His eyes twinkled. "Besides, I know of two other incidents between you two."

The Laird frowned.

"In this very chamber. I saw you kiss her, and I saw you hold her hand."

The Laird looked thoughtful for a moment, but a grin slowly spread. "I am glad that at least you do not feel those were 'incidents' worthy of worrying about."

"Nay. If I had thought either one were more than it appeared at the time, I would have said something to you then."

"But what happens if she hears the gossip?"

Alcandhor let out a slow breath. "I know not. She is very ingenuous and seems to understand little of such things. I hope she hears nothing of it, and I know not what she would do. My desire is to take her back to Zaidhron and let my sister be foster-mother to her and teach her those things her father did not."

"Let us hope then, that she does not hear of it."

The Thane rolled his eyes in agreement.

"But I do think it is best if I spend my time letting Lord Krendhal instruct me, and give this gossip a chance to die."

"That might be wise, Your Grace."

~:~

Alcandhor agreed to show Tam the hidden hallway that afternoon to quiet her. He took a candle although the key would have given enough light by itself.

"This is it? Just this corridor?" Tam looked around, disappointment on her face.

"I think it had a special use for the Enaisi, but since they are gone, we cannot know the purpose."

She lifted her hands above her head. "I feel air."

"Aye. I wish we knew some of the secrets of the Enaisi. Fresh air without an apparent source, lighting—so many things they had that we do not."

"The water and waste system used here and in Laird Hall and in Zaidhron, are those from the Enaisi?"

"Aye."

Tam thought of the structure on the Forbidden Peninsula. "Could this air not be from hidden ventilation shafts?"

"That was my thought, and although you can feel air coming through small slits near the ceiling and along the floor at the end of the hall, I never found anything indicative of a ventilation system. Remember, I was young and curious too, at one time."

"Would you mind if I searched anyway?"

"'Tis a prerogative of the young. During your free time later, you may search all you wish."

She beamed. "Thank you, Uncle!"

"Tam," Alcandhor said as they left the hidden hallway. "Go to the meeting chamber while I locate Haladhon. There is a matter I wish to discuss."

"Aye, Uncle."

Alcandhor returned with Haladhon to find Tam sitting in a chair at the table. She quickly put down the book that he had been reading. Her curiosity about those books delighted Alcandhor almost as much as her ability to make a key glow.

He sat in the chair next to her while Haladhon sprawled in another, long legs sticking out and crossed at the ankles.

"Tam, I need to ask you some questions."

She sat straighter. "Aye, sir?"

"These dreams of blackness. You are sure you remember nothing more?"

261

"Just blackness."

"Can you describe it to me?"

She fidgeted in her chair. "I–I see blackness in front of me. I feel pulled, or called to it. I fight it, and I wake up."

Alcandhor paused to consider what to ask next. "Do you ever sense what other people are feeling?"

"Aye, of course. Why?"

Haladhon straightened from his indolent posture. "Think you everyone can sense others' feelings?"

Tam frowned over at her cousin. "They cannot?"

"How would she know it is not normal?" Alcandhor explained aloud to himself as well as to Haladhon. The tall Ranger nodded, leaning back again. "Tam, do you always have a sense of feelings around you?"

"It is easier when it is a strong emotion, like hate or fear. Sometimes the feelings I feel do not seem right and I cannot understand them."

"Can you give me an example?"

Tam chewed her lip for a moment. "If someone is smiling at you and seems so friendly but you only feel coldness. I do not understand that."

Alcandhor stifle a sigh. She had much to learn about people, and those lessons would likely be at great cost. How much hurt would she go through? He shook himself—he had no time for such melancholy speculation and worry. "What emotions have you felt that you would not consider strong?"

Her eyes shone at Alcandhor. "Peace."

His mouth dropped open for a moment before he chuckled. "Aye, I sent that to you last night. You were so distraught."

"Aye. You did the same thing at Zaidhron."

"Could you tell it was sent to you?"

"Before I did not. But I recognized it last night. It was the exact same feeling."

Alcandhor smiled. "And can you send?"

"I think so but I know not if the person to whom I am sending feels it."

"Try. Send to me."

Alcandhor felt a strong wave of affection wash over him. He sent it back, reaffirming to his niece that he did indeed love her. "You have sent to me before, and I did not realize it. But I recognize it now."

Haladhon looked from one to the other. "What did she send?"

"You felt nothing?" asked Alcandhor.

"Nay."

"Tam, please, send to Haladhon."

She paused with a thoughtful expression, tipping her head, and smiled. Haladhon stiffened, his eyes wide.

"What did you feel, cousin?" Alcandhor asked.

"Bells, I am not sure!" He gave Tam an incredulous stare. "I cannot describe it."

"Strong emotions are always easier to send," Tam said. "As well as easier to feel in others."

Alcandhor bit back a grin. "And what indescribable strong emotion did you send our cousin, Tam?"

"I am not sure what to call it. I thought of him and his beautiful laugh and his jesting and how he was my first friend at Zaidhron, and I just sent all that to him."

"Bells and stars!" Haladhon muttered, rubbing the back of his neck.

Alcandhor smiled at his cousin, even as he turned his mind back to his questions for Tam. He knew she should be able to do the things he could—and more, but he needed to see how strongly. Especially prescience, since, unlike other Enaisi traits, that attribute seemed arbitrary.

"Can you send to both of us at once?"

"I have never tried."

"Try now."

She smiled. Alcandhor felt affection again from her and saw Haladhon's eyes widen.

"You felt it too?"

"Aye. I have never experienced anything like this, 'Candhor!"

Alcandhor smiled. "She is strong, that is why." He met Tam's golden eyes. "What are some other emotions that you have felt? Strong and not so strong?"

Tam hesitated a moment. "Hatred. Sadness. Love. There are so many, Uncle."

"Can you tell who each emotion is coming from?"

"Aye."

"Even in a room full of people?"

Tam gave a nonchalant shrug. "Aye."

Alcandhor shook his head in amazement. She could focus in on a person in a crowd! Did Haladhon realize the tactical advantage she could offer? "Can you block emotions? If you do not wish to feel them, can you block them?"

She dropped her head, whispering, "Aye."

Alcandhor closed his eyes, perceiving her pain. She must be thinking of her father. "I am sorry."

Tam remained quiet, twisting her fingers. Alcandhor ground his teeth. Stars, if only he had gone to Valdhor years ago as he wished, instead of obeying his father.

She raised her head, frowning. "Why do you feel so guilty, Uncle?"

Alcandhor found himself speechless and wagged his head in dismay. He would have to watch his emotions around her. He let out his breath. "I am going to have to become accustomed to this."

Haladhon's gaze flicked between the two. "Tam, can you sense everyone's feelings at all times?"

"Aye. But 'tis easier if they have strong emotions. And some people are easier to sense. My father was easy to feel. So is Uncle." She smiled at him.

"It must be because we have the gift too." Alcandhor said. At Tam's confused expression he explained, "There are not many left with this gift of the Enaisi. And none strong like you. We are called Children of the Enaisi. Some just say we are the ones who make a key glow, which does, at times, have an advantage."

"Who else can you feel strongly, Tam?" Haladhon asked. "Nandhal?"

Tam shook her head. "Nay. I feel nothing from him. But he blocks always. I...I do not like him."

Alcandhor privately agreed. A snort from Haladhon indicated his opinion as well.

"Any others?"

"Marcalan," Tam said with a shrug.

Alcandhor's thoughts halted in perplexity. "Marcalan?"

She nodded.

Alcandhor met Haladhon's stare and saw the same question in his cousin's eyes. "A key does not—cannot—glow for him. Yet..." Alcandhor scrutinized Tam. For her to sense Marcalan more easily than others should indicate thus. "Get him in here, Haladhon."

The tall Ranger strode out.

"Are there other Rangers you feel more strongly or easily?"

"Nay, sir. Not at the moment. But I have sensed one other very strongly. He is not on the grounds right now though." Tam hesitated then added, "I have felt some strong emotions at times when walking in the bailey."

"Would you be able to point out who they come from?"

"Aye, if you want me to."

"You sound certain."

"It is an easy thing. It requires no effort."

Alcandhor sat in silent amazement staring at his niece. Tam twisted her fingers in her lap.

The door opened and the two pranksters entered. Marcalan looked confused, but his eyes twinkled. "What is it? Nothing I have planned has happened yet today."

Alcandhor shook his head, feigning irritation with his younger cousin.

"Shall I pull the curtains, Thane?"

"Nay, I want total darkness for this, Haladhon. Let us go to the bedchamber. It has no windows."

They all crossed the hall to the windowless room and closed the door.

"Bring out the key, Tam."

As she pulled the key out from under her shirt and jerkin, the chamber lit up as if by many candles.

"Stars!" Marcalan whispered.

"Give the key to Marcalan, Tam, then back away."

She did, and the key dimmed but still gave light.

"Marcalan," came Haladhon's voice, "'tis not possible that you make a key glow!"

Chapter Thirty

"We are running short of firewood," Linna told Vitran.

"What can I do about it? Tear down all the doors in this place and break up the furniture?"

"It will come to that before long," Linna shot back. "And sooner rather than later if Jandhal keeps whining about how cold he is at night and sending guards to steal what wood I have."

Vitran cursed. "That is one thing I can take care of." He stormed toward the keep, cursing with each stride. He had his fill of these nobles. Useless insects.

He slammed into Jandhal's bedchamber. The man reclined on his bed, half-dressed, a bottle in his hand.

Vitran shook with rage. "I'm trying to find ways to get us out of this mess, and dealing with all the problems and crises, while you sit in here and drink, and steal wood we need to cook our meager supply of food?"

Jandhal struggled to a sitting position. "How dare you talk to me that way!"

Vitran crossed to the bed and dragged Jandhal up by the collar of his shirt. "Cause any more grief and I'll show you how much I will dare, you piece of muckhill refuse!" He threw him back down on the bed and turned to leave.

Jandhal rebounded off the bed. "Are you threatening me?"

Vitran whirled around, his eyes scornful. "And if I am?"

"I am a lord!"

"You are nothing! You are more worthless than a scullion!"

The noble lunged at Vitran in a rage, but Vitran had his knife ready. Jandhal froze, his eyes bulging, as the blade plunged into his belly. He grabbed at Vitran's jerkin, and as the steward sliced the knife up and out of the noble's body, he slowly slumped to the floor.

With a malicious smile, Vitran kicked the still figure, and walked out. Only one left.

He left the keep and glanced up at that cursed drum tower. If only he could only get to those bloody Rangers, the gatehouse would be accessible. The Rangers still held the circumference, he was sure, but he might draw Rangers into a trap with a plea for a truce—the Thane would likely come himself.

Visions of Alcandhor and his chiefs lying dead in the gatehouse cheered him. But how to rid himself of those Rangers in that tower? It seemed impossible.

He needed to think of immediate concerns, like the shortage of wood. Would it come to tearing down doors and using furniture? Vitran stopped—doors! Wooden doors! The drum tower, as all others, had a wooden door. Why had he not thought of it earlier? How could they get to that door without a deadly volley of arrows raining down on them?

His pace slowed as he crossed the bailey, deep in thought.

~:~

Alcandhor frowned, reviewing Marcalan's genealogy in his mind.

"I–I cannot make a key glow," Marcalan said, his voice shaky. "'Tis not possible."

"Your eyes show you it is possible," Haladhon said with a chuckle.

"Haladhon, hush," Alcandhor said in a soft voice. "Let me think."

"Thane, I do not accept what this means. My mother—"

"Your mother has many faults, Marcalan," Alcandhor said, "but breaking her marriage vows to your father? Nay. It belies her nature." He rubbed his forehead, trying to remember his reading of genetics and biology. He had not touched those books in years. "I will research it when we return to Zaidhron. There must be an explanation. For now, let us not mention it. Gossip would surely take wings and slander your family."

"Thank you, Thane." The relief in Marcalan's voice gave way to his mischievous lilt. "I would not wish harm to come to anyone if my mother heard accusations."

Haladhon snickered. Alcandhor sighed; considering Kalinna's demeanor, Marcalan's jest had a taste of truth in it. But still, something was amiss. Marcalan was highly-Trained; despite his affectations at despising books—no doubt an attitude adopted when he was young to emulate Haladhon—he was well studied. How could he not know the signs of one with Enaisi blood?

Alcandhor's eyes narrowed, considering Marcalan's worry at first seeing he made a key glow, and the depth of his relief. "You knew."

Marcalan's mouth dropped open, but he immediately closed it and raised his eyebrows. "Knew what, Thane?"

"How long have you known?" Alcandhor insisted, ignoring the prankster's innocent response.

A long silence followed as Marcalan stared at the floor. Finally, in a soft voice, he whispered, "Since I was young."

"Why said you nothing?" Haladhon exclaimed.

"What should I say? Whom should I confide in? I asked my father soon after starting Training why I was not tested to see if I could make a key glow as some other children were. He explained it was not necessary, that I could not make a key glow due to my parentage. Even though young, he said enough for me to comprehend it could only indicate disgrace on my mother. So I...kept silent."

"You believed your mother had—"

"I know not what to believe!" Marcalan's voice held almost a hysterical edge. "I cannot have Enaisi blood, yet I do, but to think my mother could have broken her vows to my father—I cannot accept that either. Not Kalinna!"

"Aye, it does seem against her character," Haladhon murmured.

"'Tis a vexing puzzle," Alcandhor said. "When we are back at Zaidhron, we shall have a private council with them. I will also review what I know of genes. The Enaisi did not wish their abilities to easily survive outside their own race. Traits were purposefully encoded across various genes—all dominant, if I recall, and should not be able to split and recombine, thus each of your parents inheriting a portion that could recombine in you—" He blinked at the blank expressions around him. "My apologies."

Alcandhor nodded at Marcalan. "For now, as I said, news that you have Enaisi blood will be kept quiet."

"I thank you, Thane." This time, Marcalan's voice had no humor in it. Years Marcalan had held this secret to his heart, feeling unable to trust anyone, even his closest friend or his Thane. How much of his humor covered a dread that he could be the cause of a family scandal?

Alcandhor now shared that dread, both as Thane and close friend to Marcalan. He doubted the matter would be far from his own heart until they found answers. But for now...

"Let us concern ourselves with the present." Alcandhor cleared his throat. "Give the key to Tam, Marcalan."

The room lit up as Tam took the key in her hand.

"Tam, any other Ranger you sense might make a key glow, you tell me or Haladhon immediately."

"Aye, sir."

"Let us go back to the meeting chamber," Alcandhor said.

They crossed back and closed the door. Alcandhor fell into a chair, feeling drained. He gestured for her to sit. "Tam, how far away can you feel emotion from someone?"

"I know not. I felt my father's anger and worry when I was in that ravine with a broken leg while he was searching for me."

268

"How far can you send emotions?"

"I know not that either, Uncle."

"Hmm, perhaps we can test that. Send to Marcalan so he knows what it feels like."

Turning to look at her cousin, Tam smiled.

Marcalan gasped, his eyes wide and face flushed. "Stars!"

Haladhon leaned against the wall, chuckling.

Alcandhor grinned. "Now, you prankster. Go out to the gate, and Tam will continue to send to you as you go. If you stop feeling the emotion she is sending, then note that spot and return. Otherwise return when you reach the gate."

Marcalan swallowed. "Aye, Thane." He fled out the door as if chased.

What had Marcalan so unnerved? Alcandhor exchanged glances with Haladhon. His cousin shrugged. "'Tis new to him."

Nodding, Alcandhor asked Tam, "Are you still sending?"

"Aye."

Alcandhor rose and poured a cup of tea. He grimaced as he drank it. Cold.

"Want you a fresh pot?" Haladhon asked.

Alcandhor shook his head and sat, waiting for Marcalan's return. The scamp soon entered, breathing heavily.

Haladhon straightened. "Stars, did you run all the way?"

"Aye. I could still feel her sending at the gate."

Alcandhor eyed his niece in amazement.

"Bells and stars, 'Candhor, how far away can she send?"

"I know not. But further testing will have to wait until another day. I have other things I wish to discover." Alcandhor cleared his throat and leaned forward. "Tam, do you ever seem to see things in your mind? Things that have not happened yet? Or things that are happening far away?"

"I do not think so, Uncle."

Haladhon slumped back against the wall. "I was certain she could see."

"She might and not know it. I did not discern what it was for many years. It is so natural that you do not recognize it as a special ability. Remember Tam did not realize that sensing emotions was a rare gift. Tam and Marcalan both need to be trained to use whatever abilities they have."

"Thane, I have never had any sight," Marcalan said.

"You may not realize you have it, or other abilities, either. I know not how strong you are, but you have something of the Enaisi in you.

Have you ever had the sense you could feel what others were feeling?"

"Well, aye, Thane." Marcalan cocked his head, grinning. "Especially when I have felt a thrashing coming on."

"Would that be seeing, or sensing emotions?" Haladhon nudged his younger cousin, his eyes twinkling.

"That would just be Marcalan," the Thane said dryly. "But be serious for a moment. You can sense emotions?"

"Aye, at times." A wry smile spread on his face. "Stars, to able to admit...this is freeing, Thane."

"I imagine it is. What other abilities have you?"

"I know not, really. I have tried to squelch any abilities. I...I dared not show temper."

Haladhon and Alcandhor nodded, exchanging glances. Irises darkening would have been revealing.

Marcalan hesitated, shaking his head. "I truly know not what abilities I might have. What is it possible to inherit from the Enaisi? I know of sight, and eyes that darken when angry. But what heed should be given to the stories about the Enaisi themselves?" Alcandhor stifled a groan as Marcalan's voice began to lilt. "One hears how they could delve into people's minds, and kill with a stray thought, and heal with a simple touch, and see future events as though they were already happening in front of them, and move from place to place as quick as if riding lightning bolts—some say they could even fly. Not to mention—"

"Enough!" Alcandhor waved an arm in impatient dismissal. "You sound as if you have given ear to Worshippers. Will you call them the Celestials next?"

Marcalan chortled a bit and sobered. "I give no heed to the rantings of those fanatics. I know little of the Enaisi, but I know they were no gods."

Alcandhor grimaced. "Back to you. We will have to teach you about abilities you might have inherited. You will have to study. Intensely. As will Tam. And I must determine how much of what abilities you do have." He looked at Tam and rubbed his eyes. "Stars, I wish we were back at Zaidhron. There is so much..."

"Uncle?"

"Aye?"

"What is it you hope for?"

"What mean you?"

"I feel hope in you. What is it?"

Alcandhor pulled his chair closer and took Tam's hands in his good one. "I wish not to say too much and perhaps direct—nay, misdirect you. You have strong abilities and the most encouraging is that dream of blackness." He shifted forward more, meeting her golden eyes, his breath quickening as he contemplated what she might accomplish. "Do not fear it or fight it. Let the blackness draw you in and tell me what happens when you awaken."

Tam's face turned white. "I...I know not that I can do that."

"Try, Tam. Please. Try. It is very important."

Tam hesitated, touching her tongue to her lips, and murmured, "I will try."

Alcandhor relaxed with a smile. If she could overcome her fear, his dreams might be possible after all. His heart thudded in anticipation.

"You still have not told me your hopes, Uncle."

He chewed the inside of his cheek, staring at his boots. Dare he put his dream into words? Would she mock him as others had? Alcandhor looked up and met Tam's gaze. "I wish to contact the Enaisi, if we can."

Tam sat like stone, her eyes wide.

Haladhon chuckled. "I think you overwhelmed her, Thane."

"'Tis an overwhelming idea," Marcalan said, rubbing his temples, no lilt to his voice. "Just hearing you say it, Thane, made me feel very strange."

Tam stirred in her chair. "Uncle? What is this seeing like?"

"It can be a feeling, like a premonition something is going to happen—or you might actually see something that either is not happening yet or that is happening somewhere else. It can happen while awake or within a dream. The Enaisi called it prescience, but we just call it foresight or having sight."

"When does it happen and how?"

"There is no telling. It happens when it happens."

"I think I saw something—someone—when you said you wished to contact the Enaisi."

The chamber fell silent. Alcandhor whispered, "What, or who, think you it was you saw?"

"I know not. It was a flash in my mind." She frowned. "A person..."

Haladhon smirked. "She sees, Thane Alcandhor."

"Wait, wait," Marcalan muttered, frowning and rubbing his head again. "I felt something just as the Thane said what he did, and when you said you saw someone, I felt it again..." He grimaced, shaking his head. "I cannot put it into words."

Tam and Marcalan stared at each other, bewilderment on both their faces.

"I know not how, but it is connected to you, Marcalan. I felt what you did as you remembered it. Let me send it back."

Marcalan gasped, staggering back. Haladhon caught him.

"Stars!"

Alcandhor shot to his feet, staring at Tam in shock. "You can send another's emotions back to them?"

"Send back, nothing! It was like getting hit full force in the head with a staff!" Marcalan groaned as Haladhon set him on his feet.

"I felt it, so I sent it back. I thought it would help him remember." She turned to her cousin. "I am sorry, Marcalan."

"You would make a good weapon, cousin," Marcalan said with a laugh.

Alcandhor silently agreed. He sighed, rubbing his eyes again. He needed time to absorb all this. "I am tired and cannot think anymore. I need a walk to clear my mind." He arched his back, massaging his aching shoulder as he gazed at the three of them. "We will talk later. Thank you, Tam. And Marcalan."

Tam rose and left, but Marcalan hesitated, his eyes somber.

"Thane? Truly, have you an explanation for this? I have always been told that inheritance must be direct. Parent to child. Both my grandfathers could make a key glow, but neither my mother nor my father have that ability."

"Aye. I will have to review those books. Genetics has not been my focus, and I have forgotten much." Alcandhor smiled at Marcalan to set his mind at ease. "Worry not. I will solve this mystery."

"Aye," Haladhon said with a laugh. "You have provided our cousin with new direction for his constant study."

"Ah, then perhaps you will grant me special honors for giving you new reason to keep your nose in books, enh?" Marcalan blinked, eyebrows lifted in anticipation.

Alcandhor glared at the rascal and waved a hand. "Get out of here and go back to whatever trouble you were causing."

Marcalan grinned and shot out the door.

~:~

Tavnol came toward Linna and she wiped her hands, glancing about the kitchen for Karnin, but the guard was not in sight. Was that boy going to beg her again to help him end the siege?

"Jandhal is dead," he whispered.

Linna stared in shock. "How do you know?"

"We all know. Vitran killed him."

"He what?"

"We think he means to kill Talrig, too. We think he means to become Laird." He chuckled humorlessly. "At least until the siege ends.

And that might be soon. He has a new idea. He is going to send someone dressed all in black to sneak to the gatehouse and from there to the drum tower."

"What good would that do?"

Tavnol shushed her, his eyes flicking about. "He intends to soak the wooden door to the tower in oil, then light it. As the door weakens and breaks, he will have us pile wood—taken from furniture in the rooms near the gatehouse—to feed the fire. He wants to smoke out the Rangers."

Linna's heart pounded. "The smoke will kill them!"

"Yes. And then he plans to call for a truce, and ambush the Thane and chiefs when they come. I...I will not fight Rangers, but I am afraid of Vitran. We have to stop the siege before he can do this. We are dead if Rangers die, or if we get caught trying to stop the siege, but we are dead soon anyway. I know the food is almost gone."

Linna stared at Tavnol. He was pale and shaking—as terrified as she was.

She had learned to be hard through severe lessons in life. She knew she could endure much and thought she might survive this siege if anyone could. But the look on the faces about her now shook her. Frightened and weak from hunger, her girls huddled by the fireplace. When did she start thinking of them that way? They had just been servants. Scullions. Now she felt responsible for them. She did wish Vitran had let them leave.

Linna closed her eyes. The flour was gone, and the grain. Only a few handfuls of pod seeds remained in the bottom of one sack. The gardens had been stripped bare, and the supply of tubers and roots would only feed them a day more, perhaps two, if one considered the scant portions "meals."

Linna opened her eyes and met Tavnol's gaze. "All right. But how do we get the herb?"

"I have seen where it is kept. I can get it, but you need to cover for me with Karnin. When you go in to the storeroom, distract him, and I will get the panvarin."

"You will need lots of it. Perhaps a whole jar. How will you hide that?"

Tavnol took a deep breath. "I can put the jar in the sack of pod seeds. It's almost empty. Tell me to bring it along."

Linna hesitated and nodded. Tonight the siege would end, or they would be dead.

~:~

Tam walked to the dining hall to take afternooning, a toothsome smell making her stomach rumble. She dipped a bowl out of the large soup pot swung out from the fireplace.

As she sat at a table, the other Rangers nodded to her, some smiling, but said nothing. The one surly Ranger she had seen twice the day before frowned from his place at a nearby table, disdain in his brown eyes. Tam felt a genuine interest or curiosity from a few in the room but from others a falseness—a sense of ingratiating themselves. Others ignored her. 'Twas interesting to note Rangers' attitudes toward her without a chief present.

Marcalan came in and took a deep breath as he leaned over the pot. "Mmm, redfruit stew!"

He began to ladle it into a bowl and exclaimed, "Conju! Stars, 'tis rare. Did some Rangers from the south bring conju with them?"

"Just eat, Marcalan," one Ranger said. "Need you give commentary on everything?"

"Need you have a sour stomach at all times, Gardhal?"

"Being around you is enough to sour anyone's stomach."

Marcalan sat down across from Tam with a grin. She returned his smile. 'Twas impossible to be somber around him, for her at least.

"Pay him no mind," Marcalan said, nodding toward Gardhal. "We are close friends."

Gardhal grumbled under his breath, and Marcalan chuckled. He gestured at her bowl. "You have barely eaten. Do you not like redfruit stew? 'Tis best with conju in it. It lends a sweet taste." Marcalan shoveled a huge spoonful into his mouth and closed his eyes, moaning in pleasure. Gardhal sighed loudly.

Tam dipped her spoon to capture a piece of the fruit. She chewed it experimentally. Sweet, with a slightly tough, almost woody texture. Tam liked redfruit stew, but had to admit this did improve the taste.

"Sherel," Marcalan called, "this stew is the best I have ever tasted. You have my heart."

Sherel came to the door between the kitchen and dining hall, wiping her hands on her apron. "I'll serve it up for evening meal then."

The room exploded in laughter. Tam jumped a little and belatedly joined in. Marcalan's banter continued as he ate two bowls of stew. Finally Gardhal slammed a fist on the table. "Do you ever leave off?"

Marcalan blinked, his eyebrows raised. Tam knew that innocent look already. The Rangers must too. Several groaned. "Spare us," one said.

Marcalan blinked again. "What?"

Tam sighed and rose, shaking her head.

"Where are you going, cousin?" Marcalan asked.

"I know not. Outside. I have no duties at the moment."

"I will join you."

Tam again smiled; it made her happy that Marcalan wanted to be with her.

As they left the dining hall, Marcalan said in a quiet voice, "Let us walk, and you can tell me more about this ability to feel. We could go into the garden." He leaned close and whispered, "The Rangers stay out of there out of fear of Sherel."

Tam bit her lip to stop a giggle.

They stepped outside. The overcast day had remained cool. Tam breathed in the fresh air, listening to the birds while wondering if it would rain.

They entered the garden and as they walked down a path, anxiety began in Marcalan. "This having Enaisi blood and sensing emotions, I need to learn more of what to do with it."

"I will fain teach you, if you wish."

His blue eyes twinkled and the disquiet left. "Would you?"

Relief flooded her as she smiled back at him. "I am glad you like me."

"Stars! What would make you think I did not?"

"This morning."

Marcalan stared at the sky while combing his hands through his hair. The churning that felt like fear returned. Panic coursed through Tam. Why she wanted Marcalan's friendship she knew not, but just the thought of having him displeased with her created a tight knot in her stomach. Timidly, she touched his arm. "Y–you are uneasy, Marcalan. What bothered you so much this morning that you were afraid?"

"I was not afraid, I was just..." He shook his head. "I should not be the one to talk to you about it."

"About what?"

Marcalan groaned, closing his eyes.

Would he become so afraid that he would not wish to be with her? "I am sorry, Marcalan, I will not ask about it if it makes you that uncomfortable. I do want you to like me."

He laughed, lightly tugging strands of her hair. "You need not worry about that."

~:~

Linna hoped Karnin did not see her hands shake as she reached for a seldom-used spice on a high shelf opposite the wall where the medicinal herbs sat. She turned to Karnin. Tavnol stood in position.

"Could you reach that for me?" Karnin started to grab the jar, but Linna said, "No, that one is older, try the next one. Newer herbs will have more flavor and with little substance, well-flavored broth will be welcome."

Karnin grunted, but lifted onto his toes and snatched the other jar. He offered it to her but she shook her head. "I have my arms full with these tubers. If you could carry that, and Tavnol the sack of pod seeds—"

"Why the whole sack?"

"It's almost empty. I need the rest of them for the soup."

Karnin grunted again and headed out the door. Linna followed and Tavnol last. Karnin shoved a hand in Tavnol's chest. "That sack looks heavy for one that's almost empty. Let me see in it."

Linna's heart and stomach plummeted into her feet, but in a move so swift she barely saw it, Tavnol drew his dagger and thrust it into Karnin's chest. The guard lurched and dropped the jar, which shattered with a teeth-jarring shock.

A cry came from down the hall, and another guard appeared. He ran forward and dove at Tavnol. The two wrestled but in short work Tavnol snapped the guard's neck. As the man fell with a sickening thud, Tavnol gasped. Karnin had managed to draw his dagger and plunge it into Tavnol's back. Linna's hands flew to her mouth as Tavnol fell. She stared in horror at Karnin, but the man fell back into the wall, and slid down to the floor, his eyes blank.

Linna knelt by Tavnol. He smiled weakly, his breathing labored with a slight burble to it. Red foam coated his lips. "It was brave, wasn't it? Tell my family, tell Poll, I was brave."

Chapter Thirty-one

Tam felt only a cold emptiness from Marcalan. She smiled. "You block well."

"I tried to teach myself as best I could. 'Tis the sensing I must learn better. I had to be surreptitious to avoid anyone discovering I could do thus."

"That we can continue to practice." Tam's eyes wandered over to the garden bed. She gave in to her desire and began pulling weeds.

"Are you a Ranger or a gardener?"

Tam squinted up at Marcalan, who wore an amused expression. "Both. Or I was. 'Tis a hard habit to break. I see weeds, and I start pulling them."

"Go on then, but do not expect me to help. I would not know what is a weed and what is an herb. Sherel would not believe my innocence if I accidentally pulled up something I should not."

Tam giggled. "Of this I have no doubt."

"You have a nice laugh," Marcalan said, smiling. "I like it."

Tam returned his smile. A soft yet intense probing shot through her. She straightened and looked around. Someone near could sense and was reaching out, using his ability.

"What is it?" Marcalan asked.

"I feel someone strong." Tam stood, frowning as she peered about. "Can you not sense him?"

"Nay. Who?"

"I know not yet. He is gentle. And kind. But filled with purpose. He is in the bailey..." Tam began walking. Marcalan followed.

Tam headed east, threading her path between Rangers, who watched with curiosity. A few began following her. Her target had continued south, toward the gate now. Tam picked up her pace.

Nandhal stepped into her path, sneering. "On some mission, cousin Tam?"

Tam forced herself not to react to his arrogant demeanor. Even though he blocked his emotions, she knew he wished to make her angry. "Aye, I am." She sidestepped to go on and he moved over to stop her again. "Excuse me, Nandhal, but the Thane has given me an assignment, and you are hindering it."

277

"And what is this so-important mission, enh?"

Tam glared into his eyes. "That is not your business." She waited a moment, and when Nandhal did not move, she shot out the heel of her palm, striking him in the sternum.

He fell back with a gasp, and she stalked past him. Several nearby Rangers laughed or hooted. Tam did not like Nandhal, and she did not trust him. Something about him seemed wrong—she could not feel it, but she knew it.

But for now, she wanted to find this gentle man who still prowled the bailey in a purposeful manner. There! A Ranger with golden hair and square shoulders. She strode to him and he turned, a look of surprise on his face. Unlike most Rangers, he sported a full beard.

Marcalan laughed. "Stars, Tam, you have a talent! Zandhral, she sensed you from across the bailey."

Intense blue eyes stared at her. "You are our new Second at Table? Well met. I am Zandhral and we are fourth cousins, once removed."

"Greetings, cousin," Tam said. "Uncle told me to find anyone I could sense strongly. That is why I sought you."

Zandhral's eyebrows rose as a smile spread. "Indeed. Sense you any others?"

Tam shook her head. "I would be able to sense Nandhal, but he is blocking. No others are in the bailey, but a few are at the perimeter."

Zandhral inhaled. "You can feel them that far away?"

"Aye."

Zandhral's eyes flicked over the Rangers that had gathered about them. "Walk alone with me, Tam. I have need to speak to you."

Tam glanced at Marcalan, not wishing to be away from him. He grinned, giving her a reassuring nod. She turned again to Zandhral and followed him away from the others.

He put a hand on her shoulder. "Cousin. You know we have a twig viper hiding in our kindling, do you not?"

Tam frowned, shaking her head. "I know not what you mean."

"Someone in our clan—amongst us here most likely—is a traitor. Someone who helped those that ambushed your father and our Thane."

Tam felt the blood drain from her face. A Ranger would betray his kin? His Thane? Zandhral nodded. "Aye. I know. And believe me, I feel the same way. Your uncle has me on a mission. I wander the perimeter and the bailey each day, sensing for anything that might betray such a one. But my abilities are not what yours are. I just wanted to ask you to be alert. If you have any feeling of someone worrying, a sense of hiding something, sneaking—you understand? Anything suspicious. Report it to the Thane."

Tam nodded as a face flitted through her mind. "Nandhal."

Zandhral smiled. "Aye. He blocks most of the time, so it is difficult to tell with him, but he is one we suspect."

"He is...wrong. I cannot say on, I have not the words to tell. Just a feeling." Tam tipped her head, wishing she could explain what she knew. "He is not to be trusted."

"Sight, cousin?"

Tam frowned, shaking her head. "I know not. Uncle is still teaching me about my gifts. But I–I know. I cannot explain it."

Zandhral pressed his lips together for a moment. "Tell the Thane this, cousin. 'Tis not proof, but he needs be told."

~:~

Linna snatched her sleeve across her eyes, sorrow and disbelief warring in her as she looked at the young guard's lifeless face. "Oh, Tavnol."

She exhaled slowly and stood.

Before long, she came into the kitchen dragging the sack of tubers and carrying the sack of pod seeds. She closed and locked the storeroom door. Her scullions stared at her.

"Where's the guards?" one asked.

Heart plummeting, Linna covered fear with her cook's temper. "Never you mind! Poll, take these tubers and see they are chopped for soup. You other girls, go rest in the back kitchen. I have no need of you right now." *And it will keep any of you from telling anyone about the missing guards.*

Her back to Poll, Linna quickly removed the jar of panvarin and set it among the herbs on the shelf, hoping Poll did not notice her shaking hands.

Her eyes kept straying to the panvarin. No one would likely notice one new jar among the spices, but did Linna have the courage to do this herself? Not only to dose the soup but to dare approach the drum tower?

Tavnol had been right—they were dead either way. He had already paid trying to stop the siege. His death was in vain if she did not follow through. And what would happen when the guards' shift changed and the three dead ones were discovered?

Linna glanced over her shoulder; Poll was still chopping tubers. Linna ground the panvarin, added it to the huge cauldrons, and set the pod seeds to soak. Turning to Poll, she said, "Add those tubers to the soup here, then go rest with the girls."

The sun had not yet set when Linna went to the door and called guards to come over; she wanted to serve the food before Vitran could put his plan into action. "I know it is early yet for evening meal, but the soup is ready. I think you'd not mind eating sooner."

The guards grinned and exclaimed agreement.

Linna gestured into the kitchen. "Could you carry the soup kettles? My girls are too weak." *And please be so hungry you don't notice the guards aren't here!*

The guards rushed in and carried the huge pots to the Great Hall where almost everyone ate now, even guards. To keep rations equal, they claimed. The guards came back for the smaller kettles, to take to those on duty in the towers and walls. The guards kept as prisoner were not fed in the evening by Vitran's orders. They only had one meal a day. That fretted Linna, but at least she did not have to be concerned with tonight's soup.

Linna swung out another smaller kettle from the fire and called to the scullions.

"Come, girls. Eat."

She sat near and waited for a while as the girls ate, ignoring the horrible gnawing hunger in her own stomach.

Soon Linna's girls huddled near the fire, asleep. She walked outside. High, thin clouds passed in shredded rags across the Bells. She craned her neck to look up at the drum tower. They had never shot anyone but guards yet, but what if she was wrong? What if Tavnol had been wrong? Worse, could the Rangers tell she was a woman from up there? Might they think she was a guard dressed in skirts and shoot her?

She walked into the Great Hall and saw people fallen over in chairs or sprawled on the floor. No one moved.

Linna went back outside—no movement there, either. Looking at the walls and around the bailey, she continued over to the drum tower, staring up at it, arms stretched wide to try to show them she was not armed, meant no harm. The tower seemed frightening, rising so much higher than the walls and even the corner guard towers. Her heart hammered, and she wanted to turn back. Only Tavnol's sacrifice kept her from turning and running.

Were the Rangers the traitors, as Vitran kept insisting, or the honorable men she had always thought them to be? Linna would find out now. Trembling, she unbolted the door to the tower and waited. Nothing happened. She took several deep breaths to calm herself and began the long, dark climb. Her left hand felt along the cool, white stone of the outer wall for support and guidance. Long before reaching the top, she became weak and light-headed and sat on the steps to rest, her breath rasping loudly in the silence. After her breathing became calm, she rose to continue the climb.

"What are you doing here?"

She jumped, and her hands clutched stone as she nearly fell on the steps. She stared into the blackness above her. "I–I want to end the siege."

"You are the cook, are you not?"

"Yes."

"How intend you to end the siege?"

"I added an herb to their food. They're all asleep. You can end it now. Please!"

"Continue up to our tower."

Linna began climbing again. She trembled and felt dizzy by the time the wall gave way to nothingness. She almost stumbled into the chamber. Her heart hammered as she blinked into the darkness. Did she see outlines of men in the shadows of the room?

"What is your name?" asked a voice.

"Linna. That is, Alinna, but I go by Linna."

"What herb did you add to the food, Linna?"

"Panvarin."

"Indeed? 'Tis a strong medicine."

"Yes, sir. But things are desperate. Vitran'd let us all die before surrendering, and the food is all but gone. And he'd planned an attack on your tower for tonight. We had to stop him."

"How could he attack us?" a voice tinged with amusement asked.

"He was going to have someone sneak to the door and set it afire. He was going to kill you with smoke."

"Stars, we wondered if someone would think of that." The voice still sounded amused.

One of the men stepped forward. "This woman is almost faint with hunger. It was a long climb. Vardhon, take her into the lower chamber and get her some food, while I check below and verify her story."

"You and Sandhral have just come off watch, Bardhal. Let me go below, and you stay. I know you wish to go yourself, but those stairs will take a toll and you are not rested."

A sigh.

"Go then, Madhrel. But take no chances. Vardhon and Sandhral, keep watch. If Madhrel does not return shortly, you both know what to do."

As the one Ranger went past her down the stairs, another strode to her left and opened a door. A very dim light shone within and she could see steps leading down. With a slight bow, he indicated she should go first.

"Come, Linna. Eat and rest. If you have done as you said, this will be over soon."

She walked through the door into a small chamber, and down a short flight of steps into a well-lit chamber with food laid out on the table. Would the smoke have affected them if they'd hidden here?

The lean, grey-eyed Ranger closed the door behind him and indicated she should sit. His average height surprised her. She had an image of Rangers being as tall and imposing as this drum tower of theirs. He got a clean plate and eating knife for her and sat, tossing his curly, dark hair over his shoulders.

"Please eat. Go light, though, or your stomach will rebel."

She nodded as she sat, looking at the platter of cheese, roots, and tubers. How did they have all this food? She had not known the drum tower had any large areas for storage.

As she began eating, the Ranger poured two cups of tea, set one in front of her, and sat down on the opposite side of the table with a smile. She was not used to anyone waiting on her, much less a Ranger, and it felt strange. She avoided his gaze, sipping the hot tea.

~:~

The Rangers rose from evening meal, and Marcalan came over. Tam smiled.

"Will you join us in the foreroom, Tam?" he asked. "You, as well, Your Grace?"

"If you Rangers think a stodgy noble will not hinder your fun," the Laird said, grinning.

Marcalan chuckled. "We will manage, Your Grace." He looked at Tam. "Coming?"

Tam nodded. "But I need to speak to Uncle first."

A hand dropped onto her shoulder from behind. "You do, enh?"

Tam turned, looking up into her uncle's kind eyes. "Aye. It is important."

His eyebrows lifted. "Let us go to the meeting chamber, then." He kept an arm around her shoulders as they walked out.

Once in the chamber, he lit a candle and gestured for Tam to shut the door.

"Now, what is so important?"

"I met Zandhral today. He said I should tell you Nandhal is not to be trusted."

"He felt this?"

"Nay. I feel it. Not by sensing him—he blocks most of the time. But

I just...know it. Zandhral said to tell you that."

Alcandhor inhaled slowly. "Aye. Thank you, Tam." His face seemed deeply lined in the shadows of the candlelight and Tam could feel the ache inside him. He tried to smile. "Anything else to report?"

"Nay—oh, aye. I had Marcalan practice blocking and sensing today. He learns fast."

"Aye. He has a mind quick as his tongue. I am glad you taught him. You will both have to study intensely—ah, but I have already said thus. Let me not keep you from enjoying yourself with the Rangers in the foreroom."

"Will you not join us, Uncle? Please?"

He hesitated and slowly smiled. "For a little while."

Rangers played music while others talked. They also played games, some on a board, others set up tiles on a table. The Laird asked to play kingsmen and sat down at a board.

Tam approached two Rangers hunched over a backhand board. "Know you how to play, cousin?" asked Tanadhon, looking up.

"Aye. My father taught me. He said it helped learn strategy and to think clearly."

"Join us, then. We just started."

"Uncle, too?"

"We would be honored."

From the wry look her uncle gave her, Tam knew he had planned on disappearing back into the meeting chamber to read. Tam knew not what he read that could be so important. She had peeked at several books he had piled on the table—some were in a language she knew not, and those she could read confused her.

"One game." Alcandhor sat at the board.

Playing backhand with several opponents who all thought differently challenged Tam. She had only played her father. But after awhile, she began to anticipate their moves and relaxed, enjoying the game.

She glanced up to see Marcalan grinning at her. A soft wave of playful affection cascaded over her. Careful to keep it light so as not to overwhelm him as she had that afternoon, she sent affection back. They bantered their emotions back and forth, Tam trying her best to not giggle—'twould not be meet in a serious game like backhand.

Tam quit sending to concentrate on her move and inhaled sharply— the sending continued on its own. She dared not look up at Marcalan, but could feel his surprise. What did this mean? Her hand shook as she moved her piece.

"Are you all right, Tam?" Alcandhor asked.

"Aye," Tam said. Could her uncle sense the connection? Should she ask him about it? She would have to wait; she could not say on here as Marcalan's gifts were to be a secret for now.

Tam did not understand completely why, but knew it had to do with the Laws of the Maker and Clan Laws of parentage and illegitimacy. Her father had her memorize them, but when she asked how a husband might not be father to his wife's child, her father had not explained. He said she merely needed to know the law and when she was older, she would understand. Tam only knew it must involve a deep betrayal. Perhaps Uncle would explain it to her.

"You seem distracted," her uncle said, making her jump.

"I am. I...I thought of my father," she said, hoping he would accept that explanation for now.

Alcandhor gave her a sorrowful look. "I am sorry, Tam."

"I am all right, Uncle." She pointed to the board. "It is your move. Be careful."

His eyes twinkled at her. "Think you not I see that you are scheming to steal my man? I am not blind, niece."

Tanadhon and the other Ranger snickered.

Drums caused the room to fall silent. As the message beat out that the siege was over, the Rangers all jumped to their feet.

"Move out!" Alcandhor called. He gestured for the Laird to join him, and they strode through the door.

~:~

Alcandhor led the way as hundreds of Rangers, all with bows ready and no torches lit among them in case it was a trap, approached Laird Hall. Santran walked with them, not only going back to his home, but to care for anyone who needed a healer. Drays filled with supplies rolled among them. A high mood prevailed, although Alcandhor urged everyone to remain vigilant.

As they drew near, he could see two of his bowmen standing by the open gates. They saluted, grinning, and Alcandhor relaxed, blowing out a breath. He gave the signal for the Rangers to proceed inside and held his hand aloft in greeting. "Well met, Madhrel, Sandhral."

The bowmen both returned the salute.

"How managed you this?" Haladhon asked, with a broad smile as he sauntered up behind, the Laird following.

Madhrel grinned as he and Sandhral bowed to the Laird. "We did nothing. It was the cook."

"She added herbs to their food. The entire hall is asleep," Sandhral said.

Haladhon broke into laughter and clapped his arm around Tam's shoulders. "We seem to owe everything lately to women, do we not, my Laird?"

"Indeed," the Laird said, grinning down at Tam.

Alcandhor bit back a smile as the two bowmen exchanged surprised glances.

Tam remained quiet, her wide, golden eyes taking in the activity within the bailey. Rangers swarmed the place like tiny pincebugs whose hill has been disturbed, and before long, another drum message was sent—Laird Hall was secured.

~:~

"It is over, Linna," Bardhal said with a smile as the drums echoed into silence. "Now we can go down."

The long descent seemed frightening in the dark. Bardhal kept a hand at her elbow the whole way down, which could not have been easy for him, as the steps grew narrower on the inside. When she came through the door, her heart lightened to see torches lit around the bailey; the hall seemed less morbid now. Rangers hurried everywhere. A tall one stood in the center of the bailey between the keep and the gate, asking questions and giving orders.

Bardhal took her to him. Linna had to tilt her head back to see the Ranger's face. A handsome one. If only she were younger.

"Haladhon, where is the Thane?"

"He and the Laird are somewhere in the bailey."

"I had wished to present Linna to them."

Haladhon gazed at her with a puzzled expression.

"This is the cook. She is the one whom we owe thanks for ending the siege," Bardhal said.

Smiling, Haladhon took her hand and bowed over it. "My thanks, dear lady. We owe you a great debt, as does everyone in these walls whose lives you have saved."

Linna found herself blushing. "It was Tavnol's idea. He was killed helping me get the herbs. He deserves the thanks. I'd just like to go see to my girls."

"Please. Bardhal, go with her in case she needs assistance."

Upon entering the keep kitchen, Linna stood, dumbfounded. Rangers had brought sacks of food with them and had left them in piles. They had also thought to bring wood. The girls still slept.

She began inventory of what the Rangers had brought. They seemed to have thought of everything.

"Is there any help I can offer you?" Bardhal asked.

"There...there are bodies in the hallway of the storeroom yonder. One is Tavnol, he died helping me."

"I will call Rangers to clear the bodies."

Bardhal soon returned with Rangers, who carried the dead guards out. Linna stopped the one pair of Rangers. "Be gentle with him. He is Tavnol and wasn't a traitor."

The Rangers murmured assent, and Linna forced herself to think of her work. She soon had pots filled and began adding what she wanted to start the broth. Bardhal returned, helped tend the fires, and fetched for her as well.

A young Ranger came into the kitchen. "Guards who would not fight the Rangers were found locked in back and bottom cells. There are at least six or eight score of men too weak to even walk. They are near starved. Have you anything for them?"

"Six or eight score? You're exaggerating."

"Nay. I know not an exact count. But there are many and they need help."

"There is broth on the fire. It will be ready soon."

She began several large pots of tea. Soon she had the broth ready. Bardhal called to Rangers to carry the soup kettles, and cups, back to the guards. Linna followed to help and froze in horror at the condition of the men she saw. Rangers had carried them out from the filth they had been living in. From the looks of the men, and the smell, they had been packed into the cells and the small basin and drain in each had grossly inadequate sanitation.

Those strong enough were propped up and wrapped in blankets, drinking from cups. Rangers cradled the heads of those too weak to sit, helping them to sip broth. Galran, Master of the Guards, was carried past her by Rangers.

"Is he alive?" she asked.

"Aye," one answered. "By strength of will. Others have not been so fortunate."

Linna covered her mouth in shock. She had not known Vitran had allowed this evil! She had never been told of this many men. The food she sent would not have been enough for the number here. Her stomach turned—not only at what she saw, but that she had had a part in it.

She peered into the shadows. Was that a white surcoat amid the Rangers and guards? She stepped closer. The Laird?

Chapter Thirty-two

Randhal, the young Laird, sat on the ground, cradling a guard's head in his lap, helping him to sip broth.

Unable to believe a noble, much less the Laird himself, would sit in the dirt amid the stench and filth to help a sick guard, she walked closer. Her heart broke when she recognized Tagrel, a happy young fellow, and a friend of Tavnol's. The two always seemed to find their way to the kitchen—for food or the girls, Linna wasn't certain which.

She knelt by them. The Laird looked over at her, and she could see the pain in his eyes.

"Will he be all right, Your Grace?" she whispered.

"I know not, Linna."

She stared at him in astonishment. "You know me, Your Grace?"

"You have been our head cook for many years. How could I not know you?"

And she had assumed the nobles paid no attention to servants. She gazed down at the starved guard again.

"What is his name?"

"Tagrel, Your Grace. He's a pest to my kitchen, always flirting with my girls."

"We will try to get him well, again, Linna, so he can continue to be a pest."

"I hope so, Your Grace."

The Laird gave Tagrel a sip of broth. "I thank you, Linna. I understand you are the one who dared to do something to break the siege."

"It was Tavnol's idea. He was a guard who helped me sneak the herb I needed. But he was killed."

"You and Tavnol saved many lives. These not least. They would not have lasted much longer."

"Vitran lied to me. The food I sent wouldn't have been enough to feed all these men."

"They were rarely brought food, they say. Some guards kept the food for themselves instead of delivering it to them. It is not your fault, Linna. Your actions saved their lives."

She could not bear it. She had never checked to see the food was delivered, or to see exactly how many were in the cells. If she had, they would not be like this in the first place. And they thought she saved them?

How could she make them understand she had not ended the siege, but Tavnol? Stomach churning, she looked again at the ghastly spectacle surrounding her and stood. She had to get away before she became physically sick. "I must return to the kitchen. With your permission, Your Grace?"

She curtsied and left before he finished nodding.

~:~

Tam held her arms, trying to come to terms with all she saw. Only the thread of connection to Marcalan's emotions held her steady, save those times she felt the need to block.

Passing through the gates she had choked, almost retching at the heavy, sweet stench of the rotting corpses lying by the gate and in the outer bailey. How were Rangers able to handle clearing bodies from there and the towers?

The steward, Vitran, had not even tried to properly dispose of the bodies from the keep either. He had just had them all dumped into a shallow grave dug in the east end of the bailey. Except Jandhal, the one noble he killed. He left that body where it was. Tam had accompanied her uncle as he went through the entire keep. He would not let her enter that one chamber.

A Ranger ran up to Alcandhor as they were descending the main staircase of the keep. "Thane! Vitran and some of the others are beginning to wake. The Laird wishes you and Tam to accompany him and Lord Krendhal to see them."

All the traitors had been carried, still asleep, to the prisoner cells and locked in. Law dictated prisoners be isolated to keep the accused from comparing testimonies, but there were too many to allow this, so only the nobles and others known as the leaders had cells to themselves.

Alcandhor met the Laird and Krendhal in behind the keep at the east end of the bailey.

"What will you say to them, Your Grace?" asked the Thane as they approached the cells.

"Probably very little. I merely want Lord Talrig and Vitran to see that their attempt to kill you failed, and that the two witnesses against them are here also."

Tam swallowed repeatedly to keep from gagging at the horrible odor of death, vomit, and excrement upon entering the hallway to the cells.

Talrig, pallid and eyes glazed, jumped to his feet, gaping, as the Laird, Krendhal, Alcandhor, and Tam came through the door.

"There has been a mistake, my Laird," Talrig said.

"Aye. I know. I have been informed of your 'mistake,' Lord Talrig, by two witnesses, Lord Krendhal and this Ranger, Tam. You may make a statement tomorrow when we convene the trial, unless you wish to confess now and name the other traitors."

Talrig's gaze shifted from Tam to Krendhal, and he turned even whiter and fell onto the bench. "I–I have nothing to say." He looked up. "Your Grace, may I be taken to a different cell. This one is filthy and reeks."

"Water runs in that basin, and I will see that you are given rags. You may clean the cell if you care not for its condition."

Talrig slumped, putting his head in his hands.

They left the cell—which relieved Tam. Only one more to visit, and they could be away from this horrible place.

As the nobles entered Vitran's cell, he exclaimed, "I'm not a traitor! Your Grace, I have been a loyal servant. I was simply caught in the siege—"

The Laird lifted his hands. "No lies, Vitran. We know your guilt. I have many witnesses against you. The only leniency you will get is if you name the other traitors."

Vitran's expression changed from pleading innocence to a hateful glower.

Tam felt the anger burning in the Laird rise as he glared at his former hall steward. "I do fain see you in one of the cells to which you consigned my guards. I hope you enjoy the reaping of your compassion."

Tam breathed a sigh as they exited to the fresh air of the bailey.

Alcandhor said, "Good touches, Your Grace. I would fain watch such a noble lord as Talrig scrub his cell."

"I would fain keep them in those cells as they did those guards. I never knew men could be so evil, Thane."

"Now you know why the Enaisi helped us establish such strict laws to govern ourselves. To keep evil nature in check."

The Laird ducked his head in agreement and turned to join Krendhal in returning to the west end. Tam and the Thane stayed behind to see how the work was progressing of exhuming and identifying the dead bodies in the shallow grave. She glanced away from the decomposed body still wearing a white surcoat and saw the Laird walking toward them. She inhaled sharply. He had not continued to the west side of the bailey after all but was approaching the Thane.

Alcandhor saw him as well and stepped in front of him. "Your Grace, please. You do not need to see this."

Too late. The Laird saw over the Thane's shoulder and swayed, falling into the Thane's arms, sobbing. Pain shot through her uncle's shoulder and arm. The Laird looked as if he would fall to the ground but for the Thane holding him up. How could her uncle bear the weight of the young man and endure that pain? Alcandhor slowly lowered the Laird to the ground and let him continue to weep in his arms.

Tam knelt next to them, her heart breaking for her friend, not sure what she could do except to send sympathy and comfort to him. A gentle wave of compassion enveloped her—Marcalan. Even though he was at duties in a different part of the hall, he must have felt her distress and wanted to comfort her. She sent back affection and gratefulness.

"Thane!" A Ranger ran up. He saw the bodies, and his Thane holding the Laird as he wept, and hesitated.

"What is it?" asked Tam, hoping her uncle did not mind her speaking up. She was Second at Table, after all.

"Haladhon wishes me to tell you the nobles still wait at the outer gate. They are beyond irritated at the long delay and demand to be allowed in Laird Hall."

"Let them wait." The Thane's eyes glittered like coals in the torchlight.

When the Laird's tears finally lessened, Alcandhor softly said, "Let us leave this place, Your Grace. You need see no more. Let us take you to your chambers."

"Nay, Thane," the Laird said, after taking a ragged breath. "Give me a moment, then we will go see to these supercilious nobles who are demanding to be let into my home." He stood, wiping his face and still breathing hard. "Let us greet our 'guests.'"

Haladhon still stood in the front of the bailey between the gate and the keep, his arms crossed when not directing someone or giving orders, watching all the activities. Tam had to admit that with his height and broad shoulders he created an impressive sight. How could she ever be half the Second at Table he had been? She was not even ready to take on that role, and they expected her to be ready for Thaneship in a mere five years?

"Let them in now, Haladhon," the Thane said as they approached.

Haladhon gave a hand signal and the Rangers allowed the nobles and their entourage to enter. As they passed the archway, Rangers closed in behind them.

Tam lifted to tiptoe to more clearly see the lords as they approached. Two men walked in front—one with icy eyes and a commanding demeanor, the other fat.

"About time," the heavy one snarled. He halted. "Laird! H-how...?"

"A Ranger set out to rescue me the day the siege began, Lord Paltor. I have been kept safe in Ranger Hold since my return several days ago."

"The day the siege began? But, but you said you did not know where he was!" Paltor glared at the Thane.

"Imagine," Haladhon said, his eyes twinkling. "A liar who does not like being lied to."

Paltor turned to Haladhon, fists clenched at his sides. "You dare call a noble a liar, Ranger?"

"Ranger Chief," Tam said, startled at her own boldness in correcting a lord—even if a traitor.

Paltor's gaze raked over her, his arms pushing back his surcoat as he tucked his hands in the top of his sash. "What is this?"

"Proper grammar, Lord Paltor, is '*who* is this?'" Alcandhor said, his tone derisive.

Tam bristled at the hostility that shook that heavy frame of the noble, and she clenched her fists.

"We have accommodations for you, Lord Paltor," Alcandhor continued. "And for your sons. You are charged with treason."

Shock and hatred crossed Paltor's face, and desperation rose alarmingly in him—Tam sensed his lunge even as she saw the flash of metal. "No!" she screamed in panic.

The noble stopped as if struck, mouth open in wordless shock, fell to his knees, and then heavily to the ground, gasping. His dagger clattered to the paving stones.

Everyone—save Haladhon, who, in a swift motion, retrieved the weapon—stared at Paltor, then at Tam.

Haladhon held up the dagger. "Attempting to murder the Thane. And in front of witnesses."

Rangers lifted the lord while Tam stood dazed. What had she done? Others echoed her thoughts—voices lifting one above another:

"What happened?"

"How did he fall?"

"Was it *her*? Did she do something to him?"

Alcandhor lifted his arm, and the crowd fell silent. How did he make everyone obey him without question? And he wanted her to step into that role? She could never command as he did.

Her tall cousin shook his head. "I thought you had more intelligence than that, Lord Paltor. You have put your own head in a noose." Haladhon's voice grew grim. "Take him to a cell."

Paltor began yelling insults at the Thane as they dragged him off.

More Rangers came forward to surround the remaining nobles.

The Laird took a step forward. "We have accommodations for you, Lord Zantith. And for you sons of Lord Paltor, although not quite as fine."

Rangers stepped toward Lord Zantith, gesturing for him to follow them to the keep. His guards began to follow but more Rangers with drawn swords stepped between them and their master.

Zantith turned. "What is the meaning of this?"

"We have no proof of your disloyalty yet, Lord Zantith. So you will be held in the keep, guarded by Rangers until your guilt or innocence has been determined. Your guards will be disarmed and barracked here under guard until that time."

The Laird turned to Paltor's sons. "The Rangers have proof of your treason as well as your father's." He gazed at the Rangers. "Take them to cells. Any guards who are loyal to their masters can go with them into the cells. All others will be disarmed and barracked."

The guards dropped their weapons or put their hands up in compliance. Zantith stood, stunned, until the Rangers prodded him to move. As they led him away, the Laird turned to Alcandhor. "That is most of them, is it not, Thane?"

"Most of the leaders, Your Grace, but there are still many people in the provinces who are of their view. It is going to take much to bring peace and end the turmoil. We still have a hard battle ahead of us."

"I will look to you to guide me, Thane." He held up a hand. "I know it is not your duty to be my advisor, but other than my First Minister, I know not who to trust, and you are farsighted. Laird Hall will follow Ranger clan."

Alcandhor frowned. "Be careful with such words. It goes against tradition."

The Laird choked back a laugh. "This from you?"

Tam frowned as her uncle's lips quirked up. Much was being said beyond their words, but she did not know the meaning.

Alcandhor inclined his head. "Will you try to sleep now, Your Grace? It is late and you have hard decisions to make tomorrow."

"Not until I know how this Ranger felled Lord Paltor." The Laird stared at Tam with a curious smile.

"Aye. I would like to know that myself," Haladhon said.

"I know not what I did." Tam met Haladhon's eyes and then her uncle's. "I...I saw he was going to attack. I did not see the dagger, but I...felt it." Tam stopped, not able to put her feelings into words.

"I think," Alcandhor said slowly, "that Tam lashed out with an emotional attack. Purely instinctive."

"You are a good weapon, cousin." Haladhon slapped her on the back. Tam smiled, still wondering how she did whatever it was she did. She did not remember sending.

"To think such things should be seen in my days." The Laird shook his head. "I know not if I can sleep, but I will try." He clasped his hand to the Thane's good shoulder. "Thank you, Thane."

Tam hid her surprise at the break in tradition as Alcandhor play-slapped the Laird's cheek. He grew serious. "I have Rangers assigned as your guards, Your Grace. They will accompany you."

"Thank you," the Laird whispered in a hoarse voice.

The Laird walked toward the keep, and Haladhon turned to Alcandhor. "Thane, why do we not walk back to the kitchen? I would fain have you meet the cook, Linna, who ended the siege."

"Aye. We owe her greatly. Come, Tam."

The keep kitchen bustled. Tam looked around for Poll, but none of the scullions were there. Rangers helped with the work as Linna supervised. The cook saw them come in and turned, eyes narrowed at Tam.

"You! They said you escaped with Lord Krendhal." Her gazed raked down Tam, and she murmured, "A Ranger? A Ranger lass?"

Haladhon gestured to Alcandhor. "This is the Thane, Linna."

He stepped forward, took her hand, and bowed over it. "We owe you a great debt, Linna. I thank you for having the courage to do something."

The Thane awed her, but Tam could feel anger in her as well.

"It wasn't me. I keep telling everyone but they won't listen! It was a guard. Tavnol. It was his idea, and he died tonight helping sneak the herb out of the storeroom. Please don't bury him with any guards who are traitors, sir. He wasn't."

"I will see to it he is properly interred and his family notified of his bravery. I thank you, Linna."

She curtsied and turned back to her work, but Tam stepped forward. "Linna? What of Poll?"

The cook turned, frowning, then her expression softened slightly. "She's sleeping off the herb, lass. She's fine."

Tam let out a quiet sigh and nodded her head in thanks as they turned to leave.

The bailey seemed cold after the heat of the kitchen, and Tam brought her cloak forward.

As they approached Galran's chamber, Marcalan ran to them, grinning. "There you all are! Have I missed all the fun?"

Haladhon snorted. "'Fun,' he says."

"Have you finished your duty, Ranger?" the Thane asked.

"Aye, sir." Marcalan snapped his fist over his heart in brisk salute. "We have searched Vitran's chambers, and as you can see, I came away without being thrashed by Andhrel." He swept his arm in an exaggerated bow and winked at Tam as he rose. His cheerfulness lifted the gloom from her a bit.

"Found you anything useful?"

Marcalan shook his head. "Nothing that could be used as evidence in trial. But we gathered and ordered all documents. You can peruse them at your convenience."

Alcandhor gave a despondent moan. "I had hoped we would find some record or document that would help identify all the traitors. Without proof, our hands are tied and some will go free."

Chapter Thirty-three

Did her uncle ever rest? Tam stifled a yawn as she handed him the list of names Maradhor had just finished compiling. Haladhon caught her eye and grinned at her. Stars, was he not tired either?

"Coordinate this list with these reports, Tam, so the Laird can easily read them in the morning. Then give them to Lord Krendhal."

"It *is* the morning," Marcalan muttered from behind closed eyelids, in a chair tilted back against a corner.

"Go to bed, cousin," Haladhon said. "There is nothing more for you to do tonight."

"'Tis not night, 'tis morning," Marcalan repeated. "And you have done all you can to prepare for the trial, have you not, Thane?"

"Nay. All must be prepared for the Laird."

"It seems all is in order," Krendhal said, from the table where he sat reading documents.

Tam sorted the reports by names on the list and gave them to the Laird's First Minister. He nodded thanks, added them to the stack, and stood. "That is all, is it not, Thane?"

"I still have some details to document, but aye, I think that is all until morning. I apologize for such a long night."

Krendhal bowed. After he left, Marcalan let out a loud, prolonged yawn.

"Stars, Marcalan, leave off ere we all begin snoring at these tables," Maradhor said as Haladhon chortled.

"Are you not tired?" Tam asked her tall cousin.

"Best become inured to long hours being Second at Table," Haladhon said.

"Aye, almost as bad as being a scribe." Maradhor's intense brown eyes sparkled, belying his grumbling.

"Why say you that?" asked Tam.

"Not only must scribes record everything, but we must make copy of all records. Our labors are doubled."

Haladhon crossed his arms, his face serious. "I am truly heartened I have not such onerous duty."

Alcandhor snorted. "Aye, your lack of love of books and scribing is well known. Tam, I hope you have a better love of things written."

"I have not much experience with books or writing, Uncle, but I do enjoy reading."

"Considering what the Thane has in mind for you, that is good," Haladhon said with a wry smile.

"Are we through yet?" Marcalan stretched. His chair slipped and his limbs jerked out straight. As the chair thudded upright, Marcalan laughed. "Stars! That took the sleep from my eyes!"

"Who asked you to stay up, cousin?" Maradhor asked, looking up from his table. "You could have been to bed long ago."

"What? And miss our dear Lord Talrig coming to us blubbering how he was forced to participate in the conspiracy? Stars, that was worthy entertainment."

"We did get good testimony from him, though, against Lord Zantith and a few minor nobles," Maradhor said.

"Aye, which with Paltor's testimony gives us two bearing witness against Zantith. I would like more, but it is enough to guarantee exile for him." Alcandhor ran a hand through his hair. "But still we have nothing on Lorwith. Vitran refuses to speak, and Zantith, as well. Talrig can give no testimony against Lorwith." Alcandhor slammed a fist on the table. "Hang it! He is more cunning than I gave him credit for. Imagine refusing to be in a meeting with guards present or even the other lords' sons, so no one could witness his treason." He gave a long, slow exhale. "That viper has slipped through the snare."

~:~

Billowing white clouds sailed high the next morning, urged by the wind, which flapped the banners into a frenzy throughout the bailey as people filled the west end.

As Tam climbed onto the dais, she nodded toward the crowd and asked, "Who are they?"

"They are from Lairdton," Alcandhor said. "It is an open court, anyone may attend."

Urging the throng back, Rangers escorted men whose hands were tied behind their back through to the dais.

"And those men?" Tam asked.

"They had come over the wall during the siege. If no one implicates them, we will have to let them go. We have no proof they were not merely trying to escape a dire situation."

Krendhal and the Laird ascended the steps to join Tam and the Thane.

"And are you ready for this, Your Grace?" Alcandhor asked.

"Is anyone ever ready for this, Thane?" the Laird asked. "I will do what I must."

The Thane bowed, and he and the Laird took seats. Their Seconds, Tam and Krendhal, stood behind them.

The prisoners would be tried by rank, which made Paltor first. As the Thane's attendant, Tam began to read charges against him, holding the papers with both hands to steady them against the wind.

"All lies! Filthy lies, you by-blow! I hope you die and rot without a grave, you—"

Tam stopped reading as Rangers rushed forward and restrained the howling, cursing Paltor. They fought him to the ground, his yelling finally brought to a halt when they gagged him.

Tam continued, concluding with his attempt to murder the Thane of the Rangers. "...the sentence for which is death."

Silence filled the bailey, save the snapping sound of the banners. The Laird gestured to the Rangers. They removed the gag, and Paltor stood with a sullen scowl.

"Have you anything to say, Lord Paltor?" asked the Laird.

"It will do me no good. This is no trial, it is a mockery. Charges trumped up by Rangers to further increase their power over us. You will give the verdict their Thane orders you to give. You are nothing but his puppet."

"Is this your defense?"

"I need no defense. I have done nothing and am wrongly accused." His heavy chin jutted out, his jowls wagging slightly as he glared at Alcandhor.

After a pause, the Laird said, "So be it. Take him to his cell to await his execution."

Rangers had to drag and half-carry the thickset noble who refused to walk and still thrashed his feet.

"Lord Zantith. Stand forward," Tam called.

The noble did so. Tam tried to brush the hair out of her face to read the charges against him. Why could they not hold court inside?

"Lord Zantith," the Laird asked, "what say you?"

"Would my word matter? The Rangers have done their job well. I wagered for power and lost."

"I will show leniency, Lord Zantith, if you cooperate. Would you name your partners?"

Zantith huffed in scornful amusement. "I want not your compassion, nor is it appropriate to offer leniency once trial has begun. Know you this not, *Laird*?"

"So you will say nothing further about your fellow conspirators?"

"Nay, I will not. But I will add to the charges against me. I tried to have you killed and would have succeeded but for the Rangers. I wanted power and played high stakes to get it. I have lost all. What is left but my execution?"

The Laird looked down with a slight wag of his head. His astonishment and the Thane's wafted back over Tam, who also could not believe the bold, scornful attitude of this noble.

The Laird took a deep breath. "Exile. So be it."

Zantith's light blue eyes widened in surprise. Two Rangers grabbed his arms as he took a step forward. "You would abrogate the law? Why? Why would you exile me? I would not live like that!"

"Precisely," the Laird said.

Tam's gaze followed the procession as Rangers led Zantith away, his scorn crumbled into despair. Perhaps sometimes, she mused, mercy was not compassionate.

Talrig stood forward next. He trembled as Tam read the charges. He also received exile for his part since he confessed and named other traitors, although he should have received death for his role in the murder of the previous Laird.

Paltor's sons each stood forward and Tam read the charges against them of complicity to treason. They had nothing to say for themselves, but stood sullen. The Laird exiled them all.

Vitran came next, his eyes cold and his face hard.

"Vitran." The Laird glared at the man, his hands shaking, betraying his fury. "You broke your oath as Steward of the Hall. You are charged with numerous crimes that are heinous, against my household, and my guards. You plotted with the traitors against this hall. You murdered a noble. But all the charges I have in my hands that I would read against you I now hold, as you attempted one thing which takes your sentencing out of my hands. You plotted to kill Rangers in this hall, which gives the Thane jurisdiction over you."

Tam looked down at the man responsible for the condition of the guards they had found last night. Some had died, and others were still not out of danger from their ill treatment. How could a man do thus to others?

"All the years I have had to sit as arbiter," Alcandhor spat, "and as judge, yet I have never had the inclination to truly make the punishment match the crime as I do today. My first reaction to your crimes, Vitran, is to sentence you to the same amount of time in a cell under the same conditions you forced those guards to live in."

Vitran paled but remained silent.

"However, as is recorded in the Laws of the Maker, it is not the duty of any judge to pass sentence to gratify his own desires, but"—the Thane's voice lowered to almost a growl—"to seek justice. Have you anything to say on your behalf?"

Vitran only glowered at the Thane.

"The law, again, is clear. To kill, or attempt to kill, a Ranger brings a certain sentence of death. So be it. Take him to his cell to await his execution."

Guards stood forward one by one. Those who had actively taken part in any attack against the Rangers in the drum tower had their sentencing turned over to the Thane. Some claimed duress; that Vitran had threatened them and they feared being thrown into cells. Tam had helped order the papers and knew this to be true. From testimony of guards and servants, they had a list of which guards had been Vitran's accomplices and which had only reluctantly participated. The former received the same sentence as their leader, and the latter, exile.

The Laird judged the rest of the guards. Most received exile. Some were stripped of their status and rank as guards, flogged, and given stocks for a number of days. Afterwards they would be set loose with orders to never return to Viltara Province.

Few servants could be proven to be a part of the conspiracy, but those known to be sympathetic to the traitors were also given flogging, stocks, or both, and later loosed with the same injunction to never return to Viltara Province.

The Thane and the Laird rose as Rangers led the last of the servants away. The Laird gave a dispirited smile. "I am glad that much is over."

"As am I. The gallows were assembled this morning?"

The Laird gave a slow exhale. "Aye. In the east end of the bailey. What about the exiles?"

"A message will be drummed out that a Ranger ship is needed for them. When a ship comes into North Port, they will drum a message back. We will then have the prisoners escorted to the ship."

"You Rangers have things well organized."

"Our disciplines are set, my Laird. We simply follow procedure."

The Laird nodded. "I do not look forward to this afternoon."

Tam did not either.

~:~

Uardhel held his breath, staring up unseeing into the branches of the trees until the drums echoed into silence. He curled his lip, exhaling slowly to control his anger. The siege ended. The traitors caught. Curse Alcandhor and his Rangers!

Guladhor ran toward him with round eyes, creating a swath through the greenery. "You heard?"

"How could I not hear, you fool." Uardhel snatched a handful of jerkin. "Would you have us followed and caught? No tracks!"

The Rogue ground his teeth, and Uardhel glared at him, daring him. Guladhor dropped his eyes, his nostrils flaring. Uardhel lifted his chin, allowing himself a slight smile. The man had best show obeisance if he wished to stay with this band of Rogues.

Guladhor looked up with a frown. "What do we do now with Paltor convicted and hanged? He was our security against the Rangers. Who will hide us now when they hunt us?"

"Worry not about that. Think you we have no plans other than relying on that fat noble? My worry is that with the siege now over, Alcandhor might leave before we reach Lairdton."

"You would continue on knowing Paltor is dead?"

"What has he to do with it?"

"You think so little of the supplies he promised us in payment?"

"I think more of the death of Alcandhor and the chiefs." Uardhel gripped the Rogue's shoulder, leaned close, and said in a hiss, "'Tis too close to turn back. If we make haste, we should arrive late tonight."

~:~

Tam stood amid the other chiefs, clenching her fists. The wind had died down, but the clouds had thickened, now low and menacing. Would it rain? Would that postpone the horror to come?

Shrieking about Ranger injustice, Paltor kicked and writhed, forcing the Rangers to drag him up the stairs to the gallows. It had to cause him great pain for his pinioned arms to be used to carry his weight yet the former lord seemed not to care.

"Thane, need she see this?" Haladhon whispered.

"She is Second at Table. How do I exempt her?"

Curiosity momentarily replaced Tam's dread of the executions as Haladhon hissed something about the law, his lip curled. He straightened as Alcandhor muttered to him, words unheard but his low tone chastising.

Tam's attention drew back to the gallows as two Rangers gripped Paltor. He twisted, trying to avoid the noose, while two others bound his legs.

"Think you the rope will carry his weight?" Haladhon asked.

Alcandhor shot him a disgusted look.

"I am being serious," Haladhon said, his eyes wide.

Alcandhor turned to face front again. "The rope has been tested against the force of such a drop. Even with his weight, he will not break the rope."

"I have never seen a man fear death thus," Lamadhel murmured.

Alcandhor shook his head. "It is not fear. Hatred burns within him. I think 'tis the only emotion he knows."

How a man could be so full of hate? Tam stopped blocking and realized her uncle was right—malevolence roiled in this noble, filling and overflowing him. Tam swallowed, unable to catch her breath, and blocked again. She inhaled deeply, suppressing a shiver.

Once the Rangers had Paltor positioned on the gallows, the Laird and Thane stepped forward.

Alcandhor lifted his head. "Lord Paltor, you have this one last chance to call upon the Maker for your soul's sake. I adjure you to do so."

Paltor laughed, still straining against the men holding him. "Do you really? You self-righteous, pretentious sciolist! I spit upon you—and the Maker."

Tam stifled a gasp at such blasphemy. Her uncle's shoulders bowed slightly but he took a deep breath and squared them again.

The Laird nodded, and the Rangers drew the hood over Paltor. They let go, and he squirmed. The Rangers grabbed him again, whispering with some urgency, and he cursed them.

"If he does not hold still with the noose in proper position," Lamadhel said, "his neck will not break. 'Twill be gruesome to see him strangled. Can we not spare Tam from this? Though Confirmed, she is young. No one will fault you for releasing her."

Alcandhor made a twisted face, which Tam knew by now meant he was biting the inside of his cheek while thinking.

"Aye. She may be excused."

Relieved, Tam almost took a step but stopped. All her kin would see her weakness. A Ranger did not back away from duty, no matter how grim.

The chiefs all looked at her, and she shook her head, setting her chin. "I am a Ranger. I will stay."

Haladhon turned with a worried frown. "Tam—"

"Nay, Haladhon, I thank you, but I must stay."

The Laird walked over to stand by Tam, concern in his eyes. "I have endured this before," he whispered. "'Tis best to look away. Especially for this one. He will not die easy."

Tam gave a slight nod and stiffened her shoulders. She knew not what to expect.

The trapdoor opened, and the body dropped. Paltor jerked and fought his bonds. Tam averted her gaze, but could hear the wheezing and whistling noises as he struggled to breathe. A panic grew inside her. If only she had left when the Thane had given permission, but she dare not leave now.

How long would it take? Forever and forever passed as Tam listened to the dying man. She fixed her gaze on the shimmerstone wall beyond the gallows, willing herself not to see the grisly sight at the edge of her vision. How long? She closed her eyes to will her breathing as she became light-headed. How long?

The sounds lessened. And soon stopped. The stench of feces filled the air. Tam allowed herself to look, finally. The body lay on the ground, and Santran knelt over it, blocking her view. As he rose, Rangers draped a cloth over it and carried it away.

Numbness stole over Tam, and she stood as stone, barely aware of her surroundings.

Rangers brought Vitran out next. The sullen man said nothing and did not fight the Rangers or the noose. He died quickly.

Some guards wept or asked for mercy, but most remained silent. Tam chanted to herself that these men had conspired to kill Rangers. They would have killed her as she escaped Laird Hall if they had known who she was. They were on the side of those who murdered her father and tried to kill her uncle.

Tam said nothing as Rangers bore away the final body. The Laird spoke to her, and she nodded she was all right. Marcalan stayed at her side as they walked through Lairdton. Although grateful, she could not bring herself to respond to him. To anyone.

Her mind barely registered the Ranger who ran to her uncle as they entered the bailey to Ranger Hold, and she continued on as Alcandhor stopped to hear the report: "Thane. Nandhal is missing. He did not report for duty this morning, and his belongings are gone as well. We did a thorough search of the area."

Alcandhor groaned. "Estimate when he left and when it has been a full day, drum out he has gone missing, likely Rogue."

"But that only gives him more time, and he—"

"That is our law. Twenty-six hours."

"Aye, Thane."

"Tam," her uncle called from behind. "Tam, sit with me for afternooning."

Tam did not answer but walked on toward the hold.

"Tam?"

"Let her be," she heard Lamadhel and Haladhon chime.

When finally inside her chamber, she collapsed onto the cold stone floor and silently wept.

~:~

Tam pushed up—had she fallen asleep? Her stomach rumbled. She did not wish to see anyone but neither did she wish to hide. Afternooning had long past. She stared at the embers glowing in the fireplace, wondering if she should stay in her chamber until the gong for evening meal sounded, or leave now and face her kin. Preferring Rangers' scrutiny to the sounds of Paltor's death echoing in her mind, she rose and opened the door.

Marcalan leaned against the opposite wall, his face grave. "Are you all right?"

Tam yearned to rush into his arms, but saw Rangers in the foreroom. She must not appear soft. He gave her a smile that almost broke her resolve. How could such a rascal be so understanding and gentle?

"It is almost time for evening meal," he said in a hushed voice. "By the time you wash up, the gong should sound."

~:~

Evening meal felt empty without Krendhal and the Laird. How was her friend handling the executions? Did he cry alone in his chamber? Tam doubted it. He knew how to be strong, even though young.

No one seemed disposed to talk. Her uncle asked her how she was, but made no other conversation, although he kept glancing at her with a worried look.

After the too-quiet meal ended, Tam returned to her chamber. She found it too hot again and spread out the pieces of wood in the hearth so they would die out. No wonder the Rangers all said Sherel over-mothered them. She knew as she undressed that she would not sleep. It was too early and her mind would not stop running wild with all that had happened that day.

After what seemed like hours of tossing and turning, she threw back the coverlet. She dressed and sat on the edge of the bed. What could she do? She did not want to join the Rangers in the foreroom. She wanted to be alone.

She chewed her lip, thinking. Ah, the secret hallway. Tam left her chamber, answering calls from the foreroom with a lifted hand as she headed down the hall to the dark armory chamber. She used the light of the key so she did not crash into anything. She fumbled in the back corner trying to find the place where the key should fit. There. The wall gave way.

Tam stepped inside and held the key aloft with one hand to light the way. Her other hand ran along the cool, smooth wall as she walked. At the far end she stopped. Now what? She could feel the air and raised her hands over her head. The breeze came from above. Despite the key, the ceiling of the high corridor remained shrouded in darkness. Tam needed something to climb on. A chair would not be high enough. She leaned against the wall, deep in thought. She could think of nothing that she could use to climb high enough to check the ceiling.

But did not Uncle say near the ceiling and near the floor? Tam felt near the floor with her hands. Aye. Air. She began feeling along the floor to find where the slight draft came from. It seemed concentrated in one spot. She ran her hands along the floor and up the walls—a chill air rushed past her with a soft *whoosh*, and her heart thudded as an opening appeared. The secret hallway had its own secret!

She thought of the layout of the hold. This new secret passage filled the gap between the Thane's bedchamber and the foreroom. She put a hand out on this new wall and almost tumbled as she took a step. A staircase! Her heart pounded even harder. She held up the key, but it did not help much since it glowed near her face and she needed to see what was beyond her feet. She took a deep breath. *This is of the Enaisi. I need not fear.*

Chapter Thirty-four

Tam took the key off and held it above her head. The blackness gave way to dull stone walls and steps—not the white stone of Ranger Hold. Willing her heart to slow, she began her descent, putting each foot down with extreme care.

An archway at the bottom to her left opened into a huge chamber. Books lay strewn on a nearby table. These books—not made of paper pulp like theirs—reminded Tam of the ones her uncle studied. Books of the Enaisi. She stepped around the table and saw several other tables as well. Could this be a study chamber perhaps? She had to tell Uncle!

She turned back to the archway. As she went through it, her hand ran along the edge of the wall and light flooded the room. She gasped aloud, spinning around.

The off-white, almost light grey, walls of a smooth, polished stone reminded Tam of the structure on the Forbidden Peninsula. Bookshelves and tables for studying filled the room, and charts hung on the walls. The nearest charts contained maps of their world and of the heavens above them. The nebula looked so real—although much smaller in size and the shape somewhat different. The dark spots actually looked like the outlines of bells, not the indistinct look the Bells actually had.

She picked up one of the books on the nearest table, brushed off the dust, and tried to read it. The tome contained so many words she did not recognize, it might as well be a foreign language. The Enaisi's books. The thought struck her all over again—some small part of her was of them. Of the Enaisi. She shuddered, dropping the book. If only her father stood with her, telling her not to be foolish. She almost could hear his voice in her head, and it helped her to stop shaking.

Uncle. She had to tell her uncle. She ran to the archway and bounded up the steps, now illuminated as well. She reached his door and banged on it, sending her excitement to him.

He opened the door, looking drawn. He wore only his trous and the sling.

"Uncle, please come! I found something!"

He sighed. "Tam, it has been a tiring day—"

"Please Uncle! This will make you happy! Please!" She grabbed his hand and pulled He groaned but followed. Rangers from the foreroom gathered in the hall, with Marcalan at the front.

Tam stopped. "No! Uncle alone! He has to see this first and alone!" Tam paid no attention to the look of dismay on her uncle's face as she dragged him into the armory, nor to Marcalan's laughter.

Alcandhor stopped, his mouth dropping open as she pulled him into the secret hallway—light shining at the end. "Tam? What did you...?" His voice trailed off and she felt his block give way. He ran to the stairwell and gazed down the steps. "Have you been down there?"

"Aye, Uncle! Wait until you see what is there!"

"How? What—?"

"Please, Uncle, just go down and see!"

She followed him down, waiting in suspense to feel his emotions. He stepped through the archway and gripped its side. Shock, awe, disbelief—so many emotions ran through him at once as he made his way into the chamber. With reverence, he brushed off a book and opened it. After a few moments, he looked over at Tam, tears in his eyes, joy and hope overflowing from him.

"Know you how many ways you have turned my world topside down in the short time I have known you, girl?"

She knew not what he meant. She could see how finding this chamber was wonderful. But how else had she changed things for him? Perhaps because she could make a key glow. Not knowing what to say, she just smiled.

Alcandhor cleared his throat. "Now, please tell me how you found this place."

"I was exploring the hallway above, trying to find where the air was coming from and suddenly the wall moved. Then I came down the stairs and into this chamber."

"Was it lit?"

"Nay. I used the key as a light. I started to go back to the stairs to call you, and the place lit up."

"You must have done something, touched something, to make the lights activate..." He walked toward the archway and stopped in front of a small square at the edge of the wall. He put his hand on it but nothing happened. "Tam, touch this."

She did so and the lights went out. She touched it again and they came back on.

As he turned to stare at her, a wave of exultation rose from him. His eyes sparkled, and he looked at her in wonder, murmuring, "Can it be true?"

Sounds of footsteps echoed down the staircase from the upper hallway, and a familiar lilting voice asked, "Are we allowed down there yet, or are you still showing off your secrets to our Thane?"

"Come down but touch nothing," Alcandhor called.

By the sound, Marcalan jumped down several steps at a time. He rounded the corner and caught himself by grabbing each side of the archway. "Stars!"

Haladhon and the other Rangers crowded behind him, gaping. Haladhon shoved Marcalan forward so they could all enter the chamber.

"Cousin Tam, do you try to find some way to turn things topside down every day?" Haladhon asked with mock displeasure.

"Can you believe it?" Alcandhor's arm swept the chamber and he walked over to the front table again. He sat down in the chair, not seeming to notice the thick layer of dust on it, and opened the nearest book.

"If our Thane did not have enough books to study before, he does now," Marcalan said. "Should we move your bed down here to make it easier for you? And Sherel can bring down meals. I know not what do about a priv so I suppose you will have to bother yourself to leave this place once in awhile anyway."

"Hush," Alcandhor muttered, engrossed in the book.

Tam wandered toward the back of the chamber, gazing in fascination at the shelves of books, charts, and maps. Why were these walls like those in that structure on the Forbidden Peninsula, not the white, glittery stone of Ranger Hold? Her wondering halted as she beheld the most vivid, realistic picture on one wall. One she had seen many times and that brought terror to her heart—the black upon blackness from her dreams! The blood drained from her face and her heart thudded, but she quickly swallowed her panic lest her uncle feel it and think her weak. He had said she need not fear it. She read the chart, but did not understand the words or symbols on it.

"Uncle? What does it mean, 'portal configuration'?"

She heard a crash and spun. Alcandhor had stood so fast he knocked the chair back and tripped over it in his hurry to get to her. He stared at the chart and put his hand on it, closing his eyes. "I thought this was lost forever." He straightened and looked around at the Rangers. "Maradhor, you are here. Good. I need scribes. Any of you others have a good eye and scribing hand?"

"Jonadhan and Yerdhal are both here. They are scribes," Maradhor said.

"Call for them, get what you need, and copy this chart. Each of you so there will be several copies. I will take no chances with this. Go! Now!"

"Uncle? What is it?" Tam asked in a hushed voice as Maradhor ran back up the steps. "What does it mean?"

"It means, my dearest Tam, that you have brought me one step closer to realizing my ambition. If we can learn to understand this chart, and if you are strong enough, we may be able to get the portal working."

"Do not overwhelm her, Alcandhor." Haladhon strode over to Tam and put a hand on her shoulder.

She felt awed at her uncle's aspiration, but she did not feel the shock she had that afternoon at his mention of contacting the Enaisi.

"Overwhelm her?" Marcalan crossed his arms, looking piqued. Tam smiled, peeking at him around Haladhon's arm. "She has turned everything topside down for our whole clan. I know I am certainly overwhelmed by it all. I think I need a hug more than she does."

"A thrashing would likely do you more good," Lantalan said from across the chamber where he looked over charts and books on the shelves.

"Please, give him a most thorough one, Lantalan." Haladhon winked at Tam, and she stifled a giggle. "But outside so as not to disturb our Thane's new study chamber."

Alcandhor had been studying the portal configuration chart, while chewing on his thumb. He swung around, looking about the chamber. "Where is Andhrel? He needs to see this. We need to get these books inventoried. And after this chart is done, we need all the others copied as well. And we should—"

"Thane, it cannot all be done tonight," Haladhon said.

"It can be started. And I want two Rangers guarding this place. I will take no chance that a curious Ranger will come in here and inadvertently set anything in disarray."

"Not one single mote of dust in this hallowed shrine of yours shall be touched without your leave, Thane," Marcalan said with dramatic fervor.

"I take it, then, that you personally accept that duty, Ranger Marcalan?"

Marcalan bowed. "It is my honor and privilege."

"Good." Alcandhor went back to studying the chart, rubbing his wounded shoulder in an absentminded manner. Tam stepped next to him and pointed to the picture that had drawn her to the chart. It looked almost like a circle of blackness upon darkness but with a slight glow emanating from the edges.

"Uncle, I do not remember all that is in that picture, but the blackness in the middle, it is what I see when I dream."

Marcalan stepped close, peering over their shoulders.

"Aye, Tam," her uncle said. "Remember what I said. You need not fear it."

Tam swallowed, nodding, but just the thought of that blackness set her heart pounding. What lay beyond it?

Marcalan touched the chart. "Think you the prophecy will ever come to pass, Thane, that a child will be born to us that will be as an Enaisi, having their abilities?"

Alcandhor stared at Marcalan with wide-eyed astonishment.

Marcalan chuckled. "What surprises you?"

"I am not sure. That you knew of that prophecy or that you would ask a question seriously."

"Shocking, I know. Perhaps my new cousin is a bad influence on me." He winked at Tam who had the urge to giggle at his bubbly playfulness.

Gazing up at him, she sent him a feeling of gratefulness, and he sent back to her. The sending, the connection of their emotions, began again. She must ask Uncle about this when they were alone.

Alcandhor snorted. "If she has this effect on you, I shall see to it she spends more time with you."

"You take a chance on that, Alcandhor. Her sense of humor is already beginning to bud." Haladhon crossed his arms. "Team her with that scoundrel and who knows what will happen."

"And think you she would be safer with you, cousin?" Marcalan's eyes twinkled.

"I would teach her finesse. Something you have never managed to comprehend."

"What?" spluttered Marcalan with feigned indignation. "Forget you who it was who rigged that tapestry to fall on Sarinna, hmm? That took cunning, timing, and skill to carry that one off successfully without the tapestry causing her harm by falling on her full."

Alcandhor burst out laughing and sat down in a chair, shaking his head.

"See? Even the Thane loved that one."

"Oh, stop it, Mar," Alcandhor said, rubbing his eyes, still laughing. Marcalan and Haladhon exchanged grins, and Tam's heart lightened.

Her uncle finally managed control and sighed, wiping his eyes. "I will admit, that was a stroke of genius." He started snickering again.

"What was just as entertaining was watching Marcalan beating dust out of tapestries for several days afterwards," Lantalan said dryly.

Maradhor and two other Rangers carrying supplies strode in. Alcandhor moved out of the way as they slid tables in front of the chart and spread out their papers and inkhorns to begin their work.

"Check each other's work. I want no mistakes in the copying."

Alcandhor walked over to Marcalan and slapped his shoulder, grinning.

"You have not answered my question, Thane," Marcalan said.

"Question?"

"About the prophecy. Think you a child will ever be born with full Enaisi abilities?"

Alcandhor shook his head. "Nay. I believe it not."

The Rangers all turned to stare at the Thane.

"Of all people, I never thought I would hear you say you did not believe something concerning the Enaisi," Haladhon said.

"I think it was not a real prophecy."

"But Zadhras could see. Many things he foresaw happened in his time and many more happened later," Haladhon said.

"That prophecy was given hundreds of years ago, Haladhon, and no one sees perfectly."

"But—"

"There are no more Enaisi among us!" Alcandhor said, throwing out his arm. "Their blood has thinned. The strongest we will ever see is what we have now in Tam." He stopped for a moment and smiled at her. Her heart warmed—but so did her face as she realized they all were staring at her.

"I do not foresee any like her in the future," Alcandhor continued, "much less one who has stronger abilities. And that prophecy spoke of a Teldheri child who was as if an Enaisi, able even to read minds: one of our children who has *all* the Enaisi's gifts? Nay." He shook his head. "It cannot happen."

Silence filled the chamber for a few moments. Maradhor cleared his throat. "Thane? Do you want copies of all these wall charts?"

Alcandhor shook his head. "Just that one chart tonight. 'Tis not fair to ask more of you after being on duty all day. But tomorrow I want many Rangers found who have a good eye and scribing hand. You can take shifts down here." He turned to Marcalan. "Perhaps this new duty will help keep you out of trouble."

Marcalan grinned. "Not if I can help it."

"What have I told you, Thane?" Lantalan asked. "He does not get into trouble, he simply is trouble."

~:~

Haladhon stacked the morning reports as Tam stood. This was one part of her life as a Ranger she did not enjoy, and she was glad it was over for the day.

"Thane..." Haladhon's eyes flicked to Tam. "Now that...yesterday is behind us, tell me, how was it Tam stopped Lord Paltor?"

"As I said at the time, I believe it was an emotional attack."

"But I do not remember sending, Uncle."

"In the fear of the moment, you lashed out instinctively, probably with some negative emotion or merely your own shock of realizing his intention. This can be a weapon, though, if you can learn to utilize it."

Tam recalled the moment, blinked back tears; the horror of her uncle's impending murder flashing in her mind. "I just remember thinking I could not lose you..."

"Dwell not on it, Tam. 'Tis done, and well done." Her uncle stood from his table.

Haladhon crossed his arms over his leather jerkin. "This ability of hers, Thane. How can we train it?"

Alcandhor huffed a silent laugh with a wag of his head. "She can send emotions. I think she needs no training, merely to use it when appropriate."

Tam frowned. "What emotions would I send to...to stop someone?"

"Stars, Tam, you knocked Marcalan atilt sending back his emotions, remember?"

She nodded at her cousin. "Aye. But..."

"Some negative emotion would work best." Alcandhor's expression grew somber. "You do know this is only to be used in an actual combat—not in matches or contests."

"Aye, Uncle."

He smiled, the tenderness in his eyes telling her of his love, even though he still blocked, as he mostly had since yesterday, save that little time in the chamber below. Her uncle's smile faded as the deep rhythm of a drum message began. Tam felt her stomach churn at the subject matter.

"Another one lost," Alcandhor murmured.

"What will happen to Nandhal?" whispered Tam.

Alcandhor blew his breath out slowly. "If he gives over to Rangers when they find him, he will be brought back for trial. I hope he does not fight. They would try to take him alive, but they will protect themselves. We have no evidence to convict, so he would likely merely be stripped of rank and status, perhaps of standing as well." He ran a hand through his hair. "I know not why he ran."

"It was right after the siege ended," Haladhon said. "Perhaps he feared incrimination from those inside Laird Hall."

"We know not, and probably will never know."

Haladhon shifted from one foot the other. "He never was stable."

"Aye. I gave him every chance to learn. To mature. But he persisted in his self-centered ways. He was intractable." His voice faded, and he stared at the floor.

"Is that why he has never been Confirmed," Tam asked, "even though he has several years above Age?"

"Aye."

Her uncle's ache pierced Tam. If only she could hug him, make him feel better. But this hurt went deep; it could be seen even if not felt through his block. She twisted her hands together. "I–I am sorry, Uncle."

He shook his head. "I will be fine. 'Tis just hard losing kin." He straightened abruptly. "Check on the progress in that Enaisi chamber, Tam. As soon as everything is ordered, and the books I have chosen are packed, we can leave."

~:~

Five bands of Rangers left the bailey as the drums echoed into silence. The drum tower at Laird Hall picked up the message and repeated it.

Uardhel ground his teeth from where he lay hidden in the underbrush across the clearing from the gate to Ranger Hold. He wished he dared stop blocking and sense to get a feel for the area and where the patrols might head, but he chanced being felt by Alcandhor or any other Ranger nearby with Enaisi blood.

"Who is this Nandhal they say has gone Rogue?" Guladhor whispered in his ear.

"It matters not. The Rangers are on search. These bands will begin looking for his trail so we must be away at the first chance. I want not my neck lengthened."

The two Rogues remained still, watching the Rangers, hoping they did not come close. The two of them against a band would be a bloody fight, and one they likely would not win. Fortunately, the Rangers did not approach their hiding place, but Uardhel knew they must move soon before the sweep pattern brought their ex-kin across their path.

Before they could steal away, Alcandhor, his arm in a sling, and several other Rangers left the hold.

Hatred roiled in Uardhel, and he hissed in exasperation. He dare not attack, not with the Rangers out in force. He clenched his fists, willing his mind over his emotions. He slapped Guladhor on the arm and nodded toward Alcandhor. "Follow him."

Uardhel had his own plan; he crept off toward the town. According to Lord Paltor, they had allies at the Copper Kettle, and he desperately needed more information.

~:~

Tam stood in the archway and watched the Rangers at their tasks. Marcalan stood by a shelf, leafing through a book.

"Uncle sent me down," Tam said.

"I know why you are here, you know." Marcalan's eyes sparkled as he peered over the top of the book at her. "The Thane thinks you can keep me out of trouble."

Tam crossed her arms, fighting a smile as she entered the chamber. Their connection could be disconcerting.

One of the Rangers, Jonadhan, snorted and, without looking up from the chart he copied, replied, "Our cousin seems capable of quite a few incredible things. But I have strong doubts about that."

"Aye. I doubt if anything could tame Marcalan," Maradhor said.

"'Tis good to know my reputation is quite secure. My thanks, Maradhor."

"Will you hush, Marcalan, and let us work?" asked Gardhal in irritation, as he turned from the bookshelf where he took inventory.

Marcalan shot him a farcical expression as he and Tam both sat down. For some reason it embarrassed her to be sitting near Marcalan while sensing his emotions in this way. She knew not what to call it, but she could tell Marcalan had mischief in mind. She cut her eyes over to him, and he snickered.

"What are you up to, Marcalan?" Maradhor asked over his shoulder.

Marcalan spread his arms. "I am just sitting here."

"Quit, Marcalan. I cannot concentrate on this inventory," Gardhal said.

"Oh, who weaned you with vinegar, Gardhal?" Marcalan asked.

Footfalls on the stairs made Tam turn. A Ranger came into the archway, the one who had given Tam hateful looks every time she had seen him. He looked around at the study chamber of the Enaisi in astonishment, but his gaze settled on Tam, his eyes hardened.

Tam and Marcalan rose as one.

"Ch'oralan, you have no business down here," Marcalan said.

The Ranger shot Marcalan an arrogant look. "You do not tell me where I may and may not go."

"He does in this circumstance," Gardhal said. "The Thane set him in charge of this place. Only those ordered to help in the work are allowed down."

"I need to further explain their duties to the Rangers above,"

Marcalan said. "Since they obviously did not understand their orders."

"I told them I had business with the Second at Table, and they let me come down," Ch'oralan said.

"Exactly what I mean."

"Then why is it she is here, if only those working are allowed?" Antipathy flowed from this Ch'oralan. Tam set her shoulders and her chin.

"She is our door warden." Maradhor smiled over his shoulder toward Tam.

Tam knew why this Ranger sought her out. With her uncle taking his morning walk, this would be the perfect time for him to contest her. She met his haughty brown eyes. "Why do we not take our business to the bailey and let these Rangers work?"

Ch'oralan inclined his head, and Tam started for the archway.

"Wait a moment," Marcalan said. "I will come along—"

Tam turned. "You have a duty here, Marcalan. I will be back before long. I will have to trust these other Rangers to keep you on a picket in my absence."

The Rangers all turned to look at her, grinning, save Gardhal, who rolled his eyes.

She knew Marcalan desired to go with her, as if he felt he could protect her just by being there. His concern made her happy, but on the other hand, a Ranger did not need protection. She sent gratefulness and affection to him, as she followed Ch'oralan up the stairs. Marcalan did accompany her, but only to the armory to clarify instructions to the Rangers stationed as guards there.

They went out through the foreroom to the front of the bailey and walked around to the back. Most of the Rangers followed them. Of course. Ch'oralan would want everyone to see him contest her. Would this settle matters at least among all her kin present? Or would anything make a difference for many of them?

Ch'oralan finally spun to face her, his face hard and eyes glittering. "I contest you, Tamissa, daughter of Valdhor. A lass has no right to make a claim of being a Ranger."

~:~

Uardhel arrived at the preassigned meeting place below the mill in South Lairdton to find Guladhor waiting with the others in his band.

"Well?" Uardhel asked.

"He went into Lairdton, turned, and came back. There seemed no purpose."

"Aye, there is a purpose. I found the reason from our friends at the Copper Kettle, and I met Zantith's little murmurer from Ranger Hold there as well. The Thane is still recovering from wounds and he walks twice a day, morning and afternoon for exercise."

Uardhel smiled at his band. "So our ambush is easily planned. If we situate ourselves on each side of the path between the hold and the town with bows, we cannot fail."

"But they will come after us swifter than arrows fly."

"The Thane and all his accompanying men will be dead. We will have time between his death and its discovery to flee. We journeyed here knowing this would be risky." Uardhel curled his lip. "You wish to back out?"

"Nay. But our escape—"

"We shall be on our own. If we travel as a band we have more chance to leave tracks."

His men nodded.

"Let us get into position. If he leaves the hold again, I want us ready. Our friend said he will not be staying many more days, so we cannot lose this opportunity."

Chapter Thirty-five

Her gaze locked on Ch'oralan, Tam took out her leg knife and saw several hands reach out for it. The only face she knew was Tanadhon's, so she allowed him to take it, then took out her father's knife, and handed it over as well. His intent look gave way to a wink and a nod—silent encouragement? She took a breath, not able to return his smile.

Ch'oralan stood ready. After putting their fists over their hearts, they assumed a fighting position. Ch'oralan did not try to grab her as Loch'alan had. He did not make the mistake of treating her as a lass although he contested her because she was one. He came at her solidly, as her father used to. That made it familiar ground. She did not stay on the defensive but, to use a term of her father's, brought the fight to him, matching blow for blow.

The contest continued on for many minutes; he would not call, and she would not yield. He finally caught her with a blow to her jaw that sent her reeling off balance. Lunging forward, he grabbed her by the jerkin to punch her full in the face. She bent her knees, dug in her heels, and dove backwards. He let go and sailed over her into a shoulder roll and up. Tam rolled quickly to her feet as well but saw Alcandhor's hand slap Ch'oralan's shoulder.

"Think you not she can fight, Ch'oralan?"

Ch'oralan straightened, panting. Tam flicked the hair out of her eyes, staying in a fighting stance.

"Nay, I do not, Thane."

"Despite the fact this contest has gone on past when you should have called it? You have not bested her, Ch'oralan. She is holding her own. What are you trying to prove?"

"That a lass should not be a Ranger."

Alcandhor pointed to Tam. "Look at her, Ch'oralan. You two have been in contest for how long? Yet she waits, ready to continue. You have landed solid blows on her and she stands. You are well bruised as well, yet you refuse to admit she has the strength to be a Ranger?"

Ch'oralan stood mute, his jaw set. This prejudice against her spoiled any solace Tam might find in her uncle's praise.

The Thane said, "I expected more resistance to a female Ranger by older men. Yet, it seems the young ones are having the hardest time accepting her. I think I do not understand Rangers as well as I thought."

"Thane, do you call the contest, or does it continue?" Tam asked, still in position.

"What say you, Ch'oralan?" Alcandhor asked. "If it continues, I will take off all rules of contest."

The Rangers all muttered among themselves. Tam was stunned. Only on rare occasion would the Thane call all rules off. What would it accomplish? Either she or Ch'oralan would be injured—or worse before it was over.

"I do not call, Thane." Ch'oralan sneered at Tam.

"Understand you there will be no rules?" Alcandhor met his eyes, and Ch'oralan inclined his head. Her uncle gazed at Tam, his eyes full of meaning. Understanding dawned. She nodded, trying to feel negative emotions: all the horror she felt at the hangings, the pain of her father's death...

The Thane held up his arm in a gesture of futility. "Continue."

Before Ch'oralan took one step, he doubled over, then fell to his knees, clutching his stomach. As he struggled to straighten, she intensified the emotions until he groaned and tears streamed down his face.

"I yield," he finally gasped.

Tam stopped. Her uncle gave her a sad smile. Ch'oralan climbed to his feet and backed away from her, wiping his face on his sleeve.

She spun and walked away, not taking her weapons back, not looking at her uncle or any other Ranger there. They made a path and let her walk through She hoped she could make it to her bedchamber before tears started.

Once the door was shut, she smashed her fists repeatedly on the table in anger, bruising her hands yet not caring. Why must she cry? She had never cried before! For years she dared not! Why could she not stop the tears now? Why must they make a difference of her being a female? She was a Ranger! And a good one! She could hold her own in a match with any of the younger Rangers. Ch'oralan looked to be of Age, and she had stayed with him the whole contest! Even the older Rangers respected her abilities as a fighter. Cordhan thought well of her, and Edhron, whom she admired as a fighter more than any other, did also. Why must it make a difference? Why?

She crumpled to the floor, unable to stop weeping.

~:~

Haladhon knocked at Tam's door, but there was no answer. "Tam?"

He heard her muffled voice. "Go away."

He opened the door and saw her sitting on the floor.

"Go away!"

"And if I do not?"

"I rank you," she said in a sulky voice.

He chuckled, closing the door behind him. "You mind not your rank at times, then, enh?"

She did not answer.

"I brought your weapons."

She did not answer, so he placed them on the table and sat down on the floor, facing her in the dark.

"I just wanted to make sure you were all right."

"My father fought me much harder. I am fine."

"That is not what I meant, and I believe you know it."

No response again.

"Tam. It is not going to be an easy adjustment for some Rangers to accept you. But you are proving yourself every day. Many of the Rangers who have met you accept you, and you made a favorable impression just now in contest. You cannot expect every Ranger to be swayed immediately, though. But in five years time enough will be—"

"Nay! I do not want that!" Her voice rose in youthful temper. "I want not to be Thane! I simply want to be accepted as a Ranger! I can do what any other Ranger can do! Why does it make a difference?"

"It does make a difference, more than you realize. There is so much more to being a woman than you yet understand." *And I would fain teach you about being a woman if it were possible.* He gave a deep, soulful sigh. Sad fortune that she was niece to the Thane. He reached out, found her hands, and took them in his, determined to keep his mind on helping her and not his own desires. "Tam, there are many things you do not understand. Many things you should have been taught that you were not. Your uncle would not fain have me be the one to teach you. It should be a woman, a foster-mother. If you understood these things, you would more easily understand why it is difficult for some men to accept you as a Ranger."

"What things? Please, Haladhon, can you not explain them to me? I would fain have you do it, not some foster-mother."

"I might try to answer a few questions you may have. But only if we keep it a secret. Your uncle would not consider it my place to speak to you about such things."

"Just tell me why it makes such a difference to Rangers that I am a female! I cannot understand it. I fight well—both Cordhan and Edhron said so, and they are the best fighters I have had, save my father. I can track. I know our laws. Why must I prove myself over and over? Why does it make that much difference simply because I cannot stand up to use the priv?"

Laughter and vexation warred in Haladhon, and he fought down a smile. "You are a headstrong young lass, Tam. If I answer, will you listen without protesting as you are so wont to do?"

"I will try."

Haladhon sniffed in disbelief. "Tam, you are a beautiful young lass. You understand not what that means yet. You are also seemingly a slight wisp of a thing, which makes you appear fragile or delicate. The men look at you and see only this young, small lass with huge, beautiful, innocent eyes and they fail to see the strength of your father in you, or regard the years of training you have had by him."

"I suppose I can understand what you say about the fact I am young and small . . . "

He felt for her hand and put it palm to palm with his. "'Tis dark so you cannot see, but feel the difference in the size of our hands, Tam."

She pulled out the key, and he chuckled as its glow illuminated the chamber. "'Tis better than a candle. Now, see our hands?"

"Aye."

"Your whole hand almost fits in my palm. See you the difference in size?"

"Aye."

"By look alone, which appears stronger?"

"Yours, of course."

"These Rangers know you not. They see only your youth and your size. Understand you now why some of them have a difficult time?"

"But you knew me not, yet accepted me without question."

"You had not even crossed the city when I knew you were Valdhor's daughter and Trained by him. I also knew Ranger clothes had been sent for and that a jerkin was ordered from storage with chief rank on it and showing leaf-clusters denoting a Ranger Confirmed. Remember, I knew your father, Tam, and what it meant to be Trained by him. I knew what you should be capable of, despite appearances. And I knew the Thane would not allow you to be Confirmed unless he had tested you thoroughly. I trusted them both to do their duties well."

"Aye," she said slowly. "You were certain I would best Loch'alan." *Even though I truly did not.*

"Exactly. But not every Ranger has such understanding or blind faith in our leaders. So, you will be contested. It is a burden you will have to bear."

She sighed. "If only I could grow up faster and not be so small."

"That would only take care of some of the problems, Tam. You are also beautiful. 'Tis an inconceivable notion that a lass of such rare beauty could be such a deadly Ranger."

"This I understand not. You keep saying I am beautiful, which does not matter. What has a person's looks to do with his or her abilities?"

Haladhon chuckled. "Absolutely nothing, Tam. But many people never figure that out."

She pulled her hands away from Haladhon and crossed her arms, frowning.

"Have I answered your questions enough to set your mind at ease?"

"Some of them, perhaps. But I am still so confused..."

"And let me assure you, Tam, that you are very beautiful."

"That means nothing to me, Haladhon. Why should it? I care only to be a Ranger."

"It may mean nothing now, but someday it will. Someday soon."

"Why?"

"When the time comes that you care about being beautiful, I will not have to explain it. Until then, I dare not. The Thane would have my head."

"You drive me mad sometimes."

Haladhon grinned. "I doubt it not."

"But why should my uncle get angry at you for explaining things to me?"

"On this particular subject he would consider it unseemly and presumptuous. Which is why even the little that we have discussed must be our secret."

"Then why does Uncle not explain?"

Haladhon snickered at the notion of Alcandhor explaining such things to a lass, but sobered. Tam had hit the mark. "He should. And I no longer think he can wait. I only hope his embarrassment does not interfere with his duty as your foster-father."

"You are not embarrassed. I will not tell if you explain it, Haladhon. Please!"

"Nay, Tam. I dare not. I hope my talk about why some Rangers will contest you has helped." He stood. "But I need to go. It would not look right if I were found to be in here with you."

"Why?"

Haladhon groaned. "Another question I should not answer. Suffice it to say that for you to be alone in a room with a man, as we are, is not considered proper, unless perhaps it is your uncle, since he is your foster-father now."

He opened the door, looked back at her, and threw out a parting statement to distract her from asking the inevitable *why*. "And, cousin, that contest was well fought." He flashed a grin and closed the door.

Haladhon turned to find himself facing Alcandhor, eyes dark and face set. He met his cousin's black eyes evenly, waiting for the inevitable. Alcandhor's jaw muscles jumped in what Haladhon recognized as a desperate attempt to keep his temper.

His cousin opened the door to his study. Haladhon entered the chamber and stood waiting.

Alcandhor closed the door and spun with an icy gaze. "What were you doing alone with her in her bedchamber, in the dark?"

Haladhon pointed toward the door. "Did you see her expression as the contest ended? I cannot sense emotions as you can, but I need not to know the look on her face. That child needs guidance. She is overwhelmed."

"Overwhelmed? Who is not right now?"

"Think you, man! Until a lunation ago, that girl lived alone with Valdhor. She knew nothing except his training. She was alone. Now she has been thrust into a totally different world. She is Confirmed and has been told she will be Thane in five years. She went from no family to hundreds of relatives. And I tell you, cousin, she is starting to discover who she is. Valdhor is no longer here to keep her crushed into a mindless, submissive child. That girl is not the same lass I saw in conclave. She is growing up fast and has no background of our culture or clan to give her foundation for many things that are inundating her. You need to talk with her—and now."

"Wait. Wait a moment." Alcandhor raised his good arm. "What things are inundating her?"

"I could give you a long list, cousin."

"Please do."

"Do you know what her perception of being female is?"

"Tell me." Alcandhor spread his hand with a sardonic incline of his head.

Haladhon crossed his arms, irritated at his cousin's sarcasm as well as his inability to see Tam's dilemma. "She is insulted because the Rangers take her not seriously simply because she cannot stand up to use the priv. That is a quote."

Alcandhor fell into a chair. "If only Sarinna were here."

"She is not, and you cannot wait."

"This is your knowledgeable opinion?"

"If you brush this off, you will regret it. Beyond all the ways her world has been turned topside down within the last lunation, and her grief over her father's death, that girl can feel what anyone around her is feeling. You tell me what emotions she has encountered?"

"She seems to deal fine with—"

Haladhon waved his arms. "Alcandhor, you are not thinking! She is the only female on the grounds, besides Sherel—who does not count"— *stars, no!*—"among all these Rangers. She is young and beautiful. Think you what emotions and urges she has sensed from some of them? Think of what Nandhal said to her that morning. You must have a talk with her. Now."

"But we leave for Zaidhron tomorrow."

"Four days of journeying, sleeping in camps or inns barracked with hundreds of men? You cannot wait."

"Oh, blessed stars." Alcandhor moaned, dropping his head to his hand. "How can I? You know me. All these years married, and I cannot talk openly about such things. I have not your candid attitude. What would I say?"

"You are a very private man, which is why such things are harder for you to address openly. But you will have to find it in yourself, cousin, to say what needs to be said. If I thought you would trust me to talk to her, I would offer."

"Part of me wishes you to be the one to talk to her, and part of me does not trust you." He looked up with a sorrowful expression. "I am sorry."

"Aye, my reputation sullies your trust in me." Haladhon rubbed his neck with a pang of remorse. "I think for the first time, I have some feeling of regret about my licentious ways."

Alcandhor stared up at his cousin in surprise, and Haladhon grinned. "Not much, mind you."

Alcandhor managed a small smile. Haladhon sat down next to him and put a hand on his arm. "Alcandhor, if you got beyond the trust, would you let me have the talk for you?"

"And how do we get beyond that? I know what I felt when I discovered you were in her bedchamber with her."

"What if we both had the talk with her?"

Alcandhor laughed. "Two men trying to tell a young girl about life and love and being a woman? Oh, great Bells!" He sat up straight. "Sherel is here. She could—" He stopped and shuddered even as Haladhon gripped his arm.

"Nay! You would inflict Sherel upon that lass? Granted, such a discussion should be from a woman, but Sherel has neither patience nor compassion."

"Aye. And although she has said nothing overtly, she cares not for Tam. Whether 'tis because she is a Ranger-lass or some other reason, I know not." Alcandhor combed his hand through his hair and tossed it back. "I...I will talk to her. I know not how, but I will talk to her."

"Now."

He shook his head. "Give me a few hours, cousin. I will speak with her before this day ends."

Haladhon expelled his breath in a weary sigh.

~:~

Tam remained on the floor thinking of what Haladhon had said and trying to come to terms with all the emotions she found herself almost drowning in daily. But she could not just sit in the dark. Although quiet and peaceful, it seemed too much like hiding, and her nature fought that. She decided to go back down to the Enaisi's chamber. She wanted to be near Marcalan.

As she walked through the archway, the Rangers all turned and grinned, calling welcome.

"Well fought, Tam," called Maradhor from his copy table.

"Hear, hear," said another.

Marcalan, from his seat, grinned with pride. "It was very well fought."

"And how would you know this?"

"He convinced us it would be a great loss to miss seeing this contest, so we left the two above as guards and went out to watch," Maradhor said.

"For once the vagabond was not jesting. 'Twas grand to see." Gardhal had a pleased look.

Tam glared at Marcalan, which did not diminish his grin. How could she stay irritated at that scoundrel? She found herself smiling back at him. "You are an unrepentant rascal."

Warmth flowed over her. "And you would have me no other way, my dear, young cousin."

She sent back to him, and the strange connection began again. To hide her exultation over the experience, she asked, "How goes the copying and inventory?"

"We are almost through here." Marcalan smirked. "I expect we should be finished by evening."

"Not that you have done much of anything to help," Gardhal said.

"I have not a neat hand, cousin. My duty is protect this place, down to every mote of dust."

"I see you have done that duty by collecting each mote of dust," Tam said, pointing to the clean tables.

"Oh, aye, and most carefully saved them too." Marcalan put his feet on one of the tables, his eyes twinkling. "I take my duties very seriously, Second at Table."

She avoided his gaze, again feeling embarrassed to be able to see him and be so near him when she could feel his emotions. She picked up a book and opened it, enjoying not being alone. It felt strange, this being connected to someone. She could sense his mood changes and knew he could feel hers.

She just wished she knew what devious things he could be planning that would bring on such a happy mood so quickly. She glanced over at him but he had leaned back in the chair, hands behind his head. He opened his eyes, winked at her, and closed his eyes again.

Scoundrel! She fought the urge to giggle, a difficult task as she felt him laughing in her mind. She tried to concentrate on the book, but did not have much success.

The luncheon gong soon rang, and they all filed upstairs, with Tam last to lock up. The Thane stood at the head of the table, withdrawn and blocking. Only once did Tam manage to meet his eyes during the meal and he dropped his gaze. Although he continued to block, from the look on his face he seemed embarrassed.

She could not dwell on it though because the connection with Marcalan kept her distracted. She only glanced over at Marcalan once or twice during the meal but each time he had been looking at her, a conspiratorial smile on his face. Both enjoyed their incredible secret.

~:~

Rangers rose from the table, rushing back to their duties. Haladhon slowly stood, eyeing Tam, and asked, "Where to now, cousin, since you have no task."

Dimpling, she replied, "The garden."

"Ah. Enjoy." He offered her a deep bow and a wink. Her smile widened as she flitted out.

Alcandhor stepped close and said, "I am not walking this afternoon."

Haladhon frowned. "And why? Santran—"

Alcandhor waved a hand. "I have much thinking to do about...Tam. A walk into town with jesting Rangers would distract me. I will merely walk around the bailey a bit."

Haladhon smiled. "Just take care you do not fall over."

Alcandhor shot him a disgusted look and strode toward the foreroom. Haladhon's smile faded. The Thane's preoccupation over his niece kept him from seeing that his worst fears were already budding. Haladhon needed no Enaisi blood to see what was happening between Tam and Marcalan. He must warn them.

He sent word through the guards stationed in the armory that he needed to see Marcalan and soon his cousin's grinning face appeared. "What?"

"Not here. Come with me."

Marcalan frowned and followed Haladhon outside. They walked a bit before Haladhon stopped, looking around. They stood in the middle of the bailey, no one near. Still, Haladhon kept his voice soft. "I think you are stepping into trouble, cousin."

Marcalan laughed, crossing his arms with smugness. "This is nothing new. To which prank are you referring?"

"No prank. I am serious."

"Oh? So tell me, my dear Haladhon."

"You and Tam."

Marcalan blinked, his voice and manner were both light. "What about us?"

"I saw the way you two kept looking at each other at table. How serious are you?"

Marcalan lifted his arms in a tacit claim of innocence. "I know not what you mean."

Haladhon gave a shake of his head. "Mar, this is me. You know I will keep any confidence, but I know what I saw."

Marcalan struck an indignant pose. "If you truly saw anything, so would others, including the Thane. Especially since he can sense emotions. Why has he not sent for me then?"

"He is preoccupied, in case you had not noticed, cousin." *And if you knew the reason why, you would be hiding under your cot!* "The others are not as likely to notice as much because they do not know both of you as well, and even if they did, I doubt they be likely to approach you or Tam. Why will you not be honest with me?"

Marcalan's face grew sober. "By my family name, Haladhon, there is nothing more than friendship. She sees someone she can trust and be open with, as an older brother, perhaps. No more."

"I saw the looks you two gave each other at table."

"Stars, cousin, she has been teaching me to use my abilities, to sense and block. We practice on each other. 'Tis like having a private jest to do so among people."

Haladhon stared hard at his cousin, trying to gauge his sincerity; he knew Marcalan to be an accomplished liar when it suited his pranks. "You are in earnest?"

"By my family and blood." Marcalan put a hand over his heart. "She is as a little sister."

With a hesitant nod, Haladhon let the subject drop.

Chapter Thirty-six

Uardhel ground his teeth as his Ranger informer breathlessly shared the update: the Thane was not taking his afternoon walk.

"What can we do?" the Ranger asked.

"Let me think..." Uardhel sucked a tooth, pondering how to get Alcandhor alone. He jerked a thumb in the direction of Ranger Hold. "There is no place inside the hold where one might be alone."

The Ranger shrugged. "Only maybe the crypt."

"The crypt..." His eyes narrowed. "What might get him to the crypt—alone?"

"Alone? I can think of naught. Haladhon and the other chiefs have been his shadow."

"Help me, man! That corner is isolated, we can easily scale the wall unseen and enter the crypt. What could get him inside?"

The Ranger frowned but, slowly, light came to his eyes. "He reads reports periodically throughout the day, slipping a paper onto his desk is an easy task. Do any of you have scribing skills?"

"Aye. What is your plan?"

"Someone wishing to meet privately with information of betrayal within the clan—that would get his immediate attention."

"That just might work." Uardhel imagined Alcandhor, held captive by his men. He would drop his block before running him through, so he could sense his soul leaving Alcandhor's body. He smiled. "Aye. That will work well."

~:~

From a nearby incline, overlooking the walled garden, Alcandhor watched Tam kneeling in the dirt, diligently working. Already blocking, he was hopefully safe from her sensing him. Although now would be a perfect time to talk to her, he could not face her at this moment. He turned away. *Coward,* he chided, but did not go back.

He strolled through the bailey, feeling inadequate to the task ahead of him and totally mortified. The Rangers seemed to understand he wanted solitude; few approached, and those that did, he waved away.

How could he talk to Tam about such private matters? Haladhon was right, of course, Tam was vulnerable and needed guidance. He resisted the urge to run his hand through his hair in frustration and chagrin. Thane of the Rangers—and father of three—and he had not the boldness to talk of love and intimacy.

He must attack this face on. Now was his chance to form words, plan his approach. His face grew warm as his mind worked through his dilemma, but he persevered, his ambling taking him throughout the bailey.

He found himself eventually near the crypt and stared at the stone structure, ivy crawling over the northeast side. Alcandhor was tempted to go in and rail at Valdhor's bier, but that would accomplish nothing. His thoughts were as swirling, muddied waters. What a knotted tangle! He veered away and headed back to the hold.

The interior felt cool after the warm, autumn sun. Once in the meeting chamber, he stared at the table and sighed. The morning reports had all been filed, but a sealed message now awaited in the center of the table. With all on his mind, how could he concentrate? He hesitated, sighing again; duty must win out.

He sat, opened the missive, and began to read. The untidy scrawl indicated haste and caught his full attention. Letter clenched in his fist, Alcandhor strode outside, eyes darting among the Rangers gathered in small groups. Where was Haladhon?

A contagious laugh drew him toward a group of Rangers practicing their bowman skills.

"On the mark!" Haladhon hooted. "Well done, Bardhal! Not a miss yet."

"What wager have you taken on the first of us to miss?" asked Sandhral chuckling.

If Alcandhor did not have traitors on his mind, he would fain watch four of his best bowman tickle a wager out of his tall cousin. Perhaps later...

"Haladhon."

His Third at Table turned. "Aye, Thane?"

Alcandhor held up the crumpled note with a beckoning nod. Haladhon's smile faded into a frown, and he hurried over. Wordlessly, he took the paper and read. His jaw worked for a moment, and he finally asked, "Who is this from?"

"You can see for yourself it is unsigned."

"Think you it is genuine?"

"We shall see."

Haladhon shook his head. "Tam is your Second now. She should be with you."

Alcandhor grimaced. Haladhon was right, but he chafed at any delay. "She is in the garden. Get her and meet me at the crypt."

With an incline of his head, Haladhon turned and ran off.

Alcandhor walked toward the southwest corner of the grounds, impatiently waiting for his cousin and niece. As he drew near the burial chamber, he frowned as he realized the door hung ajar. He blinked as the sunlight peeked through the branches of the overhanging trees—did he see movement inside, shadows in the darkness?

He stepped closer, peering hard through the doorway, and—too late—tried to draw his knife.

~:~

"Second at Table."

Tam rose at the firm tone in Haladhon's voice and wiped the dirt from her hands on her trous. "Aye?"

"The Thane requires your presence." He thrust a paper at her. "Read this as we walk."

Tam trotted alongside her cousin to keep up with his long strides as she read. She then squinted up at him and asked, "Nandhal?"

"We know not."

"Is Uncle at the crypt?"

"Aye, he is waiting for us."

"I cannot imagine a Ranger betraying kin."

"Neither can Alcandhor. I only hope he waits for us."

"What do you mean?"

"It might be a trap. He knows this, but his desire for information..."

Oh stars! Tam dropped her block to sense for her uncle. She inhaled as echoed pain hit in her shoulder, stomach, and face: the Thane was being beaten! Tam broke into a run. "Uncle!"

A strong wave of evil, joyous hatred crashed over her. She screamed aloud, sending to its source as she tore through between trees and around bushes.

Shock and anger assailed her, and she matched it with as much pain as she could direct; she must send him to his knees, keep him from acting—killing.

She heard Haladhon shouting as if from a distance, rallying Rangers to help them. As she neared the crypt, she drew her sword. Men were inside; she could sense them. A voice shouted, "Bar the way!"

She hesitated outside the door. She had never tried sending to so many, but she must now. *Pain!* In a moment's time, she let the torment of her father's loss, the horror of having killed and of the hangings fill

329

her and sent to all the men inside.

Groans and shouts of dismay broke the silence.

"Tam!"

She spun, still concentrating on sending. Haladhon, sword drawn, stood behind her, gasping for breath. Rangers rushed toward them, weapons at the ready.

"I am sending," she said. "Go!"

She stepped aside, and the Rangers poured inside like floodwaters. She rushed in behind them, feeling for the evil presence and for Uncle. Both were below.

She hesitated, trying to get her bearings in the darkened, smoky atmosphere amid fighting between the Rangers and the assailants, then tore for the stairs. Her left hand ran along the cold wall, her feet unsure on the steps, but she dared not slow. Once at the floor below, she peered and sensed into the dark. A momentary gleam of a blade and onslaught of hatred warned her of an attack. She ducked, slashing a counterattack.

Tam lunged forward with a straight thrust, tripped over something, and fell to her knees on the hard stone. A groan came from next to her. *Uncle!* Fear for him, and fury for his attacker boiled up inside Tam. She shot a burst of emotion at her opponent with all her strength.

A gasp, then a thud and clang of metal. Had her enemy fallen? After a moment, a growl rose before her in the dark and hatred shot through her again, making her feel as if she were going to vomit.

No! She clenched her fists, concentrating on him, sending, fighting back his onslaught of emotion.

Boots clomped the stairs, accompanied by a growing light.

"Have at me, Rogue!" came Marcalan's shout from above.

Marcalan tossed the torch to the stone floor, illuminating the chamber, and jumped the last steps, landing in front of Tam and Alcandhor.

The assailant, blond hair lank around his lean, enraged face, lunged, and Marcalan's sword swung in to parry. Her cousin jumped to his right and backstepped, forcing the—Rogue? This was a Rogue?—to turn away from Tam and Alcandhor.

Keeping her eyes on the fight, Tam's fingers brushed the hair from her uncle's face.

"Tam..." he whispered.

She glanced down. "Uncle, are you all right?"

"Worry about Marcalan. Uardhel..." Alcandhor's voice trailed off as he struggled to sit up. She pulled him upright and leaned him against the wall, keeping one hand on his shoulder to steady him.

The Rogue sent to Marcalan, who stumbled back. *Not fair!* She hurled the Rogue's own emotions back at him, then set a block through Marcalan—for Marcalan.

Her cousin's mirth rose as a froth, and he laughed.

"By-blow!" the Rogue hissed, lunging.

Marcalan danced to the side with a diagonal down-stroke. "Ha! Nay. Sorry." His blade flickered in the dim flames of the torch, flourishing in a pattern Tam had never seen, but it drove the Rogue back.

"Cannot cheat, can you now?" Marcalan taunted. "Must merely use your sword skills. Lacking a bit, are they?"

The Rogue snarled and leaped forward with a downward cut. Marcalan side-stepped and countered with another combination of strikes, hooting as the Rogue backstepped. Merriment bubbled in her cousin; he enjoyed the baiting!

"Stop playing him, Marcalan!" Tam shouted. "Finish him!"

More footsteps echoed, and Rangers, some carrying torches, crowded down the stairs.

"Uardhel!" several Rangers yelled.

"Marcalan, be careful," Haladhon called. "He—"

"Tam has him blocked. He is mine!" Marcalan continued to beat the Rogue back.

Uardhel grunted with effort as he slashed, ducked, and parried, his breath heaving, his sword and Marcalan's interweaving in a flashing dance then—both stopped. Marcalan's blade had found its mark. With a practiced saccade, he withdrew his weapon from the Rogue's chest and knocked the blade from Uardhel's grasp.

Uardhel's face contorted with hatred. He spat at Marcalan and fell.

Tam stared at the crumpled body and inhaled, trying to ease the crush of emotions not only from her own heart and Marcalan's, but all the Rangers.

Haladhon helped Tam in assisting Alcandhor to his feet, murmuring, "Santran should be called to ascertain if you have received any harm from your adventure."

"'Adventure.'" Alcandhor snorted softly. "Aye, 'twas that. But I am fine."

"Hush, Uncle. Haladhon is right."

Marcalan picked up Tam's sword—dropped when she fell, she supposed, although she could not remember—and held it out with a bow. "Your sword, Second at Table."

She hesitated in releasing Alcandhor; she felt his unsteadiness. But would he want her to say thus aloud? "You hold it, Ranger Marcalan. I am not letting go of Uncle!"

Several Rangers chuckled. Alcandhor's arm tightened around her shoulders as she gave him support, and he gave her a knowing smile.

Once outside the crypt, Haladhon whispered, "We have more than one twig viper, Thane. Who wrote that report and delivered it?"

"Aye. We must give thought to that." Alcandhor replied softly and nodded toward the hold. They began walking in that direction, Haladhon's head and the Thane's close as they continued their quiet conversation. "Is Zandhral here?"

"Aye, he is about," Haladhon glanced around. "Most likely helping clear bodies inside the crypt."

"After mealtime, we shall have a meeting."

How could a meeting help? Zandhral had been trying to sense for the traitor for a long time. They hadn't even known Nandhal was guilty for certain until he ran. Stars, one of the Rangers walking alongside right now might be the traitor!

Her uncle gazed down at Tam. "Worry not, niece."

Tam studied his face, memorizing every line, every pore, still fearful of this near miss. Still afraid of someone close trying again to kill him.

His eyes darted about; she felt the suspicion in his heart, as it was in hers. He smiled and said in a louder voice, "You rescued me just in time for afternooning. 'Twas fortuitous. Sherel is serving bata soup, one of my favorites."

~:~

The chiefs and Zandhral all gathered around the meeting table. Tam sat gingerly on the edge of her seat, feeling the tension of all those around her.

"Where shall we start?" Haladhon asked.

Alcandhor shook his head, his gaze on Zandhral.

The bearded Ranger shook his head. "Look not to me. I could not discover anything during the whole siege. I cannot fathom how to uncover the source of this treachery."

Lamadhel rapped his knuckles on the table as he spoke, his blue eyes flashing. "Someone falsified a message and either gave it to someone to bring into this hold, or placed it on this table himself. This person had direct contact with the Rogues, or else how would they know where and when to wait to ambush Alcandhor? We do not leave here until we decide on a course to uncover this traitor!"

Her great-uncle's anger unsettled Tam even more; he always seemed so calm. But now he had a depth of emotion which astonished her.

The chiefs all voiced agreement with Lamadhel, and Haladhon raised a hand. "Which leads us back to my question: where shall we start?"

Andhrel pursed his lips. "The first question, I think, is—when did the message for the Thane appear on this table? Alcandhor, had you seen any new papers or reports before or after luncheon?"

"Nay. I came back here after luncheon, and the table was untouched. I...did not stay long as I had matters on my mind." Her uncle's face flushed, and he cleared his throat. "I walked about the bailey for some time—anyone could have come in."

"Wait, wait..." Andhrel held up a hand, frowning. "Whoever it was had to leave the hold to contact those Rogues. Let us interview the gate guards."

Tam thought of the Rogues, and how they must have gained entrance to the hold grounds. "What if the traitor scaled the wall? 'Tis high, but not impossible."

Andhrel blinked. "There is that."

"No." Alcandhor leaned back, hand rubbing his chin. "Let us assume the simplest answer first. Being seen scaling the wall with all the Rangers quartered here would draw attention, and this person has been very circumspect and sly. Start with the gate guards. If that avails nothing, we shall broaden the focus. Call for them, Haladhon."

"Aye, my Thane."

As the door shut after Haladhon, Alcandhor continued, "Tam, as Second at Table, you will record the interviews, but also you will sense for truthfulness."

"Aye, sir."

~:~

The chiefs sat at the table, facing the door. Zandhral stood as door warden. He had not seen the need to be there with Tam present, but the chiefs wished it; he had been working to uncover the traitors since the beginning, after all. Also, he remained the only Ranger, outside the chiefs, known for a certainty to be faithful.

Tam and Zandhral sensed the gate guards as they were interviewed, and found only outrage at the recent attempt on the Thane, and a desire to help uncover the traitors.

With the siege over, many of the Rangers from other provinces had been conscripted as guards for Laird Hall, while others with pressing need had been allowed to return to their homes. As a result, traffic flowing in and out of Ranger Hold had been minimal. Five Rangers had passed out and back in during the time period in question.

Of those five, Tanadhon, being highest in rank and steward of the hold, was the first brought in for an interview. As he entered the chamber, he smiled brightly at Tam, but despite the light-hearted curiosity in his eyes, a sense of being prey weighed on him. Tam's stomach tightened, and she glanced at Zandhral—his eyebrows raised in surprise.

"You wished to see me, Thane?" the hold steward asked, his gaze sweeping over the chiefs.

This Ranger could act well. By his face and stance, one could not tell what he truly felt. How could one break his false face down? An idea struck Tam. But could she do it? Dare she do it?

"We wish to know if you saw anyone entering this chamber—or saw anything unusual—between luncheon or afternooning."

Tam hoped her sending only feather-touched Tanadhon as she returned his apprehension to him. She felt his heart rate increase, and flutters stir in his stomach.

Yet he appeared unmoved as he replied, "Nay, Thane."

Tam increased her sending a little bit, and he swallowed and blinked—a break in his façade. Alcandhor's gaze grew intense, as did all the chiefs. She let the emotions grow stronger; Tanadhon shifted his gaze from chief to chief, and took a step backward. From his position behind the hold steward, Zandhral tensed.

Tam was not certain of protocol in an interview, but this was a moment to be used—inwardly he had reached almost hysteria. He amazed her in only showing a slight nervousness on the surface.

"Were you alone?" she asked. "Did other Rangers help in the planning of this ambush?"

His mouth dropped open. "I know not what..." A swallow, and she felt his throat constrict. She magnified his fear, sent it as strongly as she could; as she had accidentally done to Marcalan, as she had done to Ch'oralan, and to the Rogues. He choked, almost a strangled cry.

Alcandhor's gaze pierced. His voice was low and deadly. "Were you alone?"

"Aye, Thane." Tanadhon shook, fists clenched at his sides, his shoulders hunching. "'Twas only me and Nandhal, but he ran. How..." He looked at Tam. "How did you know?"

Tam stopped sending, and Tanadhon drew a breath in sharply, straightening in release.

"Why?" she whispered. "Why would you wish to kill your Thane?"

Tanadhon's face melted into a sneer. "What other clan has Rogues? Our own kin branded as outlaw, cut off, cast out—what do I care for our clan—for our Thane, who allowed it of one of his closest friends!"

Haladhon barked a laugh. "Monadhal was my closest, my best friend. Aye, you were close to him, too, but tell me not of your feelings for him. I nearly died trying to save him from himself. He chose his path."

"You would take the Thane's part, would you not?" Rage grew in Tanadhon; Tam stilled—preparing to stop him if he acted.

"Alcandhor was not Thane when Monadhal went Rogue," Eladhrel said. "And he did speak on Monadhal's behalf."

Lamadhel stood, his hand slicing the air in a chopping motion. "Enough. 'Tis done. We have our traitor."

Tanadhon belatedly bolted for the door. Zandhral grabbed him, and the two began to wrestle. Tam shot a full blast of emotions at the traitor, and he moaned, his struggles decreasing. Haladhon rounded the table and in two strides had both hands on Tanadhon.

As he was forcefully escorted out, Tam turned to the Thane. "Who is this Monadhal, Uncle? Was he the one leading these Rogues?"

"Nay. Uardhel led this band," Lamadhel said.

"So, then, who is Monadhal?"

Alcandhor's eyes filled with pain. "Another Rogue. He is my age, as is Tanadhon. We all Trained together and were close friends. The two most affected when he went Rogue were Tanadhon and Haladhon." He shook his head. "I knew not such bitterness grew in Tanadhon though."

Lamadhel cleared his throat. "We need a new hold steward, Thane."

"With Nandhal and Tanadhon both out..." Alcandhor rubbed his eyes for a moment and straightened. "Capalan."

"Think you he is ready for such responsibility?" Lamadhel crossed his arms. "He is a good Ranger, but tends to underestimate himself."

"He has more in him than he realizes. Aye, this will be a good position for him."

~:~

Alcandhor had gone to supervise the packing of books from the chamber below. Tam hid in the meeting chamber reading a book to avoid the gazes of Rangers who wanted to see the lass who saved the Thane. Would they accept her for this peculiar ability, or would it merely set her apart?

"What strange thing have you done now, my friend?"

Tam looked up at the Laird's voice and set the book aside on the table. She stood and bowed. "Your Grace. How know you what happened?"

"News has faster wings than the birds." He chuckled as he entered the chamber. His white surcoat now had a wide purple edge on it, with gold embroidery, and he wore a leg knife. "I had planned on coming to say good-bye anyway, but when I heard of the Rogues' ambush, I hurried."

"How are you?" she asked.

He shrugged. "It is lonely. Even with Lord Krendhal. He is ever mindful that he is my First Minister and seems not aware he is also my cousin." His blue eyes filled with longing. "I wish I had kin such as you have."

"You have friends, Your Grace. Ones who care for you, not your rank."

The Laird smiled. "Aye. And I thank you." He let his breath out in a slow exhale. "But you will leave soon, and I will be alone."

"We can write. And Uncle must journey to Laird Hall often, and I am certain that I shall accompany him at least some of the time."

He smiled. "There is that."

Alcandhor stepped in the doorway and bowed. "Your Grace. I apologize. I just heard you were here."

With a slight frown, the Laird turned. "I am not my father, Thane. Do not treat me with such formality when it is just us."

Alcandhor spread his hands with a wry look. "I apologize again. What brings you here?"

The Laird crossed his arms and said in a huff, "Evening meal."

~:~

After the meal and a game of backhand, Tam and Alcandhor walked with the Laird and his escort of Ranger guards to the gate of the bailey.

The Laird hesitated, his eyes averted, before asking, "Once you are gone, to whom shall I turn?"

Alcandhor smiled. "I have a solution for that. I have asked Lamadhel to stay on here. He is my best counselor. I lend him to you."

The Laird's eyes lit up. "Ah truly, Thane?"

"Aye." Alcandhor pointed a finger at the boy. "And know you he is not afraid to grab you by the neck either."

Tam smiled at the swell of affection as the Laird embraced her uncle. He may not be kin, but he loved her uncle as she did.

The Laird smiled at Tam and turned to Alcandhor. "With your permission, Thane?"

Alcandhor inclined his head with a slight smile.

The Laird hugged Tam. "I will miss you greatly, my friend."

"And I you."

"I will write you. I still need your ear, you know."

"You will always have it, Your Grace."

They returned to the hold in silence. As they approached the door of the foreroom, Tam whispered to her uncle, "I feel sorry for him. He is so lonely."

Alcandhor put his arm around her shoulders. "If I know Lord Krendhal, that will not last long."

Tam began to ask what he meant, but a loud yell came from the back of the hold. They ran down the hallway and joined Haladhon at the kitchen door. Sherel was beating Marcalan with a broom. He had his arms thrown up over his head in defense as he laughed uncontrollably.

"I'll teach you, you scoundrel! You leave my kitchen alone!"

Alcandhor took Sherel by the shoulder, calling her name in a soothing tone. She turned and almost used the broom on the Thane before stopping. She lowered her ersatz weapon, breathing heavily. The Thane took the implement from her with aplomb.

"Thane, you have to do something about that rascal! I will not put up with it any longer!"

"What has he done, Sherel?"

"I have been going mad looking for spices and herbs that are not where they should be and thought it was simply that I was having to use Rangers as helpers in my kitchen, but it was this prankster all along!" She spun and pointed a finger at Haladhon, who was snickering. "You were probably aware of it too, you rake! Were you his helper?"

Haladhon raised both hands in innocence, his wide eyes though, still twinkled. "I have not touched one spice in your kitchen, Sherel."

She sniffed in disbelief. "I don't hear you saying you knew nothing about it."

Tam thought Sherel must be right, but did not say so. Haladhon chuckled and winked over at Marcalan who still giggled. Sherel whirled back to the younger Ranger, who cringed in mock fear though grinning broadly.

"You get out of my kitchen, you rascal!"

Marcalan winked at Tam as he passed her at the doorway.

Sherel put her hands on her hips. "You must do something with him, Thane!"

"I will have a talk with him, Sherel," Alcandhor said in a soothing voice.

Sherel sniffed again. "You will probably urge him on. For all of your observances of manners as Thane, you are like him at heart, whether you admit it or not."

Haladhon clapped a hand on Alcandhor's shoulder, grinning. "I think I will retire. Night's rest, Sherel and Tam. And to you, my scoundrel-at-heart cousin." He walked off laughing before Sherel could retort.

Tam quirked an eyebrow, watching Alcandhor chew his cheek to keep from smiling as he and Tam turned to leave the kitchen. He called behind him, "Night's rest, Sherel."

They walked back up the hallway, and he grinned at Tam as they stopped in front of their doors. Tam tipped her head. "You are a bit of a scoundrel at heart, are you not, Uncle?"

His smile grew melancholy. "I suppose I once was." He rubbed his chin. "Tam please come into the meeting chamber. I have to talk to you."

She entered and sat across the corner of the table from Alcandhor. He cleared his throat several times and studied his hand splayed on the table. He licked his lips and finally spoke. "Tam, how much did your father tell you about growing up?"

"What do you mean, Uncle?"

"A–about growing up. I mean, surely you realize you are...becoming a young woman."

"Well, aye, I suppose."

"What did your father tell you about it?"

"Nothing. Why?"

"Nothing?" Alcandhor's mouth dropped open and he stared at her for a long moment. "You mean...nothing?"

She shook her head.

"But you—" He sighed and combed his hand through his hair. Tam felt sorry for his discomfiture, although she knew not what troubled him.

"Surely you are old enough to have...your cycles, are you not?"

"Cycles?"

"Womanly cycles. Women have a cycle, which—"

"Oh, that. Aye. I have those," she murmured, feeling her face grow warm.

"And Valdhor explained them?"

"He said it is something women have happen and that I must take care it of and to be discreet about it. He was so angry that first time." She frowned down at her fists, remembering his anger.

"Why?"

She began rubbing the scars on her hands. "He was angry at anything that reminded him I was not a son. I am not certain if I was more frightened by what was happening to me, or by his anger. I had been so afraid when I called to him..."

Alcandhor groaned, and Tam sensed both sympathy and anger.

"I do not mean to make you angry, Uncle."

"I am not angry with you, but at your father. I cannot believe even he would be that insensitive."

Tam did not answer; she knew not what to say.

"Tam, understand you why you have cycles?"

"Just that it is something women put up with."

Alcandhor grimaced, fidgeting. "It is a sign you are becoming a young woman and old enough to bear children."

Tam's eyes widened. "Children?"

Alcandhor smiled. "Why are you so incredulous? Had you no thought that someday you would have children of your own?"

"Nay, Uncle. I–I never did. I had only thought about my cottage and garden until you came, then I have only thought about being a Ranger."

"You never thought you might marry? I find that hard to believe."

"Nay, I have not, Uncle. Why is that hard to believe?"

"Because I thought all girls dreamed of growing up and finding a man to marry. At least, it seems so from all the gossip and silly talk that flies around in Zaidhron."

Tam shook her head. She had never thought much about the future, living day by day, enduring her father's training. What did she care about marriage? How could she train at Zaidhron as her Uncle wished with all the extra work? "Nay. Why would I want another man to cook for and to clean up after?"

"Is that what you think marriage is?" asked her uncle in amazement.

Tam stared at him, lost.

Alcandhor lowered his head with a quiet laugh. "Oh, Tam, Haladhon was right." He rubbed his hand on the table. "You probably will begin thinking of marriage before long. That is why I wanted to have this talk with you. There are things that definitely need to be explained to you."

"What things?"

He combed his hand through his hair again. "How do I explain the lifetime of knowledge you have missed, being raised in such solitude? You have no concept of our world's mores, perceptions of propriety, the clans' customs. You have no notion of so many things that you need to know."

"Then teach me, Uncle."

A soft laugh escaped him. "If only it were that simple. Know you how babies are created?"

Tam shook her head, feeling foolish. "I have seen herdbeasts give birth, but father would not answer questions about it." Tam's frustration in her own voice made her wince. Wait! Was Uncle going to answer all those questions?

"So, you...you do not know—" Alcandhor gave a slow exhale, licking his lips again. "All right." He bored the table with his gaze. "I will try to start with the simple things your father should have told you. Like why your body is changing."

"You already told me. Because I am becoming a woman."

"Aye. And as you get to be a young woman, you are bound to start attracting men."

"Why? How?"

"There is no 'why,' it just happens. It is our nature. As boys grow into men, they become interested in women. As to the 'how,' well, you are very beautiful."

She pursed her lips, tired of hearing that. "Haladhon kept saying so too."

Alcandhor's head snapped up. "He did, did he?" His voice became hard. "What else did he say?"

"He said that I am beautiful, and Rangers who do not know me will not take me seriously because of that. Why does it not matter how a man looks, Uncle? If he is a Ranger, he is accepted. Other Rangers look not at his appearance."

"'Tis a sad fact that people are judged by appearances and not by their hearts, not by their abilities. So you must endure it."

"That is what he said too."

"Ah. What else did he tell you?"

"Not much. Just that I have to put up with Rangers not accepting me immediately."

Her uncle leaned back in his chair, relieved. Why would he be? Haladhon had said that her uncle should be the one to talk to her and would not be happy if he knew Haladhon talked to her. Stars, he was right, as usual. She really must listen to Haladhon's advice from now on.

"One of my worries is that a Ranger, or several Rangers, might become interested in you. And you need to be aware if it happens."

"What do I do?"

Alcandhor hesitated. "Tam, if a Ranger shows an interest in you, it might mean he wishes marriage. And marriage means children. You cannot marry yet."

"I do not think I would wish to."

"I am happy to hear that, but if you meet a man who makes you feel special, that you wish to be around all the time, you might change your mind. And you cannot marry yet. You are too young, and you have an obligation to our clan. 'Tis not fair, but when you are a Ranger, you must sacrifice what you want for your duty to the clan."

Tam frowned. "Uncle, how can I be old enough to be a Ranger Confirmed and not old enough to marry?"

"It is not your age, it is you. You are not ready. If you had been raised at Zaidhron and knew all these things, it might be different. But you have no concept of what marriage entails, or bearing and raising children. But even if you were ready for marriage, because you are heir to Thane, you could not marry. I am compelled by the vow the conclave made to your father to mentor you until you are of Age, and I will not have you distracted from your training."

He patted her hand absently, his attention again on the table. Tam knew now this meant he was going to start talking about things that embarrassed him.

"You will have men who will show an interest in you. They might wish to go on walks with you, might try to hold your hand, or put their arm around you. They may try to kiss you."

Tam frowned. This was truly so confusing. "But Uncle, men have put their arms around me, and kissed me. Should I not let them?"

Anger again rose in her uncle, coupled with fear. "Who?"

"Besides you? Haladhon and several other cousins have put their arm around me, and the Laird has kissed me."

"Ah, I see." Alcandhor took a slow breath, and Tam felt his emotions subside. "To my knowledge, this has been a kinship affection. Even the Laird has a brotherly feeling for you. But that is different from the emotions you would feel from a man who has more in mind than friendship. What you would feel from him would be very strong and unsettling. Since you have empathic ability, it would evoke strong physical responses from your body. He would want to be near you, touch you, kiss you. And I mean on the mouth, not on the cheek or forehead. And you might desire to have him hold you and kiss you."

Tam tipped her head, remembered the strange feelings that had come to her when walking across the bailey the day after she arrived. "I– I think I have sensed this. I did not understand..."

"Who?"

"I know not who. When I first arrived here, I felt them from some of the Rangers here on the grounds. I feel them not as much anymore."

"If they are wise, they will remember you are my niece. If any Ranger approaches you, and you feel such desires from him, do not allow him to touch you. Not for any reason, not even to match. Understand you me?"

"Aye, Uncle."

"There is so much more I need to explain, but I am not sure where to start..."

"Uncle?"

"Aye, Tam?"

"What are these feelings called? These 'desires?'"

"They are called desire, passion, lust...There are many words which describe them."

"These are the feelings one feels when one wants to marry?"

"It is often involved, aye. Although many times marriages are arranged for advantage—clan alliances, for example, or to increase land ownership, for political advantage, there are many reasons. But in my view, hopefully the two people who wish to marry are in love."

"*In* love? What is that?"

He sighed, once again piercing the table with his gaze. "Two people can have great passion for each other, and there may be no love involved. No great affection, just physical attraction. But when two people are in love, there is not only the attraction, but also deep love where they are each willing to sacrifice for the other, to put the other person's needs above their own."

Sadness swelled in her uncle, and she understood. This was part of what caused such sadness in him. He did not have *in love*. Did he not love his wife and she him? She felt it presumptuous to ask, but ached for him.

"What is it?" he asked, putting a hand over hers. Not wanting to reveal what she could sense, she thought quickly about questions she wanted answered.

"Uncle? Where *do* babies come from?"

He sighed, his eyes averted. "This is truly going to be a long night..."

~:~

All the things her uncle told her jumbled in her head as Tam shrugged on her pack. She still had so many questions. If only she could talk to Haladhon. She doubted they would have a chance on the journey back to Zaidhron.

She stifled a yawn. Did she even sleep two hours? She tugged her hair from under the straps and peered into the shadowed corner. The embers in the fireplace glowed dimly, not enough to see. She brushed her fingertips along the smooth wall until she felt her lorzwood staff. She smiled as her hand clasped her old friend.

Finally, she was on her way home. Tam frowned. No, not home. 'Twould be a long time before she considered that huge city home. A pang twisted her heart. She had lost not only her father, but her cottage.

Her garden.

With a shake of her head, Tam dismissed those thoughts. They did her no good. She had much to be thankful for: family, clan, being a Ranger, friends.

She opened the door and joined her kin in the bailey.

~~~

ABOUT THE AUTHOR

L.S. King has novels published in two series: Deuces Wild and the Sword's Edge Chronicles.

Besides having short stories published in *Deep Magic*, *The Sword Review*, *Dragons, Knights & Angels*, *Digital Dragon Magazine*, and *Residential Aliens* (the fact that several of the publications which have released her stories are now defunct has nothing to do with her, honest), she also authored a column for writers, has worked as a submissions editor and a copy editor on several magazines, and was a founding editor of the semi-pro online magazine *Ray Gun Revival*, currently on hiatus.

~:~

Check out my website: http://loriendil.com
Follow me on Twitter: @Loriendil
Facebook author page: @AuthorLSKing
Facebook fan group: Loriendil's Lair
Subscribe to my blog: http://loriendil.wordpress.com/